Fly with Me

Fly
with
Me

Andie
Burke

ST. MARTIN'S GRIFFIN
NEW YORK

This is a work of fiction. All of the characters, organizations, and events portrayed in this novel are either products of the author's imagination or are used fictitiously.

FLY WITH ME. Copyright © 2023 by Andie Burke. All rights reserved. Printed in the United States of America. For information, address St. Martin's Publishing Group, 120 Broadway, New York, NY 10271.

www.stmartins.com

Designed by Meryl Sussman Levavi

Library of Congress Cataloging-in-Publication Data

Names: Burke, Andie, author.
Title: Fly with me / Andie Burke.
Description: First edition. | New York : St. Martin's Griffin, 2023.
Identifiers: LCCN 2023016836 | ISBN 9781250886378 (trade paperback) |
    ISBN 9781250886385 (ebook)
Subjects: LCGFT: Romance fiction. | Lesbian fiction. | Novels.
Classification: LCC PS3602.U75514 F59 2023 | DDC 813/.6—dc23/
    eng/20230426
LC record available at https://lccn.loc.gov/2023016836

Our books may be purchased in bulk for promotional, educational, or business use. Please contact your local bookseller or the Macmillan Corporate and Premium Sales Department at 1-800-221-7945, extension 5442, or by email at MacmillanSpecialMarkets@macmillan.com.

First Edition: 2023

10 9 8 7 6 5 4 3 2 1

To my fellow nurses.

To those of you battling depression, anxiety, or PTSD. To any of you who have ever watched your own loved ones suffer while knowing too much about what can and might happen. To all of you who have lived humanity's best- and worst-case scenarios only to come back and do it again just a few hours later.

Fuck the pandemic and everyone who gave you a pizza party instead of a raise. Love you all.

Hope this book makes you laugh.

The stars seemed near enough to touch and never before have I seen so many. I always believed the lure of flying is the lure of beauty, but I was sure of it that night.

—Amelia Earhart

Author's Note

I started writing *Fly with Me* after several rough nursing shifts in a row, a little over a year into the pandemic chaos. When I look back on the time I spent working with that amazing pediatric ER team, I'm always struck by the number of funny bonding moments punctuating the toughest ones. Whether it was getting salty about the hand sanitizer smelling like stale tequila or finding the occasional but alarming squashed bug in the stack of repurposed theme park ponchos we were using as PPE, our camaraderie grew with each second of shared laughter.

In both my personal and professional lives, I've seen how often moments of comedy and moments of tragedy occur in a strange tandem. This might be because I'm a romance writer, but I find comfort in the idea that falling in love can happen while so many other things are falling apart. With this context in mind, Olive and Stella's story includes several heavier plot points, including scenes of caregiving and end-of-life decision-making; depictions of an acute depressive episode and panic attack; management of a parent's diagnosis with a progressive neurological disease; and an anaphylactic allergic reaction. I hope I have succeeded in handling these elements with the sensitivity and honesty they deserve.

Chapter 1

"We're not going to crash."

The entire row of fellow airplane passengers turned, and Olive Murphy realized she'd said the words out loud. And with noise-reducing headphones over her ears, she'd said it so loudly every passenger on board might have heard her.

She swallowed against the thickness in her throat.

Uncharacteristically, her stupid mouth kept moving. "There's actually only a one in three point three seven billion chance of dying in a commercial airplane crash. And ninety-eight point six percent of plane crashes don't even have fatalities." Olive tugged at the collar of her sweatshirt. "Though I guess even the people on the planes that crashed had that same statistical probability, and they still died in a heap of burning wreckage." She let loose a couple of nervous chuckles and risked a glance around her, hoping a sinkhole or vortex had appeared to swallow her whole. No such luck. She was still here.

On a fucking airplane.

She tightened her grip on the tiny white pill in her fist. Joni, the doc from work who prescribed it, hadn't told her when to take it. What if they got stuck on the tarmac for hours? Olive had only two Valium pills with her. One for the flight out and one for the flight back. Her normal meds wouldn't cut it for today.

Her mouth was dry.

There was a smell here. A plane smell. Like recycled air and metal. And death.

Okay, not actually death.

God, she was about to be ten thousand feet up in the air with the airplane smell, defying the laws of physics, the laws of nature, and the laws of Olive Murphy's guide for surviving life. All she could think about was Newton. What goes up must come down. An apple falling from a tree. A Boeing 737 full of screaming people. All splattered in a crater. Or dive-bombed into the water. The remains picked away by sharks or piranhas or whatever feasts on human flesh in the deep.

She needed to stop watching so much Discovery Channel.

Olive lifted the Valium. "Now or never."

The pill was inches from her mouth when the plane lurched. The white tablet tumbled into the aisle. A high-pitched curse fell from her mouth, giving the kid behind her an NSFW vocabulary lesson. She clung to the armrest and the seat in front of her as if the metal box had done a barrel roll. A flight attendant stepped on the pill as she passed. Her patent pump pushed the pill into the carpet.

"Oh god."

A nurse didn't need to be told the number of bacteria on a shoe that had walked through an airport. Gross. The other pill was in her larger carry-on in the compartment. Her eyes darted like a mouse in a cat's mouth right before the dramatic gulp. The walls closed in. Tunnel vision. Ringing in her ears.

Breathe.

She would calmly stand up, get what she needed, and then sit back down. This was okay. This was *fine*. She unclipped her seat belt.

A flight attendant with an enormous blond bouffant and a Southern accent pounced on her. "I'm sorry, ma'am, but you need to stay in your seat."

"I—I need something from my bag."

The woman's powdery pink lipstick spread in a placating smile. "You can get it once we're at cruising altitude."

"It's . . . a pill." Half standing, Olive clutched the armrests harder.

"Is it a life-sustaining medication?"

Olive gulped. "No."

The woman pointed a talon-sharp fingernail at Olive's seat. "Then you'll need to stay there."

Olive flopped back down, rebuckling her seat belt. She could do this. She'd faced worse over the last year. She closed her eyes and imagined what this trip would have been like if Jake were here. He'd make her laugh. He'd tell her that her mind was playing tricks on her and say if she could run a forty-six-bed ER during a full moon, she could survive this. Actually, he wouldn't say any of that. He would quote *Parks and Rec* or get her to forget she was on a plane altogether by yanking her hair and pretending they were back on a family car trip in the nineties belting out Disney songs in harmony and driving their younger sister bonkers.

But he wasn't here. And that was the whole damn point. She could do this. For him. He was why she was on this stupid plane in the first place.

They bumped down the runway while the flight attendants checked all the compartments. That blond-bouffant attendant gave her an extra assessment, as though she were an unruly student in an elementary school class who'd already been caught carving dirty words into her desk.

Olive shut her eyes tight and squeezed her phone. She blasted the music in her headphones. Brandi Carlile belted out a few particularly emotional notes.

Happy place. Happy place. Happy place.

Music. Nature. Potted plants. Mid-century modern art deco designs. Velvet tufted everything.

The plane shuddered.

She gasped, drawing more exasperated looks from the totally calm and normal people in the seats around her. Yeah, they'd probably be telling all their friends about the psycho in their row. Sandpaper lined her throat. She fumbled for her water. Water would be good.

Unless the plane landed in it.

Piranhas. Sharks.

A revving noise hit her ears even through the headphones. The plane accelerated, flattening Olive to her seat. She held her breath as if she were jumping off a diving board. A bounce. A lifting sensation. Her eyes opened. Her head whipped around. There was no more shaking. No shudder of the wheels beneath her. Smooth. They were in the air. A small *thunk* made her latch on to the armrest again.

A gnarled hand lifted her right headphone off her ear, and a gravelly voice from the aisle seat beside her spoke. "That's the landing gear going away, dearie." A woman in her nineties if she was a day smirked—actually smirked—at her and patted her arm placatingly.

"Oh, okay."

"Everything's going to be fine." She pointed. "Watch the flight attendants. As long as they're calm, you should be calm. You're not going to get sick, are you?"

"Why would I get sick?"

"I can deal with reciting horrific accident statistics better than the stench of panic vomit." With that she pulled down her eye mask and was snoring in seconds.

Olive cradled her face. This wasn't the most humiliating experience of her life. Not by a long shot. Jake used to call her proof that Murphy's Law existed. With her, whatever could go wrong usually did, especially if it involved making a complete ass out of herself. But generally, she could laugh about it.

Not today.

Nevertheless, she dutifully watched the flight attendants. They were calmly chatting. Several more minutes of smooth flying passed before one of the flight attendants shot out of their seat.

"Oh my god." Olive pulled her headphones down around her neck. Shouts from the front echoed in her ears. Wasn't there that thing a few years back when a woman got pulled out of a plane after debris hit her window? Olive tightened her seat belt. "I'm not going to die today."

The goateed man on the other side of her sighed loudly. Very loudly. It was almost a groan.

Several flight attendants spoke into a walkie-talkie while others fumbled through cabinets. Olive wanted to wake the nonagenarian beside her to beg for reassurance. But even Olive wasn't quite that pathetic yet, despite the sound coming from her mouth, which might have been a whimper.

A musical and calming female voice came over the PA system speakers. "This is your cocaptain speaking. I need to know if we have any doctors on board. We have a passenger experiencing a medical emergency."

No one moved. No one raised their hands.

Olive wasn't a doctor, so she let her shoulders slump, hoping someone with less panic coursing through their veins could help. The flight attendants repeated the request for doctors.

Another minute passed. The same voice overhead. "Do we have any medical professionals on board this flight?"

Motherfucking Murphy's Law.

Olive raised her hand, and her voice squeaked when she found it. "I'm a nurse."

Chapter 2

With the permission of the bouffant blonde, Olive leaped out of her seat into the aisle. Her headphones almost strangled her, as they'd somehow gotten hooked in an armrest. She pulled them off. She could do this. She *was* an ER nurse with ten years of experience. She could absolutely do this. The plane lurched, and Olive grabbed hold of the seats, her muscles locking up until she saw the man on the ground.

Oh shit.

They'd gotten him out of his seat and onto the floor in a small vestibule at the front of the plane. He was in his forties or fifties. Gray peppered the hair on either side of his utterly pale face. Unconscious.

Some essential gear in Olive's brain clicked into place. She rushed to the man's side. "What happened?"

The head flight attendant, a tall man not much older than she was, handed her a stethoscope. "The people in the seat next to him saw him clutch his chest and then slump over. We don't know anything else. Is he having a heart attack? The captain's working on getting us diverted."

"What supplies do we have?" Olive asked. Another flight attendant opened a black vinyl bag. She searched through it. "Can you find out what he was doing right before he slumped over?"

Olive kneeled, pressing the stethoscope to his chest. He was barely breathing. He had a pulse. Perfusion poor. Color bad. Extremities cool.

The flight attendant appeared beside her again.

"They said he was eating a protein bar and coughed a couple times."

Olive's mind processed the information as she wrapped a blood pressure cuff around his arm. Not choking, though. That wouldn't have been so fast.

The blood pressure was dangerously low.

Shit.

Protein bar.

Coughing.

She grabbed a penlight from the bag and looked at his throat. Not choking. Swelling. Allergic reaction. She breathed out slowly and grabbed the EpiPen from the emergency supplies bag. She pulled the cap and thrust it into the man's thigh.

The man gasped and gagged. She rolled him onto his side, where he vomited. His skin was still super pale, and he wasn't awake. Hypotension from anaphylaxis? Okay. Next steps. She tore his sleeve, wrapped a tourniquet around his arm, and started an IV. She let the fluid flow into him and checked his pressure again.

Still too damn low.

He was breathing better, but symptoms weren't getting better quickly enough, and there was only one EpiPen in the bag.

Fuck.

Olive grabbed the mask and bag to start giving him rescue breaths. "I need someone to check with the passengers and see if anyone else has another EpiPen. Sometimes you need a second dose."

A rash had bloomed all over his exposed skin. Olive pulled a flight attendant down to the ground and demonstrated how to give breaths with the mask.

The woman nodded nervously and picked up the motion. "I-I-I've had CPR training."

"Good, thank you. You're doing great." Olive offered an assuring nod.

There was an AED beside her. She went ahead and ripped open the man's shirt, sticking the pads on his chest.

If she couldn't fix him soon, he was going to code. Could she manage a cardiac arrest here?

The other flight attendant came back with an EpiPen in his hand. Olive flipped it open and thrust it into the man's other leg, holding it while rifling through the rest of the medications. She threw the used pen on the ground and drew up a dose of Benadryl and gave it through his IV, really hoping that Good Samaritan laws meant she wouldn't get sued for this.

The man's chest rose more steadily. His color improved. The hives weren't better, but they weren't worse either. He was breathing—really breathing. Olive stopped the attendant pushing in breaths with the bag-valve mask, and set up a continuous flow oxygen mask instead.

She took another blood pressure reading, holding her own breath as she watched the tiny needle on the gauge.

112/70.

Stable.

Olive sat back on her heels, almost gasping with relief. *Thank god.*

Two flight attendants helped her prop the man with a pillow. Olive sat cross-legged beside him, checking his pulse and monitoring the fluids dripping into him.

His eyes opened, and Olive leaned forward.

A hacking cough came first and then what almost sounded like a raspy laugh. "The packaging said no nuts. Those assholes."

Olive grinned. Tears pricked her eyes. "Well, I think you should file a lawsuit. But you're going to be okay." She patted his shoulder.

The head flight attendant pointed to her. "This woman saved your life, sir."

The man smiled. "Thank you." He held out a shaking hand.

"Anytime." Olive shook his hand but then winced. "But hopefully never again."

"We're preparing for our final descent. A medical crew is going to meet us at the gate," the flight attendant said.

"We're already in Orlando?" Olive's eyes widened. It couldn't have taken that long.

He shook his head. "Diverted to Atlanta."

"Oh, yeah. That makes sense." She tried to hide the disappointment in her voice. It was absolutely the correct decision. She could get another flight out. She could make it in time.

Her legs had begun to cramp underneath her. She was shaky when she made it to her feet, cracking her back and stretching her neck. A roar of noise assaulted her ears, almost giving her a heart attack.

Were they crashing? *No.* Not after all of that.

It . . . it was applause.

For her.

Olive pressed her cold hands to her cheeks, hoping to ease the burning. The flight attendant whose name tag she was finally calm enough to read—LEO—pulled her onto a small flip-down seat and buckled her in. Her hands, which had been so steady when she'd held the EpiPen, now trembled wildly. Two other flight attendants managed to half carry the man she'd helped into one of the first-row seats. They checked and rechecked him to make sure he was conscious.

Olive's eyes shut as a sudden wave of exhaustion crashed into her—well, not *crashed*. Just to be clear, *nothing is goddamn crashing*. She massaged her eyelids, seeing colored spots when she forced them open again.

In fifteen minutes and several more near panic attacks, the plane landed with a surprisingly gentle thump, and Olive Murphy was on the ground again. She closed her eyes and sighed.

They slowed to a crawl and then taxied to the gate.

Leo touched her arm, rousing her from a stare. "The pilots would like to talk to you."

"Uh—sure. Can I check on him now?" She pointed to the man who'd had the allergic reaction.

Leo nodded.

Olive pressed her fingers to the man's wrist to feel his pulse. He smiled at her. He had a kind, animated face, and she was relieved to see color back in his cheeks. Before she could ask his name, the gate door opened and paramedics appeared. Another round of applause greeted her as she approached her seat.

The old lady in the seat beside hers took off her mask and earplugs and peered up at her. "Did you puke?"

Olive looked at her clothes, which were still mercifully free of vomit.

"I knew it—"

"But I—" Olive shrugged. "Never mind." With Leo's help, she hauled her bag out of the overhead compartment and dug in the seat for her phone. He ushered her back up to the front and off to the side.

The cockpit door opened—was it called a cockpit or was that just what they called it in *Top Gun*? Olive froze.

Standing in front of her was the most beautiful woman she'd ever met in real life. Long, shiny dark hair pinned back into a neat bun beneath a hat. Sparkling dark brown eyes and full, kissable lips. A mouth that quirked up at the sides as if smiling was its most natural position. And right now, this captivating woman was smiling at no one except Olive.

"I'm Allied Airlines pilot Stella Soriano."

Chapter 3

Allied Airlines pilot Stella Soriano's eyes brightened. "I was so surprised to find out that the person saving the other passenger was *just* a nurse."

Okay . . .

So the most beautiful woman on the planet might be an ignorant asshole.

Fabulous.

Murphy's Law.

Olive shook Stella's hand, which, to Olive's dismay, was perfectly soft and prettily manicured. "Well, on most of those shows, whenever they show a doc touching a patient, it's usually actually a nurse doing the stuff in real life." She hadn't meant to say that, but between the nerves on the plane and helping the man, her mouth's social filter had decided to malfunction.

"Oh, I don't watch TV."

A *snobby* ignorant asshole.

With a too-perfect smile and goddamn dimples. Of course she had dimples.

But seriously, who doesn't watch TV?

Olive forced on a facsimile of a grin, slung her backpack over her shoulders, and grabbed the handle of her suitcase. "Well, I better go look and find a flight to Orlando."

Stella's lips pursed. "There are no more flights tonight."

Olive's hand tightened on her suitcase handle, her nails digging into her palm. "Well, I better, uh—I better go, then."

A smooth voice came from behind Stella. The white man

grabbed Olive's hand and shook it slowly. "I'm the captain of this here aircraft. Call me Kevin. Or Captain Kevin." He guffawed at his own joke. "Well, y'all didn't mention how pretty she is. She'll look great in the photographs. Won't she?" Captain Kevin was in his forties. Blandly good-looking with the air of someone you wouldn't be surprised turned out to be a suburban swinger or have a secret life as a niche porn actor with three families across three states.

Stella had the good taste to grimace at the captain's smarmy tone. "We hadn't asked her about the photographs yet."

"W-what photographs?"

Stella smiled. "The airline would like to pay for your flight and give you a voucher for ten free flights."

Olive decided not to mention that this was essentially like awarding an arachnophobe a collection of free tarantulas. Instead, she said, "Great."

"And we'd like to take your picture with the crew for our newsletter and website."

The airplane seemed to shrink, her vision tunneling like it had before takeoff.

Olive ran a nervous hand through her messy curls. She hadn't even had time to put any product in after her shower. She probably resembled a poodle by now. Grime from the airplane floor coated her leggings. "I'm not really dres— I look terrible. I don't think a picture would be good right now."

"You look great. Trust me, most men would disagree with your assessment of how you look." The smile from "Captain Kevin" wasn't genial. His eyes fixed on the area of her tank top that had pulled down enough to expose her cleavage.

She pulled the zipper up higher on her hoodie. Olive was too tired to hide the frostiness in her voice. "Random men's opinions on my appearance have never been very high on my priority list, but *cool*." Why bother fighting this?

Stella shook her head. "If she doesn't want to take a photo, we shouldn't—"

"I'm sure she's just being modest." And he pulled Olive close. "Smile, sweetheart."

Unnoticed before by Olive, a gate attendant stood with a smartphone held aloft.

As the entire crew gathered around her, Olive smiled.

She was sure she'd be very glad she did in about twenty-four hours if this photo actually ended up posted somewhere. But for now, she needed to get the hell away from these people so she could cry about the fact that everything was ruined, and she would be stuck in Atlanta until morning. There was no way she'd make the race for Jake.

"Thank you again for everything you did to help the passenger." Stella shook Olive's hand one more time, her face more apologetic than it had been before and a little less snooty. "Goodbye, then."

Olive walked down the tunnel to the terminal and went to find a seat where she could fall apart.

Chapter 4

As Stella had told her, there were no more flights out of Atlanta tonight. The Disney race would begin in nine hours, and she was a six-hour-and-fifteen-minute drive away. If she drove all night after working at the hospital from 3:00 A.M. until she had to leave to catch that stupid flight and *then* tried to run a half-marathon, *she'd* probably be the one being resuscitated. She knew her body, and she was too tired to drive right now. Her brain had reached a tipping point, too full to make any choices. So she'd been sitting on a bench in the airport for the last two hours, half-heartedly crunching on a bag of pretzels.

She slipped Jake's medal out of her bag and held it between her steepled fingers.

Jake's voice spoke inside her head. *"You always let Lindsay tell you can't can't can't. But I'm telling you, if I can do this, you can do this. You can do anything."*

He was wrong, because making the race tomorrow was something she couldn't do. She was happy about what she'd done for the man on the plane. As soon as she'd sat down in the first empty airport terminal chair she saw, she wished she knew his name. Wished she'd be able to make *sure* he was okay.

Saving the man's life would have made Jake so proud. She'd never gotten to tell Jake how proud she was of him because that wasn't really a normal thing to tell your brother.

Olive's phone battery had died at some point during the flight. She'd spent the day checking to see if her family had texted her back. It didn't make sense that she wished they were coming tomorrow. She closed her eyes and visualized the photo of Jake at the finish line from last year. His freakishly tall form was flanked by her parents and her then very pregnant sister. The medal was around his neck, and an amazingly goofy smile was on his face. Olive was supposed to have been there, and she wasn't.

So much had changed in a year.

Her parents probably canceled their hotel room. There was no way Heather would be coming either. She hadn't seen her sister or her niece and nephew for months. Probably for the best. Every conversation ended in threats and accusations involving lawyers and doctors and probate court.

It was all too much.

Olive's head bowed over her knees.

They would see her missing the race as another piece of evidence against her.

Selfish, thoughtless, and a complete disappointment.

For now, she might as well sleep here until she could rent a car and drive in the morning. Race or not, she had a three-day stay planned at Disney World already paid for, and she'd make the best of it.

"You're crying," said a melodic voice.

Allied Airlines pilot Stella Soriano stood in front of her.

Olive wiped her cheeks. "I know I'm crying." Fuck, she had snot dripping out of her nose too. So attractive.

"Are you okay?"

"I'm fine." Olive wrapped her arms around herself and sniffled.

"But you're *crying*." She accentuated the last word as though Olive didn't know what the wet stuff leaking onto her cheeks was.

"I *know*." Olive stood, disliking the way it felt to have this gorgeous pilot towering over her while she blubbered like an idiot. Though even standing, Olive was five inches shorter than Stella. "*I'm fine* is the socially acceptable response when you're having an emotional breakdown in public and you don't want to make people feel like they need to comfort you."

"But it doesn't actually explain whether you do, in fact, need to be comforted. Notwithstanding whether or not the person witnessing the outburst would feel compelled to comfort you. The question is whether or not you should be comforted, which, my assumption based on the tears is that you do. Need to be comforted, that is."

It took Olive several seconds to parse the meaning of those sentences. "You talk really fast."

The corners of Stella's eyes crinkled in amusement. Olive stared down at her feet, which looked so informal in their scuffed-up Chuck Taylors beside Stella's perfect patent leather.

"I get that a lot." Stella appraised her. "What's wrong, Olive? It *is* Olive, isn't it? I realized that we didn't actually give you a chance to introduce yourself, so I had to look up your name on the register."

"Yeah, Olive Murphy."

"So, what's wrong?"

Olive shifted her weight between her sneakers, looking anywhere except at Stella. "I'm supposed to be running a half-marathon tomorrow."

"Are you disappointed to miss it after spending a lot of time training?"

"No . . . I probably didn't even train enough." Olive's forehead dipped.

"Maybe it's for the best you *can't* do it, then."

Can't. God, Olive hated that stupid word.

Olive wiped her face, happy at least that the tears had stopped flowing. "It's complicated. And I really wanted to be there. *Needed* to be there."

"If it's so important, why did you decide to go out with so little schedule padding? What if there was a weather cancellation?" The words weren't impatient. But their tone was like what Olive used with pediatric patients when she asked why they decided to put the quarter/jelly bean/Monopoly piece up their respective noses.

"I had to work today."

"You couldn't get your shift covered?"

Was this woman trying to make her feel worse?

"I forgot to request off in time, and it's the last weekend we can take leave until after Christmas."

"Oh." Stella's facial expression made it perfectly clear that forgetting to do something was completely outside her realm of experience. *Well, good for her.*

"Is that from the last time you ran the race?" Stella pointed to Jake's medal.

"No." Olive slipped it back into the front pocket of her backpack. "It's—it was my—never mind."

"I'm sorry we had to divert." Her expression softened enough to make Olive hyperaware of her own surliness.

"I'm just bummed. Happy I could help that man, and obviously, getting him the medical care he needed was more important. I just . . . I had a plan."

"I get really upset when my plans don't work out too." Stella pushed her fancy rolly suitcase in a circle, like she was—what? Nervous? Excited? "You know, you could still make the race if you drove? You could get there by three A.M."

"I—don't think I could drive all night and then run. I was hoping to sleep some on the plane, but . . ."

"You're right. That's super impractical." She pursed her plump lips and focused on the blank wall beside Olive as if contemplating the meaning of life. She seemed more casual now, less of the snob she'd seemed on the plane, but Olive still had no idea how to read her. And, indeed, it was difficult to think about anything else standing near this woman beyond that she was beautiful, a bit weird, and probably straight—because, as established: Murphy's Law. Not that it mattered.

"Welp." Olive widened her eyes and pointed at the rest of the terminal. "I'm going to go try to find something to eat and a seat to camp out in."

"You're not going to get a hotel room? Didn't the airline offer to get you one?"

"They did, but honestly I just want to sit down somewhere for a while. I'll find a room if I decide to take one."

She hadn't turned her phone back on yet. She didn't want to field a passive-aggressive good-luck text from Lindsay and have to respond and tell her she wasn't going to make the race so the luck was unnecessary. The text back from her ex would probably involve a tacit told-you-so that would make Olive feel worse. It wasn't completely fair to blame Lindsay for Olive skipping the race last year, but all her jabs about having a more respectable first half-marathon time sure hadn't helped.

A sudden brightness flooded Stella's dark eyes, as if a cartoon light bulb had appeared above her head. She looked like a student government president struck by an inspiration about a prom theme or smoothie machine in the cafeteria. Honestly, everything about this woman screamed Most Likely to Succeed. "Let's go." Stella pointed to Olive's suitcase.

"Let's? What? Go where?"

"I'm going to drive you to Orlando," she said, as though this were the most obvious thing in the world.

"But I don't know you."

"We met two hours ago. I'm Allied Airlines pilot Stella Soriano." She grinned.

Olive wrinkled her nose skeptically. "You could be a serial killer."

"I'm not a serial killer. Google me. I have a"—she lifted her fingers in air quotes—"social media presence." She gestured to her phone. As a nearby gate opened, arriving travelers spilled into the terminal, the sounds of shoes and rolling suitcases making it difficult for Olive to concentrate.

"Um. What?"

"Stellaflies."

"Your?"

"Instagram handle." Stella made a tiny tsking noise through her nose. "The airline likes to trot me and the other female pilots out whenever they want to pretend they have a commitment to gender equity in hiring practices. It was highly encouraged that I maintain an account."

Olive chuckled and grabbed her phone before she remembered the battery was dead. Stella handed Olive her phone, already open to Instagram. Stella did have twenty thousand followers. Rolling her eyes at the grid, she lifted the phone to face Stella. "There are five pictures of you and you're in the pilot uniform in all of them. If you weren't standing in front of me, I'd think you were a bot who bought followers from a click farm. And these were all stock photos." With tags like *hot woman pilot.*

"But I am standing in front of you, offering to rent a car from Budget and drive you to Orlando."

Olive handed the phone back to Stella. "But why?"

"The airline gets really good deals with Budget."

"Not why that car company, why are you offering to drive me?"

"Because . . . you did something great today. You saved a life. And it's a big deal. And I'm sorry about what happened with the photo. I could tell it made you uncomfortable, and you were a good sport about it."

"That pilot's kind of an ass."

A slight darkening in Stella's eyes made it obvious that she was in complete agreement with Olive. "We better get going."

"You're sure about this?"

"Yes."

"Do you have to work tomorrow? Like fly airplanes and keep people alive and in the air?" Olive made a zooming motion with her arm, like an idiot.

"No. I was already going to be in Orlando for a few days

anyway, on leave. I go to the Food and Wine Festival every year if I can manage it." That smile. That perfect smile seemed to make the bustle of the terminal blur around Olive.

"You swear you're not going to get me in a car, drive off to a dark alley, and axe-murder me?"

"I do swear. Though if that were my plan, I almost certainly wouldn't tell you about it beforehand—well, at least until I had my axe out and ready."

Olive rubbed her eyes and mumbled into her palms. "I can check 'do something impulsive' off the list."

"List?"

"Never mind." Olive's tears returned without permission. Tears of surprise and gratitude making her voice wobble as she spoke. "Thank you."

Stella pulled out a small pouch of tissues from her bag, without even having to dig for it. She probably had one of those purse organizer things.

Olive touched Stella's elbow. "Thank you. Really, really. You don't know what this means to me."

"You're welcome." Stella grabbed her phone, and her thumbs pretended to type. "Now to find the nearest dark alley . . ."

Olive almost laughed.

"Kidding. Let's go."

What were the odds that Olive could make it through a long drive a foot away from a woman she was attracted to without completely embarrassing herself?

Slim.

Chapter 5

Stella came out of the bathroom stall wearing black jeans that hugged tightly to an objectively amazing ass and a casual but elegant boatneck sweater. She'd swapped her patent flats for spotless white sneakers. Even in her "casual clothes" she looked like an Ann Taylor model. Her hair was down, out of the tight bun. It cascaded over her shoulders in elegant waves. She was so not Olive's type—except in her complete unavailability.

"Are you okay, Olive?"

Fuck. She'd been ogling her. And something about the way Stella said her name made Olive want to stare deeply into her eyes and ask her to say it again. This was a totally normal feeling when one was tired.

"I'm fine."

Stella cocked her head to the side. "Fine like before, when you were actually having a terrible crisis, or actually fine?"

Olive adjusted the shoulder strap of her bag as it slid down her arm again. "Actually fine. Thank you again. I seriously don't know how—"

"It's fine." Stella laughed. "Stop thanking me."

Olive looked at the mirror and untwisted her hair from her topknot before pulling it back up into a pouf. There were dark purplish circles beneath her eyes. Why did she look like this after a flight? Was it something about the airport bathrooms that made people sallow? A quick glance at the woman beside her confirmed that it was not, in fact, the mirror.

Olive gave up on her reflection and grabbed her other bag.

They stopped to get coffee—well, Stella got coffee. Olive felt too nervous about tomorrow to get anything right now. She crammed a crushed protein bar from her bag into her mouth as she walked, chasing it with a couple of swallows from her Hydro Flask.

As they reached the car rental desk down on the ground floor of the airport, Stella rummaged in her wallet.

Olive was quicker and yanked out her credit card. "I'm paying for the car."

"But I want to get to Disney too." Stella waved the card away. "And I'll be driving and returning the car once we get there."

"Please let me pay for the car?"

They held a stare, giving Olive a chance to marvel at how beautiful Stella's eyes were. Stella nodded.

Olive handed over her ID, and Stella added her own to the pile. The man took the IDs and gave Olive a paper to sign. He checked her age and then her face twice. Olive always got mistaken for being younger than she was. She'd gotten carded for an R-rated movie within the last few years. No one ever believed she was thirty-four.

He tapped the driver's license. "You've got the same birthday as me."

"Really?" Olive asked.

"I'm just a couple years older, though." He chuckled. "Not really looking forward to the big six-oh, but my wife's already planning some big fancy surprise party next month. She can't fool me."

"Nice of you to play along, though." Olive chuckled back politely. "I hope you enjoy it anyway. December birthdays get the shaft too often."

"Don't they just," the man said with a wink.

Stella beamed at the man. "Happy early birthday, sir."

After thanking them both, the man handed Stella the keys and then directed them out the door. They crossed a sprawling parking lot.

"Are you going to eat anything else?" Stella guzzled her coffee and then chucked the cup into a trash can.

"I don't think so." Olive's eyebrows knit together. "You didn't want to bring the coffee in the car?"

"It's a rental," Stella said by way of explanation.

"Oh . . . okay. Rental. Right." Olive frowned, hoping her water bottle was acceptable. She'd refilled it at the airport and knew she needed to hydrate tonight.

Every time she looked at Stella, her mouth felt dry and nervous nausea roiled in her stomach. She must be more anxious about the race than she had expected.

They wove through aisles to find the well-maintained silver sedan exactly where the parking attendant said it would be. Stella opened the trunk, and they both heaved their bags into the back. While Stella nestled her oversized tote on the backseat floor, Olive found her portable charger stick and plugged in her phone. After getting in, Stella twisted the key in the ignition and took several seconds adjusting all of the mirrors and the position of the seat. Olive imagined this was what Stella looked like before every flight, thorough and meticulous.

Olive was cold—that weird cold you get when it's past your bedtime and slightly damp outside and your body can't quite keep up with your metabolic demands. She hugged her arms tightly, but a shiver rocked through her anyway.

Stella motioned to the car radio. "Do you mind if I listen to music during the drive or will that interfere with your rest?"

Olive shook her head. "I'm not going to be able to sleep for a bit. Too amped up. And I can fall asleep even with music. I sleep like a rock."

Stella fiddled with her phone for a moment before meeting Olive's eyes again. "It really was great, what you did."

"What I did?"

"The man on the plane."

"Oh, right." Olive's focus had been so wholly switched to

the race that she kept forgetting about that craziness. "Anyone would've done it."

"You diagnosed the problem and saved his life, all while in a super pressurized situation. You're a *hero*."

"I'm not."

"You are."

"I'm not." Olive knew that might have come out more snappish than she wanted it to. Stella didn't know about Jake. Stella didn't know why the word *hero* would have been a trigger. "But thank you. I'm sorry. I'm being an asshole."

"You had a long day."

"Speaking of long days, you're really going to be okay driving all night after flying during the day?"

"One hundred percent." Stella pulled a phone cord from her bag. "I've pulled a lot of all-nighters in my life."

"That's something we have in common." Olive smiled. "I work nights sometimes."

Stella plugged her phone into the car, switched the audio, and music exploded out from the speakers. Familiar music. Stella hurriedly turned down the volume.

An ecstatic grin threatened to expand on Olive's face out of nowhere. "That was Brandi Carlile, wasn't it?"

"Yep. Shoot, sorry I blasted your eardrums with that. It's not that loud in my earbuds." Stella grimaced. "Whoops."

Olive had to take a few deep breaths. Lots of people liked Brandi Carlile. Just because a person liked a gay musician didn't mean they were gay. Maybe she just had good taste?

"I love that song," Olive said, somewhat tentatively.

Stella's dark eyes glowed under the parking lot's floodlights. "Me too." With her hands in perfect ten and two positions on the steering wheel, she pulled out of the lot and accelerated to the on-ramp to the highway.

She'd never been good at picking up these things. Her whole life, she was always developing inappropriate crushes on straight girls. Joni, who prescribed her the antianxiety meds for the trip, had been the last one. She was at Olive's hospital on loan from another hospital in Colorado, and Olive awkwardly tried to hint at maybe asking her out. After Joni mentioned a boyfriend, they'd become friends instead. But the entire situation had been embarrassing and made Olive never ever want to try again. Shouldn't she have a better gaydar by now?

Wanting to break her brain away from its current trajectory, Olive spoke. "How long have you been a pilot?"

"Ten years."

"How—how do you become a pilot? Were you in the military?"

"No, it's a common misconception that all pilots start out in the military. I went to Embry-Riddle for my degree in aeronautics and then to flight school."

"And now you're a pilot."

Stella's grin was ludicrously large now as if the memories made her glow. "Yes. I think it's amazing that nurses can learn everything they need to know in an associate's program."

Olive had to remind herself that this person was spending seven hours of her life driving her so that she could run a race. Thus, Stella was obviously not an asshole. But she did seem to have a tendency toward insensitivity about certain things. Or maybe it was obliviousness. Though Olive was used to people assuming she didn't have a four-year degree. Not that there weren't amazing nurses who only had their associate's. Stella was right about that.

"I actually have a master's degree in nursing. You can get your nursing license a lot of different ways."

"Oh wow. *Interesting*. I had no idea there were regular nurses with master's degrees."

Olive didn't exactly love the note of incredulousness in Stella's voice. "Oh . . . yeah?"

Stella's teeth sank down on her lower lip for a moment. "Not that you don't seem like someone who would have a master's degree. I don't know very much about how nurses are prepared, academically speaking. But I imagine there's a wide range. With pilots there is, at least. There're a variety of pathways to become a pilot."

"Do you scuba dive?" Olive asked.

"I don't actually. Why do you ask?"

Olive chuckled. "You have amazing breath control when you speak." It seemed like she never paused to breathe at all.

Stella nodded as she merged into a different lane with a smooth acceleration. "Practice."

"Practice?" Olive adjusted her seat belt strap so she could more comfortably look at Stella.

"Male-dominated field. If you take a breath, they assume you're done talking. Of course, sometimes they don't even wait until I take a breath and go right ahead and talk over me or restate my ideas. I'm doing it again, aren't I?"

"Doing what?"

"Talking too much."

"I don't think you talk too much. I like—I like listening to you talk." As long as she wasn't making mildly patronizing assumptions about her nursing career or her experience, Olive enjoyed listening to her voice. It was energetic and enthusiastic, nothing at all like her own, which occasionally came too close to an Eeyore imitation. It also helped that when Stella spoke about her career, her eyes brightened and her perfect face seemed to glow.

No crushes, Olive. You'll probably never see her again after this.

"I was just thinking back to what I had said earlier on the plane about being surprised about it being *just* a nurse, and it occurs to me now in light of this conversation that I could have given off the wrong impression. I just meant that what you did was super impressive especially because nonmedical people like me tend to know more about what *doctors* do . . ." Stella's teeth worried over her bottom lip.

"It's really okay."

"I'm just . . . I'm used to people underestimating me because I'm a woman or assuming I'm a flight attendant rather than a pilot when they see my uniform because . . ." Her eyes went wide. "I'm not . . . shoot, I shouldn't have said it that way. I wasn't belittling what flight attendants do because did you know that they are actually really important for aviation safety, and they get treated like they are just customer service when in reality—"

"Stella, it's okay." Olive smiled, but Stella kept her attention on the road, so she didn't see it. If there was one thing Olive understood, it was that familiar anxious impulse to postmortem after a conversation and then correct any potential misunderstandings. Olive put her foot in her mouth so often, Derek had once implied she must enjoy the taste of shoe rubber. "I appreciate you saying that, though."

Stella released a short exhale and swallowed once. When she spoke again, her voice was slower, less pressured. "What kind of nurse are you?"

"Emergency room."

"That sounds exciting."

"It can be." Olive tried to stifle a yawn.

"Why don't you go to sleep for a bit?" Stella patted her leg and a shock of electricity went through Olive. So much so that Olive may have actually jolted—*god*, she did jolt. It had been a long fucking time since she'd gotten laid. A slight wrinkling in Stella's forehead was the only sign she noticed. For the second time today, Olive wanted to dissolve into the floor of a transportation vehicle.

"Yeah. I think I'll try to sleep." She checked her phone, but it was still too dead to turn on.

Stella rifled with one hand in the bag behind her seat and

pulled out a small beautifully colorful travel blanket. "Here, I get cold when I deadhead, so I always keep one with me."

Maybe Stella interpreted the jolt as a shiver.

"Thank you." Olive leaned her seat back, so unbelievably thankful to be in a car, not a plane. The blanket smelled like lilacs and vanilla. Basically, it smelled incredible. Which probably meant Stella smelled incredible. Which probably meant Stella would make a bed smell incredible too.

Calm your lady boner down, Murphy.

Stella had tied her hair up in a bun again, but a few strands fell loose, curling beautifully at the base of her neck. Heat pulsed in Olive's core. In the ever-present lady-loving battle of "do I want to be her or fuck her," Olive was pretty sure she knew where she stood regarding the woman in the driver's seat.

Who was probably straight.

And even if she wasn't, she was an extroverted, ray of sunshine, type-A pilot.

Who probably wouldn't look twice at you.

Yet she did seem to be looking over every few minutes to check on Olive, as if she were worried Olive would disappear. Maybe she was worried Olive would start crying again. Olive's last thought as she drifted off to sleep was a prayer to the gods that she wouldn't snore or drool.

Chapter 6

A gentle jostling woke Olive. Bright streetlights burned her eyes. She turned over, forgetting where she was until the seat belt shoulder strap slashed her neck. Stella had taken off her sweater and was now wearing only a thin V-neck T-shirt.

The corners of Stella's mouth flicked upward. "You *were* really tired."

"Did I—"

"Snore? Only a little. The car isn't the most ideal place to sleep before a race. You didn't even stir when I stopped. You sleep like the dead."

"You stopped?"

"There was a grocery store near the gas station. I googled the best foods to eat before a race, and the running website said peanut butter and a banana, so I got that. And a few water bottles since prehydration is important. It's been a long time since I've run a long race like this. We made good time. No traffic. The banana and peanut butter sandwich stuff are in the back seat because I didn't know if you had food allergies, and honestly, the last thing I wanted to do was to *watch* another allergic reaction. I can pull over in a parking lot for you to eat a snack outside the rental." She pointed to the window.

"Wait, wait. You *watched* what happened? How?" Olive ran her hand through her hair. Her teeth and mouth felt and tasted gross after sleeping so long. "There are cameras in the back of the plane?"

"No . . . but you don't know?"

"Know what?"

"I assumed that was part of what you were upset about?" Stella kept her eyes firmly fixed on the road.

"Upset about . . . when?"

"At the airport."

Olive angled her body toward Stella. The seat belt suddenly felt like it was strangling her. "I was upset about missing the race. What else would I be upset about?"

"Oh, well . . ." Stella's grip tightened on the steering wheel, her knuckles blanching. "You went viral."

"I went—what?"

"Going viral, like the video of you is being shared by—"

"I know what going viral means. Shit. *Shit.*" She grabbed the phone from where it had been charging. As soon as it was on and unlocked, alert messages exploded on the screen.

> Was it you?
>
> Saw you on the news?!
>
> Where are you?
>
> Gosh, you and your brother.

Most of the messages were from cousins and friends at the hospital. Nothing from her parents or Heather at a glance. Of course not.

Olive had forty voice mails, which meant her inbox was probably full. Her Instagram notifications had exploded. She closed it without scanning any of the DMs or messages. Thousands of new followers.

Palpitations skipped in her chest.

She swiped to text messages and scanned over the ones from her best friend, Derek. There was also a voice mail from Jake's hospital that had probably come in during the flight. *Shit.* She'd have to call them back later. Olive swore several more times and then squeezed her eyes shut, knuckles digging into her forehead as she leaned her weight onto her knees.

"Are you okay?"

"Going viral . . . my brother had it happen a little while ago. It . . ." Olive wasn't sure how to verbalize what had happened right now without letting the entire story spill out. Without turning—once again—into a tears and snot faucet. How many times were you allowed to fall apart in front of someone you'd just met without transitioning from "just had a traumatic experience" and into the "weird and dramatic, give her a fake number and flee" category?

A light hand touched the area of her back between her shoulder blades. The hand rubbed a few circles there and then the pressure vanished. The touch had been wonderfully calming. Olive's breathing slowed, and the ability to form coherent sentences returned.

Olive sniffed once and cleared her throat. "People on the internet can be assholes." After all, Jake had saved a child's life and gotten hurt in the process, and it didn't stop the trolls coming for him about being gay. "And that guy in the plane . . . his family might see the video and be really upset. I—I don't even know that he's okay."

"Oh, please don't worry. I—uh—well, I had scrolled through a lot of the comments left on the video. Actually, *videos* would be more accurate, since it seems a number of people were recording you. It seems like we had a group of extremely famous TikTok influencers on board near the front of the plane, so they had a full view of everything you did." Stella's voice was even faster than normal. "The response is all positive. Nothing bad. Everyone likes Mickey Mouse. And the man really looked okay when the medics got him onto the stretcher . . ."

"Wait—Mickey Mouse?" Olive said weakly.

"Yeah . . ." Stella's mouth opened, then closed, then opened again as if she were deciding the best way to explain. "I guess the man you saved is a really well-loved character actor at Disney World, so hashtag 'nurse saves Mickey Mouse' was trending for a while. It's quite a catchy hashtag. That being said, I don't know if he *does* play Mickey Mouse. It wasn't clear. Someone else said his brother is a really high-up executive at Disney. Again, unclear. Rumors."

"Nurse saves Mickey . . . trending? Like *trending* trending?" Olive rubbed her temples. Okay, she'd been worried about drooling. Now she was worried about puking in the rental that Stella hadn't even allowed herself to drink coffee in. *Shit*. "Okay. Okay. Okay."

"Take deep breaths, Olive." Stella pulled off the road into a parking lot near a service station. "Are you sure you're okay? I wouldn't love the attention either. But it's not exactly a bad thing, right?"

"Just—the internet assholes . . . these viral things can start out nice and get mean." She sucked in a breath. The air smelled different in Florida. It was at least fifteen degrees warmer than it had been in Georgia.

Stella appeared genuinely perplexed. "Why would anyone be mean to a woman who saved someone's life?"

"For my brother, it started out really nice too. Lots of attention. News stories. It was a whole thing." Olive groped for her water bottle. Her throat was on fire, the cool water a soothing rush. "But then it got really ugly. The harassment, I mean."

At least Jake never had to see those comments. The slurs. The threats. The vicious rumors. One of the last things Olive and her mother had been united about was their fight against the trolls coming after Jake on every possible platform. So much had happened since then.

"That's awful." Stella's expression was a jumble of sympathy and surprise.

It had been awful, but it hadn't been the worst of it. Seeing it happen had been the worst . . . Olive and her sister, Heather, both ended up accidentally seeing the viral video when it was shared by people who didn't know it was Jake. It was one of those doorbell cameras. The kind of thing that gets shared over and over on social media. A child's life saved by a random stranger. Olive couldn't hear the screech of tires as the driver tried and failed to stop in time, but she could imagine it. She'd *seen* Jake get hit.

"Olive?"

She looked up at Stella. Something in her kind expression eased the tangle of tension pulling between Olive's shoulders. "I'm okay."

After a few minutes of silence, Stella swiped on her phone and held up her map app. "We're almost at the park, Olive. Seven more minutes."

"The park?"

"Your race."

Right. The half-marathon. Disney World. The entire reason she was experiencing this ridiculous day.

"What hotel are you staying at?"

"Oh—uh, the Beach Club. It was my brother's favorite." Way too fancy and expensive for Olive, but she wasn't the one who made the reservation.

"You still want to run?"

"I do want to run. God, Stella, I'm sorry." Her brain lurched forward into the moment like it was a bike chain and a stick stuck in the gears had been yanked out. "I slept the entire time. I meant to wake up and trade off with you for a bit. Driving, I mean."

Stella shook her head and waved a dismissive hand as she pulled off the highway, following the directions of her phone GPS. "Oh, I can't do that anyway."

"Can't do what?"

"I can't be in the car with anyone else if they're driving.

Except my father. But he doesn't drive anymore, so that's not important. I've always been that way. Are you getting excited? I remember the last time I ran a race, I could barely sleep the night before. I couldn't wait."

Olive gave a noncommittal shake of the shoulders. "I'm really happy to have made it here. Thank you again. But . . . I think I need coffee."

"I read that coffee isn't great the day before a race because of—well, gastrointestinal issues."

"I'll be fine. I'm sure you're starving too. Thank you so much for getting the peanut butter and banana."

Her eyes brightened again. "Of course. My *pleasure*."

Olive could probably listen to Stella say the word pleasure about a million more times. It was like ASMR. If the ASMR was designed to get someone incredibly horny and make them consider doing something very ill-advised.

Stella turned left, and Olive pointed out a twenty-four-hour convenience store in the distance. The signs changed from normal road signs to festive ones. Mickey Mouse was everywhere. Stella pulled into the parking lot. Olive grabbed her bag from the trunk and went inside. She hit the bathroom first since her bladder was a bowling ball in her pelvis. The bathroom was dingy, but at least it had been recently cleaned. She changed into her running clothes, stuffing the wrinkled plane clothes into her suitcase.

After her teeth were brushed and her face washed, she put on mascara and enough makeup that she wouldn't be mistaken for one of the ghosts in the Haunted Mansion. The makeup had absolutely nothing to do with the gorgeous woman who was driving her. Nothing at all. Putting on makeup before running thirteen miles is something people do sometimes.

She braided back her wild hair as best she could. After rummaging in her bag, she found her electrolyte gummies and mini water bottles and stuffed them into her not-dorky-at-all running fanny pack. Finally, she took out Jake's medal and fitted it into the inside pocket of her leggings. She'd feel it during the entire race. She nodded to herself in the mirror and headed to get the oh-so-necessary caffeine juice from the big coffee vats. She would have preferred an IV of the stuff this morning. Could 3:00 A.M. even be termed morning?

Stella was already at the counter, with a coffee of her own, one of those fancy nuts-only protein bars, and, strangely, a yellow bag of Swedish Fish. There was no way Stella could know they were her favorite candy, right? Olive whipped out her credit card before Stella could free her own from her wallet.

"You don't have to—"

"I do." Olive offered a small smile. "And I need to know what you spent on gas."

"You paid for the rental car." Stella shook her head and held up her own card.

Olive pushed the card away. "The rental car was to get me down here. I should be paying you a lot of money for your chauffeuring services. As a pilot, I feel like you're a really overqualified Uber driver."

Stella's laughter was more restrained than Olive expected it to be. While she could talk and talk, she always seemed to be aware of her body and volume in a way that made Olive wonder if Stella was less sure of herself than she seemed. Maybe that was why she never had a hair out of place.

The girl behind the counter popped a chewing gum bubble to get their attention. "I need a credit card from *someone*."

Apparently, they'd been staring at each other for several seconds like at the rental car desk.

Olive slid her card into the chip reader. "I still owe you for the peanut butter."

Stella gave a tiny smile and nod.

They took their coffee and snacks outside and found a bench. It was a gorgeous, balmy night, and part of Olive couldn't quite believe she was sitting here. Insects buzzed around the high streetlamp illuminating the spot. The last twenty-four hours seemed too surreal. She spread peanut butter on several pieces of bread and alternated drinking coffee and water.

Stella violently bit the head off a Swedish Fish.

"Breakfast of champions?"

Stella smirked. "Not exactly breakfast for me. They remind me of my childhood. It's a guilty pleasure snack. I used to eat them after exams in college. They were my reward."

"I love them too."

Stella held out the bag. "Want one?"

"Probably another nonconventional pre-marathon food, but yes. I'd love one. They were my go-to movie theater snack choice. My favorite." The red gummy tasted exactly the way Olive remembered from the movie nights with her brother. He picked peanut butter M&M's, but it was always the weird red fish for her. Her dentist parents had always been anti-candy, so she never took it for granted growing up. Olive exhaled dramatically after she swallowed. "Ah. That's the stuff."

Stella chuckled, then put a fish on her tongue and flicked it back into her mouth. It was only mildly pornographic. "How are you feeling about the video, Olive?"

Olive's shoulders slumped. "Weird." She inhaled the comforting scent of her hazelnut coffee, staring at a cluster of pines thrashing in a sudden gust of breeze. She'd have to think about the going-viral stuff tomorrow. Not today. Today was about the race. And Jake.

"Is anyone meeting you at the race?" Stella sipped her coffee.

Olive forced down a thick swallow of peanut butter. "No, uh—my family was going to come. But . . . I don't think they are anymore."

An unreadable expression appeared on Stella's face before changing back to an encouraging smile. "Well, I think you're going to do great. And it will be great. Happiest place on earth, right? I'm sure that the races there are a blast."

Olive found herself smiling too. Something about Stella's positivity was contagious. "Right."

After they finished up their drinks and food, they got back in the car. When they arrived at the hotel, the area outside was packed for 3:30 A.M., as if lots of other people were getting in late and desperate to get to the race on time. Olive barely had time to say goodbye before a hotel staff member directed Stella to drive off to let the next car come up to the curb.

This hurried farewell meant that Olive was saved from the catastrophic mistake of asking Stella to come to the race. That would have been super weird, since (a) they'd only just met and (b) it was a weird fucking thing to ask someone to come to "watch" you run for four hours. She rushed to the concierge desk to drop her luggage, then called an Uber to take her to get her bib at the emergency bib pickup.

Her leg twitched during the ride over to the arena. All her muscles were tight. As soon as the car stopped, she flew out the door. When she said her name at the bib table, a cast member did a double take.

"We've been trying to get ahold of you, Ms. Murphy," said a slightly balding man looking more harried than anyone should look at the happiest place on earth.

Olive's face fell. What now?

Chapter 7

"You need to come with me." The man rubbed sweat from his shiny head with a towel as he ushered her down a hallway.

"Oh?" Olive flipped her phone anxiously in her hand. Was the reservation bad? Were they going to tell her she couldn't run, after all the effort to get here?

Too nervous and confused to ask questions, Olive followed and was greeted in a large conference room by three other people, two in suits, all wearing bright, toothy smiles. She focused on the suited man whose smile seemed to boast the highest wattage. "Is there a problem with my bib? Please, I really need to run today."

He chuckled. "No, we saw the footage of what happened when you saved Mr. Feldstein's life."

"Mr. Feldstein? Was that the man on the plane? Is he okay?" Olive clasped her hands in front of her.

"He's doing fine. Mr. Feldstein's a very beloved cast member here, and we'd love to do some press photos with you after the race. He'll be here tomorrow, and we thought we could get a photo op of the two of you too."

Olive frowned. "You want to do press photos with me after I run thirteen miles?" After her last long run she looked like she'd been dragged on the pavement for the last few miles. "I'm worried I'm not going to be able to physically walk back to the shuttle bus to get to my hotel after. I'm not sure I'll be in any state to take photos."

His smile didn't falter, as if working at Disney World meant he tried to imitate the Cheshire Cat. "Oh, yes. About the hotel.

As a thank-you, we've upgraded your accommodations to one of the suites."

"Oh . . . thank you. You didn't have to—"

"You saved the life of one of our own. Mr. Feldstein's brother insisted. It's the least we can do. We want to make sure you get the honor you deserve. We really hope you enjoy your new accommodations. The photos wouldn't take long at all." There seemed to be an implication that this meant press photos was the least Olive could do . . .

Olive rubbed the back of her neck. She was already sweating, and she hadn't even started running yet. "Can I see how I feel *afterward*?"

"Of course. Of course. Do you mind signing a few release forms so we can use any photos in promotional materials?" He handed her a pen.

"Sure, that's fine." She skimmed the page and then scribbled her name at the bottom. "I think tomorrow will be better. Um . . . can I go get my bib now? I probably need to find my corral." She also desperately needed to answer a few messages. Derek was going to be pissed.

"Would you like a golf cart to bring you to where you need to go?"

"No, I'm good. I'll be fine. Uh—thank you. How do I get in contact with you if I decide to do the photographs for tomorrow?"

"Pick up the phone in your room. There's a note on your account."

After an awkward goodbye, Olive trotted outside. She waited in line to check her shoulder bag and then tried to find a quiet enough space to call Derek.

Derek answered on the third ring, which was weird given the time of day. "What in god's name happened on that plane?" She heard another muffled male voice and the sound of blankets moving.

"I'm guessing you've seen the video." She tapped the toe of her sneaker onto the pavement.

"Have *you* seen the video?"

"No. I hate watching myself on camera. This is mortifying. The Disney people want me to do photos. The airline forced me to do photos. This is a goddamn circus."

"You looked hot saving him all like *Grey's Anatomy* and shit. I'm glad you were wearing those Lululemons I bought you instead of your pants with the holes." Derek Chang had been Olive's best friend since middle school, and he never missed an opportunity to give her shit about anything, especially clothes.

She adjusted her fanny pack, rechecking that she had everything she needed, switching the call to her running earbuds. "Ugh. Me too. Imagine the press I would have attracted had my crotch been visible in the viral videos."

"I shudder to think. Where are you now?"

"At Disney World." As much as she'd loved Disney as a kid, the crowds were a lot. She'd never been here alone. Her heart thumped louder.

"How'd you get there? A second flight? I checked, and it said your flight was diverted."

Other runners pushed past her as she tried to navigate the crowd, scanning the crush of people for signs. "It was. And there were no more flights. Uh—the copilot drove me."

"You met a *man*." He chuckled.

"You're a sexist asshole. Her name is Stella."

"You're talking to a male nurse, O. I'm making assumptions based on statistical probabilities. You've dated men on occasion."

"True, but she's a woman, and her name is Stella, and it doesn't matter because I'm probably never going to see her again." A group of women wearing Minnie Mouse ears and tutus shoved her out of the way so they could find the fifteen-minute-mile corral.

"You think she spent five hours chauffeuring your sexy ass out of the goodness of her heart?"

"I—I think she is a genuinely nice person. And it was six and a half hours. She's . . . something, though. Utterly gorgeous and wrong for me. Type A. She won't even drink coffee in a rental car. Kind of a control freak."

"You're talking about her an awful lot for someone you *don't* have a crush on."

Olive tripped over the curb and had to steady herself on a lamppost. "I never said I didn't have a crush on her. I said she's utterly wrong for me. She's a pilot, for fuck's sake, and I could barely make it onto the plane."

"Hold on for a sec." A muffled conversational noise. "Joni wants to know if you took the Valium."

"You're at work already?" He must have been saying good-bye to whoever was in his bed when she called. It was later than she thought, and he lived practically across the street from the hospital. "No, I didn't, but I will on the way back. Thanks again for covering my shifts this weekend, by the way."

"You know you don't have to thank me for that. But seriously, check your phone to make sure *Good Morning America* hasn't called you."

"They're not going to call me." The Disney music seemingly playing from everywhere surged in volume. She whipped her head around trying to make sure the race wasn't starting without her.

"This is the type of story they eat up. They love this shit."

Really wanting to change the subject, Olive cleared her throat. "Is Gus okay?"

"The doggo is happy and settling into a few days at my apartment. He only gave me a slightly sarcastic grumble when I made him take a walk in the rain yesterday."

"He hates rain." Olive laughed, thinking about her Great Dane mix's face when she tried to take him on walks in wet weather. An announcement bellowed over the loudspeaker. "Shit, I have to go."

"Wait, O. I have to tell you one more thing." His voice was serious.

"What?"

"Lindsay's down there."

"No." Groaning, Olive covered her face with one hand. "Shit. She said she wasn't going to use her bib. She said she was trying to sell it." Luckily Lindsay was way faster than Olive and would never be caught dead in the eleven-minute-mile-pace corral. This was quickly becoming another Murphy's Law situation. Her family had abandoned her, but of course her toxic ex wouldn't be able to stay away.

"She posted about you on Instagram. And Twitter. After the video went viral."

"What did she—never mind. I don't want to know. We're broken up."

"I know that. And *you* know that." He sighed. "But maybe sleeping with her six months ago and all the random hookups before that made her hazy about those details. She's not nice to you. Don't let her reel you back in. She's a manipulator."

"I won't. It's why I came by myself. This is for Jake. This weekend is about turning over a new leaf and checking another item off his list."

"Be careful, okay? Text me after."

"I will." An even bigger crowd pushed in on her from every angle, and she couldn't help herself from worrying over every flash of blond hair. She didn't want to see Lindsay right now.

"And you should call Stella."

"I don't have her number, and I'm not going to stalk someone just because she's hot as fuck and drove me to Disney World."

"Those sound like two monumentally good reasons to stalk someone."

"Shit, I really need to go now. People are moving and I don't know what they're doing."

"Happy running," Derek drawled.

"Un-freaking-likely," Olive answered while taking her body through the motions of a few stretches.

Chapter 8

Olive didn't expect "running" a half-marathon to involve an hour of slow walking. Watching group after group start before you was infuriating. It became even less clear why anyone who was not a masochist would do this for fun.

She felt in her pocket for Jake's medal, closing her eyes and imagining how it would've been if she'd come with him last year. He was a lot faster than she was, but he'd be back here anyway, bouncing around and making friends with everyone else in their corral. Basically, doing all the work socializing so Olive could stand back and marvel at his magnetism.

God, she missed the big, giant idiot.

It took only an eternity before her group arrived at the starting line. The music set them off running. Well, *running* might have been stretching the definition of what Olive was doing. She'd been given strict instructions by her running group to pace herself.

So she did.

Thirteen point one miles was a long way. *So. Fucking. Long.*

But she didn't stop.

She didn't take photos with characters.

She didn't look at anyone around her.

She just ran.

Thinking of Jake. Thinking about all she'd accomplished in the last year and all the things he would almost certainly never see again.

Olive didn't start crying until mile ten. That was when it got hard. Jake said he kept going the entire time when he ran last year. She would too. No matter how much it hurt. No matter how much she ached to sit down and give up. He didn't give up, so she wouldn't either. She closed her eyes, and found herself back on the last long run she'd done with her brother. She was whining like a five-year-old and practically limping down the last run of trail that would bring them back to Jake's house.

He leaned over with his paw-like hand and mussed her hair. She pushed him off and gave him a tiny, petulant shove.

He laughed once, but then his voice softened like he knew his words would echo in her brain months later. *"Fight through it. If I can do it, Olive, you can."*

Fight.

Was she fighting through this stupid half-marathon because she'd lost the other battle that counted?

With every step closer to the end, she found herself wishing against all hope for the scene in Jake's photo from last year. The proud Murphy family waiting to cheer him on at the end. The smiles and hugs. He'd been the essential piece that brought them all together.

Olive's feet faltered in their rhythm against the pavement.

"Keep moving," she said through gritted teeth.

Talking to her feet might be a new low for Olive. Jake would have teased her endlessly for that.

He had been on a long run the morning of the accident. The last picture in her phone from Jake was of the new running shoes he bought after coming back from Disney. What had happened to them after he was brought to the hospital?

Such a weird, stupid thought.

Olive's own worn shoe treads scraped against the pavement. Every step was a battle. Blinking away a round of tears, Olive scanned the festive crowd on either side of the racecourse. All unfamiliar.

The dumb crying meant she'd missed seeing the last distance marker. She checked her watch to see how much farther she had to go before she could collapse into a blob. Twelve point nine miles done. Just a few more turns and she'd be at that finish line.

Time was strange when you were running. It slowed down when it was hardest.

Olive checked her watch one more time partially out of habit, but her feet almost stopped moving when she read the numbers. That time. That *exact* time brought her back to the worst day of her life. She was sitting in a hard plastic chair with one hand in her brother's and the other clenched in a fist. Time was ticking away on her wrist as if the universe didn't realize how fucking precious every second was. An unfamiliar face appeared at the sliding glass door.

Olive checked her watch too often in those days, particularly when they knew a fresh specialist would be reviewing Jake's scans. Olive, her mother, and her sister rotated care, so he was never alone, but on that day they were all together in the room. Her father had gone for coffee. Dad seemed to always have a reason for leaving. But after the accident the Murphy women became a three-woman army against a common enemy. That glass-walled ICU room with its stuffy air and constant noise became their base of operations. They faced each assault together. First, Jake would never walk again. That had been bad enough, but then the news became grimmer and grimmer until that goddamn day when Olive checked her goddamn watch and looked up to find that goddamn unfamiliar face at the door.

Heather had been nursing newborn Cody when the newcomer knocked, adjusting his scrubs as if he'd just gotten out of a surgery. Olive never thought much about how similar the Murphy women were in mannerisms until that moment. They each tensed their hands and leaned closer to Jake, as if some instinctual defensiveness told them of the coming blow.

The final blow.

Clinically speaking, Olive understood all the words the doctor said. Despite the tears and shattering breaths, she *understood* that the new test results were unequivocal. She let go of Jake's hand, grabbed onto the bed to keep herself upright. Olive stared at the watch as she breathed against the crushing weight of the revelation.

Jake was *gone*.

In every way that mattered.

Heather left the room first, going to call her husband to come get the baby. The doctor turned to Olive, recognizing her role as medical power of attorney. He talked about choices and possible next steps.

"He wouldn't want this." Olive's voice had been somewhere between a sob and a whisper as she gestured to the room. The machines. The tubes. All of it. "He'd want us to let him go."

As the words left Olive's mouth, Olive's mom went rigid. Like the subtle vibration of a live wire, the air seemed to hum around her. After several speechless moments, she rose to stand beside her son and then erupted. She screamed until Olive's ears rang, telling everyone that "*nobody better touch my son*" before she came back. She clutched her rosary so tightly in her fist, Olive was surprised the beads hadn't broken.

The sudden pain in Olive's chest beneath her safety-pinned bib had nothing to do with the miles of running, but it brought her back into the present.

Breathe, Olive. The crowd noises from the race seemed to quiet as Olive focused on the course in front of her.

"*Fight through it.*"

But she'd already lost.

No matter how much she tried to focus on the race, the memories wouldn't stop.

She had tried and failed. Olive took steps to honor Jake's wishes, signed the paperwork, and waited beside him for her family to come back. But several hours later, her mom charged back into the hospital room with a lawyer at her elbow and a damning document alleging that Olive's "personal financial stake" in her brother's death was a conflict of interest. Her mother's priest showed up a few hours later, making it tacitly clear that the financial accusation was all just a means to prevent Olive from honoring Jake's wishes because of their conflict with their mother's religious beliefs. Olive hadn't even known about the will yet . . .

In a matter of hours, Olive had become her family's number one enemy, all because she didn't want her brother to suffer. Olive understood their anger because she was angry too. Angry because Jake was *supposed* to be right next to her right now. An ugly part of Olive was angry at him for leaving her. He was supposed to be here.

This rage against the unfairness of Jake's accident gave her legs a final surge of energy.

The finish line appeared on the horizon.

Olive forced her breaths to stay even.

"If I can do it, Olive, you can."

Last year, Jake had a group of beaming Murphy smiles waiting for him at the finish line, but Olive would be alone. Did a tiny part of her hope that they saw the viral video of her on the airplane and it reminded them that Olive wasn't a horrible person?

Maybe.

But they wouldn't be there.

Still, she kept running.

The crowd around her thinned, so only a few runners flanked her now. They appeared as stupid exhausted as she was. The finish line was less than a hundred yards away.

"For Jake," she said softly.

After a deep inhale, Olive sprinted the last fifty feet, every breath a knife in her chest, every step jolting her body with pain. When she crossed the finish line, her face was dry—her tears had been wiped away by the Florida breeze. Every other part of her was soaked with sweat.

Olive had done it for him, and now it was over. She should feel a sense of accomplishment, but part of her still felt empty. When she slowed to a stop, her muscles began to rebel in earnest. She took out his medal and ran a finger over its surface and then put it back in her pocket.

The finish line was packed with people. She wove through the crowd, grabbed a banana, and then went to get her stuff from the bag check. A dense mob of runners and their loved ones populated the open space just beyond the exit of the roped-off racers-only area.

Apparently, her heart hadn't caught up with her brain. She scanned the crowd pretending she wasn't hoping for a glimpse of her mom or sister. She locked on the exact spot where that photo of Jake and her family had been taken last year. Another family was using it for a photo shoot. Sweaty arms wrapped around one another, with matching smiles on all of their faces as they congratulated the two racers in the center.

Why was she stupid enough to be disappointed?

No one was here for her.

Out of nowhere, a hand grabbed hers, pulling her into a tight hug. Olive was hyperaware of exactly how disgusting her body was as the scent of lilacs and vanilla hit her nose.

Stella beamed at her. "Congratulations!"

A series of clicks sounded. A camera was there now, taking photos of her. It was not one of the normal photographers that were scattered throughout Disney World. This was a news crew.

A microphone pushed in her face. "How did it feel to finish the race, Olive?"

"Um, good." Just like with the photo op on the plane, playing along seemed like the only option.

"Your friend wrote on Twitter that you were running it in honor of your brother?"

"My—what? Who?"

Olive didn't know why she was asking. There was literally only one person who would have put that online. Lindsay.

"I—yes, my brother ran this race last year. It was super important to him. He—uh, got me the bib. So, I wanted to do it for him."

"How are you feeling about saving the man's life on the airplane? Being a hero?"

Olive gritted her teeth. "I'm not a hero. I did what anyone would've done. I got lucky with catching what was wrong . . ." *Hero.* She couldn't even hear that stupid word without thinking about Jake and the video. People used that word to try to make Olive's family feel better. *Well, Jake was such a hero.* Like it was supposed to make them feel fucking better about him being gone. She was going to throw up. She was going to vomit on camera in front of who the fuck knows how many people. Her ears started ringing.

A hand caught hers from behind and nudged her backward.

Stella was there, using her most Stella-like voice. "Running a half-marathon is a really big accomplishment, and Olive has had a very hectic twenty-four hours. Thank you for sharing her story. It's important for all of us to remember that what we saw Olive do on the plane is what nurses all over the country do every day. Thank you so much."

"Are you her—"

"Friend." Stella's eyes met Olive's. "I'm her friend."

For a second, neither seemed to know what to do. Olive paused in her not-so-subtle escape, and Stella appeared to have run out of words.

"You're my friend?" Olive's voice was breathless, trying to make it so low no one would hear it except Stella.

Stella nodded and then yanked her *"friend"* away from the camera crew.

Chapter 9

Olive knew her legs wouldn't actually fall off. She was a nurse, after all. The muscles and bones were all still attached to one another. But with every limping stride, her medical knowledge seemed less certain. The ground didn't seem soft, but the idea of lying down on it was more and more appealing.

Hoping to distract from her limping, Olive turned to Stella, reaching to touch her arm but then thinking better of it. "Thank you for coming today. You didn't need to feel obligated, though. But with all of that . . ." She pointed backward in the vague direction of where the camera crew accosted her. "You saved me."

"I took a short nap in my hotel room and then woke up all excited to come to Disney World. When I ran my marathon a million years ago, I would've been really upset if no one had come to see me. My dad came then, and it was really nice to see a friendly face at the finish line. He practically had to carry me to the parking lot. Speaking of which, where are we walking?"

The corners of Olive's mouth twitched. Stella spoke in paragraphs, not sentences. And *fuck* did she like that about her. "The shuttle. I'm sorry. I should've asked where you want to go. My brain's not functioning very well right now."

"Are you hurt?"

"No, just rethinking all the life decisions that led to running a half-marathon."

Olive had expected Stella to laugh at that. Not that what she'd said was funny. It wasn't really funny at all. Olive was completely out of funny at the moment.

Her phone began vibrating, which meant it was one of the few numbers that could bypass do not disturb. She grabbed it from her fanny pack.

"Shoot. My brother's hospital." Olive had given them several other numbers in case of emergencies for while she was down here. She paused her walking.

"Do you need to answer it?"

Derek had demanded she take a mental break this weekend. He'd threatened to block every hospital number and her mom's number if she didn't agree to let other people take over care decisions for a few days.

"Um. No, I don't." She put the phone away. It was pathetic how hard it was to start moving again after the short pause.

As if sensing this, Stella linked arms with Olive, taking a bit of the strain off Olive's legs. "You ran the race for your brother?"

"Yep." She was still very conscious of being sweaty, but she couldn't pull away. It felt soft and safe to have Stella so close beside her. The scent of her and the way Olive's head could lean into her shoulder at exactly the perfect angle. It was addicting.

"He's—well, that is to say, there was the implication . . . but I don't want to overstep or make assumptions because that's none of my—"

"He was going to run it with me. It's a long story." And she wasn't sure she could tell it today without completely losing it. "He just . . . can't run anymore. He's at a long-term care facility. Paralyzed. Traumatic brain injury." There. She said it without crying this time. Maybe coming here really was a good decision.

"I'm sorry."

Olive fumbled for a follow-up question that would deflect from a discussion about Jake. "D-do you have any siblings?"

"No, only child. Just me and my dad."

"Are you still close with him?"

She nodded, but then her mouth pulled downward as Olive almost tripped over her dragging feet. "Do you want to sit down?"

"If I sit down, I won't get back up. I'd really like a bed. And a shower. And room service. And a leg transplant. I'll settle for the first three." Olive's steps got progressively slower. She collected enough courage to ask a small question. "Do you have any interest in coming back to my room and having a burger with me?"

"I'd absolutely love to have a burger with you." Stella's smile should be illegal. Olive would do incredibly filthy things to make this woman smile. "That's a great idea."

Olive, however, was quickly regretting the invitation as she shunted some blood away from her decimated legs and back up to her brain. She had invited a gorgeous woman back to a room she hadn't even seen yet.

If her body hadn't been in excruciating pain, she'd be paying more attention to the lifting sensation she felt every time Stella's smooth hands brushed against her hip. Olive had always been a storm cloud, and now sunshine beamed beside her with every stride. Sexy, good-smelling, unattainable sunshine.

✳✳✳

As the door swung open, Olive's jaw dropped. "Whoa. I mean, they said it was an upgrade, but *shit*."

Stella shook her head, eyes wide. "It's amazing."

The suite was unreal. A bed that looked even bigger than a king sat in the center of an enormous room with views overlooking the pool. There was a sitting area with a couch separated from the main room by classy French doors. The décor was luxurious with calming coastal blues and teals.

"My brother made the hotel reservation. He was a really successful director at an engineering firm. He said I wasn't getting out of running the race with him this year and staying here was going to be my incentive. I've only ever stayed at the super budget hotels."

"That's why it was so important to you to get here." Stella's voice was slightly softer than her usual way of speaking. "Because of your brother."

"I promised him." Olive took a step forward. The few seconds of awestruck stillness seemed to have given her muscles free rein for lactic-acid gremlins to have a party. She needed food. She really, really needed a shower.

Staggering into the room, Olive dumped her stuff on the ground near the bed—the bed that was calling her name very, very loudly. Her half-open backpack spilled onto the floor, and she should have anticipated that Stella's reaction to that would not have been positive. What she didn't expect was that Stella would attack the spilled contents with the ferocity of a territorial honey badger. It was like mess provoked a reflexive pounce.

Olive waved her hands, sweeping the stuff back up into her bag. Her taut hamstrings screamed in agony as she leaned over. Still, Olive would prefer Stella not see that her packing strategy consisted of throw shit in one bag, throw shit that doesn't fit in the other. Stella was probably one of those people with a Pinterest board dedicated to packing strategies, a loyalty card from the Container Store, and a commercial grade label maker. She might even have one of those fancy Cricut things.

Olive took Stella's hand, and pulled her over to the couch. "Sit." She grabbed the hotel binder. "Order food. I'm going to take a shower because I probably smell like a dead sewer rat. Order whatever you want. I really, truly owe you."

Stella looked up through her lashes at Olive and blinked twice before nodding and flipping through the menu. Olive's heart flipped in her chest, a curl of heat twisting in her stomach.

The bed began calling her name for a very different reason.

Stella's gaze lifted. "What do you want?"

An ice-cold shower.

She cleared her throat. "A burger and fries. Basically, as greasy as it gets. I'm going to die if I don't have one ASAP."

"Well, we wouldn't want that." Stella crossed her legs, white jeans tight around her hips, flowy goldenrod top billowing gracefully.

Was Stella flirting?

Olive couldn't decide if Stella was flirting or the power of wishful thinking was overpowering reason. Whatever it was, Olive's general grossness was not going to work for whatever happened next.

A well-adjusted human might ask the other person how they felt.

But Olive was not a well-adjusted human. She shut her mouth and hobbled to the bathroom.

Maybe Stella would casually mention how much she liked pussy during the next conversation, and then rip Olive's clothes off, push her down onto the bed, and—

Cold shower.

Olive remembered she'd forgotten—because it was that kind of day—her toiletries out in the main room. Hers was not the type of hair that worked with hotel products unless she wanted her head to spend the next twenty-four hours resembling an ill-trimmed juniper bush or, if she brushed it, one of those troll dolls from the nineties. Olive grabbed her backpack rather than dig through it in the room and expose the aforementioned whatever-shit-fits organizational method.

Stella quirked an eyebrow at her but didn't comment from where she sat on the bed, cradling the hotel phone to her ear.

God, she looked like a vacation advertisement or a travel influencer profile photo on Instagram.

Cold shower.

Right.

It took Olive thirty minutes to untangle her hair enough to get it out of the braids. Dirt and dust had caked into a disgusting paste in every crevice of her body. It didn't help that she was so stiff it took double the time as usual for her to wash herself. She may or may not have taken a few extra minutes to ensure that her legs and underarms were freshly shaved.

When she came out, she was clean, wearing her favorite (and not at all understatedly sexy) rust-colored romper, and feeling like she might look like an appropriate person to sit beside Stella. Or under her. Or on top of her face.

Jesus.

The food sat on the table untouched but smelling amazing.

She'd waited for Olive to start eating?

Well, that was incredibly thoughtful.

And Stella . . .

Gorgeous, well-kempt, never-a-hair-out-of-place Stella was passed out. Snoring, drooling, and cuddling a pillow with her elbow tucked adorably beneath her head.

Olive stood there watching for at least forty-five seconds longer than would have been normal and not creepy. Torn between concerns about Stella's food getting cold and the desire to let Stella sleep, Olive ate a couple of fries and guzzled a bottle of warm Gatorade from her backpack. The salty calories staved off the edge of dizzy exhaustion.

She leaned across the bed and touched Stella's shoulder. "Stella?"

Stella mumbled something that might have been either "I'll be up in a minute" or "I'll kill you if you don't let me sleep." It was hard to tell.

Given that Stella had dutifully waited for Olive to get out of the shower before eating, Olive felt she could at least let Stella finish her nap.

Olive grabbed her phone and sat on the edge of the bed as

far away as possible from Stella. She skimmed through several good-luck texts from Derek and Joni and her cousins, replied to them, and then she didn't remember anything else.

Chapter 10

Golden light tinted the room when Olive woke. She was still in almost the same position she'd been in when she'd fallen asleep, near the edge of the bed on her back. The most important difference in her situation was that a long, soft arm reached across her chest. Every inhale smelled of lilacs and vanilla, and a foot twitched between her own.

It was heavenly.

She'd never woken in someone's arms before. It amazed her that she'd been able to sleep at all. Yet if she'd closed her eyes again, she could stay like this for an eternity. It felt—well, it felt like something more than she expected but also less. It felt comfortable. Like home. Not awkward.

A few of Olive's sore muscles tingled and complained. She shifted slightly as she began to wake up enough to engage in her normal pattern of overthinking. Stella woke up all at once. She leaped off Olive as if she'd been injected with some kind of panic, anti-snuggle amphetamine.

"I'm so so sorry," Stella stammered. "I'm a sleep cuddler."

Unable to stop herself, Olive burst out laughing. Being a sleep cuddler was pretty much the most on-brand Stella thing ever. Even in sleep, she went the extra mile and overachieved.

"I just . . . I always get cold, and I search for a heat source."

"A heat source?" Olive suppressed a smile.

"Yeah . . . my roommates in college used to say that I'd spoon an alligator if it ended up in my bed."

"But aren't alligators cold-blooded?"

"You know, I pointed out that flaw in their logic, too. They said it didn't matter." She sounded ruffled. Anxious and jittery. It was cute, and Olive was torn between teasing her and giving her an out.

"I didn't mind, Stella. Really. I slept amazing. I was . . . I-have-literally-no-idea-what-time-it-is-right-now type unconscious."

Stella flipped on a light, both women groaning at the searing pain against their sleep-addled irises. "Oh gosh. It's five thirty."

"We slept six hours?" As if in open rebellion, Olive's stomach made a sound less like a rumble and more like a Jurassic Park–level roar.

Stella was at the mirror, finger-combing her hair and attempting to smooth creases out of her blouse. Her hair was wavy and wild, scattered with flyaways and pillow frizz. Still gorgeous. Pink indentations ran down one of her cheeks.

Olive stood beside Stella and raised a finger to the circular marks. "You have—I think that's from my buttons." The buttons down the center of Olive's romper. At some point Stella's head had rested directly between Olive's tits. And she'd slept through it. *Jesus fucking Christ.*

Cheeks flushing, Stella covered the indentations with her hands.

"I think you're dehydrated." Olive went to get her a bottle of water from the stocked fridge.

Stella guzzled the water, and for the first time since they met, she seemed shockingly incapable of speech. She didn't say another word until she'd drank the entire thing. The food on the table was soggy and glacial, but Olive picked at it anyway out of desperation.

"You know what I really want right now?" Olive asked.

Stella tilted her head. "What?"

"Fried chicken and waffles."

Stella snickered. "That's a super specific craving."

Olive went to her bag, torn about what she wanted to do and

whether it would be weird. Jake would tell her to go for it. She held up a box that held two park entry bands. He'd picked the colors when he'd surprised her with the trip. Again, telling her the only way she'd get it was if she trained for the race with him. *Asshole. Lovable asshole.*

"Want to come with me to Disney World?" She pulled out the green band and handed it to Stella. "My brother . . . I know I should have canceled his pass or whatever. But I hoped I would have someone to bring with me."

Stella flushed. "I—I'd love to."

***

Stella scrolled on the app on her phone, looking for rides with short waits. Olive looked over her shoulder, chin almost grazing the smooth skin between Stella's neck and collarbone. They'd already done several of the classic rides that weren't too crowded.

"I know which one." Olive led Stella back into the park all the way past the teacups and Dumbo to the Barnstormer. This area of the park was always a little less crowded, and a late afternoon thunderstorm had cleared it even more before they arrived.

"All the other lines are too long, but I want to ride a roller coaster."

Stella stopped. "A roller coaster? But there's so many other rides. Why this one?"

"It was the first one Jake ever took me on when I was a kid. It's really fun. A lot of people forget about it now since there's bigger coasters here." She grabbed Stella's hand and pulled her up the ramp. There was almost no one in the line. "I know it might seem lame, like it's a kids' one or whatever, but it's great."

Stella's hand was tight on the railing, knuckles blanching. Her throat bobbed.

"Are you okay?" Olive angled her body toward Stella's.

"Of course I am. I mean, it's not even a big roller coaster, right. So of course I'm okay. Why wouldn't I be okay?" Her voice was at least a register higher than usual.

"Allied Airlines pilot Stella Soriano is afraid of roller coasters?"

Stella's eyebrows knit together. "I've never been a big roller coaster person."

Olive turned around, walking back down. "I'm sorry. It's not a big deal. Let's find another ride."

Stella shook her head and marched back up to the top where only about ten people stood ahead of them.

"You don't need to do this for me, Stella."

She shook her head. "I'm not. It's about time I try something new."

"Are you sure?"

"If you can run a half-marathon after sleeping all night in a car, I can ride a rickety . . ." She swallowed again and turned back to face Olive and away from the "rickety" roller coaster. "This is good for me."

All right, maybe Olive had a lot more in common with Stella than she originally thought.

Olive's eyes were wide as she faced Stella.

"What?" Stella asked.

"It's just . . . you're a pilot."

"Yes?"

"You love flying in metal ten million feet in the air."

"Thousands, not millions. And yeah? So?" Her eyebrows pulled together, truly not seeing an ounce of irony.

"Never mind." Olive smiled. "This one's short. We can go ride the Haunted Mansion ride or Pirates again afterward if it's too much."

Stella playfully smacked Olive's shoulder—and fuck, did it feel like another electric charge went through Olive at the touch. "I'm not a coward."

"I know you're not."

"I'm not." Stella's chin jutted out.

Before Olive could reply again, a few people in the line urged them forward as another group boarded. They'd be on the next run. Stella took in a few long breaths, extending out the exhales. Her eyes followed the loop-de-loops of the ride, darting every which way. She played with her hair, and Olive mirrored the movement.

"It's not a big deal at all. There are lots of other rides. You're sure?" Olive asked more seriously.

Stella stood a little taller. "Yes."

A voice from the front called out, "*Next.*" They stepped up and scooted into a seat. Their hips pushed together. Olive's bare knee knocked against Stella's leg as they brought the rail over their thighs.

Olive turned to her, speaking low. "You have to remember to scream."

Stella's voice became breathless. "What?"

Olive's fingers were a hair away from Stella's thigh. She leaned forward. "Scream. It's way worse to hold it in."

"Oh. Okay. During the ride. Right. I need to distract myself." Stella was close enough that her breath made wisps of Olive's hair flutter. Her full lips pressed outward, parting as she mumbled. Her tongue dragged slowly across the bottom one, making it shiny and painfully enticing. "You know, I looked up the statistics once, and I think roller coaster accidents are really rare. Something like less than point six five per million rides. So, I really shouldn't wor—"

"Stella?"

"Yeah?"

Olive leaned an inch closer. Was some combination of fatigue and nostalgia making Olive bold? PDA in public when you were queer could be a risk, but at that moment she didn't care at all. Olive would never have listed the ability to cite obscure actuarial statistics as a turn-on, but mainly seeing how much they really were alike seemed to give her the confidence she needed to ask a particular question. "Could I kiss you?"

Stella's dark eyes widened as she gave a tiny nod. "Yes."

Olive pressed her mouth against Stella's. It was cautious at first, sweet and quiet. But Stella opened for her. Their tongues met gently. Tasting. Tentative turning urgent. Olive's fingers trailed up Stella's skin, stroking her from elbow to wrist. With the rail, she couldn't fully take Stella into her aching arms. A flood of warmth pooled between Olive's legs.

Jesus.

A click signaled that they were about to move.

As she pulled away, Olive nipped at Stella's lip. "Remember what I told you."

"What?" Stella's eyes were still closed, voice low.

Olive whispered directly into Stella's ear, adding another light kiss on the smooth outer shell. "Scream, Stella."

"What?" Eyes popping open, Stella faced forward and gripped the rail with one hand. The other rested limply on her leg, palm up.

Olive wanted to intertwine her fingers there, but as she reached down, Stella grabbed the rail. They climbed the first hill before the big drop. The wheels clacked beneath them on the track.

"It's the waiting." Stella took in a deep breath and held it. When they reached the top, she looked over at Olive, smiled, and *screamed*.

Chapter 11

They were both breathless and laughing when they ran down the ramp. Olive rubbed a lingering sore spot on her leg and then looked up. "Thank you."

"For what?"

"For coming with me on the roller coaster even though it's not your thing."

"So that was a gratitude kiss?" Stella's eyes angled with something that looked like understanding. "To distract me from being scared."

"It was . . ." Was she giving Olive an out, so Stella didn't have to reject her? The honest answers were easy. *Amazing? Earthshattering? Life altering?*

"It was . . ." Olive searched for a word that wouldn't reveal too much.

"Olive?" Stella's expression was unreadable.

"Yes. Um, I *am* very grateful. I—really appreciate everything you did. Hanging out with me today. With the interview this morning. And tonight. I'm having so much fun."

Something was changing on Stella's face, and Olive was struck by the terror that the kiss had made her uncomfortable. She'd thought it was romantic at the time, but she'd literally cornered a woman into kissing her. They had a rail over their legs, for Chrissakes. What if she didn't feel she could say no? *What the fuck, Olive?* Before she could summon the courage to apologize, Stella was speaking again.

"It was nothing. I needed something to do tonight. I'd signed up to do that last flight down here, and I don't have another flight tomorrow—like I said. I could've deadheaded back home and then come back, but I love the Food and Wine Festival. It was no big deal."

"Do you want to go over to Epcot now?"

"You don't want to stay here and see the fireworks and do more rides?"

"If you love the festival, I want to do what you love." She checked her watch. "It's open for three more hours. I'll do whatever you want."

"Really?" Stella grinned.

Olive's own smile widened. "Yeah. Whatever you want." Olive's cheeks were cramping worse than her legs. She'd smiled so much today. More than she had in months.

Stella's hand twitched as if a small part of her wanted to reach out and grab Olive's, but she balled it into a fist and glued it to her side.

"So, we'd better . . ." Stella said as she pointed toward the park exit.

"Yeah. Let's go." Olive looked away to hide her disappointment.

They rushed through the park to the monorail. It was packed with bodies of every age and size. A stroller rammed the back of Olive's aching legs, shoving her into Stella's chest. She had to brace her hands on either side of Stella's shoulders so she didn't land face-first into her tits.

Oh, great, now Olive was mauling this poor woman. Fabulous.

Stella steadied her, with a delicate pressure on her shoulders. Damn, she had long eyelashes. They couldn't be real, could they?

Stella scrunched her face. "They could kill someone with those things."

"Strollers are deadly. My sister Heather's got one of those double ones, and it's like driving two grocery carts at once."

"You've got nieces or nephews?"

Olive slid her phone out of her pocket. "Shit, my phone's

about to die again, but yeah. I've got one of each. Heather's kids." She swiped to a photo that used to be her lock screen. "Well, Fiona's my sister's oldest, and she turned four last month—wow—and Cody is eleven months." She hadn't been on Facebook much, so she hadn't seen any recent photos of the kids. The last photo she had of them on her phone was from the week before Jake's accident. Cody was practically a newborn in it.

Stella squealed and grabbed the phone from Olive to get a better look at the photo. "They're adorable." She held her finger over the phone. "Are there more photos of them?"

"Yeah, you can swipe. I keep all my compromising nudies on a burner."

"You never want to swipe without permission. Never know what you might come across." Laughing, Stella browsed through the photos.

Was Olive imagining it or had Stella's cheeks gone pinker? Maybe joking about naked pictures wasn't something a normal human did like ten freaking minutes after possibly coercing someone into a romantic almost-make-out session on a roller coaster.

"Oh my god, this one." Stella's grin widened.

Olive came closer, her cheek grazing Stella's shoulder as she checked which image she was talking about. "Yeah, my niece Fiona's first trip to the fair. She loved all the animals, and she ran off because she wanted to nap with the pigs."

"She looks so cute covered in mud." Stella pointed at the picture. "That's your brother holding her? You guys look a little alike. The smile, I mean. He seems really tall."

Olive nodded. "Yeah, that's Jake. Super tall."

"Oh my god, the mud in this one. Fiona smeared it across his face?"

"Yeah." The toddler had gotten the foulest-smelling pig mud all over him that day, and he'd just thought it was hilarious, to the exasperation of Fi's parents.

"He didn't have kids?"

"No." Olive frowned. "He always joked that he was in a Carrie Bradshaw/Big relationship with his career, and he had trouble committing to anything else."

"Big *Sex and the City* fan?" Stella's eyes twinkled.

"The biggest. I wish he'd found someone, though. For a while, I was just stupidly hoping he'd marry my best friend because . . ." Olive took a measured breath. "I don't know. He would have made a great partner if he ever stopped working so much. He was the sweetest, funniest, most selfless guy."

"I get what he meant about the job thing, though. I—well, I'm not good at relationships either. When you have something that you want to put all your energy into . . . people can get hurt, you know?" Stella focused back on the screen and went through another few photos at a faster speed. "You all seem like you did a lot together with your whole family? That's great you had them all close by."

Olive was intensely curious about what Stella had meant about relationships, but given how quickly Stella had shifted the subject, Olive didn't want to pry. "Yeah, it really was." The necessary past tense stung. How long had it been since she'd seen Fiona and Cody? Olive had sent Fiona a birthday gift, but she'd never heard whether she'd received it. Cody would be turning one next month. Olive molded her face into a happy expression, ignoring the ache in her chest that accompanied thinking of her family. "Do you have much family close?"

"Not really." Stella handed the phone back. "In the states, most of my cousins with kids live in Texas but all over, and it's a big state. We're so spread out. I see them around the holidays, but I wish I had some nieces and nephews nearby to spoil."

"Do you like kids?" Olive asked.

"I do." Stella's expression grew pensive. "I think I could want a couple someday, maybe. Hard to know. My life's really about my career, so I'm not sure anything like that will ever happen. Relationships . . . well . . . In any case, I can have a meaningful life without kids. I mean, everyone says having them is super fulfilling, but it might not happen for me, and that's okay. I'm okay with it either way."

Olive raised an eyebrow. "Yes, it's okay. Whatever you want, right?"

"Right."

Olive squared her shoulders to Stella's. "It's hard to see people—like my friends and family—having kids and not really knowing if that's something I actually want. Or if I just want it because *other* people want it. And because dimples and chubby feet are adorable."

"Yes." Stella's hands flailed out and then clapped together. "Yes, exactly that."

"What do you do when you're not flying?"

"I teach flying."

"Like in a classroom?"

"In a Cessna." Her eyes lit up at the word. "There's a classroom component. But I like getting people up in the air. It's beautiful. And honestly, there's nothing like seeing someone take the controls for the first time. It's magical. Ethereal."

Flying in a small plane was the stuff of Olive's nightmares, but she couldn't bring herself to say anything that might dim the mesmerizing passion on Stella's face, so she said something idiotic. "That sounds amazing. I would love to do that. Flying."

What the hell are you saying, Olive?

"Have you ever thought about taking lessons?"

"No, they're, uh—expensive. Expensive. Jet fuel."

They had to be expensive, right?

"True, they are. I'll have to take you up sometime. It's nothing like being in a commercial jet. It's . . ." Her eyes faced the starry sky past the monorail window. "'Once you have tasted flight, you will forever walk the earth with your eyes turned to the sky, for there you have been, and there you will always long to return.'"

Hearing Stella recite the quotation should have been corny, but it wasn't. It was sweet and honest.

"Da Vinci?" Olive said, tentatively.

"Yeah. It is." A flicker of wonder passed across Stella's face. "How did you—"

"I was an art history major in college. Before I was a nurse. I was pretty obsessed with Italian painters for a while."

"Have you been to Italy?"

Olive swallowed. "No."

"Why not? Your laptop in your backpack has stickers from all over the US, so I assumed you travel all the time."

She noticed that?

"I've traveled all over the continental US. Just not . . . I've only ever flown once. I usually drive. I have a dog," Olive ended feebly.

Stella's eyes were the size of saucers. "Last night was your *first* flight? The flight down here?"

Olive grimaced. "Yup. I can't decide if that means I'm a storm cloud and should never fly again."

"You saved someone's life. I'd say it's good flight karma."

"Meh, probably better for me to stay on the ground. Just in case."

Stella poked her elbow and chuckled. "Wait, are you *afraid* of flying?"

"How much are you going to judge me if I say yes?" Olive shielded her face with a hand.

"You just said being up and taking lessons in a little plane sounds amazing. You know that commercial air travel is way safer than that, right? Incidentally, it's much safer than driving too."

"I might have had a temporary bout of insanity when I said

that." Olive watched out the window as the monorail curved on the track.

Nope. She was a lying liar McLiar pants because Stella was so fucking beautiful when she talked about flying, Olive couldn't think straight.

"Okay . . ."

Olive turned back to face Stella, tightening her grip on the metal pole. "I know all the statistics about aviation. My brother worked to build airplanes. It was pretty much his mission in life to get me on one. My mom's actually afraid of flying, so I guess it rubbed off on me. It's weird." It was the one thing Olive had inherited from her mother.

"But you never flew? Even when you were a kid?"

"Nope. Not until now."

Stella lifted a finger up to Olive's face. Olive's immediate thought was that she had something on it, but no. Stella was brushing stray strands of hair away from her eyes. Her fingers were soft as they trailed along Olive's jawline and down her neck.

Swear words and a barrage of *OHMYGOD*s stormed through Olive's brain. Every muscle locked down as if she worried a sudden movement would spook Stella away from touching her. This had to be flirting. Had to be.

As the monorail came to a stop, the crowd pushed around them, interrupting the moment. The stroller—that motherfucking stroller—slammed into Olive's Achilles tendon, harder this time. Olive hopped on one foot for a second and then limped off the monorail.

"Are you okay?"

Stella was obviously trying to kill her because she reached down and touched Olive's bare leg where the stroller had assaulted her. A shiver ran down Olive's spine. "I'm fine."

Straightening, Stella snatched her hand back as if Olive's leg had burned her. "Margaritas."

Was that a question?

"Margaritas," Stella said again in a strangely clipped tone.

Olive lifted a conspiratorial eyebrow. "I like margaritas."

"Really? Good. I need one. Now." Stella's voice was almost flustered.

"I can make that happen." Olive offered a wicked smirk.

Chapter 12

Thank the Lord for tequila.

All the awkwardness had vanished, and they were running along the boardwalk. Hysterical laughter over nothing had them pausing every ten feet or so. They'd downed two baskets of chips and guacamole with their margaritas. Salt and lime still clung to Olive's lips and fingers. Her legs felt better than they had all day, the alcohol dulling the edge of the pain. Stella had grabbed her hand to guide her toward another pavilion. Stella's fingers were gentle. They fit perfectly around Olive's.

"We have to stop here," Stella said.

"Japan?"

"Yes. For the mochi bonbons."

"Mochi?"

"It's Japanese ice cream, and it's delicious."

"Okay."

Stella ordered two and handed one to Olive. She bit into it. Cold, creamy, and not exactly what she expected texture-wise. But delicious. She ate it too fast, and then dug her thumb and index finger into the center of her forehead, which felt like it had been stabbed by an ice pick.

"Brain freeze?" Stella asked.

"Yup."

"*Ouch.* That always happens to me too." She gave Olive a pitying look. They finished their dessert and tossed the wrapping in the trash. "Let's run to France."

"I'd let you take me anywhere, Stella."

It was the tequila. The tequila said that.

Stella smirked. "But not on a plane?"

"Maybe you could convince me."

"Let me show you my favorite macarons here. Maybe then you'll want to go to real France." She grabbed Olive by the hips, veering her over to the lake side of the boardwalk.

Olive ended up facing her, with Stella's back to the railing.

Stella pointed. "Sorry, I didn't want you to get nailed by another stroller. A big parade of them were coming past."

"I appreciate that." Heat rose in Olive's chest as it had on the monorail. Stella's hand hadn't moved from her hip. It would be so easy to lean forward. Just an inch at first.

Olive could ask if she could kiss her again.

Stella said yes once.

But as soon as the thought formed in Olive's mind, the enticing pressure of Stella's hand was gone. Stella was moving again. She power walked into a narrow gap in the crowd.

"Where do you want to go in Italy, Olive?"

"I'm assuming you mean real Italy and not Epcot Italy."

Stella snorted and nodded.

Olive quickened her pace to keep up. "Well, if they invent *Star Trek*–style teleportation . . . probably Florence and the Amalfi coast. Rome. All over, really."

"Have you tried antianxiety medication?"

Olive laughed. "I brought a pill on the airplane last night, and I was so nervous, the pill fell out of my hand before I could take it. But yeah, I'm going to try that for the flight back."

"I hope that works. Italy is amazing." The billowing fabric of Stella's top swept across Olive's arm. Goose bumps rose in its wake.

"Where is your favorite place you've traveled?"

"Last year I went to the Cañón del Sumidero in Mexico with my cousins, which is like the Grand Canyon of Mexico. Super amazing. Other than that, probably Paris or New Zealand."

"Oh, wow. Did you see any hobbits?"

"Yep, Paris is full of them." Stella covered her mouth as she erupted with laughter at her own joke.

Olive joined in for good measure. Everything was hilarious tonight. Stella had made her laugh over and over again. Olive clutched at her stomach after the cackling fit subsided. Who the heck was she tonight? Her abs were sore from laughing at corny jokes?

Stella sobered. "New Zealand is *breathtaking*. Long flight, though."

Olive shook her head darkly. "I read once that when you're in a plane over the Pacific Ocean, no one actually knows where you are. A nightmare."

Stella looked like she wanted to roll her eyes. "That's not true anymore. I thought you said you knew all about aviation." She gave her a teasing frown.

"Still." Olive stopped at a food stand, buying two waters. She handed one to Stella, who thanked her and guzzled it. "Maybe someday I'll get there. For now, I'll keep trying to hit all the national parks in my car."

"Where was your favorite?"

"Grand Teton. It's beautiful. Seeing the parks was on this list. It was Jake's—my brother's. He used to work so much. I'm—um . . . trying to go to all the ones he didn't get to see. A couple years ago he made this life list to make sure he was really living, you know?"

"Yeah."

"So now I'm doing everything on it. If my phone wasn't dead I'd show you my Instagram account I made for my Adventures with Gus. Basically just me carting a giant dog around to check things off Jake's list."

"Something impulsive . . . you said check something impulsive off the list."

Olive chuckled. "Yup. I think I can definitely check that off now." Her good mood faltered as her brain returned to the full story about her long road trip last year. She shook off the memories. "Thank you for not being an axe murderer."

"Ha. You're welcome. That's really a cool thing you're doing. Finishing his list." Stella's smile was tinged with sadness—not pity, compassion. "You know you can get places even faster in a plane?"

"I've heard that. Security lines are a bitch, though."

Stella shook her head and sighed.

They arrived at France and got into line. Stella got her macarons but Olive chose a flaky chocolate pastry.

"Do you want some of mine, too?" Olive asked.

"No, I'm good. I don't get to have these very often." She took another bite, somehow managing to stay completely crumb-free. "Where do you live? You flew out of Hagerstown. Pretty small airport."

"Frederick. About an hour south—"

"That's where I live too." Excitement glowed on Stella's face. "I like to pick up extra flights from Hagerstown when I can because it's so close by. Are you at the hospital in town?"

"Yep. I live in one of the newer apartment buildings downtown near the creek. Where are you?"

"With my dad for now. Outside the city limits." A tinge of sadness passed over Stella's face, but it vanished quickly. "I sold my condo a couple years ago. It didn't make sense to keep it since I was traveling so much, and I tried to spend time with my dad whenever I was home."

Panic that was completely inappropriate rose in Olive's chest. "You're thinking about moving?"

"Not anytime soon."

"Oh, okay. Good."

"Good?"

"Yeah, I mean, your dad must like having you around for a while. No sense in paying a mortgage you don't need." *Smooth, Olive.*

"Oh, right. Yeah. It's how I bought the Cessna."

"You own a plane?"

"Not in the Kardashian way. It's a small one. I use it to teach the lessons."

"Still."

"It's a hobby. Maybe one day I'll fly all over for vacation and not just teaching midlife crisis men how to fly." She wiped her fingers clean with a napkin. "Race me to the Frozen ride?"

"That's all the way at Norway."

"Yup." Stella checked her watch. "If we each want to get another margarita first, we better get moving."

Olive groaned and then ran after her, because she would follow Stella Soriano anywhere.

Chapter 13

"You're drunk." Olive steadied Stella with a hand on the small of her back.

"You're drunker." Stella hiccuped, disproving her point completely. "You're sure you're fine with me staying the night? I could call an Uber. They have ones with Minnie Mouse ears. I love Minnie Mouse ears." Her lips pressed into a pout as she leaned against a column outside the lobby. Her words were adorably slurred. "I wish I had my Minnie Mouse ears with me."

"Your hotel is all the way near the airport. Please, stay."

"I don't want to impose." Stella stumbled again as she crossed the threshold of the hotel, hair and shirt askew, yet she looked as amazing as she always did.

Olive helped her stay upright. They stood almost nose to nose. "Hey."

"Hey." Her breath puffed against Olive's face, smelling of limes and chocolate and tequila. Her cheeks were flushed pink, lips soft and full. Her eyes focused on Olive's mouth.

"If you stay to hang out with me tomorrow, I'll buy you Minnie Mouse ears. Sparkly ones."

"Really?"

They inched closer.

"I—"

"Where have you been?" The voice was harsh, grating. And familiar.

Olive turned, and there stood the last person on the planet she wanted to see right now.

"Shit," Olive hissed.

Lindsay's jaw was hard-set. Her beachy blond hair was pulled back into a curated wild ponytail. She wore tiny denim cutoffs and a crocheted crop top. "I've been calling you."

"My phone died a few hours ago."

"I thought you were dead in your hotel room. I mean, you know running isn't really your thing. I was worried, but those assholes at the desk wouldn't tell me your room number."

Olive grunted. "Derek told me you were here. Why'd you come?"

"Maybe I still had hope." Lindsay's makeup was less perfect than normal. The expression lines of her face were more pronounced. It was almost like she wasn't lying about being worried.

Olive rolled her eyes. "Jesus fucking Christ, Lindsay."

"I know you still blame me about last year, but you brought another woman here?" Lindsay scoffed and turned to Stella. "Typical. You know that Olive's not exactly sta—"

"Lindsay. Stop." Olive almost growled the word, but before she could say anything else, Stella cut in.

"I'm not another woman. I mean, obviously I *am* another woman. That is to say, I am a woman and I'm here with her, as in standing with her, but I'm not *with*—"

"Oh, you're straight." Lindsay shot Olive an acerbic grimace that said, *You cannot be serious right now.*

"No, I mean, I'm not straight. But we're not." Stella waved a nervous hand. "No. No. No. Nothing like that. No. We just met. We're—uh, friends," she ended weakly. "So, um. Not dating."

A pang went through Olive at the sheer number of negative words in that monologue of half sentences. She couldn't even be happy about the clear acknowledgment that Stella wasn't straight because clearly Stella thought there was nothing between them. The kiss probably meant nothing to her.

Olive glared at Lindsay. "You have no right to be here. You have no right to say shit like that to my . . . friend."

"I came to see you because I thought this weekend would be hard for you, and I wanted to check in. Derek was worried about you too, but of course he's covering your shifts so he couldn't come." She sighed, almost fretfully. "Especially with all the news coverage about what happened on the plane. Must be triggering for you."

"I'm fine."

"I can see that." Her eyes ran up and down Stella in an unflattering appraisal. "Look, if you're going to be 'friends' with Olive"—her matte black manicured nails put air quotes around the word—"you need to be okay with her being hypercritical about every mistake you make and fielding sobbing two A.M. phone calls. Be ready for all the emotionally needy drama mixed with pathological commitment issues."

Olive was so shocked that Lindsay would imply that *she* was the force of drama in the relationship, she couldn't come up with a suitably biting reply. She couldn't even focus on Lindsay at all. Instead, she stared at Stella, watching an unreadable expression appear there. What was she thinking?

"Stella, I'm not like—"

"Sure you're not." Lindsay narrowed her eyes and gave a derisive snort. "I'll see you at work, Olive. Have just the bestest time ever, you kids." Her voice became sunny but mocking.

Olive wanted to retort that it hadn't escaped her that Lindsay had first dumped her for being "dramatic."

God, did she really need to use that word to describe Olive's anxiety and panic disorder?

The memory still stung. And after what happened with Jake, Lindsay's complaint switched to Olive being "boring," i.e., she was having a fucking major depressive episode after all the stress over her brother's horrific accident. Olive *wanted* to call her on the fact Lindsay was conveniently showing up at her hotel right now only because of Olive's stupid and unwanted fifteen minutes of fame. But mostly, she wanted this conversation to be over, so she didn't bother replying. Olive turned apologetic eyes toward Stella and led her over to the elevator without another glance at Lindsay.

"I'm sorry about that."

"It's fine. She's . . . ?"

"An ex. We broke up a while ago." And Olive was too drunk to explain Hurricane Lindsay to Stella. She didn't want to be thinking about Lindsay. Olive unlocked the room and kicked off her shoes near the closet. Stella lined hers up neatly beside the door. They stood facing each other, barefoot, still drunk, but their happy, floaty Disney World bubble burst by the angry blonde in the lobby.

"You work together?"

"Kind of." Olive winced.

A few wrinkles creased Stella's forehead.

Did the universe have a vendetta against Olive getting laid?

"We can share the bed. If you need a heat source." Olive offered a tentative smile. "I really don't mind sleep cuddling." She walked into the room and passed Stella a bottle of water. "I think we both should hydrate after everything we drank."

"Hydration. Good." Stella's head snapped to face Olive's. "There's a pullout bed in the sitting room. We don't have to share."

"Oh, right. Yeah."

Fuck. Where was a one-bed trope when a gal needed it?

Now would likely not be the moment for Olive to mention that the unexpected snuggle session of the afternoon had left her feeling happier than she'd been in recent memory and that their kiss on the roller coaster had so destroyed her that she was desperate to have Stella spread out in bed, where she could make her feel as amazing as she'd made Olive feel by showing up today. And along the way, she'd like to find out exactly what kind of noises she could get her to make *off* a roller coaster.

"The pullout's fine," Stella said flatly.

"I'll help you set it up." Olive stumbled on her suitcase.

"No, you've had an exhausting day."

"I'm fine." But fatigue was hitting Olive with the force of a Mack truck, and the few minutes of being stationary made her weary legs turn to jelly. She braced an arm on the king bed.

"You're dead on your feet, Olive." Stella pointed to the bed. "Lie down." She spoke in that commanding pilot's voice that gave Olive no choice but to obey.

Olive collapsed with every intention of getting up in a few minutes to undress. Brush her teeth. Floss. Seduce the gorgeous woman in her hotel room.

She heard the clicks and clacks of the sofa bed unfolding.

And then, like every other time she'd been vaguely horizontal in the last twenty-four hours, sleep swallowed her whole.

∗∗∗

The room was bright when she woke. She was still on her stomach, her cheek drool-glued to the comforter. Her romper was twisted and creased. She popped up out of bed.

"Stella?"

The couch looked exactly like it did before. The bed was tucked back inside.

"Stella?" she said again, ears straining, hoping to hear sounds of her in the bathroom. In the shower? She stood and knocked on the bathroom door, but it pushed open. Empty.

She was gone.

Olive was alone in the suite.

An Allied Airlines Post-it note was stuck to her phone, which had been thoughtfully plugged into the charger beside the green wristband Stella had worn the night before.

She wrote in sweeping, elegant cursive script, like a character in an old period film.

Thank you so much for a wonderful night.
All the best, Stella

Chapter 14

Olive's face dug into the desk in front of her hospital computer in the emergency room nurses' station. She swept a few stray dog hairs off her black scrub pants. Gus hadn't left her alone since she'd gotten back yesterday, demanding constant snuggles. She'd only made it out of bed long enough to walk him and eat some dry cereal before work.

Derek smacked the back of her head, gently reminding her they were having a conversation. "Then what happened?"

"I took some promotional photos for Disney with the man whose life I saved, who was wearing a Mickey Mouse costume—he was super nice, by the way, Frank Feldstein is his name—and then I drank around the world at Epcot, vomited into several shrubberies, and passed out next to the Frozen ride. A security guard had to tell me to leave at closing time."

"Dignity. Always dignity." Derek shook with silent laughter.

"Fuck you." Olive poked his shoulder. "And then I threw Jake's wristband into the water."

"Why?"

"It felt right. Like scattering ashes or something."

"But—"

Joni dropped into the seat beside her, putting her stethoscope around her neck. "What'd I miss?"

"The existential tragedy that is my adult romantic life."

She smirked. "Darn. Can we rewind, please?"

"Nothing happened. She left. The couch smelled like lilacs and vanilla the rest of my trip."

"You smelled the couch?" Derek wrinkled his nose.

"Um. Of course not. Who would do such a ludicrous thing?" Olive scratched at the bushy bun on top of her head. "None of it matters. I don't have her number."

"I still don't understand how you never got her number."

"Because I'm an idiot."

Joni patted her back once before turning back toward her computer to log on. "Could you message her on her Instagram or something?"

"Ooooh." Derek whipped out his phone. "What's her Insta?"

"Stellaflies."

He swiped around.

"That's a cute handle," Joni said.

"It's so fucking cute. She's so fucking cute."

"Damn, O. She really is hot." Derek adjusted his glasses. "The uniform."

"God, I know." Olive sucked in a breath. "Don't you think if she wanted me to message her, she would have left her number?"

"Maybe she thought if you wanted it, you would have asked for it."

"My phone was dead by the time I thought of it. I planned on getting it before she left, but she was gone when I woke up."

Joni handed the phone back to Derek. "I feel like it's not that risky to message her and ask."

"She has twenty thousand followers and practically no photos. I bet she never checks her DMs. She probably gets a million spam ones a day."

"Ask her if she needs a sugar daddy, I hear that's the best way to get an influencer's attention." Derek crossed his arms, swiveling back and forth in his chair.

Joni chuckled. "Maybe say hello and tell her you'd like to see her again."

"Where does she live anyway?"

"Here. Frederick. She teaches flying lessons at the small airfield."

Joni brightened. "My sister would call that *a sign*."

"What would you call it?"

"A fortunate coincidence that would make it easier for you to have a functional and practical romantic relationship."

"As hot as that sounds, Joni, maybe we can focus and let Olive tell us more about the hot kiss on the roller coaster."

Joni cut in before Olive could answer. "I'm just saying, she's a pilot so she could have lived anywhere. But she lives here. Practical concerns are important when deciding whether to pursue a relationship. Otherwise, you can get swept up in emotions."

After giving Joni an exasperated look, Derek turned back to Olive. "O, you're literally the only queer woman I know that doesn't push for a commitment on the first date."

"First of all, that's offensive for several reasons. Second of all, it wasn't a date. And even if it was, U-Hauling is a harmful stereotype. Like pretty much all stereotypes."

Unfazed, Derek put up his hand, counting off on his fingers. "First, you slept next to her for six hours—"

"In a car."

"Yeah, while she *chauffeured* you in a rental car from Atlanta to Orlaaaando."

"I paid for the rental car."

"How chivalrous of you." He kept his fingers outstretched. "And second, she came to watch the world's most boring athletic event on the planet just so you wouldn't be alone at the finish line."

"It's at Disney World. She tries to go every year."

"Olive, not even Mickey Mouse can make watching a bunch of people pant and sweat for hours and then run across an electrical cord at all interesting." He arched an eyebrow. "Third, she basically saved you from reporters while gazing prettily into your eyes."

Olive had stared at the Orlando newspaper photo for ten

minutes after Derek found it online. "That was just a very well-timed photograph."

"Then you cuddled during a nap."

"She said it was a reflex."

Joni and Derek burst out laughing, which gave Olive ample opportunity to consider banging her head against the desk again.

Derek wiggled his computer mouse. "You had a perfectly romantic kiss on a roller coaster."

"Which I cornered her into."

"I really don't think that's how it went down," Joni said.

"Then we got incredibly drunk and shared a hotel room without touching each other. She flat-out refused to share a bed with me. And then she was gone before I woke up. She left a note. *Without* her number."

"What did the note say?" Joni leaned her elbow on the desk beside Olive and played with her stethoscope.

"Thank you so much for a wonderful night. All the best, Stella."

"You memorized the note." Derek snorted.

"Um. It's like twelve words—"

"You counted the words."

Olive threw her hands up into the air. "Don't you have patients to see? I'm supposed to be doing charge nurse, management-y things. Do you want to be the charge nurse today?"

"Nope, I discharged all my patients. I'm charge tomorrow. It's your turn today, and thus, I'm completely free to mock you."

"Great." Olive began typing up audits on her computer.

"So, she said 'all the best.' Eesh." Derek raised a thick eyebrow.

Olive swiveled around on her chair to face Derek. "Is that so bad?"

"I mean, it's better than sincerely."

"Is it?" Joni said, flinching.

Olive whipped her head toward the doctor.

"I mean, I guess it is. But it's still rather businesslike, no?" Joni steepled her fingers in front of her face.

Derek lifted his hand palms up in a weighing motion. "I suppose if we're going on a scale that has 'always hot and heavy for you' on one side and a curt 'regards' on the other, 'all the best' is not as bad as it could be."

"Can we stop talking about this?"

"The more I think about it," Joni said with a sniff, "I think 'all the best' is fine. She was probably running on autopilot."

"Pun intended?" Derek and Joni said at the same time, and then, laughing, they said, "Jinx," in tandem.

"Good, now you can both shut up, and I can get some work done before we get slammed by patients." Olive typed more forcefully on the keyboard.

Deciding not to be bound by playground jinx rules—like an asshole—Derek began speaking again. "I think she likes you."

"I think I'm never going to see her again."

"Really."

"Yep." She popped the *p* with as much finality as she could muster.

"Never?"

"Yeah."

"You think you're never ever going to see Allied Airlines pilot Stella Soriano again in your entire life? Forever?"

"No." Olive took a sip of water. Her mouth was feeling inexplicably dry.

"She just walked onto the unit."

Water snorted out of Olive's nose and onto the desk, luckily missing the keyboard. Joni, hero that she was, hopped up to shield her from Stella, while Olive mopped the mess with disinfectant wipes. Derek had to jump up and leave the area because he was laughing so hard. Yeah, that dick would find himself suddenly working every holiday from now until

2024 after she bribed the scheduler into helping her with revenge.

As Olive finished fixing her face, Joni turned around and nodded to tell her that *no* she did not look like she just spewed water from her nose like broken sprinkler head. Olive straightened her scrubs and stood.

Stella wasn't in uniform. She wore tight jeans and a perfectly fitting white button-down with a beat-up vintage-looking leather jacket.

Olive's voice didn't work the first time she tried to use it. It cracked like an adolescent boy's. "St-Stella. This is a surprise."

"I'm sorry to come to your work without calling first. But I realized after I left, I didn't have your number. I looked on Instagram to try to find your account, and I found it—your dog is adorable by the way and you take gorgeous photos, and I sent you a message but then it occurred to me that your account probably has so many new followers coming in and messages, mine probably got lost. It also didn't seem like you'd been active in a while." Her hair was back in a tight bun, aviator sunglasses perched on her head like a hot female character in a reverse-gendered *Top Gun*. "That probably sounds weird that I was stalking your social media, but then again it's probably super weird that I showed up here. If you're busy I can get your number and text you later."

Derek emerged from where he'd obviously been eavesdropping and cleared his throat. "Olive, weren't you just saying you were going to get coffee from the lobby shop?"

After quickly mouthing *I'm gonna fucking kill you* to Derek, she turned to face Stella. "I—yeah. Stella, do you want to get coffee real quick? There's a Mayorga in the lobby."

Her thousand-watt smile was utterly dangerous. "That'd be great. Perfect. I could use some caffeine."

"How much coffee do you drink every day, out of curiosity?"

"It depends if I'm flying or not. Today I'm teaching." She squinted. "I had two cups at home and a third on the way to the airfield and a fourth on my way here."

"No wonder you always seem like you're jet-powered."

"People joke that the first part of their paycheck goes to the mortgage, but I always joke mine goes to Starbucks and Dunkin' Donuts."

"Guess I know what to get you for Christmas."

Derek let out a barely audible groan that he inadequately hid beneath a cough.

Olive shifted her weight between her sneakers. "Not that I'd be . . . never mind. So, coffee."

"Coffee. Yep."

Neither of them moved.

Stella's eyes darted around. "Where . . . ?"

"Oh, sorry. It's this way."

The sound of a palm hitting a forehead in the background might have been Derek, but Olive ignored it and quickly guided Stella to the double doors at the back of the unit that would take them to the elevators. Once downstairs, they stood in line and ordered, and Olive reached for her pocket, but she'd forgotten her wallet in her locker.

Stella already had a card out. "My treat."

Olive would have liked to argue, but given that she stupidly didn't even have a way to pay, she settled for blushing bright red and stammering awkwardly before saying, "Thank you."

Stella chose a table at the way back of the shop, far from any other patrons. It was that doomsday part of the late afternoon when only real caffeine addicts imbibed, and Olive was grateful for the nearly empty shop.

They sat and sipped in silence before Stella took a deep breath and set her coffee down. "I'd like you to be my girlfriend."

Chapter 15

It was fortunate Olive had already swallowed when Stella spoke, because if she'd been drinking, the coffee would have ended up splattered across Stella's crisp white shirt. Two spit takes in one day was too many.

Olive held her coffee cup aloft as if she'd turned to stone.

She should say something.

She needed to speak.

"I mean my *fake* girlfriend. To be clear." Stella shifted her weight and tapped her fingers on the table.

Nothing was clear. Not clear at all.

Olive *should* go running out of the shop while telling Stella how preposterous the question was. Escaping. That was the only way to go here. At least that's probably what any reasonable person would do.

But instead . . .

"Okay."

"Just . . . okay?"

"No, I mean . . . Okay. As in I understood the words of your question. Because I understand words." *So clever, Olive.* Her voice became a thick whisper. "Um. Why?"

"Getting promoted at an airline like mine is political. The airline's in trouble, like many airlines are these days, and they make it tough to climb to the next level in a career." There were dark smudges beneath Stella's eyes. Something had dulled them since Disney World. Was she not sleeping well? Some ridiculous part of Olive felt instinctively protective over sweet and sunshiny Stella. Like she'd do anything to stop her from looking so nervous and agitated. This wasn't the Stella who ate Swedish Fish at 3:00 A.M. and sprinted from ride to ride at Disney.

Was there more to this than she was saying?

"How exactly does this lead to you wanting to fake date me?" Olive said, trying to keep the cynicism out of her voice.

Subtext: Why the hell don't you want to actually date me?

"This could help me advance in my career by building goodwill with the powers that be at my company. I have a friend who works in event planning, and she told me they're going to invite you to our awards banquet to honor what you did on the plane."

"Invite me?"

Stella wrinkled her forehead. Adorably. That jerk. "People who had never heard of Allied Airlines are talking about us after your video went viral. Our Google searches and bookings went up sixty-five percent after the story about you saving Mickey Mouse hit the news."

"I *didn't* save Mickey Mouse."

"He *plays* Mickey Mouse." She nodded for emphasis. "Morning shows haven't approached you?"

Olive had been too occupied pathetically pining about Stella to listen to the forty voice mails on her phone. She'd only listened to the newest one in hopes that it was Stella herself, but it was just some radio station wanting an interview. Her inboxes on all social media platforms were too full to know where to start. Stella had been right about that.

"I . . . I don't know."

"I know this is a lot to ask. And I'm sorry to spring this whole thing on you. I . . . I didn't realize we didn't have each other's numbers when I left—like I said. I don't know what came over me. I knew where you worked, and I thought I'd stop by."

"It's completely fine that you stopped by." Olive forced an expression she hoped approximated a smile. "I'm really happy to see you. I'm just trying to process this. Can you explain one more time, please?"

"I've been eligible for promotion to captain for three years. I have the hours. I have the experience. But I can't wait any longer. I need this to happen *now* because . . . I just do. My company is a boys' club. I could quit and start over, or I could do something that makes me stand out. Something they can't ignore. Basically, if people find out that we fell in love after you saved a man's life on one of my flights, it might be what I need for the right people to *finally* remember my name."

There *was* more to this than what Stella was saying. Olive could sense it, but she got stuck on a single phrase. *Fell in love.* Because that wasn't what happened on that roller coaster . . . nope. It was a gratitude kiss between two *friends*.

She asked the next question that popped into her reeling brain. "Your company knows you date women?"

"Yes, my colleagues all know I'm a lesbian. Why?" Stella sat up straighter.

"Isn't this illegal? Lying about this . . . I mean something seems illegal." Olive focused on her coffee cup and played with the flap.

"My friend said the CEO really liked the publicity, and these stories tend to die out quickly, but this one's sticking around. We're a small airline, so anything like this is helpful from a company perspective."

"I thought you said you didn't like them to trot you out as a female pilot poster child."

"It's my dream to make captain. And it hasn't happened for me yet. It's easy for my bosses to ignore me when it comes time to promote. They love to say '*he* was a better fit for the team' or 'it was the right time for *him*' but it's really all code for I don't want to think about the young Latina woman because I'm different than all the other white men at the top of the ladder." Her posture went rigid for a moment before she leaned her weight on her forearms and faced Olive, her eyes filled with certainty. "But if I can prove that I can be a value add for the company in another way, even an unconventional one, it might be the thing that pushes me over the edge. I don't care about whether they trot me out on Female Pilots Week or for Pride Month as long as I have that fourth stripe on my shoulder and captain's wings." She touched a spot over her left chest, almost as if she was imagining the wings that would be pinned there.

"You've really thought about this?"

"For my entire career it's felt like they get to use who I am against me when they want to, and I know this is an extreme idea, but I thought just maybe I could use who I am in a way that will let me benefit from it. It's not just about a promotion, it's about getting the title I deserve. The timing . . . it's important to me. I need this to happen *now*."

"The timing?" Olive locked eyes with her.

At least a minute passed before Stella spoke again. "My dad."

"Your dad?" Olive leaned toward Stella an inch.

"He's sick. I . . ." Stella was always so poised and rarely at a loss for words. She blinked several times.

This made more sense. It had been clear that Stella was close with her dad. If he was ill, wanting to make him proud with an accomplishment lined up with who Stella was.

Olive didn't fill the silence. She waited for Stella to collect her thoughts.

"He wants to see me make captain." Stella's voice was quieter than Olive had ever heard it. "I need him to see me make captain."

"Okay." Olive nodded.

Olive understood wanting to make a loved one proud. The nurse side of her brain was desperate for more details about what was wrong with Stella's father, but she didn't want to be nosy. Stella didn't seem eager to share more. "I . . . still don't exactly know what you're asking. I'm sorry if I'm being dense."

Stella brightened immediately. As if the request for concrete, logistical details put her back into her comfort zone. "There are three corporate events between now and the holidays. The awards banquet, the airline holiday party, and the Pilots' Gala. Two of those events involve *all* of my bosses. The decision makers at the top. I've tried for two years to network. I've read networking books and tried to make a name for myself, but still, it's always the men who get the jobs. If you're there, I bet my boss's boss will come talk to me. And hopefully, I'll impress my CEO enough he'll remember my name the next time I put in for promotion." She focused on her coffee cup and used a napkin to wipe away a few stray drips.

"This still seems like a major risk."

"The alternative is me quitting and starting over. I've never quit anything, and I won't now."

"Couldn't there be a benefit to starting over if your company is a group of misogynistic a-holes?" Olive frowned. "I'm not judging or anything. Just curious."

Stella tapped her nails on the lid of her cup. They were both silent for a few long minutes. Olive guzzled her coffee, hoping a rush of caffeine would help all of this make more sense.

Stella frowned, her beautiful eyes avoiding Olive's gaze. "I'm sorry. This was a mistake. I'm really, really sorry I even asked. The next round of promotions comes out in January, and I got desperate when I heard I probably wouldn't be making the list again, and this was impulsive, and unfair. I didn't mean to bring up my dad. I don't want to be manipulative and now that I'm saying all this out loud it feels like I'm just asking to use you as a prop—"

"I don't feel manipulated," Olive said. "It just feels like you're asking me for a favor . . . and we're friends, right?"

Stella nodded, but still appeared guilty and unconvinced.

Do something impulsive.

Olive grabbed Stella's hand. Their eyes met.

"Let me think about it for a day, okay?"

"Really?" She nodded with the energy of a jackrabbit, tightening her grip on Olive's hand. "You don't feel pressured? I know this is an unorthodox way to try to get ahead."

Was it bananas Olive *was* considering it? Probably.

"Women need to stick together."

Stella's fingers had twisted in Olive's, her thumb stroking across her palm. Olive's mouth went dry. She jolted as the pager clipped to her collar beeped and a robotic voice said, "Call from Derek Chang."

She pushed the button, and Derek's staticky voice came out. "Sorry to interrupt coffee. We have a situation."

"Be right there." She lifted her head, surprised to find her fingers still tangled in Stella's. She pulled away. "Sorry. I have to get back. Can I actually get your number this time?" Olive handed over her phone.

Stella's dark eyes regained the twinkling quality that had been there underneath the Disney World lights. Stella's nimble fingers moved over the phone before handing it back. "I sent a text to myself, so I have yours."

"Perfect."

"Call from Derek Chang," the robotic pager voice said again.

"*Shit.*" Olive tapped the button. "I'm coming."

With a little shuffle step and a wave that could only be described as awkward *as fuck,* Olive was run/jogging back upstairs and onto the floor to help.

In Derek's defense, the emergency was an *actual* emergency. A cardiac code that lasted all the way to thirty minutes after she was supposed to get off work. Olive flew around the unit, drawing up medications, paging providers, and helping to shuffle assignments until her feet, which hadn't fully recovered from the half-marathon, were ready to fall off. After she'd given the change of shift report to the next charge nurse, she headed to the parking lot. Derek and Joni were waiting outside the double doors.

"Did you think we weren't going to ask what happened?" Derek crossed his arms over his broad chest.

"We were just curious." Joni grinned.

"She wants to be my fake girlfriend."

For at least an hour or maybe several minutes, nobody spoke.

"Before we get into all the obvious follow-ups about whys and hows . . . and seriously, why . . ." Joni's expression was mystified with a hint of amusement. "Did you tell her no?"

Olive scrunched her nose and eyes and mouth together like that Daenerys Targaryen meme.

Derek laughed.

"I think I said *maybe*. Maybe?"

"Oh man, Olive." Derek rubbed his temples, fielding a glare from Joni. "What? She's got it bad."

Joni poked Derek in the arm.

"Stella Soriano." He snorted.

"Stella Soriano?" Joni forced a smile.

"Stella Soriano." And Olive's stupid, pathetic heart skipped a beat.

Chapter 16

Rain pelted the window of Jake's room while Olive sat in the chair by his bed. At some point this should feel normal. She'd seen Jake like this hundreds of times by now. But it was always a shock. Every time she came, her brain rebelled against the scene in front of her. That thin, unconscious person on a hospital bed couldn't really be him. This person surrounded by machines couldn't be her brother. She surveyed the room, eyeing the painted light green walls. The curtains framing the windows. The large bulletin boards covered in photos.

She had picked up a sandwich on the way over. It made the room smell more like cheese and tomatoes and onions and less like a hospital. She bought the sandwich at one of their favorite restaurants before the accident. She tried to eat lunch with him at least once a week like they had in the "before the accident" times. Eating also gave her something to do with her hands. A thing to do that made her feel less awkward about hanging out with a person in an irreversible coma.

"Sorry I didn't bring you one."

Asshole move, Sis.

Olive knew his answers weren't real. But she'd known him well enough to have a pretty good idea what he'd say.

You gonna tell me about the woman who wants to be your fake girlfriend?

"It's not fair that since your voice is a figment of my imagination you know what's going on in my head."

A privilege of being mostly dead, I guess.

"Jake." Her eyes went misty.

Stop crying and tell me about her. It's boring here.

Olive dabbed her eyes with her napkin, before realizing it had some of the pepper grease on it. She ran to the sink and flushed her eyeballs to stop the burning. "God, why did you have to like the spicy sub. Damn it."

Murphy's Law strikes again.

"Bastard." She almost smiled then. He'd be dying laughing if he saw her do all that. Such a typical Olive move.

Face a mess, and eyes probably still fire-engine red, she sat back beside her brother. Her feet rested on the bottom wheel beneath the hospital bed.

"Stella's a pilot, so of course you'd love her. And before you ask, no, it doesn't make me want to get on more planes. Yeah, she wants me to be her fake girlfriend, and that's so fucking weird. But Jesus, she's spectacular."

Spectacular, eh?

"Yeah. And her dad's sick, and she wants to do this for him. She's super driven. Type A like you. Really smart and funny, sometimes unintentionally. She's flying all day today, so we're going to talk tomorrow night. I'm going to give her a final answer about the whole 'fake girlfriends' thing then. I sound like an idiot saying that aloud."

Is this one more way to put off your own stuff?

"What do you mean? I don't have any of my own stuff." Olive had spoken without thinking. "I mean, I'm working my way through the national parks you hadn't been to yet. I only have so much leave after what happened last year, and—"

You didn't take the flight back from Orlando.

Olive scowled.

She hadn't even confessed that humiliating truth to Derek. The truth of her canceling her flight and renting a car because even though she'd succeeded once she couldn't quite believe she'd be able to get on that next plane again, Valium or no.

The Jake in her mind did not seem ready to let up.

What do you mean you don't have stuff?

What *did* she mean when that had fallen out of her mouth like self-pitying word vomit?

How could she explain without seeming like even more of a wreck? She couldn't tell him that nothing mattered in the last year. She couldn't figure out the way to explain that she was going through his list, but none of it brought her an ounce of joy.

She'd *tried*. She'd been trying. She'd tried so hard to do exactly what Jake would have done. The parks were beautiful, and it felt right to be doing something to honor his life since so much of his current situation felt like her fault.

Damn it, he'd made his list, and she'd check off everything since he couldn't.

But in this, she also felt like she was failing. Lately, she felt like she was doing nothing but failing. With every passive-aggressive email from her mother's lawyer. Every realization of how long it had been since she'd spoken to her father. It was crystal clear that she was the bad guy. It had always been pretty clear that Jake was Mom's favorite child and Heather was Dad's, given that she'd joined the family business. But before the accident . . . the Murphys had always been a unit. Now the remaining ones were united against her.

A tiny curl of anger simmered in her chest.

She stood and paced beside the too quiet and too still hospital bed.

"Look, I'm trying. I'm doing the best I can. Don't you know this year has sucked? I miss you. And you're gone. I miss our family being an actual fucking family. I-I feel so . . ." She couldn't bring herself to say the word *alone*. He was technically right beside her. "And so what if I said I didn't have stuff. I'm trying to do *your* stuff. I ran the half-marathon, didn't I? That's what you wanted. And I did it." A childish urge to stamp her foot came over her.

What I wanted?

She was getting into a fight with her brother. Her brother who was in a persistent vegetative state. Super normal.

Olive looked away from Jake's face. Her race medal now hung on a hook from the large bulletin board beside his bed. His was back on the hook beside it now too. The rest of the board was covered by family photos and cards that Heather and her mother had assembled from the "before times" when they'd all gotten together for the tiniest reasons. Jake would find out Fiona took her first steps and then invite everyone to his house for a dinner to celebrate. Olive got a promotion at work—cookout at Jake's to celebrate. Derek was almost always there too, dragged along with Olive since childhood sometimes staring at Jake in a way that Olive thought maybe someday . . . That bulletin board seemed like a lie now. All those hours that used to be filled with family events were now spent doing the things on his list. Yet it didn't help.

If you don't want to talk about the list or the race, can we discuss you going viral?

"Ugh. No. That's even worse."

Going viral was one more thing that could blow up in her face. One more thing that could chip away at the only good things she had left in her life. Though . . . it had brought her Stella.

"The entire thing is ridiculous. Saving Mickey Mouse? Completely absurd." Olive harrumphed in an immature way that would have earned her a teasing hair ruffle had Jake actually been here.

Her eyes settled on the tubes and cords keeping Jake "alive." He wasn't *here*.

Not really.

Whatever was left of him was suffering, and that was all her fault.

The door opened. Morgan came in wearing bright purple scrubs that seemed to make the entire room friendlier. Her red hair was twisted into a bun on top of her head. Olive dug in her bag and tossed her friend from nursing school a sandwich.

"Oh my god, Olive. You didn't have to bring me one."

"Last week you were practically drooling over mine. I called ahead to see if you were working."

"You're the best." Morgan grinned. "Now I won't have to have a vending machine lunch."

Olive rested her chin on her clasped hands, her elbows digging into her knees. "Thanks for taking care of him. It makes me feel so much better to know you work here."

Morgan waved off her gratitude. "My job. Glad me being here makes you feel better."

Olive's attention refocused on her brother. "How's he doing?"

Morgan patted Olive's shoulder and spoke in a quiet, soothing voice. "The same."

Olive nodded. This had always been the answer. Nothing had changed in months. "Have my parents still been coming on the normal days? And Heather?"

"Yeah. She's mostly just quiet though."

"My mom still bullying the staff?"

Morgan pulled her stethoscope out of her pocket rather than answering, but it was confirmation enough. She wrapped a blood pressure cuff around Jake's arm and squeezed the pump several times.

Olive gritted her molars together. "I'll need to bring some baked goods for the break room to say thank you to you all for putting up with all that."

"Everyone would love that." After pulling her stethoscope from her ears, Morgan became serious. "Your mom wants to bring in a new doctor from California."

Above the bed was an addition to the room that Olive hadn't noticed before. Her mother had obviously added that while Olive had been in Florida. A gold crucifix that Jake would have definitely labeled as creepy in its level of detail. Perfectly symbolic of everything her mother had been doing over the past few months.

Olive sighed and dragged her fingers through her hair. "Of course she does. She's never going to stop. What'd the team here say?"

"We showed her the most recent scans and tried to explain why we felt recovery wasn't possible." Morgan adjusted the curtains. The rain outside had slowed, the sun seemed to be attempting to pierce the dense blanket of November clouds.

"It's not going to stop her." Olive couldn't hide the edge of bitterness in her voice.

"Oh, we know." Morgan checked on all the life support machine settings and safety equipment before kneeling at Olive's side. A frown of such sympathy came over her face that it tore at Olive's heart. "You're doing the best you can, Olive. We all see it." And with one more shoulder pat and a few more thank-yous about the sandwich, Morgan left her alone.

Alone, because her brother wasn't really here anymore at all.

Chapter 17

The day after seeing Jake had been busy and terrible at the hospital, so Derek insisted on an impromptu wine night at Olive's apartment after work. He invited Joni to come along. Although Joni was a relatively new friend, Olive would be glad of her opinion, mainly because she was less likely to encourage her to get drunk and call Stella and confess that she had not-at-all-fake feelings for her.

Joni had come back to the area to help care for her aunt, and Olive and Derek were already really hoping her job here became permanent. As if agreeing with Olive about Joni being a kindred spirit, Gus took up residence on Joni's lap. She gave him all the behind-the-ear scratches he could take.

"I think Olive should make a pro/con list," Joni said.

Olive's phone vibrated. A text from her mom insisting she check her email. Ugh. Not right now. Olive sucked down the last gulps of wine and then held out her glass in a silent plea. Since Derek was the best, he filled the glass almost to the very top.

He topped off his own glass too. "I think Olive should say 'fuck your fake dating trope, I'd rather be in one of those novels where the characters have hot sex the whole time in old-timey clothes.'"

Never mind. Derek was not a hero. Asshat.

"I have no idea what you're talking about." Joni squinted at Derek.

He tugged Olive's bun before grinning at Joni. "Take a trip to the romance section next time you're at a bookstore. If you know, you know."

And Olive did know. She had a few shelves of romance novels in her apartment—most of which had been gifts from Derek—and at least several of them began with this exact setup.

Joni moved from under Gus's head and went to the counter and grabbed a legal pad from her bag. She sat back down, and Gus set his head right back on top of her legs. She smiled at him encouragingly and rested the pad of paper on his broad back. "So, pros first?"

Derek plopped down next to Olive, nearly spilling her wine. "She's hot, and she looked at Olive with sex eyes."

Joni laughed. "You want me to write 'sex eyes'?"

"Right at the very top." He tapped the legal pad.

Olive rubbed a spot in the center of her forehead. "Be serious, you guys. This is—"

"Olive, this entire situation is ridiculous. How can we be serious about it?" Derek looked to the ceiling as if he were silently asking a higher power for patience.

Olive smelled her wine and then put it back on the coffee table. "Look, Stella wants to do this because her work is full of sexist tools who aren't giving her the promotion she deserves. And that's not okay. She's amazing. Really, really a good person. She deserves—"

"Could help Stella's job," Joni recited as she wrote. "And in the cons, Olive might get hurt."

"What do you mean, might get hurt?"

"You have strong feelings about Stella."

Derek nodded in agreement.

Joni put down the pen on the pad, which was still balanced on Gus's back. "And you'd be signing up to have a fake relationship for the next few months. That might be confusing and risky. You light up when you talk about her, Olive."

"She *so* does."

"I do not. And, risky?"

"Yes, risky." Joni clicked the pen on the pad. "Any time you put yourself out there, there's unknowns. There's opportunities to get hurt."

"Okay, alternative theory time." Derek swirled his wine. "Stella has real feelings for Olive, and this is a way for them to get close so that they can eventually be real girlfriends."

Joni pursed her lips skeptically.

Olive made a noise reminiscent of a wrong-answer buzzer on a TV program and gave a thumbs-down. Gus got angry enough at the loud noise that he scampered off Joni's lap and back to his inner-tube-sized bed in the corner. "She said something at Disney about being so focused on her job, she wasn't good at relationships. If she actually liked me, she would have asked me to actually be her girlfriend and not her fake girlfriend."

Derek shrugged. "Maybe she's just a terrible communicator?"

Olive's face colored with outrage. "Hey, she's—"

"I'll add that." Joni began writing on the list again. "Stella might be a terrible communicat—"

"Don't write that." Olive grabbed the pen out of Joni's hand. She stood and began pacing while clicking and unclicking the pen over and over. What if what Lindsay said at the hotel had gotten into Stella's head? Made her think Olive was some hypercritical, unforgiving, and emotionally parasitic mess.

No . . . If she believed that, she wouldn't have come to see her yesterday. After a few minutes of silence, she crossed her legs and sat beside Gus, giving him a few apologetic tummy rubs. "She communicated really well. She looked me in the face and said, 'I want you to be my girlfriend.' And then made it impeccably clear a second later she meant *fake* girlfriend."

Derek grabbed the pen from Olive and the pad from Joni. "Stella might be completely bonk—"

"She is not bonkers. She's desperate."

"Why?" Joni said pensively.

"Why what?"

"I know you said it had something to do with men being promoted above her, which I can definitely understand, but really, why? Like why now?"

Olive opened her mouth to mention what Stella had said about her dad, but as if in answer to this question, Olive's phone began vibrating on the coffee table.

Closest, Derek snatched it first. "It's her. It's her." He leaped over the couch. "Speakerphone? I'm thinking speakerphone."

Olive pushed the part of his hip that had been ticklish since they were kids, and grabbed it from him. "Not speakerphone. Goddamn it. Gimme."

She fled to the bathroom and locked the door. She squinched her toes into the carpet, like that would ease her thundering heartbeat.

After taking a breath as if she were about to dive into the deep end, she swiped to answer. "Hey, Stella, how are you doing tonight? Did you have a good day at work? It was good to see you on Monday. Nice to talk to you."

Yup, Olive was the *coolest*.

"Hi, Olive." Stella's voice was always like sunshine but it seemed to quiver tonight. "I called to apologize. To be honest, impulsive is not something that really works for me, and I was in a bad place, and disappointed by some bad news . . . at work . . . I wanted to call and tell you over the last day I've been rethinking everything, and I don't think it's a good idea because I don't want to put you in this position. Basically, I'm sorry I showed up at your place of employment and asked you such an incredibly inappropriate favor. There is absolutely no excusing my behavior, and—"

"Stella."

"Yes?"

"Breathe."

"Okay."

And Stella did. She took several deep breaths, drawing out

the exhales as she seemed to always do when she was nervous or stressed.

Olive looked away from her reflection in the bathroom mirror. "Because I was going to say yes."

"Yes, what?"

"Yes, I'll be your fake girlfriend."

"You'll what?"

Olive dug her fingers into her mess of hair, massaging her scalp. "Didn't you show up at my hospital on Monday and ask me to be your fake girlfriend, or did I have an aneurysm?"

"I did, but—"

"I accept."

"You can't mean that. Me even asking you was absurd."

"I'll go to the events. It's fine. I'll need to check my schedule, but my hospital actually already sent me a few emails about publicity events after the whole stupid viral video thing, so I think they'll be into this. They keep telling me they're trying to leverage the press coverage into getting a few more donors to redo the waiting area of the ER. They want me to do a few of the interviews to stir up more press. Guess everyone likes this story, like you said."

"Are you sure?"

Nope, not even a little bit. "Absolutely." Olive leaned on the bathroom counter, the ceramic cold beneath her fingers.

"We should meet to iron out the details."

"When?"

"How about tomorrow? I could come to your place. If that's okay with you?"

"Yeah, I'd be totally into that. I mean, it sounds good. Logistics. Schedules." Olive's nails clacked a nervous timpani beat that she hoped Stella couldn't hear through the phone.

A muffled snort came through the door, so Olive kicked it, causing Derek to curse loudly.

"I have no idea how to thank you for this." Stella's voice still sounded embarrassed.

"You helped me get to the race. You helped me survive the weekend. I owe you."

"You really don't. I—um—had a great time too."

Olive cradled the phone close. "Really?"

"Yeah."

Knees unsteady, Olive sat on her vintage chartreuse bath mat. "So, I'll text you my address. Is six okay? I can make dinner."

"You don't have to feed me. I can pick something up."

"I like cooking for people." She hugged her arms tighter. "Please?"

A pause.

"If you're absolutely sure."

"I am."

Stella made a couple of noncommittal noises as if she were deciding whether or not to tell Olive something. "So, I have celiac."

"Oh, that's fine." *More than fine.* "I'm used to cooking gluten-free. How did I not notice this when we were eating together?"

"Disney's one of the best places for me. I know what I can eat there. They're great with special diets."

"That's why my brother liked it too." Olive smiled broadly, then caught sight of her ridiculous expression in the mirror and tried to clamp down on it.

"Your brother had celiac?"

"Uh-huh." Olive was already planning the perfect menu.

"You're still good with cooking? I know it can be a major burden."

"It's not. Stella, you could never be a burden."

Chill.

"Thank you. So, I'll—um—see you tomorrow, then?"

"Tomorrow," Olive repeated through a smile so wide her face hurt. "Come hungry."

She held the phone tight to her chest for a minute until a smack on the door jolted her from her happy fantasies. They weren't even dirty ones. Just mental images of Stella sliding Olive's signature gluten-free dish on a fork. Then Stella would tell her how delicious everything was before dragging her to the bedroom, ripping off her clothes, and—

Okay. Maybe they were a *little* dirty.

Derek's voice interrupted the fantasy. "Olive Murphy, I swear to God, if you don't—"

Olive swung the bathroom door open, narrowly missing hitting Derek in the face. Six eyes were fixed on Olive if you counted Gus's. All were expectant.

"So, I might have told her yes." She spread her fingers in a jazz hands *surprise!* motion.

Derek walked over to the legal pad, tore off the pro/con list, and basketball-style dunked it in the trash. "Of course you did."

Chapter 18

"I love your place." Stella handed over her coat.

Gus lumbered over to the door. He was old and lazy but still managed to get thoroughly excited whenever a new friend came.

"And oh my god, Gus is even more adorable in person." Stella kneeled and let Gus lick her a couple of times on the face while scratching his chin. Olive was pathetic. Truly pathetic because she was currently jealous of her goddamn dog.

Stella stood and walked farther into the apartment with Gus trotting behind her. "But seriously though, your place is amazing."

Olive laughed as she hung Stella's coat on the antique rack by the door. "Thank you."

"Why'd you laugh?" Stella asked as she checked that the coat was straight on the hook and plucked a piece of invisible lint from the shoulder.

"I guess it's a little cluttered compared to what I think you'd like."

"Oh, well, it's not like I'm some uptight . . ." She stopped in the process of straightening and restraightening her shoes beside the closet door so that they were perfectly perpendicular to the wall. She kicked the one shoe so it was intentionally crooked. "I'm not."

Olive cocked an eyebrow. "Okay."

Stella's attention immediately caught on the wall above Olive's velvet tufted couch. "Wow." She let out a breath.

"You like it?"

"You have good taste." Stella's finger hung in the air, drifting over the eclectic gallery wall as if she were tracing. "It all fits.

I love the colors. I could never put something like that together. The vintage European cities travel posters with the art. Wow."

"Thank you." Smiling, Olive watched the curtain of Stella's hair sway as she appraised the wall as if it were a masterpiece in a great museum. "Do you want wine or gluten-free beer?"

Stella whipped her head around. "You have gluten-free beer?"

"My brother liked it, so I thought you might. But if you're not a beer person, no pressure at all."

"I'd love it. I haven't had a beer in years. It smells amazing in here, by the way."

"It's Dijon chicken with wild rice. With green beans. Nothing fancy. Sound okay?"

"Like heaven. I've been living on gluten-free freezer meals and bananas."

"You don't cook?" Olive handed her the beer, enjoying the touch of Stella's fingers on her hand as they grazed hers.

"Not much. I work a lot. We have a service that brings meals for my father." She sighed. "My dad and I got spoiled having my grandmother living with us. She was an amazing cook. The only thing I used to cook with her were tamales at Christmas. It's not that I don't like cooking. I can use a recipe but sometimes I get impatient when it doesn't turn out like it should. It's a cliché but nothing tastes the way my grandmother made it."

"Recipes are tricky. I don't cook from recipes much. Baking, sure. But—" Olive's phone dinged. "Sorry. Let me silence . . ."

DEREK
You made her the pound cake, didn't you?

She clicked the phone on vibrate, but Olive didn't put it down quick enough to avoid seeing his next text.

DEREK
So this isn't operation fake dating, so much as operation make Stella your actual girlfriend.

Derek
What could go wrong? <facepalm>

He was such a dick.

"What is *that*?" As if she knew the contents of the messages from Derek, Stella's perfect mouth had fallen open. Her gaze fixed on the peninsula of the kitchen counter where a dessert was presented on a teal vintage Pyrex cake stand.

"It's a pound cake."

"No . . . that can't be. Is it?"

"Yes, it is."

"It would be rude to ask about eating dessert first, right?" Stella approached the cake looking less like Stella and more like a jaguar circling a small animal of jungle prey.

"What if we do a tiny piece and call it an appetizer?" Olive widened her eyes comically, trying not to laugh.

Stella did a happy dance that made Olive want to wrap her up in her arms and kiss the crap out of her. Stifling those completely useless instincts, Olive eased a knife from the block and cut Stella a sliver. She grabbed a spoonful of strawberries from the fridge, a dollop of whipped cream, and a mint leaf.

"It's a masterpiece," Stella said in that breathless voice that threatened Olive's sanity.

"It's got all the major food groups. Grains, dairy, fruits, vegetables."

"Vegetables?"

Olive pointed to the mint leaf. "It's kind of a green. It's vegetable-adjacent."

"I'm not complaining." She slid her fork into the dessert, making sure to get bits of strawberries and cream with it. She lifted it to her mouth and closed her lips around it. "I feel like it's bad form to call the person making you a delicious dinner a liar, but there's no way that's actually gluten-free."

"Well, I guess since I'm agreeing to be your fake girlfriend,

I am a liar. But in this case." She held up a hand. "Scout's honor."

"And you're sure we can't just eat cake for dinner?"

"Go sit. Balanced diet. I'm a nurse, remember? I want to make sure my fake girlfriend eats vegetables."

Eesh, Olive needed to stop calling her her fake girlfriend. She was making this weird.

Her conscience or internal Derek or whatever it was popped up like a Whac-A-Mole head.

It just is weird.

She took an internal monologue mallet to that thought and settled her attention back on Stella.

A muscle feathered in Stella's jaw, but then she took another bite and the enraptured look returned. She took a third bite of cake. "I'm feeling super spoiled."

Olive sipped from her own bottle. "Well, you did drive me all the way to Disney World."

"You need to stop thanking me for that."

"Are you still hungry right now? The cake didn't spoil your dinner?"

"Still starving." Stella licked her spoon.

Holy fuck. Bridgerton *dude has nothing on Stella Soriano.*

Yep, and that was an actual moan as Stella's lips closed around the last forkful of cake.

"I'll just—" Olive tripped over her rug, slamming her hip into the counter.

"Are you okay?" Stella hopped up. Before either of them could make another decision, Stella was running a thumb over Olive's hip. "That sounded like it hurt."

"I'm fi-ine." Olive smiled, trying to ignore both the awkward crack in her voice and the throbbing. She focused on the fact that Stella's hand was touching her and pretended no other parts of her were throbbing.

Stella's mouth parted, and Olive turned back to the range,

stirring the rice so vigorously the pot almost fell off. No, she couldn't kiss her again. That was what screwed everything up the first time. If she kissed her again, Stella would probably run away or, more accurately, fly away.

"Go sit, and I'll bring you a plate. You want everything?" Olive said directly to the microwave.

"Yes, please. I'm not picky other than the whole dietary restriction thing."

Dietary restriction. Safe topic. Perfect.

Olive spooned food onto a plate, arranging it neatly. "When were you diagnosed?"

"When I was a teenager. I was anemic and really tired. I had migraines. My entire leg went numb for a few days."

"Holy shit."

"My dad just thought I wasn't sleeping enough. The doctors tested for everything. MS. Lots of other scary things. But I tested positive for celiac. It was like magic for my body. I don't even miss gluten because I feel so much better. I was lucky that a lot of Mexican cooking is corn-based because my grandmother didn't have much trouble making things gluten-free. A lot of what she made already was. What about your brother? Do you mind me asking about him?"

"No, it's fine. Jake had some vague symptoms and got tested. My mom and aunt have it too, so we're pretty familiar with the signs."

"Not you?"

"Nope. My younger sister doesn't either." Gus leaned on Stella, his not-at-all-subtle way of demanding more attention. "Push him off if he's annoying you. He's relentless."

"It's fine." Stella actually hugged Gus, wrapping her arms around his thick neck and kissing the top of his head. "I love big dogs."

Of course she does.

"Any pets?"

"No. My dad's cat died a few years ago. He's allergic to dogs. I'm not, though." Gus arched his neck back and licked her nose.

Olive pointed to the small mid-century table that barely fit in her kitchen nook. "Please come sit."

Stella grabbed her beer and pulled up a chair to the table. She inhaled deeply as Olive placed the assembled plate in front of her. "You're like a magical unicorn, Olive."

"What? Why?"

A magical unicorn? That had to be a good thing, right?

Stella blushed. "Cooking gluten-free. I really appreciate this. Some people think it's a fad diet . . . but it's really serious for me. Still, I feel awkward bringing it up. With my cousins in Texas, sometimes they think it's the same as keto or like a 'crunchy' thing. They'll give me stuff covered in white flour and act like I should suck it up because it's not an allergy. I have to explain every time."

"That's what Jake said. He basically had to educate everyone at his job about it."

"You said he built airplanes?"

"Yeah. He was always obsessed with aviation." Explaining the full situation with Jake was what she'd do with a real girl-friend. This wasn't a date. This was a dinner to discuss a some-what mutually beneficial plan. Derek was wrong. She was *not* desperately trying to inception Stella into being her real girl-friend with baked goods. She wasn't.

"Please, eat." Olive smiled.

Stella took the cue, draped her napkin in her lap, and took a few dainty bites. "It is unreal how good this is. Thank you."

They chatted through dinner about their respective jobs, swapping stories about patients and passengers. Stella was funny, incredibly funny and witty when she told stories about macho pilots from when she'd started out after flight school. Olive found herself laughing almost as much as she normally did on nights with Derek. Strange.

When both their plates were half empty, Olive put her fork and knife down. "We should probably work out the details about what fake dating means. What do I need to do to help you?"

"Oh, *right*." Stella hopped up, and ran to her bag where she pulled out a binder. An actual three-ring binder. She handed it to Olive and sat back down.

"What . . ."

"You don't have to look at that now. I don't know why I gave it to you during dinner. It's all the details of the three events I need a date for. What to wear. Who the people are that I need to talk to who will best optimize my ability to network with the right people. The people who make promotion decisions, that is."

Olive pushed her plate out of the way, so she had room to lay out the binder. "It's color coded."

"It's organized." Stella pointed to the contents.

Olive flipped through pages. "There are custom tabs and small photos of the different executives."

"Yes?" Her voice was factual. Like the binder was the most normal thing ever. But this was some Paris Geller–level shit.

"Never mind, nerd." Olive winked at Stella.

"Oh, you think this is nerdy? You should see my label maker."

God, Olive wished *that was an incredibly oblique euphemism.*

"You are the *biggest* nerd."

"Well, you're the one who agreed to fake date me." Stella's cheeks flushed.

"Touché." Olive guzzled her beer, wondering if she should move on to bourbon. "I need more alcohol for this." She stood and walked to her brass bar cart. She twisted off the cap and didn't even bother to get ice.

"I've been thinking about how I could compensate you for your efforts."

Olive almost spilled the bourbon as she splashed it into a glass. "Well, now I feel like a fake hooker."

Stella's cheeks became a deeper rose pink.

Olive sat back down. "It was a joke, Stella."

"Oh, right. Okay. If you feel uncomfortable . . ."

"I don't feel uncomfortable. A few parties. How bad could this be? Chatting with some pilots. Oh shit, that pilot from the flight will probably be there. Captain Kevin or whatever."

"Yeah." Her eyebrows pulled together. "Kevin will be there. But we shouldn't have to talk to him. He generally ignores women he doesn't want to sleep with." There was an edge to her voice.

"Was there a time when he didn't ignore you?"

Stella scraped her nails over the paper label on her beer bottle. "It was a long time ago. Never anything since. Things were worse when I started. The Me Too movement helped a lot."

"I'm sure." Rage pulsed in Olive's chest. Maybe she could figure out a way to "accidentally" kick him in the balls at one of the parties. "I'm so sorry."

"It's fine." Stella set the beer bottle down. She scooted it a few inches closer to her plate on the placemat as if to make sure it didn't drip condensation onto the wood table. "I want to take you to Italy."

Olive choked on the bourbon, making her throat burn. "What?"

"You said you've never been. You were an art history major." She pointed at the gallery wall with its lush colors and assemblage of various European masters from different periods. "Seeing that, it makes me certain this is the right thing to do. I get really good deals with other airlines." Stella fiddled with the salt and pepper shakers in the middle of Olive's table.

"That's absurd. You can't take me to Italy."

"I don't have to come with you or anything. I would buy your ticket and maybe set up a hotel room for you with my travel points."

"In case you forgot, I'm terrified of flying. And that's over *an ocean*. We talked about this." She made a swimming motion with her hand.

"You got on a plane to Florida and back."

"I—uh."

Stella's mouth pulled to the side, eyes narrowing.

"I only made it to Atlanta."

"But what about the flight back?"

Olive grimaced, but didn't answer.

Stella arched an eyebrow. "You didn't . . ."

"I canceled the ticket, rented a car, and drove." Olive shrugged as if the revelation didn't make her want to shrivel up inside. "With a good audiobook, driving is great. I drive all over. It helps that I can take Gus on my trips."

Stella shook her head. "Okay, so if I can get you to be comfortable with flying, I'll get you a ticket to Italy."

"It's still too much." Her hand curled into a fist as it rested on one of the plastic-covered pages in the binder.

"It's really not. You haven't been to these events."

"They're that terrible?"

Stella played with her food. "They're long. Lots of people. Not bad, just overwhelming. Crowds make me nervous sometimes."

"That's something we have in common. You're so poised, though. Like you were with the reporters."

Stella shrugged. "I can fake it."

Olive flipped a few more pages. "Stella . . ."

"What? Is there a typo?" Stella lurched forward in her seat, reading the words upside down.

"You have a tab in here for PDA. This is something we need an entire section on?"

Her blush spread, and her ears went pink. She pulled at the collar of her ivory cashmere sweater. "I thought it was something we should discuss."

Olive pretended to adjust an invisible monocle like she was

a grizzled librarian investigating an ancient text. "The binder has spoken. Hand-holding is fine. A quick kiss on the cheek is good in some situations. Arm around the shoulders. What excellent news. Hugs are completely appropriate. Good, because I was worried." Olive widened her eyes in mock concern.

Stella clicked her tongue. "I think things work out better when there are clear expectations."

"When did you make this?" There were pages and pages of information here.

"Today. I didn't have to fly for the airline. The weather was too bad, so I canceled my lessons."

Olive coughed, interspersing the word *nerd* between pointed hacks.

After giving Olive's ear a playful flick, Stella hid her face behind her hands.

"You really can't take me to Italy."

"Honestly, I'd buy you a ticket to Italy for making me a few more of those pound cakes. Are they made of fairy dust?"

"No, just a shit ton of butter." Olive flipped the binder closed. "Okay. If we can figure out a way to get me on a plane, I'll think about it. In the meantime, I need a favor."

"Anything."

"So, the local news is doing a thing about me saving the guy on the plane. They called me today."

"Not surprised. It was really amazing."

Olive shook her head, dismissing the compliment. "Anyway. In addition to having a fear of flying, I don't like public speaking or anything close to it. But my hospital thinks it would be cool, so I'm going to try. But the way you handled the reporters at the race . . . any chance you could do that?" She drummed her fingers on the table, nervously.

"Are we going to say how we met and that I'm your girlfriend?"

"Uh . . . yeah, I mean I think that makes the most sense? It's a pretty good story. It would probably help with your plan too."

Olive took a bite of chicken and chewed slowly, watching for Stella's reaction.

Stella grinned. "I think it's a great idea."

Deliberately staring at the plate, Olive asked a question she'd been dying to ask all evening. "Out of curiosity, and I only feel comfortable asking you this because I'm your fake girlfriend, but why don't you have or want a real girlfriend?"

Careful.

"Oh, that's easy. I'd be a terrible girlfriend." It was as if she'd answered a question like what's your favorite season or who's hotter than Rachel Weisz in *The Mummy*—the obvious answer being no one. Stella's answer was easy, given from the gut without the slightest hesitation. She thought she'd be a terrible girlfriend?

Olive thought back through their day together in Florida when Stella had been that perfect mix of fun, sweet, and spontaneous. "Why?"

"Past experience." Stella gave a nonchalant shake of the shoulders. "I work too much."

"That's it?"

"I have goals. And a deadline. I told you I have to make captain now. Literally my entire life I've had this goal in mind, and I'm so close. I . . . I can be a little . . . *focused* when I have a goal."

"Isn't focus a good thing?" Olive eyed the binder meaningfully. "And what did you mean by past experience?"

"The last time I had a girlfriend . . . well, both last girlfriends."

Olive tried not to sit up straight and beg for details because the thought of Stella being with someone else touched a never-before-felt nerve of unreasonable jealousy. "So, what happened? With the girlfriends, I mean. Like you broke up?" Yeah, that was definitely not too eager-sounding. Nailed it. "Toxic exes. I get it."

Stella shook her head. "Nadine and Laura weren't toxic. They were actually great. They were both really good people. We had similar interests. Lots in common. They were kind and we had fun together."

Okay, this sucks. Is she still in love with her ex? Olive's mind was like a fried circuit breaker in a 1990s movie, spluttering and sparking and overheating.

"With Nadine, I wasn't there for her. I was young, and I don't think . . ." She took a bite of food, chewed, and swallowed as if she needed a moment to decide how to explain. "I wasn't in love with her, but I did love her. Does that make sense?"

Olive nodded.

"When we were together she was having a tough time in school. I was so focused on my own grades. On my own flight hours. All of it. I was *so* focused that I didn't notice what was going on with her. I can be kind of a lot." Stella's focus flickered to the binder. "You might have noticed."

Olive wanted to reach out and grab Stella's hand, but she didn't. "For what it's worth, I like your intensity."

Stella waved off the compliment. "Nadine ended up failing out of school, and she was too embarrassed to tell me before she packed her bags and left." She sighed. "I was so type A that my girlfriend wouldn't tell me she needed help. Yikes. She deserved so much better."

"Stella, that wasn't your fault. You were what, nineteen? Twenty?"

"I still should've noticed. And with Laura . . . she got hurt too. It made me wonder if I'm even capable of falling in love the way other people do. I forget birthdays. I don't notice things, and people get hurt because I'm not there for them the way I should be." Her expression tightened like even talking about this made her relive the guilt.

"Just because you haven't been in love *before* . . ." *Wow, could Olive be any more transparent?*

Stella shrugged. "The bottom line is that when people emotionally rely on me, they get hurt. I know myself. I know what I'm capable of, and right now, I want to become captain." The word *captain* seemed to shake Stella out of thinking about her exes. That small sparkle reignited in her dark eyes. "I adore my job. I pick up as many flight hours as I can. I volunteer with my company's CSR programs. I teach flying lessons because I love being in the air. And then I have to help my dad."

"What do you mean help your dad? You said he was sick. I'm sorry, I don't mean to pry. Just tell me to shut up if this is none of my business. Sorry for all the personal questions."

"No, it's okay. He has Parkinson's. I . . . handle all the logistics with his care. I'm good with logistics." Another head twitch toward the binder.

"I'm so sorry." Olive frowned. "How's he doing?"

"Worse in the last year. He's started forgetting things more. I . . . don't know how long he'll be around. Or how long he'll be himself." Stella smoothed her hair, even though there wasn't a strand out of place.

"That's so hard. I bet he feels super lucky to have a daughter who cares for him so much."

"We've always been a team."

Olive understood that feeling, but she wanted to ask why Stella worked around the clock if she was also worried about all the time she'd miss with her dad. Olive would have given anything just to have another run with Jake. But that certainly was none of her business as a fake girlfriend. She'd probably already pushed the bounds of what was her business with the last question about her exes. This line of questioning would probably lead to a conversation about Olive's family. She wanted Stella to like her, so she should probably stay away from that particular topic.

Stella blotted her mouth once with her napkin before spearing a bite of green bean. "Well, I better finish this because the cake is staring at me."

"Oh, it's staring at you, is it?"

"Yep." Stella lifted her voice into a squeaky Muppet-ish range. "Please come and eat me, Stella. All those vegetables are not as delicious as I am." Her voice returned to normal. "Seriously, though, what did you put on these green beans?"

"Shallots and butter."

"God, I love butter." Stella sighed as she chewed. Such a lovely contented sound.

"Me too."

Olive tapped the binder. "Do I get to keep the binder for reference?"

Stella lit up. "Of course. I have my o—" Her mouth snapped shut.

Olive smirked. "You have your own copy?"

Stella's cheeks flushed again. She finished her beer with the bottle tilted up at the ceiling. Olive grabbed another beer from the fridge and placed it in front of Stella.

She swept her hand gently across Stella's arm, leaned close, and whispered, "I like nerds."

✳✳✳

It was 9:30 P.M., and Olive picked up her phone from on top of Stella's comprehensive guide to fake dating. She was cuddled up by Gus on the couch and wishing Stella had stayed over longer. Olive finished her third beer, enjoying the haze. She didn't really like beer that much, but she hoped it would take the edge off the disappointment from the awkward hug at the door when Stella left.

She swiped to call Derek. He answered after two rings.

"I had hoped you weren't texting me back because you were having extremely hot sex with Stella."

"Nope. Not even a little bit." She pulled the afghan from the back of the couch and draped it over her legs, thinking about how nice it would be to have a sleep cuddler keeping her warm right now rather than a slightly smelly Great Dane mix. Feeling guilty about the thought, she nuzzled Gus's face.

"But you like her." There was an edge of genuine concern in Derek's voice.

"She's a really nice person, and she's going to help me with a couple interviews and flying."

"Flying?"

"Yup, she's determined to fix me."

"Fix you?"

"Just my fear of flying so I can travel." Olive paused and then her voice lowered to a mumble. "She hasn't known me long enough to know all the other ways I'm broken."

"If this is about your family—"

"I have to fill out a questionnaire." A change of subject would be best. The topic of her family always made Derek furious.

He hesitated. "What are you talking about?"

"For Stella. We need to know things about each other, so it'll be believable. Realistic." She flipped back to that page and grabbed her pen.

"This girl is so extra. She's hot. But she's extra."

"Extra gorgeous. Extra smart. Extra really fucking good at kissing."

"Oh, drunk sad Olive." He sighed. "This shit's going to blow up in your face."

"Yep."

"Does that make you want to change your mind?"

"Nope. Not even a little bit."

"You got it real bad, O."

"I know."

Her phone buzzed. A text. Not from Stella.

LINDSAY
Why haven't you returned any of my calls?

Fuck. She was so done with this.

OLIVE
Because you aren't my girlfriend and I don't have to
call you back.

LINDSAY

Why won't you tell me who that girl was at Disney?

OLIVE

A friend. Not your business. Why do you care?

LINDSAY

Of course I care. I don't want you getting a crush and getting hurt.

Olive snorted.

Lindsay had a nose for drama. She could sniff it out a mile away. She also had a knack for making Olive feel like complete shit.

"Olive, are you there?"

Oh yeah, Derek was still on the phone.

"Ugh, I'm so sorry. Lindsay's texting. Asking about Stella."

"What'd you tell her?"

"To leave me alone." Olive adjusted a throw pillow to support her neck, a tension headache brewing.

"Good." Even through the phone, Olive could hear the relief in her best friend's voice.

LINDSAY

I want to see you. I figured when stuff calmed down about your brother, we'd hang out again. When you had more time. That type of girl will break your heart

LINDSAY

You need someone who will call you on your bullshit so you don't get into that self-pity zone again. I know you think I'm a sociopath, but I just want the best for you

Olive groaned.

"What? Just block her damn number. What's she saying?"

Olive tucked her phone beside her ear, skimming over the

questions on the page in front of her. "Rewriting our history to make it seem like she didn't dump me for having a depressive episode after my brother went into a coma and break up with me several times before that for having generalized anxiety disorder. Although, in her defense, at least Lindsay probably wants to actually fuck me rather than pretend that she's fucking me. So, there's that."

Also, Lindsay was almost certainly right about Stella breaking Olive's heart one day. Olive didn't need to bring that up though.

Derek sighed.

This kind of conversation with Lindsay sent Olive to a dark place. She pushed the binder on the coffee table and threw the beer bottle into her recycling bin. "It's always the same." She lowered her voice to a level Derek couldn't hear. "I might as well enjoy this while it lasts."

She sat back down and grabbed the thick three-ring binder. She flipped to the page with the questionnaire and pulled it out from the clear page protector. She hadn't noticed before that Stella had already filled out a copy about herself in her elegant cursive.

"Still there, Olive?"

Some mix of the alcohol and the exhaustion sent her into a fit of hysterical laughter as she read over the questionnaire. "Oh, I'm still here, so . . . I need your opinion on something . . ."

She was still laughing later when she *may* have sent out a few ill-advised drunk texts.

Chapter 19

STELLA
Getting killed by a meteorite. Getting mauled by a
bear. Being born with an extra finger or toe.

OLIVE
Is this a riddle or the most disturbing game ever of
would you rather?

She waited for a response, but since Stella's text had come in
at 4:30 A.M. (an ungodly hour and a half before Olive's alarm
went off), who knew when she'd get back to her. She peeled
herself out of bed and turned on the shower. A few minutes
into the shower, she leaned out to check if Stella had texted
back.

Nope.

After giving Gus a quick walk, she got ready and drove
the ten minutes to a parking space at the hospital. Her phone
buzzed in her pocket. She grabbed it with enough force that it
Frisbeed out of her hand and into the back seat. She went to
reach for it and then the car inched forward in the space.

"Fuck." She slammed on the brake and pushed the gearshift
into park before diving into the back seat to fumble for the
stupid phone.

DEREK
How's the Stella-hangover. I hope you didn't actually
send those texts.

Olive made a sound very similar to a growl and then froze.

The texts?

Oh shit.

Had she sent the texts?

She swiped back to Stella's message and scrolled up.

> OLIVE
>
> I'm reading over this questionnaire, and I think this is
> all just an ill-disguised attempt to psychoanalyze me.

Oh no . . .

> OLIVE
>
> For example, when I find out from your questionnaire
> answers that you speak three languages, should I lie
> on my own questionnaire because I am so incredibly
> turned on/intimidated by your excellent linguistic cre-
> dentials or should I be honest?

Oh god, she had actually typed out the words *turned on* . . .
about Stella being a polyglot. Olive had truly out-Murphyed
herself.

Don't drink *and text beautiful women. Don't drink and* text
beautiful women. Don't drink and text beautiful women.

And that wasn't the only thing she had texted.

> OLIVE
>
> Favorite color? Seems like a gimme but then you
> put that your favorite color is a very specific Pantone
> shade of periwinkle. Thus just saying "green" seems
> inadequate. I really do like emerald and chartreuse?
> Now I have to decide which is more impressive.

Olive leaned her head on her steering wheel so hard the
horn beeped, making the person who was for some reason

sitting in the parked car in front of hers give her the finger out their back window.

Yeah, fuck me, indeed, thought Olive.

There was one more text. The one that ostensibly Stella had been answering in the previous two texts.

> OLIVE
>
> Biggest fear. Well, at least this one's easy. Flying. Well, not the flying part. The crashing into a pit of fiery wreckage or an ocean abyss part or body being vaporized part. The being torn into a million parts part.

Thinking that it was too early in the morning to overdose on embarrassment, Olive stuffed the phone back into her scrubs pocket. The extra five minutes spent drowning in mortification meant she didn't have time to get coffee from the shop on the way in, and she would, therefore, be a very angry nurse until she got a break and the caffeine gods smiled on her.

Joni was already at the desk clicking through charts when Olive set her stuff down at the nurses' station.

"I brought coffee today. And donuts." Joni pointed absently at the back.

"Have I told you how you're my new favorite person and how you can never ever go back to Colorado?"

"No, you haven't." Joni grinned, pushing her wavy red hair out of her face. "Better not tell Derek. He'll be mad to be usurped."

"Derek didn't bring me coffee today. Consider yourself notified. Tell Colorado you're staying forever."

"We'll see." Joni laughed.

Olive went to the break room. She poured herself a cup of liquid happiness and gulped it down and stood with the posture of a coke-addicted Wall Street investment banker waiting for the high to kick in.

She checked her phone again.

Still nothing.

She hoisted up her proverbial big-girl pants and then sent off one more text.

> OLIVE
> If those are your biggest fears, they are awfully spe-
> cific and they do not align with what you wrote on the
> form which is the very intentionally vague "failure"

No reply. Stella was probably flying.

After four hours of patient care, the phone buzzed again. Olive ran into the supply room and grabbed it out of her pocket. Because she was apparently a freaking teenager today.

> STELLA
> Those are all things more likely than dying in a plane
> crash

Olive burst out laughing, apparently startling the resident who'd been crouching in the back corner, hiding from the attending doc—the one who was much scarier than Joni. Olive thought for a second and then began typing.

> OLIVE
> The Oxford English Dictionary definition for phobia:
> an extreme or irrational fear of or aversion to some-
> thing.

> STELLA
> While I do enjoy lexicology, I'm confused.

> OLIVE
> It's not rational.

She watched for the tiny typing bubble, but it didn't appear.

It would be best to go out and act like a professional. Acting giddy over a couple of text messages was the least Olive thing ever. Somehow this had gone from Olive making a fool out of herself to the most addictive kind of witty banter?

As she caught sight of her face in the reflective surface of the blanket warmer, she noticed her mouth doing this incredible bizarre thing.

Smiling.

No, she had important nurse shit to do. Olive took out her notebook with her to-do list and began checking things off.

She had to have a few long conversations with underperforming team members, and go in with Joni to give some extremely bad and emotional news to a patient. Then ten people all came in at once for a fender bender, all of them acting like they were in a gruesome wreck for the amount of attention they demanded.

It was nine hours into her shift before she sat down to eat lunch—leftovers of the food she'd made for Stella. She had forced Stella to take the rest of the cake, and Stella had only barely argued. She'd glowed and said she couldn't wait for her dad to taste it.

> STELLA
> Giving birth to conjoined twins.
>
> OLIVE
> I mostly date women, so I feel like that would change those odds.
>
> STELLA
> Dying falling off a ladder
>
> OLIVE
> If the point is to also make me afraid of ladders, you're succeeding.
>
> STELLA
> Did you know that cows kill way more people than sharks every year?

OLIVE

What does this have to do with flying?

STELLA

Just thought it was interesting how often fears don't make sense.

OLIVE

Next time I see a cow, I'll make sure I run in the other direction.

OLIVE

Glad we had this talk

STELLA

I'm a veritable smorgasbord of useless information.

OLIVE

Ha.

A call came in on her pager, and Olive had to stuff her phone back into her pocket and run to help with an aggressive patient. After a Mt. Olympus of charting after that fiasco, she sat down long enough to drink a cup of doomsday hour coffee and check her phone again. Not that she was planning her whole day around when she could check her phone. Because that would be pathetic.

STELLA

Being struck by lightning.

OLIVE

Please stop.

But . . . she hoped she wouldn't actually stop. Ever.

STELLA

Are you working on Tuesday?

> OLIVE
> No.

> STELLA
> Come fly with me.

Pressing the phone to her chest, Olive swiveled in her chair. After a barely audible chortle came from behind her, Olive turned. Joni was silent, but her facial expression dripped amusement.

"What?" Olive barked.

"Nothing." Joni hunched over her computer again, muttering something that included the words *phone cuddling* and *Derek's gonna die.*

> OLIVE
> Is it possible to hear that question NOT in a Frank
> Sinatra voice?

> STELLA
>

> STELLA
> You passed the test. Now come on. I'll make it worth
> your while.

Olive's eyes widened as she considered whether another kiss from Stella would be enough of an incentive to get her phobia-riddled ass on a tiny, scary death plane. The fact she was considering it probably meant she liked this woman far more than was reasonable given she'd known her less than a week. Derek was right, the stupid asshole.

Her phone buzzed, and she swiped to answer before realizing that it was not Stella.

"Hello, is this Olive Murphy? This is Joe Roberts from NBC Four."

"Oh, hi." Something tightened in her chest.

"Are you still interested in coming down to do an interview about what happened on the plane last week?"

"Yeah, so, I had a quick question. I—uh, I met the pilot . . . Well, actually she drove me down to Disney World afterward, and now we're dating, and she's my g-girlfriend." At some point, Olive would need to stop stammering over the word. "Is there any way she could come too? She was there after all."

"You fell in love with the pilot of the plane you were on when you saved Mickey Mouse's life?"

"Um. Yes? But he's not actually Mickey Mou—"

"Can I call you back?"

"Sure. Are you still okay with me talking about my hospital in the segment?"

He sounded distracted. "I think we can work that out. I'll be calling you back soon."

"Okay. Thanks."

> STELLA
>
> To be clear. I was talking about bringing you Swedish Fish.

> OLIVE
>
> 👎 Fiery wreckage > Swedish Fish.

> STELLA
>
> That looks like you're saying that fiery wreckage is greater than Swedish Fish.

> OLIVE
>
> Damn it. I mean that the risk of fiery wreckage outweighs the benefit of Swedish Fish.

> STELLA
>
> But these are your favorite candy.

A photo came in of Stella with a bag of Swedish Fish. One fire-engine-red fish held between her straight, white teeth.

Olive was in so much trouble with this woman.

> **OLIVE**
> Swedish Fish selfies are playing dirty.

> **STELLA**
> Oh, I can do dirty.

Shit. Okay. Here for this.

> **STELLA**
> I feel like that came out wrong.

Damn it.

No more texts came in for a while. After finishing some more work, Olive pressed the phone into her forehead, and it started buzzing right into her skull.

She swiped, again hoping for Stella and seeing another random number instead.

"Joe?"

"No, not Joe. This is Steve." His voice was very different, one of those smoked-a-pack-and-a-half-a-day-since-1976 types of voices.

"Hi, Steve."

"Quick change of plans."

"Oh, I understand if you don't want me to come on anymore." A small part of her rejoiced at getting out of it.

He laughed, a Hollywood smarmy laugh that happens right before a big company buys up all the land in a cute small town to put in an oil refinery. "We'd like to have you on today."

"But it's 5:30 P.M. I can't get there today."

"No, *TODAY*."

"I told you I'm really sorry but I can't get there today. I'm still at work, and I don't get off for—"

"The *TODAY* show."

Olive dropped the phone. It clattered on the floor, and Olive scrambled to pick it up.

Who's on first. Her life had devolved into a bad Abbott and Costello routine. *Jesus Christ.*

"Are you there, Ms. Murphy?"

She grabbed the phone off the floor, making a mental note to clean it with an alcohol wipe. "Um. I don't think I can come to New York."

"We can film you in DC. We already talked to Allied Airlines about Stella Soriano coming. That's your girlfriend, right?"

Shit. They hadn't talked about *TODAY* when they discussed an interview. Olive had said local news and maybe a radio show. Would Stella be mad?

"Yeah. I should probably ask her—"

"We verified with the airline. She's available."

"Oh. Great."

"So, you're still available on Thursday morning, right?"

"Yeah." Nausea hit. Olive's ears were ringing, but she managed to force out a few more words. "I'll be there."

"Great. See you then. Will email the full deets."

An unironic *deets.* Wow.

"Coolio." Olive winced. "Bye."

> OLIVE
>
> So slight change of plans with this interview . . . 😳
> And any chance you can borrow one of those airsick
> bags from your plane? If things go bad with this, I'd
> like to keep my panic-puking on theme. ✈

Chapter 20

The scent of vanilla and lilacs washed over Olive as Stella adjusted the collar of Olive's teal dress. The dressing room was illuminated from the Hollywood lights around several mirrors. Stella was in uniform today, pilot-wings pin gleaming on her chest. They'd spent last night talking on the phone about their story, basically deciding to keep it identical to the actual story of their relationship. Which, to Olive, begged the question of *WHY THE FUCK WEREN'T THEY ACTUALLY JUST REALLY FUCKING DATING?*

But . . . Olive decided to put off that discussion for another day especially given how certain Stella seemed that any time she was in a relationship the other person would wind up hurt. Despite this . . .

Things were good.

Great, actually.

Stella slipped her hand in Olive's as they sat in two stools waiting to be called. They'd discussed talking points with the interviewers beforehand. And Joni had given her a prescription for Zofran in the hopes that there would be no stage fright panic-puking. Although Olive had been joking, Stella did bring her a tiny Allied Airlines airsickness bag. When Olive unfolded it, she found a small note.

You won't need this. We got this.

We got this. Just something else to make Olive's heart do that dumb, delighted little spasm.

They did have a plan though.

For the past three days, they'd texted around the clock. Stella had raved about the cake and how much her dad liked the leftovers Olive had sent home with her. They'd joked about Swedish Fish, unlikely death scenarios, and everything else. She'd been so preoccupied with Stella that it was easy to ignore the texts from Lindsay. And not overthink about the lack of recent actual contact with her mom and Heather. Olive also evaded some of the slightly judgy but ultimately caring texts from Derek, who seemed baffled by the entire situation.

They'd straightened Olive's hair for the interview, and it felt like she'd had a head transplant. It didn't move the way it normally did, giving her an odd, out-of-body feeling. She was checking it in the mirror one last time when Stella ran her hands through it. Olive fought the urge to lean into her touch. But they were alone here. No one was watching, so she didn't have the fake relationship as an excuse for potential cuddle initiation. That wasn't listed in the PDA section.

"You look lovely, Olive. Your hair is so soft like this. And so much longer. But I like it when it's curly too."

"I hardly ever straighten it. I used to. But it was a pain. Derek said all the heat was ruining the texture."

"I like it wild." Their eyes met in the mirror. "But you're—it's beautiful today."

They were standing so close, Stella's hip was pushing up against her. It was a slight nudge of friction just inches from a very sensitive spot.

"You look nice too. I like you in the uniform." Olive's finger traced the outline of the wings on Stella's chest.

"Come on another flight, and you'll see me in it again."

"Where are you going on Saturday?"

"Cincinnati," she said in an exaggerated, seductive whisper.

"Hard pass."

"What's wrong with Cincinnati?"

"What's *in* Cincinnati?" Olive drawled.

"You're such an East Coast snob."

"*I'm* an East Coast snob?" Olive poked Stella's arm. "You're the one who said she always needed to shower after coming home from the Bible Belt."

"All that self-righteousness makes me itch." After affecting a tiny grossed-out shudder, Stella doubled over laughing and braced a hand on the small of Olive's back.

"You ladies ready to go?" said the voice of a PA from the door. The woman tilted her head. "You really do make an adorable couple."

"Thank you." Stella's smile wasn't the same as it had been a few seconds ago.

They sat together opposite a perfectly polished woman in a purple dress, all mic'd up and ready to go. When the camera went on, Olive found she could breathe through the anxiety as long as the familiar smell of lilacs and vanilla kept her calm.

***

"You were absolutely amazing, Stella. Thank you," Olive whispered into her ear as they went back to the green room to get their stuff. Stella's smooth hand was still tight in hers, ostensibly for the pretense of their arrangement. But no one was watching them now.

"You were too."

"My hospital's going to be thrilled about this. Maybe we really will get some donations to the department. You never know. New donors can really help with equipment and budgets."

"I'm glad I could help. I don't know how nurses do what you do. When you told me about that patient threatening to kill you the other day . . ." She shook her head. "I like having an impenetrable door between me and the general public most of the time. I don't like that you have to deal with that."

Because she was concerned for Olive's safety?

"It's all usually less dramatic than it sounds."

A buzzing came from Stella's pocket. When she lifted the phone, worry erupted on her face.

"What's wrong?"

"My dad fell. *Shit.* He says he made it back into the chair, and he's fine." She began furiously typing on her phone.

"Did he hit his head?"

"His caregiver didn't say. I'll ask." She typed more. "He told her to tell me to stop coddling him."

"Tell him your friend's a nurse, and she's the one asking. Sometimes dropping the nurse word makes people pay attention."

"Okay." Her thumbs beat another *rat-tat-tat-tat*, faster this time. "He says he didn't hit his head, and his caregiver—he has someone who comes to help him a couple times a week—insisted on telling me."

"Men."

They both sighed in tandem.

"I know we talked about getting lunch, but I don't think—"

"Let's go. I know better than to ask to drive. But we can go straight there. I can take a quick peek at him if you want."

"You'd do that?" Stella squeezed her phone, eyes wide.

"Of course. If we swing by my apartment, I can grab my blood pressure cuff and stethoscope and be more thorough."

"That would be perfect. It's so hard to get him to go to his regular doctor's appointments to get his meds adjusted and blood drawn. An emergency visit is almost impossible."

"Say your friend is a nurse busybody."

And Stella kissed her on the cheek. "Thank you."

"A quick kiss on the cheek is good in some situations?" Olive quoted the PDA section of the binder.

"This was definitely one of those situations."

Olive turned away to hide her burning cheeks. "Let's go. It's no big deal. We're friends, right?"

"Yeah."

They headed out to Stella's car, which was, obviously, spotlessly clean. The Prius had that new car smell that Olive loved but could never get to stick around in her own car since she usually at some point left old taco wrappers in it too long. Stella yanked the gearshift into drive, turning on a playlist low in the background.

"What's your dad like? What was he like growing up?"

"Strict but strong. He always had clear expectations for me, which was good. I do well with that. He was a great provider. Worked really hard. He's brilliant. Won tons of awards at work. Always wore a perfectly pressed black suit and tie and came home telling stories about meeting with important people on Capitol Hill about aviation policy. My grandma came to live with us after my grandfather died. They raised me together since he worked a lot."

"Is your dad a pilot too?"

"No." She shook her head with regret. "He wanted to be. My grandfather was a Mexican fighter pilot in World War Two. He trained in the US during the war, then worked in aviation back home in Mexico after. He met my grandmother on a trip to Texas, and he married her and got a job for an airline there. My dad grew up wanting to be a pilot more than anything. Just like his dad was. I'll have to show you some of the photos of my grandfather."

"Why didn't he?"

"He joined the US Air Force, but then the day before he was supposed to start, he had a seizure." She pulled her mouth in an expression of regret. "And that was that."

"That sucks."

"It did. He got degrees in engineering and public policy instead. My first memory is him taking me down to Gravelly Point in DC and us watching the planes take off from National. He's this tall guy, and he'd put me on his shoulders, point to the sky, and say Stella Sofía, you're going to fly one of those someday."

"Did that feel like pressure?"

Stella smiled, sadly. "He said I loved planes more than Barbies. My grandmother said it all started when I was a baby, and he'd zoom me around the room like an airplane. My first word wasn't *Papi*. It was *up*."

"That's the best story." Olive wished she could hold her hand and make her happy again. It wasn't that she seemed sad, rather more wistful or regretful. "Did your dad have more seizures?"

"Nope. Just the one. Destroyed his dream. And now I'm so close to doing everything he didn't get to. He's ecstatic about it. I owe it to him to not let anything stop me."

"You love him so much."

"Sure do. When I was growing up, he was never a feelings-type man. But he was always everything I needed. He paid for my college so I wouldn't have student loans. He worked so darn hard every day. He made sure I had everything I need to—"

Stella's hands tightened on the steering wheel. She wasn't crying, but there was such an outpouring of emotion in her brown eyes. This is what flying meant to her. This beautiful connection between her and the father she clearly loved so deeply. No wonder becoming captain was her entire focus.

"Pull over." Olive pointed at the shoulder.

"It's fine. I'm fine."

Olive touched Stella's face very lightly, wiping away a single tear with her thumb. "We've talked about what it means to say you're fine when you're crying."

"I'm not *crying*," Stella said, but despite this, she flipped on her blinker and left the road. After shifting into park, she sniffled but kept holding tight to the steering wheel. "I don't know when something like this is going to be the catastrophic thing."

"That's brutal. What you're doing by living with him is huge, and I'm sure he appreciates it."

She blinked over and over again, as if determined that no other tears would join that first one. She spoke more quickly than usual, which was a feat. "My grandmother passed away a few years ago. I think he was ignoring his symptoms while taking care of her. He actually got really mad when I told him I was moving in, but it's worked out. I made him believe it was so I could afford my plane."

"But it wasn't?"

"No. I'm frugal. It would've been fine."

"But you wanted to be there for him?"

"Yeah. Of course. He's had to make some tough decisions. He retired ten years sooner than he expected and he feels like he's a burden. But he's not. When my grandmother got sick a few years back, that was tough, but this is completely different." She took her hands off the steering wheel long enough to flex her fingers once before grabbing on again as if she thought it might fall off. "I'm getting this all out now so I won't do it in front of him."

All out appeared to still be referring to that one, reluctant tear. "Not a big crier?"

"I want to be strong for him."

"You are."

After a few minutes, Stella pulled the car back into drive and merged onto the highway again. They didn't speak for the rest of the ride. Stella parked in front of Olive's apartment building, and Olive ran up to get her blood pressure cuff and stethoscope. As the car started moving again, nerves tugged at Olive. She could handle going over to assess her friend's father. That was normal. It happened all the time. People called her with medical questions, asking her to come check out a kid's rash or asking if whatever thing their baby was doing was normal.

Olive's knee bounced up and down.

This was different.

She was meeting the father of the woman she had an unrelenting crush on.

And from everything she said, he sounded like an intense man.

Olive took a deep breath. Everything would be fine. She'd be her normal take-charge, nurse self. He wouldn't know what a mess she was. Today especially she looked the part in her TV-ready shift dress and sensible flats.

Stella pulled into the driveway of a perfectly tasteful brick bungalow. Neat landscaping. Well maintained. A man with a stainless steel cane stood in a doorway.

He was not what Olive expected.

Not one bit.

He wore a flowy multicolored shirt over . . . were those leggings? A few beaded bracelets jangled on either wrist. He smiled a shaky smile at Olive and Stella as they walked up the sidewalk to the front porch.

His voice shook slightly, a tremulous quality Olive had seen with other patients with Parkinson's. "So, here's Olive. It's good to meet you. I'm Hector." He extended an arm, which rose and swayed from side to side. Chorea. A side effect from the meds. "Come give your fake girlfriend's old man a hug."

Sweet Jesus. Olive's mouth fell open.

Chapter 21

"Papi, I said no incense unless I was home." Stella sniffed the air as she helped her father back into the wheelchair by the door.

"Jocelyn lit it during yoga."

"Who's Jocelyn?" Olive asked.

"The caregiver I'm currently thinking about firing." Stella's teeth gritted together.

"Be nice to Jocelyn, Mijita. She's going through a very tough divorce right now."

She hooked his cane onto the handle of the wheelchair and wheeled him back into the living room. "You're only supposed to try yoga poses when the physical therapist is here."

"What can I say?" He reached a shaking hand to her chin and then flicked her nose, which took a couple of tries. "I forgot."

Stella ground her teeth together. "Not funny."

"I'd say *too soon*—that's what the kids say, right, Olive?"

Olive nodded feebly.

"But if I waited to make the *too soon* jokes, and I was too late, I'd be dead."

Olive thought it was possible that Stella's brain might explode.

It was hard to tell about such things.

Stella began cleaning nonexistent messes, which involved stacking and restacking books and coasters. Everything was perfectly neat, but it wasn't the minimalist wonderland Olive expected. Stella's father obviously loved color as much as Olive did. There was color everywhere, with photos of planes in frames mounted on an exposed brick wall. On one wall was a large set of Catholic religious iconography with a collection of colorful candles beneath it.

There were a few blankets with similar patterns to the one that Stella had let her borrow in the car on the way to Orlando. On one wall, there were some black-and-white framed photos of a pilot with an old fighter plane who, she assumed, must have been Stella's grandfather. Throw pillows were neatly arranged on a gray sofa, and a medical grade recliner chair stood in the corner with an iPad on an accessibility stand. Hector pushed up from the wheelchair and moved to the recliner. Stella adjusted the cushion behind him and put a blanket over his legs.

His shoulders were hunched, his shirt loose as if he had lost weight recently. Muscle wasting? Stella had said he was diagnosed two years earlier. This was not a good sign. No wonder Stella was worried.

Olive hadn't said anything beyond a flabbergasted nice to meet you, so it was probably time to begin speaking. "How are you feeling, Mr. Soriano?"

"Call me Hector." He smiled. "Right as rain other than the fact I have Parkinson's."

"Can I take a quick look at you? I think it'll make Stella feel better."

"Do what you must." He extended a hand to gesture to the seat beside him. "Especially if it will make my daughter stop harassing me."

"I don't harass you."

He huffed rather than responding.

Olive took out her stethoscope and blood pressure cuff. "You remember everything from the fall?"

"Yes."

"You didn't hit your head?"

He smiled at her. "No."

"Okay. Where did you hit?"

"My elbow, hip, and knee."

A small yelping sound came from Stella, but Hector silenced it with a pointed glance.

"Hector, I'm not a doctor, but I can at least see if I think there's any cause for Stella to harass you into going and getting an X-ray. At the end of the day, everything's your choice for your care, and I'll give you my best opinion. But that's all it is, one person's opinion. And whatever you choose to do is your choice."

"She seems smart, Mija."

"She is."

"Not sure if I'm nearly as fun to take care of as Mickey Mouse . . ." He chuckled.

Olive groaned. "It wasn't Mickey Mouse."

"*Papi.*" Stella began pacing and picked up his mug, which had an accessibility lid and spout, along with a plate that still had half a sandwich on it. She'd known Hector for only a few minutes but Olive bet that getting Hector to use that accessible cup had been a battle. "I'm going to clean up." And she took it through a door in the back that Olive assumed led to a kitchen.

"I was still eating that." Hector shook his head and extended his arm, bending despite the shaking. "You see, I can move everything."

Olive felt from his shoulder all the way down his arm. She was right about the muscle wasting. "I won't check your hip. I'll take it as a given that it's not broken since you were standing when we arrived."

His voice lowered. "Probably won't be standing too much longer. But I still can for short periods of time. I know it makes her feel better. Makes me feel better too."

Olive nodded. "That makes sense."

"Life." He shrugged, lifting his hands as if to say there's good and bad. "So, tell me, how is my daughter as a fake girlfriend?"

"Wha-what?" Olive's ears were on fire. "She's—she's . . . Well, we're friends. And she's a really great friend."

"Perfect answer."

"I didn't realize she would've told you."

"We made a pact a long time ago not to ever lie to each other. And while I can't say I exactly approve of the way she's doing things, I understand. I had that kind of drive once too."

"You're a good dad."

"Bring me that book over there if you will." He pointed to a leather-bound scrapbook on a bookshelf in the corner.

Stella popped her head in from the kitchen. "Do you want coffee?"

"Yes," he called back. He made a hurry-up movement.

"Olive, what about you?" Stella asked.

"I'm okay, thank you."

As soon as Stella went back into the kitchen, Olive grabbed the book. It took him a couple of tries but he got it open to the first page. "That's me and Stella's father."

"You're—"

"I know what it's like to keep secrets from parents, and they can drive a permanent wedge in the relationship like they did for my ex-partner and his parents and to a lesser degree between me and my father. I didn't want that for me and her."

"She said her grandmother lived with you. Helped raise her."

"She did." He shifted his weight. "Her other father left when Stella was very young. He was from a very conservative family. She doesn't remember him. She knows nothing but openness in all of the relationships that matter. She's never lied to me about anything important. Not that she tells me everything." He arched an eyebrow pointedly. "But she's never lied. We've always been a team."

"Why are you telling me all this?"

"Because I want you to know that Stella's never been ashamed of who she is. And she's not ashamed now. She has a lot of guilt over the way her previous relationships played out . . . always so hard on herself. So, this fake girlfriend situation . . ." He turned a page, the edges worn from years of loving perusal. Photos of baby Stella covered pages, turning to toddler Stella. Stella in a Girl Scout uniform. Stella on a trip to Mexico based on the neat notation beneath it, beside a group of ten other kids who must be her cousins. Stella in a marching band uniform with braces. Stella with a soccer ball. The same beaming smile in every single one. "I suspect you know by now that Stella can be single-minded about a goal. And even though I miss her sometimes when she works a lot, I know what becoming a captain means to her. So please don't judge her based on this. With everything that's happening with me, she's—"

"Papi, *no.*" Stella came into the room with a gallon-sized cup for herself and another for her father. "Not the photo album."

"It's my job to show your friends where you come from."

"It's mortifying." A blush covered every visible inch of her neck and face.

Olive grinned and pointed to a photo of Stella holding what looked to be a box turtle, wearing a tie-dyed camp T-shirt. Braces with neon rubber bands on display. Wire glasses perched on her nose. "You're so cute."

Stella rolled her eyes and sipped her coffee, walking around the room muttering something about headgear and stirrup pants and whether Polaroid photos created toxic gases when they were lit on fire.

"I still need to check your knee, Hector."

"Have at me."

She rolled up the leggings. There was some bruising, but his range of motion was good. Olive also checked his pulse and blood pressure and listened to his heart. Everything seemed normal besides the typical manifestations of parkinsonian symptoms and common medication side effects.

"Well, he looks okay. He can move everything."

"Ha." Hector pointed at his daughter.

"But." Olive crossed her arms, shifting into boss-nurse

mode, brandishing her folded stethoscope like a teacher brandishes a pointer stick. "I still recommend calling your physician to check in. I don't know about what meds you're on. I don't know your medical history. You're welcome to tell them a nurse came by to check on you. But it's my recommendation that you call."

"Ha." Stella pointed at her dad.

A few hours later, they'd called the doctor and all eaten dinner together. It was odd for Olive to be a part of such a normal family dinner. Olive and her father had never been close. He'd been a 1950s-style father, complete with horn-rimmed glasses, short-sleeved button-downs, and emotional detachment. She couldn't help but marvel at the easy way Stella and Hector interacted. They were friendly and teasing. Open.

Most surprisingly, Olive didn't feel awkward at all for being there. After more coffee, for Stella of course, and tea for Hector and Olive, Hector wheeled himself away from the table. He kissed his daughter and even gave Olive's shoulder a paternal squeeze.

Stella had followed to help him, leaving Olive alone at the table. Olive was washing dishes when her phone started buzzing. She was expecting it to be her mother or Heather, but it was Lindsay.

She ignored the call.

After she'd stacked the last dish on the drying rack, she grabbed her phone again.

> LINDSAY
> Can I come over?

> LINDSAY
> I need to get my mason jars and that blender bottle.

> LINDSAY
> Ignoring my texts is immature.

Olive flicked away the messages. When Stella returned to the kitchen, she'd changed out of her uniform and was in a pair of leggings and an Embry-Riddle sweatshirt. It was the most casual Olive had ever seen her.

Olive crossed the kitchen to throw out the meal-prep containers in the recycling bin, and when she came back Stella wrapped her arms around Olive's neck.

"Thank you." Stella's mouth was almost touching Olive's collarbone.

"It's nothing."

"It was huge."

"It's not a big deal."

She released Olive from the hug, gratitude glowing on Stella's face. Her voice got more passionate but not any louder, ever aware that her father was in a room ten feet away. "I worry about him and then he worries about me, and we're both just as stubborn as each other. You really put my mind at ease. I don't ever want him to not tell me something is wrong because he doesn't want me to worry. Does that make sense?"

"Yes. And you're welcome, then." Olive tapped her toe on the kitchen floor, nibbling on her lip. "Are you excited for the awards banquet next weekend?"

"Excited to have the chance to get moving on the plan."

"Right." Olive cleared her throat. "The plan."

"Hey, speaking of the plan, we should probably take some photos for *the 'gram.*" Stella finished her sentence with a slight wince.

"The 'gram?" Olive said, laughing.

"I'm cool. *Shush.*" Stella put a finger over Olive's mouth, and Olive damn near fainted. Was it normal to want to suck on someone's fingers? "Tomorrow's supposed to be the last beautiful day for a while. I'm teaching lessons in the morning, but would you want to meet and go hiking in the afternoon?"

"Hiking?"

"We won't have time for a national park, but we could go to Harper's Ferry?"

"Oh, yeah. Hiking. That'd be fun. Taking some photos would make sense. The whole point of this is for your company to notice the relationship, right?"

Stella gave a couple of quick, slightly frantic nods. "Right. And on that topic, I need to ask you to help me with something else, but it's a little embarrassing."

Chapter 22

It would not be a stretch to say Stella climbing out of a cockpit was now Olive's sexual orientation. The sun glinted off her dark hair, which was coiled into a tight bun at the nape of her neck. Aviators were perched sexily on her nose, and she was wearing fitted jeans, sturdy hiking boots, and a soft-looking flannel that made Olive want to nuzzle her. Which was not creepy at all.

It had taken Olive several hours to decide what to wear. Was this an athleisure type of hike or more of a rough-it type of hike? She stood near the airfield where Stella had told her to park and was actually happy with her choice of attire. Beat-up jeans and an old thrifted Kate Bush concert T-shirt with a hoodie. She guzzled the rest of her third coffee of the day and then put the empty cup back in her car.

Olive had stayed late over at Stella's house the previous night, helping her develop a social media strategy complete with choosing presets and filters and brainstorming ideas for how to leverage her followers to continue to make a name for herself at the airline and as a leading female pilot in the industry in general. Olive hadn't posted anything on her own Adventures with Gus account since it blew up after the viral video, but helping Stella with hers felt less intimidating.

Stella shook hands with her flying student and then trotted over to meet Olive.

"Thanks for meeting me here," Stella said, grinning. "Ted was running late, so I wanted to give him an extra few minutes so he could get his full hour of flight time in."

"That's okay. You want to drive, right?"

"If you don't mind." Stella offered her an unsure quirk of the lips. "We can pick up your car before dinner."

"Sounds good."

They crossed the parking lot to Stella's ever immaculate silver Prius. They hopped in and drove toward Harper's Ferry. Olive knew better than to offer her any sort of snack now. Stella would probably have a heart attack before eating in her car given that she wouldn't even drink coffee in a rental.

They arrived at the start of a trail and headed out together. Olive tried not to focus on the brush of Stella's hands against hers in the spots where the trail narrowed. She shoved her own hands in her pockets to avoid the temptation to intertwine her fingers with Stella's. She kept pace easily, even though Stella's legs were several inches longer than Olive's. Olive was gladder than ever about her race training. It was a beautiful day. Maryland had teased them all by staying warm now more than a week into November, which meant the coming cold snap would be more of a gut punch.

They'd stopped every now and then for Stella to point out a particular tree or landmark. Stella had Girl Scout written all over her, even if Olive hadn't seen the picture of her in the green vest and pigtails yesterday. Most of Olive's hiking over the last year had been either alone or with Gus. And she wasn't so much hiking as showing up at the national parks and wandering around until she felt the box on Jake's list could be honestly checked off or until aging Gus began huffing and puffing. Hiking with Stella would be an entirely different experience.

Sweat formed on Olive's head, so she took off the sweatshirt and wrapped it around her waist. Stella mirrored the motion by pulling off her flannel. Underneath she wore a tissue-thin white T-shirt that matched what she'd been wearing in the car to Disney.

Stella pointed. "There's a beautiful view up ahead. Is it okay if we do it there?"

"Do—do what?" Olive stuttered out words, before her brain caught up with the filthy fantasy that began playing in her mind as soon as the words *do it* came out of Stella's perfect mouth. "Oh, take photos."

"Right. What did you think I . . . ?"

"Rest and eat a snack," Olive said without hesitating, unsure if Stella would buy it.

"Did you bring snacks?"

Olive grinned, feeling heartened by the unperturbed expression on Stella's face. Her cheeks were glowing from the hike and the sun, but she didn't seem like she realized that for a second Olive wondered if Stella was propositioning her for sex. And then imagining them having sex.

And now her underwear would be uncomfortably wet the rest of the day.

Jesus, Olive needed to get laid.

"What did you bring?" Stella said. "I should have thought to grab stuff, but I had to take my dad to an appointment early. Thanks for thinking of it."

"Oh, you thought I was going to share?" Olive kept a straight face.

Stella's eyes widened, and she shook her head several times. "No, of course, I mean I should have brought my own—"

"Stella." Olive touched Stella's nose. "I was kidding. Of course I brought stuff to share."

Stella grinned and gave an adorable chirping "*yay*" before pulling Olive up the hill. The view was stunning. Golden afternoon light pierced the clouds at the perfect angle. Trees in the distance were still painted with autumnal reds and oranges. They flamed bright as the sun struck them.

Stella pulled out her phone.

"No selfie stick?" Olive asked playfully.

Stella rolled her eyes. The most openly sarcastic gesture Olive had ever seen her make. "Nope."

They took several selfies with the light giving them that natural lens flare effect. It all looked perfect as Olive looked over Stella's shoulder at the shots. Stella handed over the phone. Olive cropped the photos and then edited them, narrating each step of the process. When she finished, she offered the phone back to Stella.

"I just don't know how you do that." Frowning, Stella shook her head. "I can do the presets stuff, but somehow you just make the photos look more professional just by how you changed three things."

"I took some photography classes, but honestly, I'm not really any good with that stuff. I don't have the patience for it beyond the quick phone-app edits." Olive looked away and pushed a hand in her pocket.

"You just have an eye for it, though." Stella's hand made the slightest of contact with Olive's hand before pulling back. Olive followed the movements of Stella's fingers, and then their eyes met.

The sounds of nature seemed to swell within the pause of their conversation. The breezes and birds filling the lingering silence between them.

"Do you . . . want to have snacks now?" Olive asked, rummaging in her backpack for her water bottle. Her mouth was too dry.

"Yes, please." Stella's voice was chipper, containing no evidence of the heat that stroke of her fingers had created in Olive.

Olive pulled out a thin picnic blanket and set out several colored Tupperwares containing trail mix and popcorn. Cut mixed veggies. Dark chocolate squares. Along with a yellow bag of Swedish Fish.

"This is a feast." Stella beamed at her. "Can you be my new hiking partner always?"

Um. Yes.

"I'd like that." Olive covered her gleeful reaction to Stella's excitement by stuffing her mouth with trail mix.

They both settled themselves on the blanket and began munching. Stella confessed she hadn't eaten since breakfast. Nothing made Olive happier than feeding someone, so she smiled and pushed the trail mix and popcorn toward Stella. But when Stella started eating all the Swedish Fish, Olive tried to grab a few.

"Hey."

"I have an addiction." Stella held one in her teeth as she had in that photo from a few days ago. Her dimples on nearly explicit display.

"Wait. Leave that there." Olive grabbed one of her own and picked up Stella's phone and swiped to the camera. They both smiled goofily with the candy held in their mouths. "Post that one on Instagram." Olive laughed.

"No way." Stella giggled and reached for her phone to check out the photo. She swung her hair around. It had come loose from the bun and cascaded down her back for most of the hike. Now it thwacked Olive in the face.

"Ouch." Olive poked Stella in the ribs.

Stella laughed harder. "Stop. I'm ticklish."

"Oh, are you?" Olive smirked.

And somehow after a tangle of twisting limbs, they were both horizontal. They faced each other, their bodies close enough Olive could smell chocolate and cherry flavoring. They stayed there for several minutes, just breathing, a sudden quietness settling between them as their laughter stilled.

Olive could almost count Stella's eyelashes from here.

"You get freckles after being out in the sun," Stella said softly.

"Yeah, I do." Olive wet her lips, her gaze drifting down to Stella's mouth.

"I'm having fun today." Stella's voice was even quieter now.

"Me too."

A soft pressure swept over Olive's leg, gentle and unexpected. Stella's leg? If Stella moved any closer, Olive would kiss her again. Her entire body seemed to ache to taste her, the memory of that kiss on the roller coaster making her lips tingle. So little space separated them. The increasing chill in the air made her warm breath even more welcoming as the sun dropped lower. Olive angled her head slightly.

The pressure on Olive's leg changed. Olive looked down expecting to see Stella's foot leaning against hers, but what was actually there was an enormous black snake.

"Motherfucking Jesus goddamn Christ." Olive pulled Stella back and leaped to her feet. She had to clutch at her sternum to prevent her galloping heart from jumping out of her chest.

"Oh my god," Stella said. "That was a surprise."

"A surprise? It's a fucking anaconda."

Stella actually took a step toward the demon slithering over their perfect picnic.

"It's a garter snake. Not poisonous. It'll go away so we can get your blanket and the stuff packed."

"I'm burning that blanket," Olive said, speech still a challenge through her heaving breaths.

Sure enough, a few minutes later, the snake decided it had accomplished its purpose of fuckblocking a horny bisexual and decided to find another unsuspecting victim. Reptilian asshole.

The moment was more than ruined, more like atomic-bomb-level torpedoed, so Olive and Stella packed up the picnic and headed back down the mountain.

"I should've known better. I've never gotten along well with nature," Olive said without thinking as she slammed the Prius door. "I'm sorry I freaked out."

"A snake crawling on anyone's leg would freak them out. You didn't know it wasn't venomous. But what do you mean you don't get along with nature? You have national park stickers all over your laptop. I thought hiking was your favorite thing?"

"What?" Olive scrunched her still trembling fingers in her hair. "No. I—uh . . . it's a long story. My brother wanted to visit all the national parks." Olive rubbed a spot of tension in the center of her forehead. "And he can't now, so kind of like the race, I was doing it for him. I go visit the park and take photos for him."

Olive decided not to mention that her extended "road trip vacation" from work last year had been the result of a mild mental breakdown after dealing with shit with her family and losing it at work one day. Her boss had told her to take some time off to "heal," and she'd been granted several weeks of FMLA. Driving to the parks was the only thing she could make herself do. Since nothing else she *should* be doing for Jake worked, she could at least check some things off his list. Most national parks were theoretically drivable, and Olive had had nothing but time.

"Visiting the national parks was on the same list you mentioned before?"

Olive nodded, a lifting sensation forming inside her chest at the idea of Stella remembering the things she said. "To be honest, I tend to have disasters whenever nature's involved."

"Disasters?"

"Yeah. Murphy's my last name. And well, Murphy's Law is an apt description of how things with nature tend to go for me. It's like I'm cursed."

"Like what?"

Olive ticked the minor catastrophes off on her fingers. "Sprayed by a skunk, almost pushed off a mountain by a goat, stung by a bee, pooped on by several birds—which I maintain isn't good luck no matter what superstitions say—uh . . . oh, and attacked by a squirrel. And now I guess, slithered on by a snake."

"Can we go back to the squirrel story because—"

"No." Olive gave a tiny shudder, remembering how the snake had felt on her leg.

"Well, then what's your ideal vacation, Olive 'Murphy's Law' Murphy?"

"I don't know really. Exploring new cities? Countryside is nice, but with French wine in my hand rather than bear repellent or an emergency first aid kit. I'd like to see all the cities I've read about. All the art I've studied."

"Where?"

"Everywhere? Europe, Asia, Australia, South America. I've priced out elaborate cruises across the Atlantic to try to get me to Italy. Been saving up. But the timing was never right. I love art and architecture—I took this amazing class on ancient and classic architecture during my art degree. Oh, I'm dying to go to Egypt. The pyramids and Cairo. The temples in Luxor. But I really would like to travel. I just . . ."

Planes. Fear. One of the other many ways Olive had failed herself during her more than thirty years on the planet.

"It's nice to hear you talk about this. I can tell you have a passion for it." Stella reached and swept stray hairs away from Olive's eyes. "I think you'll get there someday."

Olive turned to Stella and blinked twice. Had anyone ever looked at her like this? With such . . . something. Olive couldn't easily define whatever emotion was twinkling in Stella's eyes. But whatever it was, it pushed away all memories of the snake.

Chapter 23

Gus yanked the leash forward. Olive had spent the last two days rehashing the hike in her mind. Stupid snake. It was like she was going through Stella withdrawal. Her dreams had been utterly depraved lately, so full of everything she'd wished she'd had the opportunity to do on that mountain.

"Gus, no." The cold snap last night meant her hands were almost numb as she gripped the hand loop harder to keep Gus from attacking the bunny peeking out from behind a tree. Maryland fall was entirely unpredictable. She should have worn her heaviest coat. A gust of wind blew down the sidewalk, stinging her cheeks. Gus sped up as they turned to the sidewalk.

Her watch began vibrating. Her chest lifted at the thought of Stella calling.

But it wasn't Stella.

Olive's stomach turned over.

Why would Heather be calling her now, after the entire family had been ghosting her for more than a week? She fumbled in her pocket, the tingling of her fingers making it difficult for her to grip the phone. She tucked it to her ear and adjusted her grip on the leash so she could also hold her keys.

"Hey."

"Mom needs something from you," Heather said by way of greeting. "Her lawyer emailed you some documents last night. We need your signature authorizing payments from Jake's accounts. This next consultation is out of network. She wanted me to check in with you because it's urgent, and she hadn't heard back."

"I got off late last night. Haven't even checked my email yet this morning." Olive tried to keep the bite out of her voice. "I'm out taking Gus on a walk now."

"Okay."

Silence lingered on the other end of the line.

Olive sighed, hoping the frustrated exhale wasn't audible to her sister. "That's all?"

Heather took a couple of breaths. "Fiona saw you on the *TO-DAY* show. I had it on while I was getting them ready for daycare." Heather's tone was difficult to read. "Everyone at work—like the hygienists and the receptionists—are all talking about it too."

"Oh?"

"You weren't going to tell us?"

"What do you want me to say, Heather? I don't want to talk to you if it's going to end the way that all our conversations inevitably end." Gus wrenched the leash forward, probably to go after a squirrel that had scurried up into the trees.

"What? With me trying to figure out why you could give up without fighting for Jake?"

"Jesus Christ, Heather."

"Language. You're on speaker. Cody's in the back seat."

Olive sighed, deciding not to mention that Cody wasn't even a year old yet and probably wasn't offended by vaguely blasphemous profanity. "Sorry."

"I'm in the middle between you and Mom, and it sucks for me too, you know? You want me to go against Mom's religious beliefs and take her son away? I know you're not a mom, so you don't understand . . ."

"Just because I'm not a mom doesn't mean I loved Jake any less than you both did." She swallowed to suppress the trembling in her voice. She had not been prepared to be ambushed with this conversation. "Do you really think after everything that the doctors have said Jake's going to wake up? Tell me honestly."

Heather didn't answer for several minutes, and when she did

it was in a quieter voice. It was barely audible over the babbling of her son in the seat behind her. She sounded just like the timid baby sister who had been begging to follow Olive and Jake everywhere during their summer vacations. "How can I tell Mom not to believe in miracles when I want to believe in one too?"

What could Olive say to that?

"I'll sign whatever Mom wants."

Neither sister seemed to know where to go from there, but Heather didn't hang up. Olive heard Cody babbling.

Heather cleared her throat. "The *TODAY* show thing . . ."

"Sorry if it confused Fiona."

"You're really dating *her*?"

"Stella," Olive corrected, stupidly. Olive didn't think lying to her family would be an issue since it wasn't like they ever talked to her about anything personal anymore. But the idea of telling a flat-out lie bothered her. "Why does it matter?"

"She seems different than your usual type."

Here we go again.

"What's my type?"

"Angsty. Dramatic. Like, you know, Lindsay." Yeah, Heather and Jake had been united in their dislike of Lindsay. "The pilot woman seems . . . nice? And driven. Successful. But, like sweet?"

"She is." Olive huffed a laugh. Of course the only girlfriend Heather would actually approve of would be a fake one. Her sister had joined their parents' dentistry practice a few years earlier, fulfilling all the expectations that Olive's parents once had for Olive. As soon as Heather became an adult, she never missed an opportunity to make it clear what she thought of Olive's life choices in the most little sisterly way possible. She'd always been on Mom's side.

"Well, I guess I think you should try to hold on to her." Her tone was tentative, but not biting. "About Cody's birthday . . . the party's on the fifteenth at five, but I was thinking—"

"Shoot." Olive grimaced, holding the phone to her forehead.

"Stella's big corporate event is on December fifteenth, god, I'm so sorry. I didn't think . . . I didn't know his party would be that day." Honestly, she hadn't thought she would be invited to Cody's birthday party. She hadn't been invited to Fiona's birthday party this year "for Mom's mental health" or some bullshit. She switched the phone to speaker long enough to add the party date and time to her calendar. "Maybe could I stop by before—"

"I was just going to say that it might be better if you dropped by on his actual birthday maybe. Instead."

"Because you don't want me to be around Mom."

"I'm just trying not to choose sides. Every time you're in the same room together, you both—"

"What do you want me to do, Heather? I'm supposed to just be cool with the fact she's telling everyone I'm trying to profit off my brother's death?"

"You can't think that's what she really thinks. She's just devastated. Lashing out."

"Lashing out against *me*. She got a lawyer against *me*. Against me trying to do what Jake wanted."

"Can you just do the paperwork for her? I'll figure stuff out about Cody's birthday and text you."

"Fine."

"Mom's really not . . ."

"Really not what?" A sudden baby shriek meant Olive had to pull the phone away from her ear.

"Sorry, buddy, I'll change your diaper soon," Heather said in an exhausted voice. "Olive, I have to go, Cody's freaking out. It's probably for the best that you have a conflict with the party." The call ended.

What was she supposed to say to that? She was sick of being treated this way by her family.

As she walked back into her apartment, Olive stifled the urge to throw the phone against a wall. This was too frustrating a conversation to have before caffeine. She poured herself a cup of coffee and sat on the couch. She'd been working nonstop since Disney, with the interview with Stella and the hike on her only off days until today.

Her niece had seen her on TV. Everyone was talking about the interview?

She'd known that could happen. But she'd been so focused on her crush on Stella she hadn't considered the implications for when the fake relationship ended. When this ended, Stella would be one more failure. One more thing her family could point to in this legal battle and say she was an unreliable mess. God, if they ever found out that this was only a fake relationship . . .

Gus started whining. "Sorry, buddy," she muttered. She dumped kibble in his bowl before returning to the couch with her phone and laptop. After a few seconds of indecision, she did what Derek explicitly told her never ever to do. She opened Twitter and typed in the stupid hashtag.

Her thumb slid across the screen. Stella had been right. It was mostly positive.

She shut her eyes when the video came up and shut the app to bring up Google.

The response to the *TODAY* interview was also generally positive except for the requisite religious or conservative trolls who always had something to say anytime a queer person did anything. Fuckheads.

She scrolled over to Facebook. Another app that hadn't been opened in a while. Her mother had never figured out what was private and what would show up on the newsfeed. Unfriending her mother had seemed petty. But now she wished she had. So few of her real friends ever posted on here anymore. It was mainly photos of kids being posted for the benefits of boomer parents and boomers themselves posting various boomer-y and often incredibly ignorant political takes.

She scanned the page of her notifications. She'd been tagged at least a hundred times about the *TODAY* show. Mostly by her various older cousins.

That's when Olive saw it.

A post from one of her mother's friends to her mother.

Mary Ellen—is this your daughter?

And from her mother.

Appears that way.

And a response from the friend. **She looks happy** 😀 **Glad she's doing well.**

And her mother posted, **I'm sure she's happy. She's had a very profitable year.**

"Fuck you too, Mom."

Olive sat quietly for a long time after that. The phone squeezed in her fist. The worst part was that on some level she agreed with her mom. After all the shit that had happened in the last year, was it tacky to be on TV smiling like that?

Profitable.

The word reverberated in her head.

Who else had seen that?

Her mind spiraled, thinking through all the possible worst-case scenarios. When Stella found out what was going on with her family, would she hate Olive for it? Hopefully not.

The impact of the last weeks hit her like a wrecking ball in slow motion.

She'd gotten on an airplane. An actual airplane.

Her hands trembled as they had at the time, remembering the feeling of the pill slipping from her fingers. The terror as the lifting sensation made her stomach sink.

That long walk down the aisle after volunteering to help.

She squeezed her eyes shut, trying to guard against the image of the pale man on the floor. What if she'd done something wrong? What if she hadn't figured it out in time? Frank Feldstein would have . . . and people were filming it . . .

"He didn't die. He didn't die," Olive whispered.

A deep pain began to expand below her sternum. Her hands shook. Weight seemed to press in on her ribs. She hadn't had time to process any of it. Not the stress of being on the plane. The horror of wondering whether she'd be able to save the man's life.

The race. Remembering that Jake wasn't beside her. She'd spent every step of those 13.1 miles with nothing but the medal in her pocket to keep her company.

She closed her eyes and returned to the moment at the finish line. Reporters closing in on her. A microphone in her face. Cameras. Asking questions. Delayed nausea at the memory hit her in the gut.

But then Stella was there.

Stella.

Without thinking, she swiped to Instagram. It was like she wanted to see Stella's face for some stupid reason. Because seeing her face at the finish line had been like being pulled out of the water after almost drowning.

Olive didn't follow many people, so the first photo to load was from Stella herself.

But it wasn't the photo of them from the hike that popped up. That perfect, golden hour photo of the two of them wasn't on her feed at all. Olive frowned and focused on the image.

This one also didn't match the earlier photos on her profile. Instead of looking like a stock photo tagged with things like *airline uniform hottie* or *sexy professional pilot* or *lesbian pilot fantasy sex dream*—okay, that last one definitely said more about Olive than the photographs on the feed—it was a selfie of Stella. A selfie with impeccable cropping and a perfect use of the preset Olive had chosen. A selfie of Stella with another woman.

Chapter 24

The woman beside Stella in the photo was gorgeous. Sleek chestnut waves framed an elegant face with a perfectly straight nose and green-sea-glass eyes. Sure, her kind of pretty was rather generic for Olive's tastes. She had that influencer look with her perfect contouring and lashes. Fuck, Olive was being an asshole. The woman was a knockout.

Could this be her ex Nadine? Or the other one? What was her name? Laura. Oh god, what if this was Laura?

They were both knockouts. Sitting together at a table with wineglasses and candlelight. Both perfectly polished, looking like they were in a gay dating website advertisement or an episode of *The L Word.* This is what Hollywood-acceptable queer women looked like. Hot like Aubrey Plaza in that problematic Christmas movie where Kristen Stewart definitely should have dumped her semi-closeted manipulative girlfriend.

Olive scrolled to the caption.

Embry-Riddle class reunion. #WomeninFlight

Well, she'd used the hashtags they had discussed. And they had talked about Stella doing this whenever she was with other pilots. Maybe that was all this was? But she was still having dinner with a gorgeous woman, and Olive had no idea who it was.

Didn't Stella say Nadine dropped out of school? Then it couldn't be her . . . If it wasn't, who was it? It could be Laura. Stella hadn't mentioned Laura's job, and it wasn't tagged.

Or it could be a date with some other random pilot? Stella said she wasn't in a relationship—couldn't be in a relationship—but was she seeing other people? Casually?

Olive hadn't thought to ask. She swallowed against the acid burning the back of her throat. Stella *could* be sleeping with other people, even exes. They'd never discussed monogamy. Especially given that they weren't having sex with each other, what right would Olive have to stop Stella from sleeping with other people?

Stella hadn't texted much since the hike. Was it because she was hooking up with someone else? *Fuck.*

Why hadn't Olive asked any questions about this?

Why would Olive ever think that someone as gorgeous as Stella would want to be with someone like her? Just like Lindsay said. Just like Heather said. No one thought Olive was good enough for someone like Stella. They were right. It didn't make sense. Olive was a loser who was afraid of flying and estranged from her family.

Her breaths sped up faster and faster. Pressure built in her chest.

She covered her head with her hands and intentionally slowed her breathing. It had been months since she had a full-on panic attack. After Jake's accident she went a few months where she had them every single day.

Gus hopped up on the couch and looked up at her with a perplexed expression. Olive dragged her fingers through his fur several times. Petting a dog was supposed to give endorphins. She needed endorphins. Like Elle Woods said, endorphins make people happy.

And happy people don't feel raging jealousy after seeing a random Instagram photo of their fake girlfriend having dinner with some green-eyed aviation goddess.

Even after minutes of petting Gus, she wasn't happy.

She was panicked, rethinking all of her choices. That ugly voice that spoke so loud on her bad depression days was making her fixate on every doubt. Every negative thought.

She was breathing faster than she had during the half-marathon.

Was this all a mistake?

She picked up her phone. A pang hit in the middle of her chest. That pang had been there for a year. Jake wouldn't answer his phone.

Derek was working today.

None of her other friends knew about what she was doing with Stella—well, besides Joni, and they weren't at the talk-me-off-the-proverbial-ledge stage in their relationship. She hated that a part of what Lindsay said was true. She *had* called her crying at 2:00 A.M. after they broke up. She *had* been desperate for help when her family had turned against her. She *was* a mess.

"What do you think I should do, Gus?"

Gus's powerful tail thumped the sofa a couple of times in response to his name.

"Maybe this was a stupid decision."

Olive leaned forward to take a sip of coffee. It was freezing. The entire apartment was freezing, actually. The furnace hadn't caught up with the plunging temperatures.

Her phone dinged, and Olive jumped and dropped it. She must have flipped it off vibrate accidentally while she sat fidgeting.

> STELLA
> Want to get dinner tonight? My last flight got canceled because of that blizzard in Akron.

No. She couldn't face Stella like this. Lindsay had broken up with her the first time after the panic attacks got worse. She couldn't let anyone else see her like this. Stella had specifically said that she didn't want someone else to emotionally rely on her. She couldn't tell Stella the full extent of what was happening. Stella would bolt.

OLIVE
I'm sorry. I'm having a bit of a freak-out day.

STELLA
What are you freaking out about?

OLIVE
Just everything. I'm sorry. I need a little space right
now. I'm good tho.

See. Take that, Lindsay. Olive wasn't being emotionally needy.

STELLA
Oh okay. Space. I understand. This has all been moving quickly. Take all the time you need.

God, she's an amazing girlfriend.

The trouble was that she wasn't actually Olive's girlfriend.
She'd probably never be Olive's girlfriend.

Something essential seemed to crumple beneath Olive's ribs.

She didn't leave the couch for hours. She hadn't had a day
like this in a long time. Everything was impossible and nothing
would be better. Ever. On days like this her entire body ached.

She mustered the energy to take Gus on a walk at noon.
Then was back on the couch. As she was getting ready to take
him for another walk before she gave him dinner, her phone
rang.

The image of Stella on a date passed through her mind again.

But, of course, Stella was wonderful so she was giving her
the space she asked for.

Olive's mother's lawyer was calling. She hit the button to ignore the call.

The documents.

Olive hissed a curse under her breath, hurrying over to grab
her computer as she slid her finger across the screen. Another
email had come in. Actually from her mother this time.

It had ***TIME SENSITIVE*** in the subject line.
In the body of the email there was no greeting.

My attorney said he would be calling if we don't hear from you soon. We're lucky to get on this doctor's consultation schedule at all. Heather said you were "busy," but excuses like that don't really work when I know your heart's not in this anyway. We need this done today.

Olive fought an urge to call her mother and yell at her. She couldn't lose it on her mom right now. In her current mental state, horrible things would come out of her mouth. They'd all be true. But they wouldn't make anything better.

She spoke to her computer as she clicked and typed through DocuSigned forms. "I'm authorizing the payments right now, but just keep acting like I'm the worst person in the world. I totally deserve it." Her sarcasm was lost on Gus, who was still waiting by the door, nosing his leash.

When she finished going through the paperwork, her feet were heavy as she stood. She trudged over to the door. Once she got there, she stood still for a few minutes. In the fog of the day, her brain couldn't keep up with what she was supposed to be doing. As if he could understand her lack of direction, Gus nuzzled her hand.

"Right. Walk. Outside. Now." Olive's version of a pep talk today sounded more like the speak-and-spell in *ET*.

She forced herself through the walk, fed Gus, and fell into bed at 6:30 P.M.

Going to bed early had the unfortunate side effect of her waking up at 5:30 A.M. Her clothes were twisted around her as if she'd been thrashing in her sleep. A slight stickiness coated her skin. She'd woken up several times after bizarre dreams— nothing like naughty Stella dreams. Nightmares where the world was crumbling around her, and she could do nothing to stop it. Dreams about Jake. That day when the cops showed up at her apartment with grave expressions on their faces. That first moment when she saw him afterward. He was barely recognizable. The video of the accident.

She grabbed her phone, eyes burning from the bright screen.

There were texts from 8:00 P.M. last night, and she hadn't heard them come in.

> STELLA
> I'm worried that our arrangement is adding to your stress

And then at 8:10 P.M. she sent another text. *No. No. No.*

> STELLA
> I think it was unfair to ask this of you.

> STELLA
> It might be best for you if we don't take this any further. I'm sorry.

Chapter 25

"Shit," Olive said for about the fiftieth time as she reread the text messages from Stella. A canyon would be worn into her floor soon from the number of times she'd paced in the living room. She'd texted her back, but Stella didn't seem to be up yet.

Today looked better than yesterday. This was how it always was when she had a down day.

She ticked away the minutes until she could reasonably expect a response. She got out of the shower and finished getting dressed, checking the screen at least seventy more times.

"Fuck it." Olive swiped across her phone. She waited as the phone rang over and over.

Stella answered on the fourth ring. "Good morning, Olive." She sounded muted, but not like Olive had woken her.

Olive paced back and forth in her bedroom. "I'm so sorry to call so early. I fell asleep early last night, and I didn't get your texts."

"It's okay. I was at the gym. Just got back. I just saw your text."

"When are you working?" Olive braced for Stella's answer. She needed to fix this today.

"I have to leave in a couple hours. Why?"

Olive sat on the couch, elbows braced on her knees. "Can I take you for breakfast. Please? I need to explain and apologize."

"You don't have to apologize."

Olive nodded as if Stella could see her. "I really do."

"Can you meet me at Silver Diner? It's on my way to work, and—"

"It's got good gluten-free food."

Stella's voice shifted as if she might be smiling now. "Exactly. In an hour okay?"

"Of course. I'll be there."

Olive scrolled through the rest of the messages on her phone. A bunch from Derek asking if she was having a down day—how did he always know? And several from Lindsay.

> LINDSAY
> We need to talk.

> LINDSAY
> Are you really so self-sabotaging you can't even an-
> swer my calls anymore? I'm just trying to help you.

> LINDSAY
> After everything I did for you, it's really sad to see this
> is who you really are.

She did what she should have done months ago. She swiped to block her number. Nothing good came of seeing anything Lindsay wrote to her. She needed to make *better choices*.

The irony of the "better choice" being begging her fake girlfriend to take her back over scrambled eggs had not escaped her.

Olive hustled to get Gus settled, giving him a short walk. She was so distracted she did the walk before diffusing her hair, which meant long curls of icicles hung off her head when she got back. She did the best she could with her hair and then ran out the door.

She arrived at Silver Diner twenty minutes early. Plenty of time to have an almost-freak-out when she realized she had no idea what to tell Stella.

Nothing had changed exactly.

Her family was still a mess.

The idea of fake dating still made her uneasy.

But the idea of losing Stella now felt unbearable because she hadn't felt this way about anyone in a very long time.

She couldn't say *that*, though.

A hand tapped her shoulder from behind. Olive whirled around, and before she could figure out what to say, the worst thing ever came out of her mouth. "Who was with you in the photo on Instagram?"

Oh fuck.

"Shit, I mean, not that it's any of my business. And good morning." Olive gave a half smile. She should have hugged her. Damn it. "Thanks for meeting me," she ended shakily.

"My roommate from flight school. Angie. We had dinner last week. And I'm—uh—glad you called."

So, definitely not one of the two exes then. Why didn't Olive feel relieved?

The hostess called them over to the desk and then ushered them to a table.

Olive rubbed her eyes. "I'm sorry for texting you what I did last night. I was having a bad day. It happens to me sometimes, worse since my brother's accident where I have these dark days where I have trouble functioning. I shouldn't have taken it out on you."

Stella shook her head. "It's reasonable. I'm the one asking you to be my fake girlfriend." The last two words were heavy. With regret? "In any case, I'm really sorry you were having a bad day yesterday. I'm sorry if I'm making you stressed. I know that having me around can be *a lot*."

"No. You're not *a lot*. Except maybe a lot of—like—good things. Cool things." *Smooth.* To reinforce the point, Olive shook her head so quickly she might have pulled a muscle. Being in your thirties was awesome. "No. No. My sister called. And I haven't told you much about this, but the big picture is that my family and I are not on good terms right now."

Stella's brow furrowed. "That must be really hard."

"My niece saw us on TV and then my sister made a couple comments and that made me want to actually check out what's going on with the viral video of me from the plane. And my mom . . . Well, she posted something that upset me. It shouldn't. I should be used to it by now."

Pity lined Stella's eyes as she reached across the table to pat Olive's hand once. "I'm sure that must be incredibly stressful." Her head tilted. "Out of curiosity, was this related to why you were asking about Angie?"

Olive internally cursed her word vomiting.

"I guess it made me realize that I didn't know if you were . . . seeing other people."

"You thought I was . . . oh. No. Like I said, I don't do relationships. I'm not seeing anyone." Stella gave a humorless laugh. "That's why I needed to convince a relative stranger to be my fake girlfriend."

"Not having a relationship doesn't mean . . . well . . . I'm sorry if this isn't my business." Olive's cheeks burned. The word *stranger* still clanged in her ears, interrupting her train of thought.

"I'm not sleeping with Angie," Stella said quietly. "She's actually married. But I'm not sleeping with anyone right now, if that's what you're curious about. I haven't had a lot of time for that lately." Her lips pressed together as if she were actively stopping herself from saying more.

"Oh, okay." Olive fiddled with the stack of jellies on the table as if she were playing Jenga. "I think . . . is it okay with you if while we're doing this, we don't see other people?"

"I suppose I assumed that would be true, but I can see how that might not have been clear in our initial conversations."

"I didn't see a tab in the binder for monogamy . . ."

"That was remiss of me." Stella offered a tight smile, but the expression vanished too quickly. "I think this is more complicated than I expected. I meant what I said in my message.

I don't ever want to be the reason why someone else is more stressed."

"I know you did. And thank you, but I'm fine. I swear."

Stella nodded once and frowned.

Interrupting their conversation, a server came by and filled both their mugs with coffee. While the server took their orders, Olive dumped way too much sugar into hers since she was distracted. Stella concentrated on stirring her own even though Olive knew Stella drank her coffee black.

After a few minutes of silence, Stella spoke. "On a similar subject, and you definitely don't need to answer this because I'm in no way entitled to know all your concerns and, please, tell me if I've overstepped by even asking. Because the last thing I want to do is make you more stressed or uncomfortab—"

"Stella?" Olive rested a hand over Stella's.

"Yeah?"

"You can ask me whatever you want."

One side of Stella's mouth perked upward. "Okay." She took another breath and then let it out. "The woman. The blonde at the hotel."

Olive waited for the question.

Stella merely lifted her shoulders in an inquisitive movement.

"Lindsay." Olive took a sip of coffee. She hadn't been expecting to have this conversation, but she wanted to be honest. "She's my ex. We were together four years. My brother loathed her, incidentally, though he tried to be nice about it. After Jake's accident, I sort of fell apart. Lindsay got over it real fast."

"What do you mean?"

"I—uh—I had . . . well, have. I still *have* panic attacks sometimes. And I battle depression. Always have. She didn't really like that broken side of me."

Stella's fingers tightened on Olive's. "You're not broken, Olive."

She said the words with such defiant certainty that Olive almost believed them.

Unable to decide how to answer that immense statement, Olive finished the story of Lindsay. "Well . . . bottom line was she broke up with me. A few times. We'd still—um . . . like, get together once every few weeks."

"For sex?" Stella said, in a slightly flat tone.

"Yup." She hiccuped the word. Super poised. "But that stopped. And then we broke up for good. Six months ago, I had a really bad day. And we hooked up again. And . . . I don't know . . . I realized it was bad for me. I told her how I felt and ended things."

The server appeared again bearing plates of steaming breakfast.

"Makes sense." Stella cut her toast with a somewhat excessive savagery. "But she came to Disney to see you?"

"She bought the bib to run it with me before everything happened with Jake, but I thought she sold it. She used to just text me sometimes, but since the viral video thing, she's been kind of relentless."

"About what?"

"About you." Olive risked a glance at Stella.

"Ah. Okay." Stella chewed for several seconds and then swallowed audibly. "But you aren't still hoping for . . . to get back together with her?"

"God, no. Oh my god. Absolutely not. We were terrible. And she's manipulative. I'm just embarrassed it took me so long to realize that."

Eyes brightening slightly, Stella nodded. "Okay."

"The ex-lovers talk. An important milestone in every fake relationship."

Stella's mouth drooped, cheeks flushing. "I mean, it's important that we know these things, so the relationship is believable and credible."

"Oh. Yeah. Right. That reminds me, I still need to finish the questionnaire."

"Yes, you do . . ." Stella's forehead bunched. "So, you're sure you're still up for this?"

Olive turned her palm over and squeezed Stella's hand. "Yes. I'm sorry I freaked out."

"You're allowed to freak out about this. It's a weird situation I've put you in."

"Hey." Olive shook her head. "I don't feel like this is a situation you've *put* me in. You were amazing in the TV interview. I could never have done that without you. Never. And if I get to dress up, drink free booze, and eat a free meal, how can I complain?"

Stella's smile reached her eyes this time. "They do usually have pretty good wine at the banquet."

"Can't wait."

Olive smiled. Her heart lifted at the idea of being excited about something. This was almost like actually being excited for something, which she hadn't been for a year.

Which reminded her that she really needed to call Derek to beg for his help for one particular thing.

Chapter 26

"You need more female friends," Derek said, as he finger-combed product into Olive's hair. Gus had fled from the smell of the hair product and was hiding out, probably on Olive's bed.

"Why? You've been doing my hair since Homecoming 2002. You and I go to sappy romance movies. We shop together. It's our thing."

"I know it's our deal, but you don't usually take eight hours to find a dress and then refuse to believe my opinions when I tell you you look good in shit. Eight hours, Olive. You made me skip the gym to go to the mall when it *opened*. Why do you punish me?" He added a few more pins to the style. "Why didn't you ask Joni to come along too? I could've used the backup when you kept doubting me."

"I don't know if we're at the help-shop-for-a-formal-event level of friends yet."

"Eight hours."

"So whiny. I made you dinner afterward. And sent home leftovers."

"We went back and bought the first dress you tried on."

"I had to be sure."

The sigh that came out of Derek's mouth could have blown a pirate ship off course. "So . . . speaking of all the various women of your intimate acquaintance . . ."

"Ew. Don't put it like that. Makes me sound all loose and slutty."

"You would be loose and slutty for Stella in a heartbeat."

"God, so true." Olive gazed wistfully at the ceiling. "Um, so what about my lady acquaintances?"

"Lindsay texted me the other day." He twisted Olive's hair into an updo and added a few bobby pins.

"Why? She knows she's your least favorite person." Technically, Derek had been friends with Lindsay first. She was a respiratory therapist at the hospital. She mainly staffed the ICUs these days, so their paths crossed less.

"I'm less confrontational than you are, so I haven't gotten to the point where I've been able to tell her to fuck off in writing. Yet."

"What'd she say?"

"That she wants to talk to you."

Olive sighed.

"You haven't talked to her since she ambushed you at Disney?"

"I blocked her number."

Derek whooped. "Thank Christ."

Olive let loose a breath. "I don't think letting her be in my life is good for me."

"Yeah." Derek tightened his hold on her unwieldy hair.

"Ouch."

Ignoring her moaning, Derek pulled her hair tighter as he twisted it into the elegant hairstyle she'd found online for tight curls. "No pain, no gain. Beauty hurts. All the hair-care sayings. You know I was taught well."

"That reminds me . . . How's your sister? And your mom?"

"Haven't heard from *that* sister." He shrugged, possibly tugging her hair harder than was necessary. "Mom's praying for me. Her whole Bible study ladies' group is also *praying* for me. The implication being exactly what you would expect."

"Eesh. Want to talk about it?"

"Nope," he said in a clipped tone.

"You know, Stella's dad's gay too."

"Really?"

"Yeah."

"You met him?"

"Nurse thing."

"She called you for a medical opinion?"

"You know the drill. She didn't call me though. He had a fall on the day of the *TODAY* interview." She sighed. "Parkinson's. It seems like an aggressive type. Pretty precipitous downturn."

"That sucks. Must be tough on her." He added one more pin and a spritz of hair spray. "Bet she was happy to have you with her."

"Seemed like it."

"Any sex yet?"

Olive grimaced as Derek pulled a section of her hair tighter. "Nope. Just me and Alyson working out my constant sexual frustration."

"I think it's really weird you named your vibrator."

"Alyson Hannigan's story arc as gay Willow on *Buffy* was a big part of my sexual awakening. It's an homage."

"It's weird as fuck, O." He spun the swivel chair around, so Olive could see her reflection. "All righty. Voilà."

"Oh my god. Thank you so much." She grinned and hugged him. "I owe you so big. I'll buy you coffee before work when we have shifts together for two weeks."

"Soy milk only, please. Keeping svelte."

"Oh, are you?"

"And speaking of. I've got to go soon but I want to stay for the *She's All That* moment. Go put the dress on." He made a *please scurry away* gesture with his fingers.

"The *what* moment?"

"God, you're a traitor to our golden age of early 2000s teenage rom-coms." He gave her a knowing look, like a trivia host giving the contestant another shot.

The reference clicked into place. "Oh, Rachael Leigh Cook. 'Kiss Me.' Red dress. Stairs."

"Ding, ding, ding." He tapped his nose. "Paul Walker was very important to *my* sexual awakening."

"Wasn't he the bad guy in that movie?"

"I didn't say it was a healthy part of my sexual awakening." He again motioned her to go to her room. "What time is she getting here? She's picking you up?"

"Yes, fifteen minutes? Shit, cutting it close. What are you doing tonight?" She ran to her room, leaving the door half open, and made to shimmy out of her shirt. She pulled on black tights and the black long-sleeved lacy minidress Derek plucked off the clearance rack at Nordstrom. Gus raised his chin, tilted his head, and then let it flop back down. He was obviously unimpressed.

"Going to the gym."

"Why?"

"Health. Wellness. Good habits."

"A dude?"

He snorted. "Oh, Olivia."

"That's not my name, jackass." She looked at the dress from every angle, turning in front of her full-length bedroom mirror and frowning. "Are you sure this dress is—"

"Good god, Olive. If you make me answer that question one more time I'm taking the dress back and you can go to the banquet in your pajamas. Is the dress on? Get your ass out here."

Her phone buzzed.

STELLA
be at your door in 5

OLIVE
I can come out. you don't have to park.

STELLA
already parked.

OLIVE
okay.

Olive's heart fluttered. When was the last time she felt this way? Picked up at the door by a gorgeous date? It *did* feel like some cheesy, waltzing romance song should be playing in the background. Goddamn it, Derek was right. Butterflies had taken up permanent residence in her abdomen since Stella asked her to be fake girlfriends. They acted like they were in some kind of butterfly mosh pit every time Stella's name appeared on her phone.

"Come out. Come out," Derek chanted from the other room. "Or I'm leaving. Don't you want me to do a final check?"

"Yes, *fuck*. Okay."

She slipped on her low heels and walked through the door to her tiny living room. "Well?"

Derek beamed at her, grabbing her hand and twirling her once. "You look fantastic. The dress is great. All of it."

"Thank you again for doing my hair."

"You're right. We have our deal. And you're watching that new Netflix rom-com with me next week. Don't forget."

"I won't."

A knock came from the door.

Derek grinned and began swiping on his phone.

"If you play the song, I swear to god I'll kill you."

"You're no fun, Olive Murphy." He pulled Olive into a hug. "You look hot. She's gonna be all sexy in uniform. But be careful. Okay?"

"I know what this is."

"You say that, but—"

Another knock.

Olive grinned. Derek shook his head, resigned.

She opened the door, and he was right. Stella was sexy as

fuck in her uniform. She was also holding a houseplant. This was basically the beginning of a porno in Olive's mind.

For a second, Stella too appeared speechless. Her dark brown eyes turned to molten bronze as they caught the light. She looked like someone had doused her with water. She swallowed once, throat bobbing, and met Olive's eyes.

Stella held up the plant. "I was going to get you flowers but then I remembered you have a lot of plants around your apartment, and I've read something somewhere about the negative environmental impact of cut flowers. Also, this is a snake plant, and it's supposed to be good for air purification and since you're a nurse I thought that might be important to you. Side note, the fact that it's a snake plant is not a clever joke about the hike. It's coincidental. But on my way over it occurred to me that flowers were the more classic choice, and I have in fact just given you an extra chore."

God, she was gorgeous when she talked a million words a minute. Gus came into the room and greeted her with a couple of low woofs.

Olive took the plant in one hand and kissed Stella on the cheek. "I love it. Thank you."

Derek let out a low whistle, which was probably to remind Olive that he was still in the apartment.

"Oh, hi, I'm Stella." With typical Stella efficiency she shook Derek's hand. "You must be Derek."

"Heard about me?"

"You're Olive's best friend who works at the hospital with her who she's known since middle school."

"All true."

"She picks out all your shoes, and your favorite movie is *Burlesque*."

"Olive? *Dude.*"

Olive cringed. "It wasn't a secret."

"Didn't have to be the first thing you said about me to your uh—friend."

"She also said that you're the smartest nurse she works with, and your softball skills are legendary in the hospital league."

"Better." He grinned. "All right, you cool kids. Curfew's ten P.M. I got a shotgun and a rake—"

"Shut up, Derek." Olive hugged him. "Thank you again."

A difficult to define emotion shadowed his face before he grabbed his keys from the counter along with the Tupperwared dinner Olive had made him. "I'll come by after the gym and walk Gus."

"Thanks."

With another slightly concerned look at Olive, he headed out the door.

Olive checked the hem of her dress for stray threads. "I'm nervous I'm going to trip when I go get the award."

Stella rested an assuring hand on Olive's arm. "You won't, but trust me when I say that wouldn't even make the top ten most embarrassing things I've seen happen at these parties."

"Phew. That's a relief." She forced a smile.

"You ready for tonight?"

"I studied the binder."

Stella's expression faltered. "That's not what I . . . thank you."

"Least I could do given how elegant the font was on the binder tabs."

"You're mean." Stella narrowed her eyes.

"Is that Helvetica or something fancier? No way it's just Times New Roman."

"It's Perpetua."

"Oh my god, ladies and gentlemen, she actually knows." Olive adjusted the plant and when she turned back Stella was right behind her.

"I'm sorry . . ." Her mouth rounded in an O. "Hey." She

rested a hand on Olive's hip. If it moved a little it would cross the boundary into ass territory.

Olive stifled the urge to shimmy the hand a few inches lower, and she lifted her chin to face Stella. "Hey." She wet her lips. "I was just teasing."

"I know. You know what?"

"What?"

"You're going to have fun tonight."

"Am I?" Olive smiled.

"I'm going to make it my mission."

"Well, I've heard that when Stella Soriano makes something her mission, nothing can get in her way."

"Heard that, did you?"

"Sure did."

Stella's lips parted.

Olive's thighs tensed, rubbing together as lava seemed to boil her insides.

They were inches away from another kiss.

Lilacs and vanilla. And sparkly brown eyes.

Stella turned and went to the sink. "They said at the store to water the plant once after you got it home and then weekly in the winter."

"Oh, okay. Thank you for making sure you got care instructions. I should probably name him."

"You name your plants?" Stella arched an elegant eyebrow.

"It's not weird. Plants have personality. See that fiddle-leaf fig over there? Total diva. Her name's Celine."

Stella erupted in laughter. "As in Dion?"

"The pothos is totally chill. His name is Dan."

"Dan?"

"Sure. Seemed right at the time."

"You think *I'm* a nerd. You're a complete dork too."

"Birds of a feather." Olive checked her watch. "We better go."

"Oh yeah, do you want me to go down and get the car? I know you don't wear heels much." She gestured to Olive's shoes. "I—uh, you look good in heels though."

The corner of Olive's mouth upturned. "I can handle a few blocks."

"That dress is really amazing. You look . . . stunning."

So yeah, maybe Derek was right about the dress.

Chapter 27

Stella handed her keys over to a valet, and they both walked up the steps into the hotel lobby. The drive had taken an hour and thirty minutes, so Olive was attempting to smooth the wrinkles from her dress. Stella reached over and squeezed her hand, offering a smile.

An Asian woman in a classic black dress held a clipboard in her hand. "Hello, Stella. This must be one of our guests of honor tonight. I'm Ruth, the director of our corporate social responsibility office."

"Olive Murphy." Olive shook her hand. "Thank you so much for the invitation."

"You'll be seated at the front table. Stella will be beside you. She's also being honored tonight because she did the most hours of community service of any of our employees last year."

Olive gave Stella a quizzical expression. "You didn't tell me." She shrugged.

"The bar is right through there to your left," Ruth said, gesturing to the door.

Thank god.

"Dinner is first and then the award presentation. Your award is last, and then we'll get several photos of you with our executive team."

"Okay. Thank you." Olive exhaled like a runner at the starting line of a race.

Stella's hand tightened on Olive's, helping still the shaking. "I'll take her to get a drink." Stella flashed Ruth a smile.

"The best words I've ever heard."

"What do you want?" Stella asked as they approached the bar.

"White wine is fine."

"Coming right up." She turned toward the bar and ran into two women, one in uniform and the other in a lovely purple dress. "*Hi!*" Stella wrapped her arms around the woman in purple and shook hands with the one in uniform. She gestured behind her to Olive. "This is my girlfriend, Olive."

The white woman in uniform wore a small trans flag pin on her lapel beneath her captain's wings. It said MY PRONOUNS ARE SHE/HER. She extended a hand to Olive. "I'm Esther. It's wonderful to meet you. I've heard so much about you. Though I suppose we've all seen the video. Mickey Mouse, huh?"

Olive's cheeks burned. "It wasn't Mickey Mouse."

"This is my wife, Margaret." Esther gestured to the elegant Black woman at her side.

Margaret was smiling. "What a beautiful romantic story. Esther told me all about it last week. You both were wonderful on *TODAY*."

"Nice to meet you both."

Stella's eyebrows furrowed for a moment. "I'm going to get Olive her drink. I think she's going to need it tonight. Can I get either of you anything?"

"No, we're good. We'll guard her for you." Esther winked at Stella.

"Thank you." She rushed off toward the bar.

Olive swallowed. "Guard me?"

Esther grinned. "Oh, you know. People talk. And people are excited to meet you. It's not every day the airline has something go viral. And with the story about you and Stella . . . it's exciting stuff."

Margaret nodded. "Stella told Esther you're afraid of flying."

Olive grimaced. "Yeah. I am. But it's not rational. I know the statistics."

Margaret cupped her hands around her mouth as if she were a child whispering a secret on the playground. "I was afraid of flying for many years too."

"You're not anymore?"

"When Esther was deployed, I could either get on a plane or I wouldn't get to see her. I figured out how to manage it because I was more scared of not seeing her than the thought of crashing. I was worried some other girl would catch her fancy."

Esther gave her wife a sweet smile that clearly said she had eyes only for her.

Olive grinned. "I like your pin, Esther."

"Thank you." She smiled. "Stella wears a pronoun pin on her uniform too when she flies. Ever since I transitioned, she made it a point of being a supportive friend to me. Don't tell her this because it will inflate her ego, but she's my favorite copilot."

"That sounds like her."

Esther rifled in her purse and produced a business card. "You text me if you ever get serious about conquering your fear of flying. I might be able to help. I'm not too far from where y'all live."

"Text you?"

"I take Margaret up in my plane, and it made her more comfortable. I've even given her a few flying lessons." She gave the offer with an intense gaze. It wasn't politeness. She was serious.

Margaret nodded. "Understanding things made it better for me."

"You fly in a little plane too?"

"Yes."

"How did you—"

The lights flashed, indicating the ceremony was going to begin soon.

"Call us if you ever want to talk about it. Fears are very real, but Margaret figured out some good strategies." Esther patted

Olive's shoulder and then took her wife's arm and led her to a table.

Stella returned and pushed a wineglass into her hand. "Sorry, there was a line."

"No, that's fine." As the stage light lit up, she sucked down two-thirds of her wineglass. "Thank you."

Stella gestured for them to walk up to the front table. Stella's name was printed on a small card next to her own.

Olive reached for a roll from the bread basket and put it on her plate, buttering the pieces and chewing slowly. Karaoke was on Jake's list because he had stage fright like she did. If she successfully walked across a stage in front of one hundred people, would that count? She hadn't been on a stage since her mom forced her on them as a child.

"Are you okay?" Stella whispered.

"I'm fine. I didn't eat much today, so the wine's going to my head."

"Oh okay."

She couldn't admit she was afraid, because that would be pathetic. She'd have to explain that she didn't attend her graduations because walking in front of people made her nervous. Stella already knew about the flying thing. How many fears were too many?

Stella was rifling through her purse. She broke off a piece of what looked like a protein bar and stuffed it in her mouth.

Olive gave Stella a curious look. "Isn't there going to be a full dinner?"

"They don't ever remember my food restriction."

"That's not righ—"

"It's fine. I'm not super hungry anyway."

"I—I brought you something for afterward because I knew half the time there isn't very much food at these things. I thought we could eat it on the way back or something."

"What?"

Olive pulled a small Tupperware out of her bag.

"You *didn't*?" Stella's eyes glittered.

"Cake for dinner is perfectly acceptable on special occasions." Their fingers touched as Olive handed her the cake.

"I think cake for dinner is always acceptable, but I didn't think I'd get the chance to eat anything as delicious as this tonight." Stella gave the Tupperware a tiny hug. "I'd feel ruder about eating outside food if they hadn't failed to accommodate me at the last few events."

"But that really is unacceptable. You should say something."

"I don't want to stir up trouble. It's easy to get labeled." A few older white men joined the table, every single one of them rocking the slightly cliché, 1980s-style mustache that really only looked good on Goose in *Top Gun* (R.I.P. Goose). All of them wore crisp uniforms with polished captain's wings gleaming on their chests. Stella shook hands all around, and they introduced themselves. Olive was thankful when the servers began passing out salad bowls because it gave her an excuse to take a minute to breathe. Stella was oddly silent.

The men continued their conversation, content to talk shop without attempting to include either Stella or Olive in the conversation. A group of women arrived at the table. They looked like they were also in uniform, but theirs consisted of a different colored long-sleeved dress for each, with a scarf and pin. All of them had their hair coiffed into identical French twists.

The choreography began again, handshakes, introductions, etc. Olive gleaned from their conversation that all the men were also being honored tonight for various achievements. The last to sit at the table was an ancient man. All heads in the room had seemed to follow him as he walked through the room. He walked straight up to Olive.

"Now here's the little lady who's gotten everyone talking about our airline again," he said in an aristocratic Southern accent.

Olive stood and extended a hand, her fingers aching from the number of handshakes she'd had so far. He didn't shake it, though. He brought it to his mouth and kissed her knuckle.

"I'm honored to meet you."

She'd never had her hand kissed. And as a nurse, she didn't even like the germ-sharing aspect of a handshake. This was so much worse. She suppressed a gag.

"Please sit, Miss Murphy." He came behind her chair and pulled it out for her.

"Oh, I don't need—"

"Nonsense. We treat our honored guests well at Allied."

Olive reached a hand behind her to find Stella's with the one that wasn't covered by this stranger's mouth germs. "This is my girlfriend, Stella. She's one of your pilots."

"Ah yes, I heard about your little love connection. Anything to keep us in the press. Delightful."

"She's being honored tonight too." Olive forced a smile.

Stella tensed beside her.

"Oh? Is she?"

"Yes. For community service."

"That's wonderful. It's important for the community to see all of our philanthropic efforts."

"I'm sorry, I didn't catch your name, sir," Olive said. She knew his name, of course. There had been an entire tab dedicated to him in Stella's binder.

Stella coughed.

"I'm Jack O'Halloran. CEO of Allied Airlines."

"Nice to meet you."

"The pleasure is all mine, I assure you."

The servers came to the table with trays of food. Olive took advantage of Jack O'Halloran's distraction and reached inside her purse and rubbed hand sanitizer all over her hands. The salad came, each with a pile of crumbling croutons on top. It tasted amazing, but Olive's guilt grew as she saw Stella poking at hers. O'Halloran had been going around the table talking to the menfolk and asking them about their golf game and investments. He hadn't said anything to Stella.

Olive cleared her throat. "I don't know much about what's involved in running an airline, Mr. O'Halloran, but it must be tough."

"Call me Jack, and you're correct. It's tough to make any money these days. Competition is fierce in this industry. Times are tough."

"I'm sure. Must have to be picky about your team members. I'm an assistant manager in the emergency department, which is nothing like this, but I know that having a good, diverse team is really important."

"One hundred percent. I make sure we only hire the best. Excellence in the air. I wrote that motto in 1976."

"Stella has told me a lot about how much a pilot has to know. All the hours she puts in in the air. It seems like so much."

Jack's gaze hovered over Stella for a moment. "How long have you been a pilot with the airline, Miss Sanch—uh . . ."

"Soriano, sir. I've been flying for fifteen years. I was hired fresh out of flight school."

"Lifetimers. We love those here. These knuckleheads—" He gestured to the three males at the table. "They've all been here over forty years."

"Wow. How long do you have to be a pilot before you can become a captain?" Olive asked in an innocently curious voice.

"No one becomes a captain in my airline unless they have ten years of experience and three thousand flight hours."

"Oh, okay. Is it hard to get that many hours, Stella?"

Stella's cheeks had paled. "I think I achieved that during my first six years with the airline. It does require a lot of hard work."

"Did you now?" Jack's attention, for the first time, had turned to Stella completely. "That's quite a feat, Miss Soriano."

"Thank you," Stella said in a slightly strangled voice.

"Are there a lot of female captains?" Olive looked around as if to search, glancing at the group of males seated opposite them.

"We have a very high percentage of female employees at Allied. Many women in our leadership structure."

"Oh, that's good." Olive held his stare.

He folded his hands in front of him. "But, as far as female captains go, I suppose we have two. Oh, and, er—Esther Caldwell should be counted in that number. I guess."

Olive's jaw tightened.

Stella sat forward. "Esther's been one of my best mentors. She's an amazing pilot and an amazingly strong woman."

"Yes. I've always admired her. And her service during the war speaks for itself as well, of course."

Stella nodded.

"Well, based on your flight hours and experience, I'm amazed you haven't made captain yet, Miss Soriano. Is that something you want?"

"Very much so, sir. It's all I've wanted my entire life. I completed the command course a few years ago."

"I'll have to make a note with my assistant for you to meet with me sometime. She told me about the *TODAY* show interview and the press it generated. We have a couple folks retiring this year. Always good to promote good representatives of the company." His eyes fell on Stella's full plate of food. "Do you not like the food?"

Stella's eyes widened. "I—I—uh—"

Olive lifted her chin, drawing courage from a place she had no idea existed inside her. "Stella has a medical dietary restriction."

Jack gave the plate a serious look. "Did they not accommodate you?"

"They—it's fine."

"My granddaughter has an anaphylactic peanut allergy.

They should know how to do this in this day and age. But I can see you're trying to be diplomatic about it. You *will* get appropriate food in the future." He spoke like a man well accustomed to absolute authority.

"Thank you, sir." She turned to Olive, eyes bright in a quiet expression of excitement.

Chapter 28

"You didn't have to walk me to the door." Olive fingered the stitching on Stella's uniform lapel.

"It's the least I could do after watching you go to bat for me with the CEO. He tends to make people freeze up."

"I said what was true." Olive never did well with people in small group situations except in the hospital. It was weird. Something about wearing scrubs gave her confidence. People tried to intimidate her in the ER all the time. Maybe the dress had done it tonight. Or something about having Stella at her side made her tap into that same confidence she had when she was working. Jack O'Halloran was a person. And if Olive could handle managing a bunch of narcissistic doctors' personalities, she could handle Jack O'Halloran.

"But you didn't have to do that."

"Wasn't this the plan?" Olive let her hand drop from the lapel, letting it fall slowly so it stroked down Stella's front.

"Yeah, but I guess I wasn't expecting it to go this well so quickly."

"I'm glad it did. You deserve to be promoted."

She beamed. "Thank you."

Olive stood in front of the stairs to her apartment. "Come in. I made fried rice last night."

"You're sure? I already ate your cake."

"I've got more of that too."

"I'd love to come in. I'm starving, to be honest."

Olive kicked off her heels at the door while Stella, as always, neatly lined hers up. "Where's Gus?" Stella looked around.

"Derek probably came and got him after going to the gym. He's practically a shared dog. He was my brother's dog, and then I adopted him. With both of our weird shift schedules, we both walk him. Gus pines if I'm gone too late. Sometimes Derek just caves and takes him home with him."

"That's a good arrangement."

"He's a special dog. Been with me through a lot." Olive sat Stella down on the couch and then heated up a bowl of the veggie rice. She stirred, sending tendrils of steam into the air, and brought it to Stella.

"You're okay with me eating it on your couch?"

Olive chuckled. "I eat here more than my table."

"If you're sure."

Olive still felt twitchy after a night spent with a crowd of people she didn't know. "Do you want a drink? Tea?"

"Oh my god, tea would be great."

"Any particular—?"

"Anything hot's great."

She brewed each of them a cup of her favorite peppermint tea. She put a mug in front of Stella and sipped her own. Olive settled beside Stella, who had dug into the rice. She made a couple of low purrs as she ate. Stella's tiny, low moans when she tasted something delicious were vaguely explicit.

Stella's full lips closed around the fork slowly, savoring each bite. "You're an amazing cook."

"I make simple things."

"Simple and heavenly."

After Stella finished the rice, she put her fork into the bowl. Olive made to reach for it, but Stella leaned forward at the same moment, knocking against Olive's head. Olive flinched, and Stella's thumb ran over the sore place on Olive's forehead. "Are you okay?"

Olive set the bowl on the coffee table. She shifted her shoulders, squaring them to Stella's as Stella continued to touch the sore place on her forehead. Their eyes locked together.

Stella's eyes focused on Olive's mouth. "You really look beautiful tonight. Not that you're not always beautiful. You are. But tonight you were breathtaking. I really love this." Stella's attention lowered. She traced the design of the lace where it spiraled and swirled over Olive's collarbone. Her finger stopped just before it would meet the bare skin. Her hand lifted to touch Olive's oversized stud earrings, just skimming against Olive's neck beneath her earlobe. "I . . . I was so happy you came tonight. What you said and did . . . you amaze me. Really."

Olive dipped her head in a wordless thank-you. Her voice was low when she spoke, trying to seem casual even though every nerve ending was firing as Stella's finger twisted a piece of hair that had escaped from the rest. "And I didn't even trip when I got my award. That's a victory for me." Olive swallowed. "Being with you made me feel less scared."

Stella's gaze fixed on Olive's. "Same."

"Really?"

"Do you remember on the roller coaster?"

"Uh . . . yeah."

Stella's head tilted a fraction to the side, her lips pressing outward and voice lowering like she was telling a secret. "I really was scared then."

Olive fought a smile. "I know."

Stella's finger that had traced the lace now touched the corner of Olive's mouth. "You knew what to do though. Just like tonight."

Olive reached up and cradled the back of Stella's head.

As if Olive's desire created a gravitational pull, Stella leaned forward, her hands finding Olive's waist. But she didn't cross those final inches. They just sat together. Close enough Olive could count Stella's long black eyelashes.

"Stella, you need to tell me if it's not okay for me to kiss you."

"Olive."

"I'm sorry, I shouldn't have—"

Without further discussion, Stella touched Olive's chin, angling her face to hers and pressing her warm lips against Olive's very ready mouth.

Olive pulled away in surprise. "K-kissing wasn't in the binder."

Stella's eyes darted between Olive's, twinkling. "I think we can go off book for a little while now. If you're okay with that?"

Olive didn't make a pro/con list. She didn't think about just how brutal it would be when all of this ended.

She pressed her lips to Stella's. They'd escaped their careful, stable orbit. This was a collision. This was combustion. This was explosion.

After weeks of waiting, Olive needed this. She didn't want this to ever end. She pushed Stella horizontal. It would be so easy to pull open each of those buttons on Stella's perfectly crisp shirt and use that tie for a very different purpose. One that certainly would not have been outlined in the Allied Airlines code of conduct. She undid Stella's tie and slid it free from her collar.

Shit, she never realized she had a uniform kink.

All she could think of was how Stella's wings would look pinned to a black lacy bra right before she ripped it off her. With her teeth.

Olive twisted her tongue with Stella's, tasting her, running the tip along the seam of her lips. Their bodies pressed against each other. Olive had worn black silk underwear, and they were drenched. It was lucky she was wearing tights or she wouldn't have been able to hide it.

Was Stella as soaked as she was?

She hooked her fingers into the belt loops of Stella's pants, linking their hips together. Olive was desperate for any friction to soothe the ache blooming at the apex of her dripping thighs.

Just kissing.

She could do that.

She kissed along Stella's jawline and inhaled the vanilla and lilacs of her silky hair. "I love the way you smell."

"Do you?"

Fuck, even Stella's voice was different now. Low and throaty, as the irresistible words pushed through kiss-swollen lips.

Stella kissed her chin. "I love your hair. It's soft but the curls are amazing. It looks different in the light. So many colors." She combed her fingers through the loose tendrils.

"Take it down for me?"

"Okay." Stella sat up and turned Olive around and kissed her neck once. Twice. Three times. And one last time, right at the base of her scalp.

A shiver skittered down Olive's back right along the pathway of the zipper she was desperate for Stella to pull. Nimble fingers combed through her hair. Stella slid the pins out one by one, dropping each one into a neat pile on the coffee table with a tiny plink. With every pin she kissed a spot of bare skin.

Olive reached behind her, stroking a hand down Stella's cheek along her dimple.

How far is this going to go?

Her hair fell loose. Stella's fingers dragged down her neck in a caress that was otherworldly in its softness, nails grazing against her, setting her skin on fire.

"Stella."

"What?"

"God, that feels amazing."

"I'm glad."

Olive twisted and straddled her, letting her released hair curtain around their faces. Stella's pilot shirt had gotten pulled free of the top of her pants. Olive's dress rode high on her thighs, the wetness saturating the tights beneath it.

Their lips pressed together again. Each meeting. Each

wanting. Stella's hair was half out of her bun and Olive figured it was her turn. She swept the hair free, loving the silkiness against her knuckles. They rolled, so each had a shoulder against the couch. Olive's leg rested over Stella's hip.

As their bodies began to move together, Stella pulled away. "Olive, I think . . ."

"Yeah."

"I think it's late. And, I know I . . . uh . . . it's not that I don't want . . . but—"

"Right." Olive moved her leg off Stella's hip. Her eyes opened. And because her mouth, brain, and lady parts were completely disconnected, Olive whispered something incredibly stupid: "You could stay here tonight."

"I'm not sure that's the best idea." Stella frowned. "This was—"

"I swear I'll be nothing but a heating source."

"I need to get home." She kissed Olive once on the forehead. "I really had so much fun tonight. Thank you. For everything. I'll text you tomorrow, okay?" She stood from the couch and within five minutes the front door opened and closed.

It took ten minutes for Olive's brain to recover from whiplash. Once she made it to her bedroom, she hung up the dress because Derek would kill her if she didn't, and then she flopped onto the bed, turning over to stare at her nightstand drawer.

"Well, Alyson, guess it's just you and me tonight."

Was talking to her vibrator a new low? Yep. Yes it was.

Chapter 29

Even four days removed from kissing Stella on the couch, Olive couldn't look at the teal-green velvet without thinking about the easy way their bodies had twined together there. It had smelled like Stella for two days. Now, Derek leaned back on her couch with the oversized dog in between them. They'd had a horrible shift and were each on their second glass of wine. Derek topped off his glass and grabbed a piece of pizza. His eyes widened for a second as he did a slight head nod toward a cream-colored sweater on a hook at the door.

"That's not yours."

Instead of responding, Olive followed his example, pouring until she killed the bottle.

"Is she coming here a lot?"

"We're friends, Derek. Stella came over for lunch a couple times. She ended up canceling a few flying lessons because of the weather. We hung out." They hadn't had any more kissing. Olive liked having her around. "She likes Gus. Friends."

"That's it. Friends. Nothing more?" He lifted his hand and then a black tie dangled down as if he were a magician doing a scarf trick.

"Oops. Where was that?"

"Suspiciously deep in the couch cushions." The tie swayed from his hand, and his lips quirked to the side.

"We might have made out. Nothing else. Clothes on." Olive hoped she didn't sound too sullen as she said it. "Except the tie."

He sucked in more wine, grimacing. "Jesus, Olive. Why are you doing this to yourself?"

"That was on me. There was this moment, I was still amped up from the award thing, and she was hot, and we had a great time. I'm an adult. It's my choice."

"So, she said she can't be a girlfriend because she'd be a bad one, and she doesn't have time for one . . . But she keeps canceling stuff to hang out with you, her fake girlfriend? Who she makes out with. Are we in high school again?"

"She's not canceling stuff *for me*."

"Sure. So are you going to invite her out with us tomorrow for the unit happy hour? Joni chose the bar this time since she's actually going to come and might bring her twin sister."

"Can't. I'm—"

"Hanging out with Stella."

"Staaaahhhp. We aren't just hanging out. We're going shopping for a dress. I need another one to go to the next event, and with all your whining about our last mall excursion, I decided to ask Stella. This perfect dress is in a store in Ashburn."

"Are you getting dinner before?" He swirled his wine with one hand and petted Gus with the other.

"People have to eat."

"And are you going home after?"

"She was going to come over so we could watch that new show on Netflix."

He put the tie down on the coffee table as if it were Exhibit A in evidence. "You guys are in a real relationship."

"We're friends."

"You're dating." He threw his hands into the air.

"We're *fake* dating. It's supposed to look real. That's the point." The weird thing was, Stella hadn't posted any of the photos they'd taken together to Instagram. Olive couldn't shake a nagging worry over that.

Derek let out a sound of feral exasperation. "This is the most ridiculous existential debate I've ever had. What's the difference?"

"We're not having sex."

He shook his head. "I can't with girls." He shook his head again and held up a hand as if shielding him from the situation that was Olive's life.

"It's a good thing you're gay."

"Damn straight. I want a dude, I do it the old-fashioned way. I swipe right on my phone and ask him very respectfully if he'd like to come home with me and take off my pants. And then we take turns. Like gentlemen. None of this weird longing and giggling over text messages."

"Fuck you, I don't giggle."

"Correction. You used to never giggle. Now I see you giggling over your phone like a damn teenager. Kissing on the couch also probably like a teenager. Won't be surprised if after the next event you end up with a hickey like Kristen Daniels gave you sophomore year. When's the next event?"

"Next week." She started to respond to the low-blow hickey comment, but a text came in on her phone.

> STELLA
> Dog attack, beesting, and wild wombat attack
>
> OLIVE
>
>
> STELLA
> Okay, I don't have hard data on the wombats, but one can assume it's pretty rare but still not as rare as a plane crash. I have a keen intuition about statistics.
> Fun fact, did you know they poop cubes?

"She's texting you, isn't she?"

Olive held up the phone.

"I feel like I need some context. Otherwise, you ladies need to seriously work on your sexting skills."

"Things more likely to kill you than a plane crash. In theory."

OLIVE
The fact remains that if I don't get on a plane, my chances of dying in one are pretty much zero.

"She's still trying to get you on a plane?"

"Yes." Olive leaned her head back onto the couch.

"Why don't you do it?"

"Uh, because I've been terrified of flying my entire life."

"So?" He ran a hand over his face. "If you're insisting on engaging in this fake relationship, then you should get something out of it."

"She wants to take me to Italy." A wicked smile played on Olive's mouth and she didn't even attempt to hide it.

"Goddamn it, Olive, I'm leaving."

Derek finished his wine and left, literally slamming the door behind him. Olive flinched. If he hadn't walked out of her apartment this way many times before, most recently as a result over which contestant deserved a rose on *The Bachelor,* she would have been more concerned. Also, she was the only reason he ate any home-cooked food, and he'd forgotten to get his Tupperware out of the fridge.

She finished her wine and grabbed her phone.

Stella answered on the second ring. *"Hey!"*

"Where are you tonight?"

"Tampa. Leaving again soon."

She slid down, putting the phone on speaker, resting it on her chest, and closing her eyes. "Can fake girlfriends miss other fake girlfriends?"

The half bottle of wine was speaking very loudly tonight. She needed to stop letting anything with a cheap screw top talk for her. It had no shame.

"I think so." Even tipsy, Olive couldn't miss the uncertainty in Stella's tone. Or was it worry? "Friends can miss friends."

"Right. Friends. You're my friend, Stella," Olive said like a completely chill person would say.

"You're my friend too, Olive." It sounded like she was smiling again.

Olive stretched out all her limbs and then yawned. "You still want to come with me to go see that dress and get dinner tomorrow?"

"Yes."

"That's nice . . ."

"Olive, are you falling asleep?"

She yawned again. "No, why?"

"Let me take you flying."

"I'm too drunk to talk about this."

"I'm shamelessly taking advantage of your weakened and altered state."

"Let's talk about it tomorrow, okay?" More yawns, one of those horrible multiple yawns where your eyes begin closing and then become glued shut by the end.

"Go to sleep. I'll see you tomorrow."

"Good night."

She opened her eyes enough to end the call. The door opened. Then the fridge. "Hi, Derek."

"Now I'm really leaving."

"Enjoy the chicken cacciatore," she mumbled. "I put the fancy peppers in it because they're your favorite."

He kissed her once on the forehead. "I love you, Olive. Sleep well." He petted Gus. "Bye, fella, try to explain to your mommy Olive that she's in a *fake* fake relationship."

Unfortunately, her stupid best friend did have a point.

Chapter 30

Olive Murphy was too old to sleep on a couch. Maybe if it wasn't a couch she'd bought at a thrift store two years ago because she loved the velvet and didn't care that it was obviously too squashy, she wouldn't have woken up and been unable to move her neck to the left. Sometime during the six hours she'd been wedged between a Great Dane mix and a pile of books that seemed to have fallen on her without waking her up, her spine rebelled. The settled spasm forced her head into a permanent lean, giving the world an oddly tilted appearance.

Her alarm went off again. She silenced it and flipped on the coffee maker. She had a short shift today, getting off at 3:00 P.M., which would leave her enough time to shower and get dressed before Stella picked her up. She peeled herself off the couch and dragged her lazy, slightly hungover ass to the bathroom. The vision in the mirror was atrocious. She rubbed her face to work blood flow back into it before hopping in the shower.

She'd been drunk.

And called Stella.

Fuck.

She really couldn't let that happen again.

She could have said all the things swimming around in her head after the conversation with Derek. He had a point. They *were* essentially dating. But Stella was so sure that dating her would lead to the other person getting hurt like her exes had been hurt. Though honestly it didn't sound like Stella was that into her exes in the first place. Maybe she *did* want to date Olive

212 * Andie Burke

but she was scared of hurting her. Maybe one of the exes made Stella believe she was incapable of a relationship?

Unless she was being friend-zoned.

Shit, was she being friend-zoned?

Maybe Stella would be interested in dating someone, but maybe not her for a million reasons. Olive's cheeks burned at the memory of Lindsay literally telling Stella that Olive was an emotionally needy mess. Was that why they couldn't be in a relationship? With this alarming thought echoing in her head and her neck making her feel increasingly like a person in a horror film during an exorcism, Olive took Gus for a walk before work. After she got back, she went through her usual morning routine and made it into the car on time, which was a miracle given that her neck was only barely functional.

Drinking a hot beverage at a forty-five-degree angle was exactly as difficult as one would imagine. So, when she arrived at work, she was pitifully crooked, pulsing with anxiety, and also speckled with coffee. A great start to a Murphy's Law kind of day.

Her first patient sneezed directly in her face.

Fan-fucking-tastic.

She ran to the nurses' station and used fifteen tiny alcohol wipes to rid the exposed areas of any germs. Thank god she was wearing a mask. She saw a few more patients, though no more face sneezers, and then settled in to do some management/administrative work while waiting for orders.

Derek was off today, so she wouldn't have to face another round of philosophical debate over the existential question of what it actually means to be dating someone. She couldn't handle it. She would work and then go hang out with the only person she knew who wasn't interested in talking about what their relationship meant. Stella.

It was after 2:00 P.M. when a flash of blond hair caught her eye from the other side of the unit.

Shit.

Lindsay sometimes had to cover for her ER colleagues when they were at lunch, but thankfully less often lately because of her new ICU lead responsibilities. Still, Olive did not need a run-in with her right now. Olive's stomach growled, a reminder that she hadn't eaten anything since getting to work eight hours earlier. Not the best choice when slightly hungover. She was scheduled to leave work at three, but she was still supposed to take a half hour to eat, and now was definitely the right time for that.

Olive checked in with the rest of her team to make sure she could take a quick break, and then ducked into the staff room before there were any other chances for a confrontation. She and Lindsay had never brought their drama to work with them, but Lindsay must have noticed by now that Olive had blocked her number.

Honestly, Olive was lucky she hadn't just shown up at her apartment.

As she finished the last few bites of her food, Olive's phone began buzzing.

Olive grinned at the name on her phone screen.

"Hey, how's it going? Did you get back early?" Another check on her watch had told her that Stella was still supposed to be in the air.

"No, I'm really sorry. Bad weather. The flight's delayed until who knows when. There's a line of really bad thunderstorms with high winds coming through. Probably won't be back in time for us to go to Ashburn."

Disappointment settled in her stomach. At least she'd be able to hang out with Joni and Derek tonight instead. "Where are you going to stay if it's canceled?"

"Airport hotel, probably. It won't be too bad. Not as fun as Disney."

"I'll really miss seeing you tonight."

214 * Andie Burke

A pause.

Shoot. That wasn't the emotionally independent Olive she needed to be.

"Same," Stella said finally. "Think you'll still go try on the dress?"

"I might try to order it instead." Olive sighed. "I better go get back to work. I leave in an hour. I'm . . ." Olive hesitated, but then went for it. "If you get back late, I'm meeting some work people at this bar The Blue Side. Just if you happen to get back in town. I'd love to see you. But like no pressure. I'm cool. We're cool. Everything's—uh—cool, either way."

Olive could tell being *not* emotionally needy was getting off to a spectacular start.

But inviting her wasn't weird. Platonic friends who were pretending to date invited other platonic friends they were pretending to date to their work happy hours, right?

"I'm not sure I'll make it back, but I wish I could." Stella's voice still sounded stiffer than usual.

"Thank you," Olive said again, rather stupidly. "I—uh . . . yeah. I wish you could too." Why was this all suddenly so awkward? She hadn't wine-vomited all her feelings into the phone last night. Everything should be the same, yet nothing about that call seemed like the usual playful Stella.

> OLIVE
> I guess I'm coming out tonight.

> DEREK
> Excellent

***

Derek's hip bumped Olive's, and he handed her a beer. They clinked bottles together, turning their high-top stools to watch a country singer kill it on the stage with a cover of "House of the Rising Sun." Most of the unit had shown up tonight. Since

Derek and Olive had taken over as day charge nurses, they tried to organize a few events per month.

Olive put her head on Derek's shoulder. "I like this place. Why haven't we come to this bar before?"

"Because we're creatures of habit."

"You said Joni picked?"

"Joni's sister loves it."

"Maybe we should branch out more often." She turned back to her plate and took a bite of her salad. She pulled out her phone, but it was one of those phantom vibrations that happen when you're waiting for a message. Not that she was actually waiting.

"Hey." Joni pulled Olive into a hug and then gave Derek one as well. "This is my sister. Suzanne."

Suzanne grinned. "I feel like I should kiss the hands of the people that helped me get my sister out to a bar." Suzanne was very pretty. Joni was beautiful, so this wasn't surprising, but despite being twins, they looked nothing alike. Suzanne was tall and slender with hazel eyes and dark brown hair.

Olive laughed. "We all agree, then, that Joni needs to have more fun here because we want her to stay."

Suzanne winked at Olive. "I'd cheers to that, but I don't have a drink yet."

"I can fix that." Olive took a step toward the bar. "What do you want, Suzanne?"

"Raging Bitch, please."

Olive chuckled. "I feel like there are so many jokes I could make, but they're all tired, so I'll abstain."

Suzanne smirked. "Thank God."

"What do you want, Joni?"

"Any beer. Not picky."

"Got it."

While she was waiting for the beers, Derek appeared beside her. "Suzanne's bi and single," he said.

"Oh?"

"And hot."

"These are all objectively true facts." She focused on liquor bottles lined up behind the bar.

"So?" Derek's tone was suggestive.

"So *what*?"

"Is a fake girlfriend going to stand in the way of you hanging out with Suzanne?"

"Just because two women fuck women and are in the same place doesn't mean they'll fuck each other." Olive tapped her fingers on the bar with the rhythm of the song.

Derek gave a quirk of the head in Suzanne's direction. "Olive, two months ago you'd have been all over a woman like Suzanne. Hot teacher energy."

"Joni said she was a guidance counselor."

"Whatever. The point is that you were saying there's no harm in this thing with Stella because you're not interested in anyone else."

"I'm *not* interested in anyone else."

"Because of Stel-la." He drew out her name as if Olive didn't know who he was talking about. He exhaled. "Stel-la is in the way of you getting a perfectly good orgasm from that smokin' woman over there. I'm not saying you should marry her, just go and fool around. Break the Lindsay cycle."

"Alyson and I are doing fine, thank you."

Derek took Joni's bottle from the bartender, leaving Suzanne's for Olive. Olive pushed through the crowd back to their table. "I've got your Raging Bitch."

Suzanne lowered her voice into a conspiratorial half whisper. "But where's my beer?"

They all laughed.

"That was pathetic." Joni smacked her sister on the shoulder.

"Yeah, pathetic," Derek agreed, but he wasn't looking at Suzanne; he wasn't even looking at Olive. No, his eyes were on a blond woman at the bar, sipping what Olive knew to be a vodka tonic—always very light on the tonic.

Lindsay.

Chapter 31

Derek tugged on Olive's arm, redirecting her focus to Suzanne. "Just ignore Lindsay."

Olive sucked down a few more swallows of her drink. "She showed up here because she won't leave me alone. Shouldn't I let her say what she needs to say? Preferably not at work."

Derek seemed to be measuring Olive's expression, and uncharacteristically, Olive couldn't read his thoughts. Before Stella, Derek had been worried Olive would jump back into bed with Lindsay again. Now, he was worried Stella would break her heart. She wasn't sure where that left his anxiety over her love life at the moment, but at the very least, he seemed torn.

"If she needs closure, I'm going to give it to her. I'm sick of this shit."

"She just wants what she can't have." Derek gritted his teeth.

"Probably." Shrugging, Olive walked over, trying to seem more confident than she felt.

A smirk pulled at the corners of Lindsay's mouth. She swirled her tiny straw with her tongue, giving it a seductive lick. Real subtle. She wore a low-cut shirt and a fringed miniskirt with tights and high-heeled boots. Olive found herself immune to everything that used to draw her in. The sex with Lindsay had been good, but the dose of self-loathing afterward made it a million kinds of not worth it.

When Olive reached the bar, she tried to keep her expression bored. "Why are you here?"

Lindsay's voice held rehearsed innocence. "I was invited. It's a happy hour. You know I like being happy." She swirled her drink.

Olive was about thirty seconds away from changing her mind and walking away and telling closure it could go fuck itself.

"For what it's worth, blocking my phone number is immature and petty. Even for you." Lindsay slid off her stool.

"What do you really want, Lindsay?"

"I told you, since you're kicking me out of your life forever in favor of some woman who is trying to latch herself on to your fifteen minutes of fame . . . Sorry, I know you must be so busy with all the interview requests." Lindsay's right eyebrow arched up into a spike, her tone full of derision. "So super cool to be so famous now, but yeah, so, when can I come by to get my shit from your apartment?"

"If I find any of your stuff in my apartment, I'll mail it to you. Like this is really about some mason jars and a blender bottle."

Lindsay leveled an appraising look at Olive. "I can tell that you aren't thinking critically about this situation." Lindsay sighed. "Is this Stella ridiculousness about the last time we broke up? Are you trying to make me jealous with her?"

Olive stiffened. This was what Lindsay did—stir up drama. When they first met, it seemed like Lindsay genuinely cared about everyone. Olive had thought that was why she was in other people's business. But her "concern" had always been mostly schadenfreude, and when Lindsay had a vendetta, all hell broke loose.

Lindsay settled a hand on Olive's forearm, her fingers cold and damp from holding the drink. "Olive, I really am worried about you."

Olive laughed bitterly, shuffling backward a few inches. "Oh, that would be new. Wouldn't it?"

Lindsay snorted. "The fact that you won't have an honest

conversation about this is revealing enough." Lindsay's eyes narrowed, something almost like concern showing on her face. "You *actually* really like this woman. Wow. It's not just about the interviews, is it? There's something not right here with this thing between you two."

Olive mustered enough self-control to feign skeptical pity. "I have no idea what you're talking about."

"She made it pretty clear at Disney what she thought of the idea of being with you. And when I texted you later you called her a friend. That's not what you said on TV. It's all lies. And more than that . . ." It was Lindsay's turn for pity. "She's out of your league, babe. Like I said, I'm legit worried about you. I really can't believe that you're prioritizing some woman you *barely* know over attending your only nephew's birthday party."

Olive narrowed her eyes. "How—"

"For some reason I still have permissions to your Google calendar." She smiled. "Sort of seems like if you were actually in a relationship with someone else you would have removed my permissions to that, but I'm not judging . . . I get keeping options open . . ."

"That's not what's happening."

"What I *am* judging is that with *everything* going on in your life right now, I can't believe that woman is making you prioritize her over your family."

Did that particular dig feel like a tablespoon of salt poured in the gaping wound from not even *being invited to her nephew's party? Yes. Also, what the actual fuck?* "Why were you even—"

"I was just checking my own calendar tonight, and your stuff was still there, and I saw all of the events you're doing for this woman. *Yikes.*"

Olive tried to seem cavalier. "Jealous isn't a good look, Lindsay. Just because I'm spending time with someone else . . ."

"Babe." Lindsay's bottom lip pouted. "I know this year's been really hard for you." Now she sounded patronizing. "And being carted around to some of this woman's corporate events is hardly 'spending time' with her." She lowered her voice to a whisper. "Are you even fucking her or is that not included in whatever messed-up 'arrangement'"—Lindsay's fingers curved into accusatory air quotes—"you have with her?"

"Fuck *you*, Lindsay. That's not—"

Lindsay's face went feline. "Hit a nerve? Hmm."

Olive scowled.

"Out of curiosity, did she ask you out right *before* bringing up these events? Because seems a little sus to me. That interview, which everyone is saying was so adorable . . . something was off. I mean, it's clear you have a crush but—"

"Just stop. This is pathetic."

"I'm pathetic? Do you remember how you said 'I love you' on like the third date but then were too scared to move in together even though we'd been dating for years?" Lindsay chuckled. "It's a good thing I didn't scare easily, but that woman with her sexy little bun and uniform . . . she's not going to want to be tied down with you after this little excitement over the video is over. Maybe this is a good fit after all since you don't ever know what you want in a relationship." The problem with Lindsay was that she generally used her incredible intuitive powers for evil, but what if she was right? She was certainly right that they weren't sleeping together.

"This is none of your business."

"After all we've been through together, how can you say that?" A hurt that almost looked genuine passed across Lindsay's face. "I put up with your moods. Those phone calls. And now you're acting like I'm evil because I wasn't willing to be your emotional support girlfriend every minute of the day? Is this still about you missing the half-marathon last year? Because that was *your* choice."

"I know it was my choice." Olive's heel hit the bar behind her. "But then my brother got hurt. I was barely holding it together, and you always made me feel like garbage. Now I'm finally doing better, and you want me back?"

Lindsay halved the distance between them. Her voice went low and breathy. "I never said I was the type of person who can handle that messy stuff. It's not what I'm good at." She raised an eyebrow suggestively. "You know what I'm good at, Olive, and it has nothing to do with dressing up for boring-ass business events . . ."

Tightening her hold on her elbows, Olive turned to face the bar. She felt a soft pressure on her ass. Fury churned in her chest at the possessive nerve of that touch. Would she be kicked out of the bar if she shoved Lindsay off her and screamed everything she wanted to say to her? "Move your hand. Right now." Olive spoke through a clenched jaw, turning to move her ass out of reach.

"Why?" Lindsay's voice was coy and inviting, and she puffed her breasts slightly outward as she leaned back on the bar. Her eyes flickered over Olive's shoulder before they settled on Olive again. "I'd be willing to fuck you in the bathroom. If you need a reminder of what it's like to be in a *real* relationship. Wouldn't be the first time for us in public. Do you remember at that bar in Adams Morgan—"

"Jesus Christ, what is your prob—"

Then Lindsay's mouth was on hers. Tongue pushing against Olive's tight mouth. Every muscle in Olive's body went rigid. As Olive pulled away, Lindsay abruptly ended the kiss herself.

"Oh, I'm so sorry." Lindsay's voice was as poisonous as Olive had ever heard it. She wasn't apologizing to *Olive*.

Olive's head whipped around. Stella stood behind her. Derek was a few steps back, his face screwed up with anger and frustration.

So many emotions. Shock. Fear. Anger. Olive could barely keep track. Her chest heaved with stuttering breaths. "I—I—I . . ."

Stella, however, didn't appear angry at all. If anything, she was amused. She offered Lindsay a glance that so plainly said *Is that the best you can do?* and then faced Olive.

"Hey. Sorry we couldn't look at the dress today." She rested a firm, comforting hand on Olive's shoulder. "The flight still managed to get out, though. The weather wasn't as bad as we thought it would be."

Olive tried to speak, all of the syllables turning into incomprehensible stammering. "It wasn't—I mean, I didn't—"

Stella smiled at her, not even giving Lindsay a moment of attention. Those dimples were just for Olive right now. "I think I know what it looks like when my girlfriend is being kissed by someone she wants to kiss."

Stella touched Olive's chin lightly. She gave Olive a small questioning look. Olive answered with a tiny nod. And Stella kissed her.

All of the stress and worry melted away as the soft lips coaxed at her own. Olive's body relaxed into Stella's long, soft arms. Stella's lips seemed desperate for more, opening and deepening the kiss. Her gentle hand found the place where Lindsay had touched Olive minutes before as if she were reclaiming it. *God,* if only she was. She pulled Olive closer so their bodies pressed against each other.

Something about knowing they had an audience was weirdly hot. Maybe it was the beer, or the taste of Stella's tongue on her own, but she kept the kiss going.

Derek cleared his throat.

Stella kissed her cheek, before pulling away. "Hi, Derek. Nice to see you again."

"Hello, Stella." Derek's eyes were wide but not unfriendly, more incredulous.

"Are you okay?" Stella said in a low voice only Olive could hear. They were still close enough for Olive to feel Stella's hot breath on her lips as she spoke.

"I am now." Was this real between them? It felt so goddamn real at times, it hurt.

"Buy me a beer?" Stella asked with a flirtatious wink.

Fake girlfriend. Fake girlfriend. Fake girlfriend.

"Of course." Olive pulled Stella away toward the opposite side of the bar. As if watching a train wreck, Olive couldn't stop herself from glancing back at Lindsay. Cold fury was etched in every line on her face, every bit of it focused on Stella. If it weren't for the comforting touch of the woman beside her, Olive might feel worried about it.

Chapter 32

Olive was walking Stella out to wait with her for her cab at least an hour beyond the time a person in their thirties should leave bars to avoid feeling like a zombie the next morning. As they walked out, hand in hand, a high-pitched shriek shattered the cold late-night silence.

Olive twisted around searching for the emergency that necessitated the scream, and found three people jogging up from the parking lot.

"Oh my god, it's the couple from the *TODAY* show," said one of a group of women. The women were all wearing oversized vintage-looking coats and thick hipster glasses. "You know, the pilot and that nurse that saved Mickey Mouse."

Olive groaned. "I didn't save Mickey—"

"Ermigod. I love you guys. Your story. All of it." The hipsteryest hipster shook both Olive's and Stella's hands.

When her hand was released, Olive's body locked up and suddenly she had no idea how to stand next to Stella. They had gone from that carefree, casual tipsy PDA to a level of awkward generally reserved for fourteen-year-old reluctant homecoming dates trying to pose in front of Styrofoam columns and fake ivy walls. Though maybe Olive was just having flashbacks to that year she and Derek had gone to that awful dance together before either of them were out. Holy shit, that'd been awkward. But now? It was the same even though it was usually so easy to touch Stella.

Where was Olive supposed to be touching Stella that would

imply *We are comfortable doing all the sex things* without looking like she was *trying* to emulate said sex things in public?

Olive realized she'd been staring back and forth between her hand and Stella's perfect ass for a couple of seconds before the giggles of the group of women brought her back to the moment.

"Can we take a quick video of you so we can put it on my TikTok? We'll tag you, Stella."

"Stella's not on TikTok." Olive couldn't help laughing. The idea of Stella being on TikTok was so absurd.

"Uh . . . she totally is. Unless this isn't you?" The girl swiped and held up a page that yes did look exactly like Stella doing one of those choreographed dances with a group of younger kids who looked a little like her.

Stella grimaced. "My cousins made me do it last summer."

"Why aren't you following her?" said one of the girls to Olive.

"How did you not know that?" said another of the group.

Recovering from her shock, Olive squeezed Stella to her side, feeling Stella go rigid against her. "Oh, right. Just slipped my mind. Forgot about all those TikTok dances I've seen you do, hon."

Olive made a note to self to please never call Stella "hon" again, because it definitely gave *Cracker Barrel waitress delivering biscuits* vibes rather than *want to do all those aforementioned sex things to your biscuit* vibes. And why was the word *biscuit* just so dirty?

Focus, Olive.

"Sure, we'll be in a video," Stella said, giving Olive a tiny nudge. "Won't we?"

"Oh, yeah. Right. Sorry." Olive winced as she rested her chin on Stella's shoulder. The small muscles around Stella's mouth were tight, so even though she was smiling, it didn't reach her eyes.

"So, uhhh . . . can you guys just smile?" One of the group of women was holding up her phone. "And like look normal."

Olive's cheeks burned. *Normal?*

Stella nodded encouragingly, which gave Olive only enough time to force a grin before the women flashed a few poses and then eventually skipped away from them and inside the bar with calls of thanks.

As the door slammed, Stella pulled away from Olive. Her posture was back into the stiff pilot mode she used when she was working or for their interview, but didn't have its usual warmth. "Didn't you read the binder?"

"The binder?"

"In the questionnaire I mentioned that I had the TikTok account underneath the part where I listed all of my social media handles. I—uh—I don't want to seem like a hard-ass about this, but if people find out, I'm really going to look ridiculous. This isn't a joke for me, okay?"

Olive reached to take Stella's hand, but Stella was already walking toward the curb where her cab would be arriving. "I'm sorry. I'll read over everything, okay? I know it's not a joke."

"Because if this is too much for you right now . . ."

Olive locked eyes with Stella. "I said I'd do this. I'm sorry I wasn't taking it seriously tonight. I'll even make Stella flash cards if I have to."

Stella chuckled. "I'm really good at making flash cards."

"You know I might not have your questionnaire answers memorized, but I think I would have guessed that."

A streetlight near the parking lot made the misty night air glow gold.

"Least we could do a convincing kiss in the bar tonight," Olive said, her voice more gravelly than usual.

"You think we were convincing?" Stella said, sucking on her bottom lip.

"I'd always be up for more practice before the next event if you think we need it." Olive kept her tone light, as if she were kidding, as she tucked a strand of Stella's hair back behind her ear.

Stella laughed, and it was back to her normal laugh, not the one she used when she was worried about being too loud or too unprofessional. "So when should I schedule your pop quiz?"

Okay, this was venturing into an incredibly sexy tutor role-play fantasy, and Olive was just about at her limit for turn-ons tonight. Every potential reply occurring to Olive involved the word *cramming,* which just seemed inappropriate. Olive needed to get home before she said something stupid.

After a check on the road to see if the cab was pulling up yet, Olive pulled Stella into her arms. "Thank you for coming out tonight."

"I'm glad I got back in time." Stella's cheeks were pink, because of either the wind or a blush. "Derek and Joni are great. Glad I could hang out with them."

Olive nodded. "Me too."

The lack of a kiss seemed to hum between them. But the cab pulled up in front of them. With another small wave, Stella got into the cab. After watching the cab's taillights disappear down the road, Olive went back toward the bar door, but movement caught her eye from the shadowy part of the parking lot. Beachy blond waves.

Lindsay gave her a broad, ominous grin as she hopped into her car.

The bar door opened. Derek came out and stood beside her.

"What are you looking at?" he asked.

"Trouble."

Chapter 33

OLIVE
Mint chocolate chip is disgusting.

STELLA
False.

STELLA
It's not fair for you to tease me about my answers
when I haven't seen yours.

Olive sent a photo of the first and second pages of her filled-out questionnaire from where it was perched on her lap next to Gus's enormous head. She'd worked most of the last week since the happy hour, and every day she had been waiting for another confrontation with Lindsay. Had Lindsay heard them talking? What was that terrifying smile about?

STELLA
Birthday cake is not a real ice cream flavor.

OLIVE
It absolutely is, and BONUS doesn't taste like tooth-paste.

STELLA
And then you put that your cake flavor is champagne
which is not a cake flavor.

OLIVE
Champagne cake is amazeballs.

> **OLIVE**
> Do you still want to fake date me after I used the word amazeballs?

> **STELLA**
> I'm still thinking.

Olive chuckled and sipped her coffee, spilling a couple of drops on the third page of the survey and then hastily mopping them up with her hoodie sleeve.

> **STELLA**
> I can't believe you put that your most embarrassing moment was what happened in Disney World. That's cheating. Nothing you did at Disney was at all embarrassing.

> **OLIVE**
> Your adorable TikTok dances with your cousins shouldn't count either then. Those weren't embarrassing either. I created an account just so I could follow you.

> **STELLA**
> I figured the User1578940301 that was liking the videos was you. Or at least I hoped it was.

Olive laughed and began scribbling down answers to the questions on the back. Most of the questions were designed to make events easier, focusing on ordering choices or things that could naturally come up in conversation that would be weird for partners not to know about each other. Like secret TikTok accounts. But some just seemed random, like question ninety-one. Favorite smell? Olive's given answer: freshly cut grass and cake batter, but not at the same time (actual answer: lilacs and vanilla). Stella's answer: petrichor or cherry Slurpee. Who even knew the word *petrichor*? And cherry Slurpee?

Question eighty-one: Did you ever play team sports? Olive's answer: veteran hospital softball league right fielder, which involved a specialized skill of standing in one spot and hoping the ball didn't come near her. She wasn't sure if she should mention that one time when she tried to play hockey like Jake and got a concussion in her first practice in peewee league. Stella's answer: soccer, volleyball, and track. With a note below that Stella only joined the teams when those sports didn't interfere with marching band. Who was this woman?

She was adorable.

STELLA

Why did you just put April 25 next to the question that asks for your ideal date?

OLIVE

Derek is going to view you asking that as a major strike against our fake relationship.

STELLA

Huh?

OLIVE

It's a reference to one of his favorite movies. Never mind. But uh . . . my ideal date would be a museum or really exploring a new city.

STELLA

That actually sounds perfect. Thought any more about Italy?

OLIVE

I had one of my plane crash nightmares just a few nights ago actually.

Olive could imagine those tiny lines of frustration around Stella's eyes. They always appeared whenever Olive talked about air travel being dangerous.

> STELLA
> AIR TRAVEL IS SAFER THAN DRIVING!

Oooh. She coaxed all caps and an exclamation mark from her. She must really be mad. They continued back and forth for a while about air travel. Olive sent Stella a link to a transatlantic cruise. Stella sent back a link to an article about an outbreak of foodborne illness on a ship.

Rude.

There was a lull in messages while Olive continued to fill out the other half of the survey while skimming through the pages of the thick binder.

> STELLA
> People magazine just called me. Did they call you?

> OLIVE
> I had a couple missed calls yesterday, but I hadn't checked my messages yet

> STELLA
> Would you have time to do a FaceTime around 4:30? I could come over there after I'm done teaching today?

> OLIVE
> Sure.

Six hours later, they sat together on Olive's couch, Olive hyperaware of exactly where Stella's thigh was in respect to her own. Stella's laptop was open before them with a Zoom call on the screen. Gus was curled in a very large ball on the floor near their feet, and Olive was mildly concerned that his snoring would distract them from the interview.

The woman on the screen had kind eyes and short auburn hair. "Well, we've all seen the video. I'm so glad to be talking to you both today. What a story."

"Thank you for having us." Stella smiled. She had lots of different smiles. The professional one. The excited and enthusiastic one that deepened her dimples. The sweet one. And the wicked one she made as Olive removed her necktie.

Olive had been gaping. She swallowed. "Yes, thank you."

The reporter smirked into the camera, noticing the small wordless glances between Olive and Stella. "So, tell me. Was it love at first sight between you?"

They both laughed.

Olive surprised herself by finding words first. "Not exactly. I mean, obviously I noticed her. Who wouldn't? She's stunning. But I don't think it was until she offered to help me get to my race that I knew what a kind person she was."

"She drove you all the way from Atlanta to Disney?"

"Yes."

"And what about you, Stella?"

"After we all got off the plane, someone tagged me in the video of Olive saving the man's life. It was remarkable. *She* was remarkable. Calm and collected despite the huge amount of pressure. I remember thinking, *I'd love to get to know that person.*" The look on Stella's face melted something in Olive.

"What were you thinking in those moments in the video, Olive?"

"I approached the situation like I would any patient. Once I got into the zone it was easy for me to forget I was on an airplane and focus on what was in front of me and how I could help him." Olive's fingers scraped along the velvet couch cushion.

"I imagine being in the tight quarters of an airplane made it much harder."

"For sure. I was using unfamiliar equipment in an unfamiliar environment. And I'm afraid of flying, so—"

"You're afraid of flying?"

Olive's eyes met Stella's. Olive chuckled. "It was my first time on a plane."

Stella patted Olive's hand. "I keep telling her that flying is the safest way to travel, and Allied Airlines in particular has very high safety ratings."

Olive lifted her palms in a *meh* gesture. "And I keep telling her that statistics never fixed a phobia. But flying Allied Airlines was a pretty good experience overall, despite the fact that I only got to sit in my seat for a few minutes."

"So, your fear of flying is cured, then?"

"Uh . . ." Olive pursed her lips comically.

They stared at each other, probably both reliving their text exchanges. The corner of Stella's mouth twitched.

"Well, watching you both together, you can see how in love you are. I'd love to get some background on each of you. Olive, I was looking into you and found out about your brother—"

"I'm sorry, can I ask you something off the record?"

"Of course."

She clasped her hands together. "Is it okay if we don't talk about my brother?" Talking about Jake was a sure way to lead to a meltdown, and if she answered questions about him, they might look into the full story of what happened to him and the legal battle with her family. She hadn't told Stella the full story about what was going on with her family yet. It wasn't that she didn't trust her. It was more that talking about it just made it feel more real. She hadn't entirely processed it yet. These moments with Stella felt so separate from what was happening with her family. She liked it that way.

"That's fine. I understand."

A wrinkle deepened in Stella's forehead. She spoke in a low voice only Olive could hear. "Are you okay?"

"I'm fine."

"Well, then let's talk about Stella and her career. How long have you been a pilot, Stella?"

As she answered, Stella reached over and squeezed Olive's hand.

Olive was getting far too used to this feeling. Maybe everything that Derek had said was right. The next event was in two weeks. If this was how Olive felt now, how much harder would it be to let go of her after the events were over?

After the interview finished, Stella ended the call and smiled at her. "I have a surprise for you."

Chapter 34

Stella came back from her car with a hanging bag and then reached inside. She pulled out a V-neck dress in a deep green velvet. It had a slight vintage flare. Different enough from what she had worn to the awards event, so that it would look okay in photos and it wouldn't clash with Stella's uniform. It had been the perfect dress.

"I thought it was out of stock," Olive said in a breath. "When I called the store the next day, they said it was out of stock." Shipping wouldn't have gotten it to Olive in time for the event, so she had given up and started looking for other options. None of them seemed to measure up, though.

"I called around and they happened to have a few sizes at a mall near the airport in Akron. You kept sending me other dress options, but you didn't seem as excited about any of them like you were about this one. I thought you should at least get to try it."

Olive hugged Stella. "Oh my god. Thank you."

"If Derek's stories about you at high school dances were any indication, I know dressing up isn't always your thing, so I wanted you to have something special to wear."

"Derek used our high school dances as opportunities to cosplay John Hughes movies, so I'm not sure he had room to talk." Olive smoothed the fabric. "Wow. I love the color even more in person." She walked into the bedroom and stood in front of the full-length mirror with the dress held up to her front. "What do you think?"

Stella followed her into the bedroom and stood behind her,

looking at the reflection in the mirror over Olive's shoulder. "It looks very pretty with your eyes."

Olive smiled. "I'm really excited for the party. You said this event is usually the most fun?"

"Less stuffy. A lot more women at this one. I can't wait to introduce you to more of my friends. I think they'll all be at this one. Usually a lot of the women end up skipping the Pilots' Gala for a variety of reasons."

"I'm excited to meet them." Olive hung the dresses on the back of her closet door. Stella had even grabbed the couple of sizes Olive planned to order. She faced Stella.

Stella's hair was down, loose onto her shoulders. A flush was across her cheeks. She'd dressed in that white button-down for the interview with a classic gray blazer. The top button had come open now, and there was a gold necklace hanging there.

What was it about buttons that made Olive so desperate to rip them open on Stella Soriano?

There was a gorgeous woman in her bedroom. And for the sake of this arrangement, she was off-limits. They hadn't spoken about their make-out session since it happened.

All it would take was a step. Olive could cover the distance between them in a single stride. Stella was right next to Olive's bed.

Stella took a step toward Olive. Her lips parted just enough for a slow exhale.

Olive leaned forward, looking up at Stella, but not reaching out to her.

"Tacos," Stella said with a sudden change in posture, folding her arms over herself.

"What?" Olive near crashed into her mirror as she stepped back.

"Question number seventy-five. On the questionnaire. It's the only one that was the same. We both said our favorite food is tacos. Can I go get us tacos?"

"Tacos."

"Yes, tacos." Most people wouldn't notice how forced Stella's smile was. They would just see the grin. But Olive was learning the nuances of Stella's face. What she showed the world, and what she hid from it.

"Tacos would be great."

***

Stella went to pick up food while Olive finished up answering some emails. There were a bunch from her mother's lawyer. Heather still hadn't texted Olive back about when she could come by to see Cody for his birthday. Was this another level of getting frozen out by the family?

"Tacos," Stella said in a loud, singsongy voice as she came through the door. That top button was rebuttoned now.

They assembled the food on the coffee table. Olive had decided that it was her job to immerse Stella in all the aspects of their generation's culture she had been avoiding, so she flipped on a must-watch trashy television show about women in dangerous stilettos selling billion-dollar real estate in Hollywood.

Stella had made the mistake of dropping a chip, which Gus gobbled up, and now he was drooling on the carpet watching every move Stella made. Stella petted him several times before Olive told him to cut it out because he was not supposed to eat people food anymore. Stella, for all her insistence that she never watched TV, kept turning up the volume loud enough she could follow what was happening as the plastic-surgefied faces on the screen yelled insults at one another over some very dramatic perceived slight. When the first episode's credits rolled, Stella pressed the button to watch the next episode, but then turned to Olive with a serious expression.

"I'm sorry they asked about your brother. I think if we do any more interviews in the future, we should tell them ahead of time that you aren't comfortable with questions about him."

For a second, Olive had forgotten about that awkward moment during the interview, since the heat of that moment in her bedroom had entirely eclipsed it. "That's a good idea."

"But you can talk to me about things. Anything, if you need to." Her eyes were painfully earnest.

Could she, though? Some days she felt like she could spill everything to Stella, but this wasn't like her to feel so comfortable. She hadn't moved in with Lindsay because something about their relationship didn't feel right. It wasn't because she was afraid of emotional intimacy, but still, Lindsay's words from the bar echoed in her head. Was this reticence to share part of the problem or just the result of Lindsay's reaction to her anxiety? Would she end up messing everything up with Stella because she was such a fuckup in general?

"Thanks. It's still an ongoing thing with my family. Talking about it sucks. That's why I don't mention it much. Not because I don't—uh—trust you."

"Okay." Stella stacked the empty taco containers and swept up nearly invisible crumbs with her fingers. "What are you doing for Thanksgiving?"

"Working." Olive had worked every holiday in the last year. Let the people with families who wanted to see them have their time. She'd take the time-and-a-half pay.

"I'll be working too." Stella crunched another chip.

"Oh? Not with your dad?"

"No. It's easy to pick up hours around the holidays."

Olive wanted to ask about why she didn't want to be with her dad, but she didn't want it to seem like she was judging.

"My dad and I will probably go out for a Thanksgiving meal the night before. Any chance . . . would you want to come with us? He really likes you."

Olive was startled into silence for a moment. When she recovered herself, she spoke with genuine regret. "I'm working the day before and the day after, actually. We do it that way so people can travel."

"Oh, right."

"I do miss watching the parade, though." Olive rested her head on her fist.

"Maybe next year you'll be off." Stella smiled, but then the expression faltered as if she hadn't meant to say that at all.

Next year?

They finished their meal, and then Stella rushed off, wanting to check on her dad. Before leaving she made sure all of the take-out trash was thrown out and the cushion she'd been leaning against was back to its baseline level of fluffiness.

God, she's adorable.

After an awkward hug at the door, Stella was gone.

Olive immediately opened the calendar app on her phone to calculate the next day she was likely to see Stella again. After she counted the days the second time, she looked down to see Gus staring up at her.

"I'm not pathetic."

He whined a little. While she knew intellectually that the whine was about wanting a walk and not an expression of canine judgment, she still shoved her phone into her pocket.

"What? You don't think I can just be cool about this whole thing? You don't think I can just be totally nonchalant about the fact that I'm probably not going to see Stella for at least twelve and a half days?"

Gus didn't deign to respond, but he did give a small head shake in the direction of his leash.

Olive rubbed at her temples. "Yeah. Me neither."

Chapter 35

"Olive, are you okay? I've been calling." Stella's voice was slightly panicked. "I haven't heard from you since you said you picked up extra shifts after Thanksgiving."

"I'm dead." Olive rolled over on the couch and clutched her blanket to her chest, wincing as she crushed her tissue box beneath her. She should move. But that would require energy.

"That seems unlikely given that you're talking. But I've been worried. Really worried."

"I have pneumonia."

"You have *what*?"

"I'm on antibiotics. I should still be"—a coughing fit erupted, one of the ones she hadn't been able to stop for the last week—"able to go to the thing tomorrow. I think. I've been on the antibiotics for more than twenty-four hours, so I'm not contagious."

"I'm coming over."

"No, I'm gross. You don't have to—"

"Text me what your essentials are and what you need, and I'll stop by the store."

"Derek brought me some stuff yesterday. I think I just need more stuff."

"You sound delirious."

"I took some cough medicine. It's the good shit." Olive leaned back enough to turn up the humidifier.

"Text me if you can. Otherwise, I'll be there in an hour."

Olive's voice spluttered out between coughs. "I'll be here."

Stella chuckled. "I know you will. Get some rest."

After an impossible-to-determine period of time, a knock

woke Olive. She pulled her blanket over her head like a Jedi cloak and stood.

Nope. She fell. Horizontal again.

Shoot.

One more try.

All right. Vertical. This is what vertical feels like on codeine.

Like floating. But also, weird and detached. Like a balloon head. That was a thing in a commercial, right?

Olive laughed, which, of course, turned into more coughing, which hurt.

A lot.

"Olive, are you okay in there?"

"No, just floating." She tightened the Jedi shawl around her and headed to the door. "I'm fine," she said while simultaneously hacking into her elbow.

Stella was wearing her typical flight instructor clothes, aviator sunglasses pushing her hair away from her face.

"Oh, Olive." She dropped several bags of groceries and hugged her. "Why didn't you call me. Who's been walking your dog?"

"Gus is with Derek." Olive stumbled as she meandered back to the couch. *Horizontal good. Vertical bad. Stella pretty.* Her voice was mostly a combination of slurs and mumbles at this point. "Fake girlfriend shouldn't have to deal with real sickness."

Stella was silent for a few moments. Olive remained immobile, her body having completely betrayed her. The crinkle of paper bags. The refrigerator opening and closing. The scrape of pots and pans.

"I brought you soup. I didn't know what kind to get, so I got all of them, including some plain broth. I got you a wide selection of teas. Yogurt since you said you were on antibiotics, and Gatorade. I also brought ginger ale, because ginger ale is always nice when you're sick." Pressure moved the couch beside her.

Stella pulled the blanket away from Olive's face and pressed her cool hand on Olive's forehead. "And oh my god, you have a fever. You're burning up."

Olive may have leaned in to Stella's touch a little. "I started the new antibiotic yesterday. Fever should be gone by tomorrow."

"Do you have fever medicine?"

"Out on the counter." Olive flailed a hand. "Ginger ale, please."

"Of course." More movement in the room. "What did you take? Not that high-out-of-her-mind Olive isn't adorable, because you absolutely are, but seriously?"

"Mough cedicine. With cocaine. No, that's not right. That's illegal. With codeine." She added another slur of garbled syllables. More time passed and there was a cool compress on her forehead.

"I have your ginger ale."

Olive blinked. How much time had passed? Stella was wearing that Embry-Riddle sweatshirt again. She recognized it even though the lines were blurred, partly because her contacts weren't in and partly because all of reality was a blur right now. She sucked down ginger ale from a straw and threw a couple of pills Stella offered down her throat.

Stella combed the sweaty hair off Olive's face and kissed her forehead.

"Rest. I'm going to make you the soup."

"Jake made soup when I was sick once."

The sounds of cabinets and pots and pans came from her tiny galley kitchen. "He sounds like he was a good brother."

"The best. I got sick a lot the first year I was a nurse. He brought me soup. I miss him."

"I'm sure you do."

"I missed you when I didn't see you."

The movement stopped. "I missed you too."

"Where did you go?"

"Orlando, Tampa, Cincinnati, Austin."

"I can never spell Cincinnati. How many cs? How many ns? How many ts? It's all a mystery."

"It definitely is. Gosh, you're so high."

"You said I was adorable. I didn't forget, see." Olive tapped her temple.

"You *are* adorable. I don't want you to forget that I think you're adorable. Why would I?"

Olive muttered something akin to "fake girlfriend" but hoped Stella hadn't heard.

And then a delicious steamy smell was wafting into her nose. She opened her eyes. "Soup?"

"Yeah. Soup."

She sat up and leaned against Stella while she ate, with a long, slender arm draped gently over her shoulders.

***

Olive came out of the shower. She was finally blessedly clean, with her head feeling clearer than it had in a week since the slight cough went to her chest and exploded into misery. She wore her coziest pajamas, which consisted of a concert T-shirt she'd stolen from Derek in high school over her most stretched-out sports bra paired with threadbare thermal pants. Her wild, wet curls were dampening the neck of the T-shirt. She'd barely bothered to finger-comb them, and her head was still throbbing too much to pull them into a tight bun. Certainly not come-hither attire, but she was sick, goddamn it.

Stella stood in the bedroom, pointing to things as if she were checking off items from an invisible checklist. She'd taken her hoodie off and was just wearing a tank top. "I changed your sheets. They were a mess, probably because of the fevers. I organized all your medications, so it'll be obvious which ones you need to take on a schedule and the as-needed ones. I also changed the water in your humidifier and topped off your ginger ale with ice and a new straw. There's two more cans of soup on the counter, but I thought maybe I could bring you back something."

"Thank you. I'm sorry I was a mess when you got here. Fever plus codeine appears to have an interesting effect on me. You didn't have to do all this." Olive gestured to the much neater room.

"I wanted to."

"Thank you. I really appreciate it."

"You're welcome."

"I need to talk to you about something."

"What?"

"I was thinking a lot this week. Mainly because I was so sick I couldn't do much else other than binge *Selling Sunset* and think between coughing fits."

"I hate that I wasn't here to help you earlier."

"That's the thing."

"What's wrong?" There was a panicked look in Stella's eyes that Olive did not like at all, but she couldn't lose her resolve. "We don't have to talk about anything right now if you're still feeling terrible."

Olive scrunched her damp curls, absentmindedly. "I'm feeling a lot better now that the fever's gone and the codeine's worn off. I need to say something now or else I'll lose my nerve."

"Your nerve?" Stella said in a soft voice.

"I don't want to be sick and wonder if I can call you." Olive rubbed the spot on her head that kept aching.

"Neither do I. You can always call me."

"When you're here doing really nice things for me . . . I'm having trouble remembering what's real, and what's fake." She shut her mouth and clasped her hands in her lap. "And maybe I'm still a little high."

"What's . . . real?" Stella's dark eyebrows pulled together, the wrinkle between them becoming a crevice.

"Do you like me?"

Stella sat very still, shoulders slumped, knees locked tight. "I do like you, Olive."

"I know I'm not in the best state to be propositioning any-one right now. But I'm not sure what this means." Olive ad-justed the collar of her T-shirt. "This." She gestured to the space between them.

"It means I'm . . . just happy with the way things are. I don't want to hurt you. I really, really don't want to hurt you. I know how I can be." Stella fidgeted with her hands, as if she were checking that her nail polish wasn't chipped.

She kept saying things like that, but here she was being at-tentive and caring and all the things she said she never was with her exes. Olive was too sick to be anything other than confused by it.

"Isn't friends easier?" Stella seemed to be focusing her eyes on anything except Olive. "We both have a lot going on right now."

Olive sucked in a breath through her nose. Her brain did still feel hazy. "So, we're friends. Friends who make out. I mean, we made out after the banquet. Then we never talked about it again."

"Friends can make out."

"Can they?" Olive sipped her ginger ale, mainly because she was too chicken to look Stella in the eye.

"We're two consenting adults, Olive. We can do whatever we want. The most important question to my mind is are *you* okay with what we're doing? After we kissed after the banquet, I got really worried I was sending you mixed signals, but then at the bar . . . I don't know what came over me. Since then I've just been trying to figure things out too." Stella's cheeks turned pink. "I didn't want to do anything else that would confuse you. Or confuse me. I know myself, and I really can't do the relationship thing with expectations and it just kills me to think that it might look like I'm intentionally messing with your head or being—"

"Stella." Olive grabbed one of Stella's warm soft hands and held on. "I don't think that. I *am* okay with what we're doing. I just wanted to check in about rules and expectations . . . and whatever." It would be nice if the *whatever* could include more making out.

Weirdly, she wasn't lying. Despite all of Derek's concerns, she *was* okay with it. It wasn't like she had been desperate for a girlfriend. After Lindsay, she'd specifically not wanted anything serious again for a while. She'd wanted space to figure out her family shit and get her anxiety and panic attacks under control. Having Stella in her life made her happy. So what if they called it friends. Did it matter?

Stella twisted a piece of her hair around a finger. "I don't want to continue if you aren't comfortable."

"I *am* comfortable." Fear bubbled inside Olive. What would it mean if this was over? No. It couldn't be over.

"I wish you had called me to tell me you were sick."

"I . . . I didn't want to seem needy."

Understanding spilled over Stella's face. "You're referencing what your ex said." A bite Olive hoped was jealousy infused the word *ex*. "You aren't like that. What she said revealed way more about her than it did about you." Stella squeezed Olive's hand more tightly and forced Olive to look at her. "Please call me if you need me. Anytime."

"Okay." Olive leaned on Stella's shoulder.

"And this, this friendship . . . this is what you want?" Stella's tone sounded unconvinced and unsure.

"Yes, it's what I want. I don't want a commitment. I like kissing you. I'd like to do anything with you. I wasn't really looking for a relationship either." Olive *had* said no relationships until she finished Jake's list anyway. Maybe an arrangement like this was perfect for her too. "What about you, Stella? What do you want? Right now. This exact second. What do you want?"

Fire seemed to blaze between them for a moment. The silence dragged on slightly longer than would be normal in a casual conversation. Stella's lips parted as if there were something she wanted to say, just on the tip of her very talented tongue. What was she not saying?

But Olive's lungs decided to pick that moment to shudder and rasp enough that she dissolved into a brutal coughing fit. Her ribs ached. Pain flashed in her head as she kept coughing.

Stella's expression changed, shifting back into what Olive was beginning to interpret as *captain mode*. She straightened, brows wrinkling as her eyes scanned Olive's body. "Well, first you need to take off your shirt."

Olive's persistent hacking barely allowed her to articulate, "W-what?"

Chapter 36

After the coughing fit slowed, Olive blinked and tugged at her neck. The room was a million degrees now. "You want me to what?"

"Take off your shirt." Her tone was matter-of-fact. Not exactly how Olive imagined her saying these words for the first time. And Olive certainly had imagined her saying them.

Stella turned to rummage through a shopping bag on the bookshelf behind her and pulled out a round blue tub, holding it up like Vanna White or a model on *The Price Is Right*.

Oh.

"In my family we have a very specific way of doing Vicks. My abuela swore by it. Do you mind if I show you?"

Olive stood and tripped over her feet. Stella rushed forward and caught her, interpreting the fall as illness-related delirium rather than the fact that all the blood in Olive's brain had gone to a very different part of her body at the thought of Stella rubbing hands all over Olive's chest.

"Still dizzy?" Stella swept her fingers across Olive's forehead with a featherlight touch that seemed too teasing to be real.

"Uh—" After her voice cracked, she cleared her throat and tried again. "Yeah. Still not feeling great."

"This will make you feel better. I promise. Sit."

Olive sat so quickly it was as if she were Gus with a treat dangled in front of his nose.

Stella's fingers grazed the worn hem of the T-shirt, and Olive offered her a tiny nod. The cotton pulled over her head, leaving her in nothing but the bra that Olive profoundly wished wasn't an old and discolored gray.

"Lie down." Stella's words were more clinical than Olive would like, but again, Olive obeyed without question. "Close your eyes."

Olive closed her eyes and felt Stella's nimble fingers working through her hair. She fanned the tangled waves out on the pillow beneath her and smoothed it. The touch was so delicate, Olive shivered.

"Are you okay? Chills?"

"Um. Yeah. A little, but I'm fine." Olive coughed again, covering her mouth even tighter with her elbow to try to spare Stella from any more of her germs.

Olive heard the untwisting of a lid before Stella spoke in a low, sympathetic voice. "You're okay if I put some of this on you? No allergies, right?"

"No allergies."

"Okay, good. Scoot over just a little."

Olive slid over and felt the bed shift. Shit. Stella Soriano was in her bed. Stella Soriano was *in her bed,* and Olive's shirt was off. She could almost feel the heat of Stella's breath on her bare skin as she spoke again.

"My grandmother always started at the temples." Stella rubbed some of the ointment in a smooth, circular motion from her temples to her ears.

Tension in Olive's forehead eased, and her body melted into the pillow.

"She always put it on our feet with socks too. I bought you some fuzzy cheap ones at the store, are you okay if I . . ."

"Anything." Olive gave a tiny fake cough this time and tried to make her voice sound less like she was in a low-quality porno and more "normal" hoarse. "I mean, sure, anything would be great. Anything, like, to help with the cough, I mean." So smooth.

The bed shifted once more, and Stella moved down near

Olive's feet. She rubbed the salve into the arches, the toes, the heels. Olive's mouth went dry, and she stifled a moan at how fucking good it felt. Jesus Christ, this woman had missed her calling by becoming an airline pilot. She had magic hands.

Once Stella seemed satisfied the Vicks was applied thoroughly, a bag rustled. Olive opened her eyes to find Stella pulling out a pair of furry magenta socks. She ripped the tag off and moved back to Olive's feet.

Olive pushed up to her elbows. "Oh, I can put them on—"

"Just relax." Somehow having Stella slide soft socks onto her feet was unexpectedly erotic. Although it occurred to Olive that Stella doing absolutely anything was erotic. Olive would probably want to fuck Stella after watching her brush her teeth or boil an egg or do her taxes.

Olive's entire body grew warm as fucking Stella was now all she could think about. All the ways she wanted to fuck Stella. Starting with those damn magic hands on Olive's . . .

"Be right back," Stella said, completely oblivious to the X-rated fantasies that had taken root in Olive's brain because of some socks. Oh god, did this mean Olive had a foot fetish now? No. Only people like Elvis and Quentin Tarantino had foot fetishes. She calmed her brain, reminding herself that kink-shaming was bullshit, but her thoughts wouldn't slow down.

"Are you okay?"

Olive jumped at the sound of Stella's voice. Her eyes popped open. "I'm fine."

"You're supposed to be relaxing, but you look really tense." Stella held a steaming mug in her hand. "I was supposed to make you drink this before the Vicks, but I got distracted."

Distracted? By Olive? Olive internally begged that Stella was distracted by her own similar horniness.

"Sip a little and then I'll finish up applying the Vicks."

"Chamomile?"

Stella nodded. "My favorite. I hated it when I was little and forced to drink it, but it does work wonders when you're sick. I also use it for insomnia now."

Olive drank a third of the tea before Stella seemed satisfied. She took the mug back and slid it onto the nightstand next to Olive's ginger ale. This time, Olive didn't need to be told what to do. She scooched over, lay down, and closed her eyes.

Stella sat beside her. "Are you okay if I rub it on your chest, or do you want to do it?"

"You doing it is fine." It came out more like a croak.

"Do you need more tea?"

"Nope. Throat's fine." She shut her eyes and tried to remember what arms were supposed to do when they were relaxed. After a couple of twitching movements, she glued them to her sides. Warm softness shifted beside her. She heard another twist of the lid. Olive opened her eyes a slit in time to see Stella lean over her. Her perfect breasts were right at Olive's eye level. Olive closed her mouth to stifle whatever treacherous sound threatened to come from her.

Then a warm hand was on her chest. The circular motion was similar to what it had been on her temples, but over her sternum instead. Olive's spine begged to arch into the touch. She felt her nipples harden and couldn't decide whether she wanted Stella to notice or not.

She shifted, letting her thighs rub together as she took a deep inhale.

This was torture. Pure, unrelenting torture. Stella's fingers rubbed over the areas of tension along Olive's collarbone and upper ribs. Those muscles that were sore from days of coughing now loosened.

"Take a deep breath, Olive."

She did. Her chest rising into the gentle comfort of Stella's palm.

"Again."

That hand was inches away from the two peaks that were begging to be set free. Begging for some attention.

Only Stella's fingertips touched Olive now, tracing a pathway from her ear to her shoulder and up her neck in leisurely strokes.

"How are you feeling? Is it any easier to breathe?"

Breathe? No. It wasn't any easier to breathe. Olive wanted the woman in front of her so much it burned away all the oxygen inside her.

"Is your fever coming back?" Stella pressed the back of her hand to Olive's forehead. "You're all flushed again. Maybe that tea was too hot. I can get you a compress—"

She started to get up, but Olive's pneumonia-addled brain robbed her of all sense. She grabbed Stella's arm and nuzzled it. Actually. Fucking. Nuzzled it. Even with the heavy scent of menthol in the air, she could still discern the lilacs and vanilla of Stella's skin beneath it.

"Please just stay with me," Olive said. She didn't want to let go of her. Everything she'd said about being okay with keeping things casual *might* have been complete bullshit.

Stella didn't say anything else, but she shifted into a more comfortable position and rested her chin on Olive's shoulder. So, Olive did what anyone would do after having a Vicks massage from a gorgeous woman while suffering from both lady blue balls and a mild-to-moderate pneumonia. She slept for twelve hours and woke to the smell of coffee already brewing. Because Stella stayed.

Chapter 37

Stella leaned down and handed Olive a steaming mug. With dismay, Olive realized that Stella was in her uniform. She sipped from the mug. The coffee was perfect. Exactly the right amount of milk and sugar, as if Stella had watched her habits. Knowing Stella, she probably had.

Stella sat on the edge of the bed. "How are you feeling?"

"Better. A *ton* better, actually. My chest still hurts, but the sleep was amazing. The Vicks seemed to have done the trick." Olive reached for Stella's arm, their eyes meeting at the same moment as they touched. "Thank you for coming over and checking on me last night."

And for the best massage of my life.

"You're welcome." She bit her lip. "I have a short day today and then the event tonight. But can you please call me if you take a turn for the worse again?"

"I'm going to be fine. Just needed sleep. And I slept like a rock last night. I'm so sorry about the event—"

"No, please don't say anything else about it. I'm glad you're okay." She paused for a beat, shifting her weight so she was closer to Olive. "I . . . I was really worried when I called."

"You didn't need to worry. I'm fine. Though I still feel like I'm in breach of contract."

Stella frowned. "I don't want you to feel—"

"It was a joke. Not a good one. But—" Olive coughed delicately. "I'm sick."

Stella's forced laugh was brittle. "After today, I'm out of town for a week and a half."

"Oh?"

"Just the way my schedule worked out."

"That must be hard, to be away from your dad that long."

It would be hard for Olive to have her away that long. But they were *friends*. This was why Stella didn't want a relationship, Olive realized. Because she didn't want to feel tethered to anyone else. Her mind was functioning better now. The memory of the ill-advised, aggressive nuzzling of the night before made her cheeks burn.

"It is. I scheduled a lot more hours with the caregivers. My dad understands. Me making captain is the more important thing to him too."

"If he needs anything, I'm close by. I mean obviously not in the next few days, but when I'm feeling better. I'd be up for anything to help him."

"Thank you. I really appreciate the offer."

Olive sipped her coffee, willing the caffeine to fill her veins. "I think he likes time with you more than he cares about you making captain, though. When I was there he just seemed like he missed you when you traveled . . . He kind of made it sound like he understands that it's important to you, so he wants to support you—"

Stella whipped her head around. "What do you mean?"

Olive set down her coffee and pulled the comforter up to her neck, feeling suddenly chilled. "It was the sense I got from talking to him. You know him better than I do, but he said something about not wanting to get in the way of your dream, which made me think—"

"He has wanted this for me for my entire life. He worked so hard to support me." Stella's tone was almost snappish. "I can't afford to get complacent. You saw him. We—" Her voice broke. "The neurologists don't know how long he's going to be *him*. You saw him on a good day. He hid his symptoms for a long time. Then he had outbursts, and everything has gotten bad so quickly. He was seventy-five when he was diagnosed. The older you are, the worse it can be. The more at risk for early death, and doctors see really concerning neurological signs that could mean dementia."

Parkinson's was one of those devastating diseases that wasn't technically fatal, but it still robbed its sufferers of their quality of life, some more quickly than others.

"I didn't mean to—I know it's important to him. *You're* important to him. I meant . . . I don't know. I was trying to make you feel better. It seems like he loves you so much. I meant that he's proud of you. I think he'd be proud of you no matter what. You're lucky to have that."

"I know I am. You met him retired. He was finally able to fully be himself now, and this disease is robbing him of his life that he deserved. He was going to travel around the world, but now he doesn't feel like he can. He spent all that time working in the government having to be careful about who knew he was gay. He did all of that to give me my dreams."

"He sounds like a great dad."

"I get to be a gay, Latina pilot. I get to be out. I get to do so many things that he never got to do, and I owe it to him not to waste this chance."

"No one could ever think you were wasting your chance." Olive wrapped her arms around Stella's waist. "I'm sorry for what's happening to him. And you. Being a caregiver is hard."

"I have to know that I gave it everything."

"You are giving it everything."

Stella checked her watch. "I have to get going."

"Oh, right. If I feel better this afternoon maybe I can still—"

She shook her head. "Pneumonia can be serious. Please don't even offer what you're thinking about offering."

"I wanted to go with you." Olive's posture might have been

described as a pout. "I had the perfect dress. What if me not being there ruins everything about *the plan*."

"I know you did." Stella gave a half smile and touched Olive's nose. "We still have the big Pilots' Gala. You can wear the perfect dress then. That's the most important event, anyway. This event was more about me getting to show you off to my friends. I mean, because they've heard so much about you."

Olive felt her chest puff out a little at that. She grinned. "You're sure?"

"Stay in bed and rest. I'll see you in a couple weeks."

Weeks.

"Oh—right." Had part of her been wanting Stella to offer to come over again tonight? "I hope you have safe flights."

"Flying is very safe. We've been over this." A hint of the twinkle returned to Stella's eyes.

"Have we?" Olive smirked back.

"Yes." She patted the area over Olive's knee. "Can I get you anything before I leave?"

"No. Thank you again for all you did last night." Olive rubbed her chest, sleepiness overpowering her mouth's filter. "I wish you didn't have to leave."

"I . . . me too." Making Olive jolt, Stella rose from the bed without warning. She stood in the doorway, and her hand curled around the doorjamb while another one of those confusing frowns pulled at her perfect mouth. "Feel better, Olive."

Then she left.

Olive's lips tingled. She'd expected a goodbye kiss, which was stupid since she was sick. A hug? Something. After drinking a third of her coffee, she slid it onto the nightstand and flopped back onto her pillow. This was an ill-advised move because it made her headache spike. She rolled over on the pillow Stella had lain on. It smelled like lilacs and vanilla. Olive brought the comforter over her head.

***

A voice called out from her living room. "Proof of life?"

She'd been having a dream. An incredibly good one. About Stella. Involving teeth and breasts and toys.

But now she was wide awake. The massage last night had only intensified what had been brewing inside Olive since Disney. She'd had Stella in her bed, and she'd been too sick to do anything about it.

Derek cracked the curtains, letting a small stripe of light into the dim room.

"Go away. I'm dead. Light is the enemy." She pulled the pillow over her head. Even that small amount of light burned her eyes.

"Can't go away. Here to provide sustenance for the invalid." The mattress shifted as he sat on the bed. "Sorry I couldn't come by again until now."

She lifted the pillow slightly to see him. "Thanks for covering my shifts. You didn't have to come today. I'm sure you're exhausted."

"It's selfish, really. I miss your cooking. I'm a stakeholder in your full recovery." He brandished a sandwich from her favorite bistro downtown. "Did you have a sudden upswing last night?"

"What do you mean?"

"Your place was a disaster on Wednesday—I mean, I'm not judging. You were sick as fuck. But it's spotless now. And your fridge actually has food in it. Maybe I should eat this sandwich. Joni said you still sounded like death warmed over yesterday when she'd talked to you."

"Oh. Um . . . Stella came by." She pulled the pillow over her face again.

"That explains why your couch cushions are organized by color."

"She brought me soup. And gave me a tit massage with

Vicks VapoRub that almost gave me an orgasm." Olive kept the throw pillow over her head. Hiding from his reaction was a best practice.

"Because the store was out of cough medicine, she thought a homeopathic oxytocin release was your best bet," he said dryly. She knew Derek well enough that she could imagine his eyebrow waggling.

"Essentially. She said something about it being what her grandmother used to do."

"I bet she wasn't thinking about her grandmother during the tit massage."

"Just a friend helping out another friend."

"Sounds like I need to find some new friends."

"Because you don't want me to massage you into horny oblivion?"

He made a disgusted noise. "Yuck, no. No offense."

"None taken. I don't want you anywhere near my lady parts either." She coughed once.

"So, we're agreed."

"Definitely."

"You want my advice?"

"No."

"Talk to her."

Olive lifted the pillow off her head and held it to her chest.

Derek pushed the sandwich into her hand. "Also, eat this. You still look like shit. How much weight have you lost?" He took her pulse.

"I did try to talk to her last night. I got out of the shower and was all about to have an honest conversation about me liking her and how I wanted to be real girlfriends. But then I realized—"

"After the shower?"

"Yeah. I was high as a kite on codeine when she got here, but I finally felt coherent enough after the shower, so then—"

"You were naked and tried to have a relationship-goals conversation?"

"I was not naked."

He crossed his arms over his chest.

Olive took a bite of her sandwich and chewed, following it with a swallow of disgustingly cold coffee. "I was wearing pajamas. I only took my shirt off later. Before the Vicks massage. Everything else stayed on." *Unfortunately,* her brain added silently.

"Look, Olive."

"And if you'd stop interrupting me, I would explain. We *both* agreed that we were happy, so why change anything. I think she puts a lot of pressure on herself in relationships and has a bad history with them. She likes me. We're friends. Why mess with that?"

"You both agreed? What did you say?"

"I said I didn't want a commitment either."

"So, you lied."

"No, I didn't—don't. After Lindsay, you know I wanted to be single. Finish up Jake's list without someone being all negative all the time or putting any pressure on me to just get over it. I'm not some emotionally needy person." That last part probably sounded like a non sequitur.

But Derek's reaction told Olive he understood exactly where those words were coming from just like Stella had. "Just because Lindsay was toxic doesn't mean you don't want a girlfriend. It also doesn't mean it would be wrong for you to want something more with someone you obviously care about."

"I'm happy. Things are good. Stella and I are real friends. We're not in a relationship because we don't want all of those expectations and pressure."

"I feel like our conversations are turning into Groundhog Day, so I'm going to quit."

"Quit what?"

"Saying anything against it."

"Oh. Really?"

He patted her shoulder. "I want you to be happy, Olive. After everything you're going through with your brother, your family, and Lindsay, of course I want you to be happy."

"Okay then. Thank you. I *am* happy."

"Good. Now eat your damn sandwich."

Chapter 38

"This is super nerdy behavior." Olive yawned, scratching her hair, which was pulled into a tangled knot on the top of her head. Her cough was pretty much gone, but her chest still felt scratchy in the morning. She wore sweatpants and a sweatshirt, feeling downright schlubby compared to Stella in her neat yoga pants and matching zippered hoodie. After a week of not seeing her, she'd been thrilled when Stella got back and called. Less thrilled when Stella said she wanted to pick her up at 5:45 A.M. and go to a grocery store and buy a magazine.

Stella's walk was a lot more like a jaunt than should be possible at 5:45 A.M. "How often are we going to be in a major magazine?"

"If it's always going to be the result of a person almost dying on one of your flights, hopefully never again."

Stella snorted.

"It's so early." Olive squinted as the sun peeked over the horizon. "And cold." Stella had heard from the reporter last week about when the magazine was coming out.

"Stop whining." She pulled at Olive's hand and dragged her through the double doors of the grocery store. "We're going to be in a magazine. This is the day it comes out, and I want to see it and remember this." She held up her phone and they both smiled for a selfie.

Would that one actually get posted to Stella's account?

Olive's smile might have resembled a yawn. "You know we could have read it online, right?" None of the selfies they'd taken together had ended up on Stella's Instagram yet. Stella had been taking lots of other photos of herself, on planes and of planes and of other aspects of life as a pilot, all with the presets and editing techniques Olive had shown her. But still there weren't any photos with Olive on Stella's feed. It felt too weird to ask her about it. Weren't they supposed to have the relationship visible?

"My dad hates reading on a screen. I told him I'd buy him a copy and bring it to him later after breakfast at your house."

"At six in the morning?"

"Oh, Olive." She shook her head and touched Olive's chin. "You're not excited?"

"I'm excited to be back in bed."

"Noted." Stella squinted wryly.

Feeling guilty and not wanting to be the Eeyore in the situation, Olive pulled Stella toward her and kissed her nose. "But I'm excited you're excited." She couldn't explain that she was mostly nervous. Nervous of the aftermath after what happened with Jake. Too much press could lead to negative attention. You never knew what a reporter could dig up. There were no guarantees about what would be in the article. This was a crapshoot.

"It's here," Stella squealed, pulling the glossy cover off the shelf. There was a small photo of them from the *TODAY* show interview at the bottom corner. Olive pulled another copy off the shelf and flipped through the pages. Her eyes scanned the words, all of her muscles tense.

It was a puff piece, but a sweet one. True to the reporter's word, there was no mention of Jake or Olive's family in the article. She hadn't bothered telling her family about the interview. She'd missed a bunch of documents sent by her mother's lawyer while she was ill, and Derek had finally insisted on calling Heather himself about it, explaining that Olive was legitimately ill and needed to rest and couldn't manage nonurgent requests. The lawyer's emails and calls and texts slowed but didn't stop. A few days ago, she'd managed to catch up with everything.

Yesterday, she'd gone to see Jake for the first time in weeks. His color had been a bit off, though that might have been simply because Olive hadn't been there in a while. Maybe he'd always looked like that.

Olive shifted her attention back to the glossy pages in her hands. Stella did a good job of being an ambassador for her airline. She talked about the planes, her career, and what it was like being a female pilot. Every quote glowed with enthusiasm. It seemed to capture their relationship too. The reporter caught the witty banter between them as they recounted the story of their trip to Disney World.

Stella's phone began buzzing in her hand. She nearly dropped the magazine, eyes widening as she took in the name flashing in front of them.

She pressed the phone to her ear. "S-Stella Soriano."

Olive took the magazine from her, and cleaned out the rack, knowing that Stella also wanted to buy a couple of extras. She grabbed one for Derek too. He'd mock her for it, but he'd also be excited as fuck to see her photo in it.

"Thank you so much for calling, Mr. O'Halloran. Yes, I am an early riser." A pause. "Uh-huh, we have that in common."

Olive turned back to look at her, her own excitement growing for Stella. More muffled conversation.

"Jack, right. Okay." A pause. "I can make that work. I'm not in the air that day. Sure. I'll email her to schedule it."

After a few more thank-yous and goodbyes, Stella beamed as she slid the phone back into her bag. Olive grasped her hands.

"The head of PR sent him the article when it dropped last night. He said he was impressed about everything I said about the airline and that this was exactly the type of press we needed." She threw her arms around Olive. Her hair was in loose waves from where it had been coiled into a bun before. "He said he wants to find a mentor for me, so I can get ready to take the next step in my career."

"Congratulations. I'm so happy for you. You're getting every-thing you wanted." Her hand pressed into the small of Stella's back.

"Thanks to you. I can't tell you what this means to me."

Their eyes met. Olive tucked a loose hair behind her ear. Stella mirrored the motion, a slight crinkling of her nose the only sign of whatever was unsettling her eyes.

∗∗∗

Stella insisted that she would cook while Olive took Gus out for a walk. She wandered the early morning streets, clutching her heavy coat tightly around her. Gus paused to sniff a fire hydrant and then sat. Gus, being a rather ancient dog, tended to need breaks on walks. Olive sat on a cast-iron bench in front of Carroll Creek.

There was a woman in her apartment cooking her eggs.

A woman she really liked.

Olive spent the last two weeks post–*VickXXX VapoRub: The Porn Edition* analyzing everything from many different angles. Derek had made good on his promise to stop trying to talk her out of doing . . . well, whatever she was doing with Stella. She'd fallen asleep more nights than not after long conversations with Stella about something and often nothing. Stella brought up Italy a couple more times, but Olive couldn't imagine what that would look like. Her and Stella traipsing through the Ital-ian countryside together? It was too perfect. And Olive's life was too fucked up with the drama with her family to imagine a future like that.

Even Alyson, her trusty vibrator, had seemed less useful in the aftermath of feeling Stella's hands on her body. Her sex fantasy life had become nothing more than a sea of images of Stella. Her imagination was out of control.

They weren't "together."

Olive *should* care about that.

Because she didn't *just* want orgasms. What had haunted her dreams more than anything was the sound of Stella's voice when she brought her coffee the morning after the Vicks massage. The sweet, sunny personality that brightened everything around her.

Friends can make out.

Given the amount of time they spent talking and texting, they were definitely real friends.

Gus interrupted her reflections by trying rather ineffectively to chase a squirrel and almost yanking Olive's shoulder out of its socket. For an old guy he could move quick in short bursts. She checked her watch and then pulled on the leash to lead Gus back toward her apartment.

As she opened the door, the smells of coffee and peppers and onions greeted her. Such a welcoming scent. The attempt to chase the squirrel had exhausted all Gus's energy. He went over to his bed, plopped down, and was snoring in seconds.

After taking off her coat, Olive headed over to the kitchen. "The eggs look great."

Stella used a spatula to plate them and handed Olive a mug of perfectly made coffee as well. "Thanks. I lived on omelets in college. I can make seven different kinds depending on what's in the fridge. Easy meal. *Eggcellent* meal."

Olive groaned before laughing. "You're like a forty-five-year-old father of five trapped in a hot lady body."

"Puns are seriously underrated. It's unfair to denigrate them as nothing more than dad humor. My dad *is* an expert at them, though." Stella cut a small piece of the omelet off with her fork and fed it to Olive.

Olive smiled as she chewed the bite of perfectly seasoned breakfast. "Not surprised Hector's a punny guy, and wow, these eggs are great."

"Now, if you had had mushrooms in the fridge it would have been even better."

"Mushrooms are disgusting." Olive pulled a face.

"You didn't list mushrooms on question thirty-two."

"There wasn't enough room on the paper to list all of the foods that are hard passes for me. I stuck to the most relevant ones."

"Caviar and escargot were relevant? I feel like you're going to be really disappointed with the food at the Pilots' Gala."

"They were just the grossest things I could think of at the time. Are you deducting points from my test score since I didn't give comprehensive answers? I don't want to get a B." Olive affected a grimace. "In case you're springing that pop quiz on me, I remember *all* of your answers on thirty-two. Hating pineapple on pizza though? Such a cliché."

"Very good. You definitely get an A." Stella's smile was wicked again. "So . . . hot lady body, huh?"

"Like you don't know." Olive was much shorter than Stella. She smiled, raising her chin, and placed either hand on the counter, playfully trapping Stella between her arms. Stella kissed her once and twisted out of Olive's arms. Olive sat on the counter with her eggs and mug beside her and enjoyed the view of Stella bending over to pick up a couple of stray pieces of green pepper.

Olive grinned. "You know I think you're hot."

"That doesn't mean I don't want to hear you say it."

The voice. That bedroom voice that turned Olive's purple cotton underwear into a puddle. It was back again.

Olive grabbed Stella's hands and pulled her closer. "You're hot. And sexy. And gorgeous."

Stella gave tiny flirtatious nods after each compliment.

"We never actually finished that conversation about whether friends can kiss." Olive drew closer to Stella, letting her breath flutter against the delicate hairs escaping Stella's ponytail.

"I think they can kiss." Stella was breathless as she spoke. "If that's okay with you. You were sick before, so it didn't seem like the time . . ."

"I like kissing you." Understatement. Olive leaned in but then pulled her lips away from Stella's at the last moment in favor of trailing down her jawline to her neck.

"Same."

"That last make-out session earned top grades." She kissed the notch of Stella's collarbone. Then her chin. "A plus for technique."

Stella pulled Olive's mouth to hers, practically knocking Olive over with the force of the kiss. Olive's hands moved from the countertop, to grip Stella's soft hips. One slid upward, teasing at the bottom of Stella's sweatshirt until a tiny nod encouraged it to keep moving.

Olive traced the curve of Stella's ribs as she pulled away from the kiss. Her finger followed along Stella's ribs to the soft skin between sternum and navel. She closed her eyes, listening for the answer. "So . . . can friends do more than kiss?"

"Yes."

Oh shit. Okay.

Olive's finger hooked beneath the hem of Stella's pants, pulling their bodies flush together once more. Her hand shifted around to cup Stella's ass. A soft urgent sound left Stella and she braced a hand against the counter, causing her coffee mug to shudder and spill a splash over the granite.

Stella's eyes darted as if she wanted to grab a rag.

Olive grabbed her hips. "Leave it, please."

"But . . ."

"Please." Olive's words were soft. They hummed against Stella's mouth. There was a question there. Stella gave a tiny nod.

Olive's legs straddled Stella's waist, her inner thighs feeling the curve of Stella's hip bones. Stella reached for Olive's pants, the tips of her fingers slipping beneath the waistband farther this time.

Their eyes met. The fire in Stella's reflecting the heat that was certainly in Olive's own.

"Do you want to do this?" Stella murmured. "Really, do this?"

"Yes." Olive's gaze settled between them; she watched her hand as it dipped further, so teasingly close. Watching Stella's breath catch with each inch nearer. "Do you?"

"Oh my god, yes." Stella crushed Olive into a kiss.

Chapter 39

Despite the fantasies Olive had about fucking Stella on pretty much every surface of her apartment, she'd rather start with a bed. No matter what happens in romance novels, the cold granite counter isn't the most comfortable surface against bare skin despite how those first teasing touches had gone over. Stella seemed to be thinking along the same lines because she pulled Olive to the bedroom, kissing her every step of the way. She pushed her gently toward the bed and reached for the drawstring of her hoodie.

Stella pulled off Olive's sweatshirt. When she found that there was nothing underneath, her movements became more frantic than Olive had ever seen them. Her hands settled on the tie on Olive's sweatpants. "Is this okay with you?"

"Yes."

Oh my god. Oh my god. Oh my god. The words echoed in Olive's brain.

Stella pulled on the tie, loosening the knot with her deft fingers. A warmth between Olive's legs told her she'd be ready for absolutely anything Stella had in mind. Stella's perfect mouth trailed down her neck and along her collarbone. The pants slid off her in a single movement. Her teeth grazed the bone, leaving a small tinge of pain that was unbelievably perfect and infuriating.

"More please," Olive whispered.

"Wait." That throaty guttural voice was back.

Olive's leg pressed at Stella's waist, hoping to urge her to touch her, lick her, bite her, fucking anything at this point. The cool air of the room caused her nipples to peak and her breasts to ache with need. Goose bumps rose on her skin.

"Stella." It was a moan, nothing but a low moan.

Stella's body moved downward, crawling and kissing, her perfect soft stomach settling over the parts of Olive most wet and wild with desire. And then she started with Olive's tits. She pulled a nipple into her mouth, sucking one while her fingers pinched and flicked the other.

"Oh my god."

Fuck. Olive could almost come just from this. She'd never been that into nipple stuff before, but she was quickly realizing that it'd never been done like this.

"I know you like this because you make the most amazing sounds when I touch you here. So responsive." Stella's voice was almost a purr. "I would fuck your tits. They're so damn perfect." As if to illustrate the point she licked around the shell-pink edge of Olive's nipple.

Stella was into the dirty talk. Unexpected, but Olive was absolutely here for it.

"Yeah?" The vibration of Stella's throat had another pulse of arousal heating her. "What else do you want to fuck, Stella?"

"Everything."

"Everything?" Olive breathed.

"Your mouth. Everywhere. But we'll start with this." The fingers that had been so deft at rubbing the tension from Olive's chest when she was sick now slid down between her folds. "You're so wet."

She nodded, tangling her hands in Stella's shiny dark hair.

Stella's fingers explored her, now saturated with slickness. She began to circle Olive's clit. Sliding them along the tender places, and Olive lifted her hips to find more friction.

Olive gasped. "Oh god."

"First . . ." Stella nudged what felt like two fingers against her entrance, opening her in a way that let the coolness of the room into the soaked depths there. "Is this okay?"

"Yes. Literally anything. Please, Stella." She arched toward her again.

Stella refused to be hurried. Her other hand traced the outline of Olive's hip. Her eyes were on Olive's pussy in a way that made Olive want to immediately fall apart beneath her. She looked hungry for her.

Stella shifted her weight and pushed inside her, reaching toward her G-spot.

Olive jerked, arching with her head tilting back. Stella pushed upward again, kissing her exposed throat before plunging her fingers in deeper.

She pulled out again, bringing her fingers back to circle on that tiny bundle of nerves at her center while Stella's perfect mouth returned to her breasts. "Right here?"

"Yes."

She flicked and alternated between slow and quick movement. It was exactly what Olive needed. Leisurely and intoxicatingly hot.

None of the impatience she'd experienced from other lovers. Time had no meaning.

Stella's long hair had fallen loose. It brushed over Olive's breasts in a heavenly sweep. It was all almost too much. The ache became a tingle she felt all the way down to her curling toes.

Olive's breaths quickened.

"Come," Stella said in that low voice, laced with sultry command.

"I'm com—"

The words turned into a high-pitched scream of pleasure, hips bucking, heart racing as Stella urged her to more, leading her through the aftershocks of the orgasm in a way that nearly had Olive delirious.

"Jesus," Olive panted.

"You're stunningly beautiful."

Almost drunkenly, Olive sat up. "I want to see you."

Stella only wore a spaghetti-strap bralette beneath her fitted hoodie. Her nipples were hard and pushing against the thin fabric. Olive ran a hand over one, loving the tiny moan Stella made at her touch. She bent forward and sucked at the cotton, letting her other hand wander down.

"Oh my god," Stella breathed.

"Are you still okay?"

"Yes." All raspy and deep.

Olive slid down, kissing her ribs, her navel. Her soft skin right below her bikini line. She pushed her hands beneath the elastic band, gripping Stella's thighs. Olive traced the lacy edging of Stella's black bralette, making her shiver. "This is pretty."

"Oh?"

"But not as pretty as your tits." Olive eased Stella's bralette over her head and nearly gasped at the perfection before her. She licked one of the soft brown nipples while teasing the other between her thumb and index finger. Stella's pelvis arched, pressing into her.

"You could have seen them any time you wanted."

Olive would contemplate that statement later. Holy shit.

Olive grabbed the top of Stella's pants. Stella nodded, and Olive pulled them down. In a moment, Stella was on the bed. Olive knelt in front of Stella, her knees digging into the soft rug beside the bed. If there had been any doubt of whether Stella wanted this too, it was gone now. Stella inched toward her, almost breathless with need. Olive opened her slowly, feeling how desire was flooding every inch of the soft skin there. She stroked her, while Stella's long beautiful legs bowed out on either side.

Stella whispered her name.

Olive kissed along her smooth thighs. On one leg. Then the other.

She dragged her tongue over Stella's clit. Once. Twice. Stella's legs began to fold in, but Olive eased them back open. She sucked over the bundle of nerves. Stella's breasts heaved, that lovely bounce building the ache between Olive's own legs.

"Yes. Please," Stella breathed. "There."

Olive's fingers had been softly caressing her hips. She lifted her head long enough to see the ecstatic expression on Stella's face. The way her full lips parted. Her eyes half shut. She coated her fingers and teased at Stella's entrance.

"What do you want, Stella?" She said the word with her mouth on Stella's clit, flicking the tip of her tongue against it with each word. She tasted fantastic.

"I want you inside me."

"Aye, aye, captain."

Stella laughed. "Shut up and fuck me."

"With pleasure."

Olive pushed into her, curling her fingers deeply. Stella arched toward her.

Fuck.

Olive's own pussy was tingling so much, she could almost come from feeling Stella's reactions to her. She worked Stella with her tongue and fingertips against the silky deep places.

Tinier gasps now. High-pitched and sweet. Olive slowed her fingers and then started them again, reacting to every nuance of the way Stella's beautiful folds clenched around her. A loud cry filled the room. Stella's body bucking, thrashing, and grinding against Olive's fingers and mouth.

"On top of me, now, please."

How could she already be aching for more? Stella crawled down Olive's body, leaving her pussy open to Olive, her knees on either side of Olive's waist.

Okay, this woman was hot from literally every single angle.

"You even taste perfect, Olive." Stella's tongue swept up along her center.

"Holy fuck." Olive's mouth was almost too dry to speak. Still tasting Stella on her own tongue. She reached up and pushed her fingers into Stella once more. She probed her deep places as Stella fucked her with her mouth.

"Jesus Christ."

Stella's hips were moving against her, urging her on. Olive was moving too. She could barely think. The world blurred. Instinct took over, fueled by need. And then Stella's fingers were on her clit again, in a quick, intoxicating rhythm.

"Olive, don't stop." Stella contracted around Olive's fingers once more.

Her own body was on the brink too.

She felt Stella's eruption against her own. She held on to Stella's legs as if they were the only thing preventing her from levitating into the air. "Fuck." Her legs were around Stella's head as she moved through the continuous waves. Crash after crash of pleasure surging into every part of her. Stella hadn't stopped moving either. Hadn't stopped licking and sucking. And the wave Olive thought was the end was simply a precipice of another peak.

"Oh my god." She came again. Her whole body trembling. Spots popped out in her vision. Tears coming to the edges of her eyes. "Stella."

When Olive's body was still again, Stella came up and kissed her.

She rested her head on Olive's chest, and with her other hand she pulled the comforter over them both.

Chapter 40

Olive grinned at Stella and drew the comforter up over their heads to burrow them both in warmth. The bed was a disastrously crumpled mass of blankets. Stella must have been sex-addled as fuck because she hadn't tried to make the bed any of the times they'd rolled out of it. A reasonable efficiency of effort, since they had been in bed for the better part of the two days since the magazine article came out. Stella had gone home several times to check in with her father and Olive had walked Gus, but otherwise they'd been happily cloistered in this room.

Olive woke in Stella's arms. This was quickly becoming the only way Olive ever wanted to wake up.

Moonlight peeked through the curtains, the rustling shadows of trees the only movement in the room.

It was still dark outside, but Olive would have to get out of bed soon. She already dreaded leaving the warmth of Stella's soft body. Stella wasn't flying today, but she did have some lessons scheduled for later. Olive had to work. *Womp womp.*

With regret, Olive wriggled out of the covers, trying not to disturb Stella from sleep. Stella turned over with her eyes still closed and found Gus. She nuzzled her beautiful face into his fur.

Sleep cuddler, indeed.

After Olive was cleaned up for work, the smell of coffee hit her as she opened the bathroom door. The bed was neatly made and empty of either animal or human. Stella stood at the kitchen counter wearing an oversized sweatshirt and tiny, thin red shorts that barely covered her perfect ass. She spun around and held out Olive's favorite mug.

"Morning." She was wearing her glasses, dark brown hair twisted into a wild ponytail. Eyes still slightly hooded from sleep.

God, she was beautiful.

"Thank you," Olive said, accepting the coffee and checking her watch. She was actually on time since Stella had volunteered to walk Gus this morning. Gus was smitten with Stella. And in a curious way, this made Olive think Jake would have adored Stella too.

Olive reached down to pet behind his floppy ears, and he licked her nose. "Hey, buddy."

"My dad wanted to know if I could bring Gus over again today after my lessons."

Stella had shocked Olive by letting Gus decorate the back of her car with dog fur. Olive had covered the seats in an old sheet, but they were still furry just from the one car ride yesterday. Stella didn't seem to mind, but she did mention investing in a shop vac at one point.

"Always. You're going to spoil him with all this attention during the day. He's used to just having the dog walkers come."

Stella kneeled beside the dog, who immediately rolled onto his back to demand tummy rubs. If her hand stopped moving, he nudged her with his nose. "How can I resist this sweet face?"

The look on Gus's face was sloppy adoration.

"You still want to come over tonight?"

"Yep." Stella nodded. "You get home by eight?"

Olive yawned. "Uh-huh." She took a few more gulps of the coffee while locked in a stare with the beautiful woman in front of her.

"Shouldn't you be . . . ?"

"Yeah. Leaving. Right."

"You okay?" Stella stroked a finger across Olive's forehead, as if to ask about the thoughts swirling there.

"Just tired."

"It's amazing to me that you get up this early for work and you aren't a morning person."

Olive nodded with half-asleep eyes. "Me too." Olive touched Stella's cheek and guided her into a kiss. "Thank you for walking Gus."

"Anytime." Stella grinned.

An alarm went off on Olive's phone, and she grabbed her travel mug of coffee and headed out the door.

When she arrived, Derek was already there, since he was the charge nurse today.

Their department's scary director was nosing around the unit. Olive moved all the nurses' water bottles and coffee mugs to the break room, since this particular director tended to pick out a nurse and yell at them over something petty when she was in a foul mood. Olive used to love working nights because she never had to deal with management, but after everything with Jake and adopting Gus, she'd moved to days. At least she got to work with Derek more.

The less-experienced nurses knew the drill by now. Hide from Mrs. Crawley and always find something to do that would allow you to look busy.

Olive had come out of a patient room when Mrs. Crawley cornered her. "Hello, Ms. Murphy. Haven't gotten the pleasure of seeing you for a while."

Olive avoided saying that it was because it was a universally acknowledged truth that Mrs. Crawley was afraid of both patients and germs; thus she found the emergency department deeply unsettling. No one knew how she'd gotten her job. Rumors abounded on that particular subject.

"Uh—yeah, nice to see you too." Olive was, of course, holding a handful of blood specimen tubes in a biohazard bag.

Mrs. Crawley's mane of tightly permed auburn curls didn't

move as she angled her head, nose creasing in disgust. "Why don't you get rid of those, and we can chat. And please wash your hands as well."

Olive was glad her face was hidden behind a mask, so it would hide her sarcastic scowl. "All righty."

She slid the bag into the pneumatic tube transport system with gritted teeth. She washed her hands because, of course, she was going to wash her hands. She washed her hands several million times a day. All nurses did.

Olive headed back to the nurses' station. Mrs. Crawley looked incredibly odd sitting in a swivel chair. She was better suited to the large leather monstrosities used in movies whenever an evil businessperson is canceling Christmas.

"The executive board wanted me to come say thank you."

"Thank you?"

"For being so positive about the hospital in the *People* magazine article and on the *TODAY* show."

"Oh." Olive relaxed a bit, and sat in the chair beside Mrs. Crawley. "You're welcome."

"The organization especially wanted me to come make it clear to you that your *partner* would be welcome at any of the hospital holiday events. There are exciting things happening because of your story." She affected a conspiratorial voice. "We're even in talks with the Disney company on coming here to give a seminar on customer service."

"Customer service?"

"To help improve what you all do here every day."

"Nursing?" The idea of nurses being mainly in the business of customer service seemed to be fairly pervasive at the executive level. Wonderful.

"Exactly." She gave a little wink. "So we'd love for your partner to come to our events. She just exudes that right attitude. Something about your two faces made a couple very, very generous"— she dropped into a raspy whisper—"VIP guests offer to donate a sizable amount. We've decided to use the money to refurbish the fish tank in the waiting room. Isn't that wonderful?"

"For the fish, I guess?"

"Always those extra ways to make our guests feel welcomed here. Helps bring the right sort of people in our doors."

"Patients?"

"Same thing. So will you be attending?"

Olive forced a smile to cover her internal cringe. The hospital holiday events were generally potluck and awkward, so she and Derek usually opted for taking the staff to a local pub instead. "Thanks. I—uh—think I have to work that night." If she didn't, she'd make sure she had another excuse, but something about the conversation made her feel bold enough to ask a question. "Any chance any of the generous donations will be making it possible to increase pay for the staff nurses here, because compared to other area hospitals—"

"We have a few big retention events planned. Don't you worry yourself about that."

"Events?"

"Pizza parties are always a huge hit."

"Sure, but—"

"Well, let me know if I can do anything for you. I hope things are going well with you and . . ."

"Stella."

"Yes, that's right." Mrs. Crawley patted her on the shoulder. "Very nice chatting with you."

Olive swiveled to face her computer. A million thoughts cascaded through her head. *Would* she have invited Stella to the work holiday event? It was a few days after Stella's holiday party. The black cloud over her future beyond the party seemed to billow like an opaque taunt.

Derek plopped into the chair beside her. "What'd Crawley want?"

"To thank me for not shit-talking the organization and to

make sure I knew Stella was invited to holiday events. And to say a few other things that I'd tell you, but your head would explode."

"Already heard about the fish tank." Derek gave a noncommittal nod and faced his own computer. A few minutes later, he spoke again without taking his eyes off the screen. "So, what *do* you think will happen between you and Stella after her work holiday thing? And where have you been the past few days? More Stella time?"

"Uh, so . . ."

Just at that moment, Lindsay came around the corner. Her mouth was a smug smile. "Derek, I'm surprised you're encouraging Olive to be this delusional about this woman."

"Lindsay, when are you going to take a goddamn hint," Derek said.

"I have Olive's best interest at heart, and you're just enabling her." Lindsay's hands went to her hips. "It's pathetic."

"Can you stop talking about me like I'm not here?" Olive stepped forward and put a hand on Derek's shoulder. He didn't need to fight this battle for her.

"Leave Olive and her relationship alone. None of your business."

"She doesn't have a relationship. Can you just stop lying. Has she actually gone *crazy* this time?" Lindsay pushed the curtain of her shag bangs out of her face. Her lip curling in a scowl. When neither Derek nor Olive spoke again, opting instead for cold silence, she huffed. Her attention went back to Derek. "Olive's just going to get herself hurt again when this psycho pilot breaks her heart. Some fucking best friend you are. Someone has to do something . . ." She stormed off.

Olive rolled her eyes and gestured to her body. "Again, I was right here."

"Maybe your Lindsay cloaking device finally kicked on."

"If fucking only." Olive focused on the double doors to the

hallway that led to the ICU elevators. "She's not going to legitimately try to fuck things up for me, right?"

He shrugged.

"*Right?*"

Derek frowned. "Like do what? Key your car? Make a slam book? This isn't high school. What could she do?"

"I don't know. She just seems really angry."

"Given how Stella handled it the last time Lindsay tried to butt in, I can't imagine her trying that again. People here were talking about her little scene at the bar."

"I think she heard me and Stella talking outside after."

Derek shrugged. "She'll get bored and move on. Don't let her get in your head. It's what she wants. More attention. You and Stella are still just friends, right?"

Olive affected the most innocent of angelic expressions. She led him into an unoccupied patient room. She grimaced. "Right, so about that."

"Olivia . . ."

"We slept together. Surprise." Olive did that same small jazz hands motion she had weeks earlier as Derek palmed his face.

Chapter 41

"I don't want to get up," Stella said in an adorable faux whine, rolling over and wrapping herself around Olive.

Olive pressed her lips to Stella's. "I don't want to either."

Gus had taken over half the bed. Stella was more of a push-over and a lot more vulnerable to Gus's whimpering. Stella had spent half her nights the last two weeks in Olive's apartment when she was in town. The others Stella slept at home, since some days her dad's caregivers came later than others. Stella and Olive had been up late last night because Stella insisted they go out after dinner to buy a small Christmas tree for the corner of Olive's apartment living room. They decorated it together, and Stella spent hours making sure the ornaments were distributed evenly.

"So, bed all day then?" Stella said with a pointed snuggle. They had some variation of this conversation multiple times on every morning they had spent together that neither of them had to go to work. For someone as type A and driven as Stella, she sure seemed content to spend a lot of hours lazing in bed. Olive had zero complaints, given the various ways Stella had been channeling her eagerness.

Gus rolled over, collapsing the makeshift tent over their heads and disrupting the moment. He was obsessed with Stella. She seemed likewise enamored of the oversized fur creature. He nudged his head under her hand.

"Real subtle, Gus," Olive said as she stretched.

"He's such a good boy." Stella scratched behind his floppy ears.

284 * Andie Burke

"He sure is."

"Oh, my dog walker wanted to verify that you could still come tomorrow . . . No pressure if—"

Stella kissed her. "Absolutely. I'll drop the big guy off later and leave the key with your neighbor again?"

"Oh. Yeah. Right." Olive stifled a frown. Stella had been clear that anytime she used Olive's spare key it was just *borrowing* it. "Neighbor would be good. She works from home, so she's usually around. Good plan."

Just stop talking, Olive.

After a few more minutes cuddling, Olive couldn't ignore her bladder anymore. They had drunk a lot of Christmas cheer last night. Olive rolled out of bed, hating the coldness of the room assaulting her bare skin. She grabbed a throw blanket that was half draped on the end of the bed and wrapped it around herself like a cloak. "It's so cold."

"Agree. Come back." Stella patted the place beside her on the bed.

Evidence of Stella was everywhere. Her lotions and travel-sized toiletries all lined up. Neatly, of course. Despite Stella's fastidiousness about order and cleanliness, she didn't seem to mind Olive's relative chaos. They functioned together perfectly. Shouldn't this be harder?

They bickered and bantered about stupid things, but it wasn't like having Lindsay around. Olive wasn't always worried about ruining everything by screwing up. She'd stopped worrying about being too needy because it all felt . . . easy. The only time she worried at all was when she remembered that the *reason* everything was easy was because it wasn't a real relationship. Despite all the shit happening with her brother, she felt happy.

Olive opened her nightstand drawer and then smirked at Stella. "How about we shower together instead."

Stella straightened, reading the suggestive angle of Olive's mouth correctly. "I think that sounds like a very good idea."

✳✳✳

They'd both lost track of time. Again. Hot water glistened down Olive's torso, over her ribs and the swell of her abdomen. The cool tile pressed against her spine.

"I feel like you should write a detailed review on Yelp for this apartment building," Stella said from where she was positioned on her knees.

"Should I?" Olive muttered.

"Yes. This is very important. The public needs to know how nice this bathroom is." Stella brushed tender yet teasing kisses across Olive's pelvis. Her eyebrow cocked wickedly as she adjusted the angle on the vibrator inside Olive.

Gasping, Olive leaned her head back, eyes shutting. Her back arched off the wall. "How should I start the review?" Her words came out haltingly.

"Luxury bathrooms. Perfect amount of space for mind-blowing cunnilingus. Tile is not too hard against the knees. Water pressure is good for stimulating sensitive areas." Stella's voice was low and almost as erotic as what her hands were doing with the toy.

"*Oh god.*" Olive moaned once. "How about you keep doing that, and I'll write the review later. Mind-blowing. Awful confident, are we?"

"I'm pretty sure you like this." Stella's tongue began to explore as if to demonstrate the point.

Olive tangled her fingers in Stella's wet hair. "What was your first clue?"

"The way you screamed the first time I started doing it. I suspect you'll be screaming louder since we added your old friend to the mix this time." Stella pushed Olive's legs wider, spreading her in every possible way before leaning down.

"I'm glad Alyson is waterproof." Stella chuckled. The slight shudder against Olive's clit made stars flash in her vision.

"Oh god—ah. Me too." Olive's eyes closed. *"Shit."*

Stella sucked on that throbbing spot between Olive's legs. Every movement of Stella's mouth had Olive whispering curses. Her hips thrust forward to meet Stella, urging her to keep going. Keep going. God, please keep going. Time seemed to shudder as they moved together. Stella gave her exactly what she needed, where she needed it. The vibration pulsed deep inside Olive, the sensation almost too much. It built and built until every cell in Olive's body cried out in another release.

Olive almost blacked out, and as Stella predicted, her screaming was probably loud enough to provoke a noise complaint.

Stella eased the vibrator out of her and clicked it off. Olive shuddered at the sudden empty feeling.

"I should put the Yelp review in soon, so that it goes in before the obituary." Olive leaned back into the tile and shut her eyes.

"Obituary?"

"Woman fucked so well in a bathroom that she hit her head on the tile and died of a mind-blowingly amazing orgasm."

Stella tutted mournfully. "Such a tragedy that would be."

Olive wrapped herself around Stella, hugging her tightly and enjoying the soft press of Stella's breasts and nipples against her upper chest while the hot water flowed over them both. "That was amazing." She kissed Stella, her teeth tugging on her bottom lip.

Stella leaned her forehead against Olive's. "What were we supposed to be doing?"

"Showering."

"Check."

"Three cumulative orgasms between us is lovely, but we should probably also do normal shower things. Like clean ourselves."

Stella cupped Olive's breasts. "I'll start here."

Olive laughed and grabbed her body wash and held it out to Stella. "Wash, then lunch."

"Okay." Stella smiled and offered a mocking salute.

Olive was mesmerized as the bubbles and water slid over Stella's perfect curves. "You really like to play up the pilot captain thing, don't you? I'd complain, but it's led me to discover many new things about myself."

"Like what?" Stella got a glazed look on her face, her deft fingers moving in a slightly slower lathering motion.

"Like how much I want to peel your uniform off you and tie you to the bed with one of those neckties you wear. Or use it as a blindfold. I have many, many ideas."

"I'm glad I'm sleeping with someone with such a creative imagination. You're putting that art history degree to work."

Sleeping with. Not girlfriends with. Was that intentional? Dropping that in to remind Olive that only part of this was real? The rest a mutually satisfying friendship. And fuck, Olive was satisfied. Her lady parts would probably be aching for days. The happy pain reminding her of the time they'd spent in bed. On the couch. On the floor. And in the shower.

Friends.

Friends who were attracted to each other and wanted constant sex. It was a natural thing. Casual. No commitment beyond the last work event a couple of weeks away right before Christmas. They hadn't talked about what it would mean when it was over yet. They hadn't talked about anything relationship-wise since Olive's pneumonia.

Olive frowned for a second, but Stella kissed the drooping corners of her mouth. "I know you're hungry." She passed her a bottle. "Shampoo, Olive. Then I really am going to buy you lunch."

Olive blinked and wiped the water from her eyes. "We can never shower together if we have to be somewhere on time."

"Good thinking."

They finished their shower, and then toweled off. They shared a couple of kisses tasting of toothpaste before Olive headed to her closet to find clothes. Stella's things were still out in the living room.

Olive pulled on her clothes, dusted her face with a small amount of makeup, and ended with a sweep of mascara.

Her phone was still plugged in on the nightstand, and it was vibrating. A sinking sensation dropped into her pelvis at the name flashing on the screen. This wasn't good. She swiped to answer.

"What's up, Morgan?"

"You told me to call you if anything changed."

Olive's legs shook, and she sank down onto the bed. "What's wrong?"

"Can you come in today? The doc here wants to call your family in for an emergency meeting."

Her face screwed up with tension. "Is everything . . ."

"Let's talk when you get here, okay?"

"I'll be there as soon as I can."

The past two weeks had been too damn perfect to last.

Chapter 42

Stella opened the door. "What's wrong?"

"My brother." Olive covered her face, a chill shaking her shoulders. "I just got a call from his facility."

"What happened?" Tender concern lined her face.

"I don't know. They're calling us in for an emergency family meeting."

"What does that mean?"

"He might have taken a turn for the worse. Or they might have gotten some new test results. I don't know."

Stella wrapped an arm around Olive. "Do you want to tell me more about him and what's going on with your family? I know you haven't been ready before, but I know he was important to you. I know about the video, but there's more, right?" Her eyes were round and questioning without being intrusive.

"Jake . . . Jake was this enormous teddy bear. He was six foot seven. Hockey player. A goalie, actually. He was the best older brother. Overprotective but not in a toxic way. Just in a . . . I-knew-he-cared way. He was also good at everything. My younger sister is similar. Type A. Perfect grades. He was an engineer and built planes, but I think I told you that." Olive blinked several times, scrunching her face and then relaxing it. "I used to make him laugh by refusing to understand about how planes work." Olive gave a watery laugh. "I'd say it was magic." Olive was pretty sure she was repeating herself, but her brain was functioning like a rusty gear.

Stella shook her head and brushed away a tear from Olive's cheek.

"He had this health scare. It was really bad because he lived alone and his cleaning lady found him passed out. He ended up being fine, but I guess it scared him. He said he had an epiphany and made this list."

"Do something impulsive," Stella quoted. "And the national parks."

"Exactly. So, he started doing all these really amazing things. He had always worked too much and never had a steady partner. Afterward he made so many changes. Started putting down roots. He joined this adult hockey league and then started running to cross-train. When he signed up for the Disney half-marathon, I said I'd run it with him, but I got scared and flaked on him." Not a great time to mention that Lindsay had psyched Olive out so much about training and pace that she lost all confidence and canceled last minute.

"It's a lot of training," Stella said sympathetically.

"It is. But I felt awful about it. He made the reservations for the fancy Disney hotel the next year—this year—to make sure I didn't change my mind about training. And because he just liked hanging out with me, and we had a ton of great memories at Disney as kids."

"What a good brother."

"He was."

Stella was quiet. She tightened her grip on Olive's shoulders and kissed her damp hair.

"This might be too much to ask, but do you . . . do you mind driving me to see him? I . . . I just have a bad feeling about today."

"Of course not."

Shit. Was that Olive's neediness? Was that exactly the type of thing that would scare Stella away?

Stella pushed the wild tendrils of hair out of Olive's face. "Whatever you're thinking right now . . . I'm glad you asked me to take you."

Olive gave Stella a quizzical look.

Stella nodded.

After they finished getting dressed, they grabbed their stuff and headed out to Stella's car. Stella turned on Olive's favorite music and then Olive put the address for the care facility into her phone.

"What else was on Jake's list?" Stella's voice was more tentative than usual.

"Do something spontaneous. Run a half-marathon. Do something that scares me. Make a difference in someone's life. Go mountain climbing. Visit all the national parks. Go whitewater rafting. Do karaoke—I'd rather die before singing in a room full of people. So not sure that's ever getting checked off. Figure out what I really want and not be afraid to ask for it. There was other stuff too, like adopt a dog. That's when he got Gus and started doing less work travel. It was a long list."

"Sounds like a good one."

"So . . . the full story on what happened to him." Olive leaned forward, bracing her head on the window. "He was training one day—running outside on one of those weirdly warm winter days. It was a Saturday afternoon, and he saw a kid run out in the street in front of a car after a ball. He was always incredibly fast despite being a big guy. Never lost the hockey reflexes. He pushed the kid out of the way. A ring camera caught it. That's how it went viral. I . . ." Olive's voice shook. "I saw the video." She rubbed her eyes. "My sister did too."

"Oh my god."

"The car hit him. He was thrown. He had a traumatic brain injury—a bad one. Spinal injury too. Paralyzed from the neck down. After a few weeks, well, at first, we *all* thought he'd wake up. But then, the doctors ran some more tests and said he'd never recover."

"I'm so sorry, Olive." She gripped the steering wheel harder. Olive was glad they were in the car. She didn't know if she could get the rest of the story out with Stella making eye contact. All the details of the fight with her family spilled out as Olive focused on the wall of trees outside the window. Stella didn't speak. She listened. Brandi Carlile sang low in the speakers as the car flew over the back roads that would take them to Jake's facility. They passed cows and horses roaming over winter grass pastures beneath a crisp blue sky. Olive took a couple of deep breaths before continuing, her exhales clouding the window glass.

"God, Olive, that's horrible."

"My mom's Catholic. She had this extreme reaction to the idea of withdrawing care even though I know it's what he would have wanted, but she got lawyers involved and made it seem like I had a conflict of interest, but it's all just because she seems like she believes there's a chance of some supernatural recovery." The coolness of the glass was soothing against Olive's forehead. "She acted like I was Kevorkian or something . . . but I just didn't want Jake to suffer more." Tears slid down Olive's face too quickly to be wiped away subtly. "He'd want to die peacefully if there were no other options."

Stella pulled over to the side of the road, the car bouncing over a couple of potholes. She handed over a package of tissues from the center console and rubbed Olive's lower back.

"I'm sorry. This is why I don't talk about this. I really wanted to honor his wishes, but I couldn't. I failed. I failed him for flaking on the stupid race. And I failed him when it really, really mattered."

"Olive, you were trying to be a good sister to him. No one would blame you for that."

"I can't imagine what it's like for my parents to lose their son. But I lost my brother. I wanted him back." Her voice shattered on the last word. "Everything in my family fell apart. Everyone sided against me."

Stella wrapped her arms around Olive. "I'm sorry."

Olive wiped her nose on a lump of tissues. "I know too much. Being a nurse sucks sometimes, and I have to watch him waste away, knowing he'd never have wanted this. Knowing he'd be angry as fuck at me for not fighting harder against my mom."

"He'd understand. You did all you could."

"I tried. I really did. My parents aren't rich, but they have more money than me. I couldn't fight her lawyers." She sniffed. "Oh, and with the video, before everything was going on with my parents, the family of the kid he pushed out of the way put the story online—what Jake did in saving his life. But trolls being trolls, someone found out that Jake had a DUI ten years before when he was really depressed. They also found some old profile photos of his from a gay dating website, and everything got so horrible I had to shut down all his accounts. He became a meme. It wasn't really known he was on life support. Cruel people saying cruel things. It was *a lot.*"

"I can't imagine."

"I—It was a really bad time."

She kissed Olive's forehead. "I'll come inside with you, if you want. You shouldn't have to do this all alone."

Olive rubbed her cheeks, opening her eyes wide to will away the tears. "Fuck, I just wasn't prepared to deal with my mom today . . ." Olive sighed. "You don't have to come, though. I know this can be a lot for some people. I can just—"

Stella shook her head. "I'm coming."

"Thank you."

"It's what friends are for. Do you usually go alone?" Stella pulled back onto the road; they were only a few more minutes away.

"Derek comes with me sometimes. He'd kill me for telling you this, but he had a major crush on my brother growing up— like when he was this star high school hockey player and we were in junior high. He was also upset that my parents weren't honoring Jake's wishes."

Stella flicked on the blinker and then turned into the facility parking lot. "I'm glad you have someone to go with. It's not fair for no one to be on your side. You were fighting for what Jake wanted."

Something about hearing Stella support her. Hearing Stella say Jake's name. It made the burden Olive was carrying feel slightly lighter.

"I'm glad you're coming with me today."

Stella took Olive's hand in hers. Her fingers were a soft, comforting presence.

After a few more moments of silence, they both got out of the car.

As she led Stella through the familiar double doors, everyone waved to Olive. Signs of Christmas decorated the lobby: a garland and twinkle lights. The extra sparkle and color gave an odd sense of artificial homeyness, almost unsettling.

Olive paused when she reached Jake's hallway. "He's back here. You're sure?"

"Yes. Goodness, Olive. I'm fine. Stop trying to take care of me and let me be here for you." She hugged her.

Olive buried her nose in Stella's hair and inhaled. "Okay."

She pulled away and led her down to her brother's room. The room was bright with sunlight coming in through the window. Her mother must have been here recently because a small fake poinsettia decorated the tiny table beside the bed along with a host of Christmas cards, probably from Olive's parents' parish.

Stella stood close, her hand hovering near Olive's elbow. There was pity on her face, but it was steeped in kind concern. She wasn't disgusted or scared.

Olive brushed hair out of her brother's face. She'd need to cut it soon. She checked his fingernails to see if they needed to be filed again. Her scan faltered as she took in his appearance overall. Small muscles tensing as her hands curled into fists. He had lost weight. Overall, his color was even worse than when she'd visited three days ago. She hadn't been imagining the ashen tint to his skin before.

"Is that your medal?" Stella's eyes were on the bulletin board behind the bed.

"Yes. His is behind it."

"Did you put up all these photos and posters? You printed all the ones from your Instagram account of you and Gus?"

"Yeah. My sister and mom brought in a lot of photos too."

She touched one of the photos of Jake with Gus. There were so many photos with the entire Murphy family together. There were even a couple of childhood photos of Jake and Olive on the St. Rose's church stage together. Her mom must have added those as an extra dig. "Is this your mom?" Stella pointed to the photo of her mom bringing a molded pound cake with an absurd number of candles and whipped cream to put in front of Jake. Toddler Fiona had insisted Jake wear a party hat. "Is that the same cake?"

"Yeah. My mom and I tried out a bunch of gluten-free ones to figure out which would be good. That was Jake's first birthday after he found out about the celiac."

"You and your mom baked together?"

"Yeah. A lot back then. We weren't super close or anything, but we did cakes together a lot for the family . . . especially after Fiona was born." Cody's first-birthday party was next week, and her sister had still not gotten back to her about when she could come over to see them. Her mom probably already had a plan for his cake for the party.

She brought up a finger to trail along the newest additions to the board, seeing where Olive was conspicuously absent without commenting on the change. She scanned all of the decorations giving the room color. "I love those photos of you traveling. Doing all the things on his list?"

After a polite knock, Morgan entered. "Hey, Olive." She hugged her.

"Thanks for calling. Stella, this is my friend Morgan from nursing school. She works here."

"Nice to meet you." They shook hands, and then Morgan focused on Jake. "I wanted you to get here so we could talk before anyone else showed up."

Olive sat in the chair by the window. Her legs had been shaking beneath her. "What's wrong?"

"We have some new results from that doctor your mom called. And we have reason to believe Jake's declining."

She handed over a manila folder. "Do you want me to go over it with you?"

After opening it and reading over the first few pages, Olive shook her head. No surprises there. "No. I just need to think." She pulled the chair up beside Jake.

"I'll be back to check in with you in a few minutes, okay?"

"Thanks, Morgan." Olive folded her hands together, squeezing them into a tight ball. A warm, soft hand covered hers. She looked up. She'd almost forgotten she wasn't alone now. "You know, I don't ever hold his hand." Olive focused on her brother. She hadn't held his hand since she dropped it that day in the ICU. "My mom and Heather always do. It felt weird. When I'm here, he's always in my head telling me what he thinks."

Stella stroked Olive's knuckles with her thumb.

"I'm glad Morgan works here. She gets it. She tells me what's going on, and I know she doesn't believe what I'm sure my mom says about me."

"Your mom . . ."

Olive's mouth tightened. "I know she's just hurting too. But it kills me, what she's doing. She's choosing to cling to the memory of my brother over listening to me. I understand it." Something constricted in her throat, but she forced the words out. "I really do. I wish I could blame her for it. But honestly, I'd pick Jake over me too." Her eyes couldn't blink quickly enough to keep them clear of what was brimming. "She needs someone to blame. And if this is really the e-end . . ."

Stella didn't speak.

She wrapped Olive into her arms and held her as she cried.

A knock came on the door. Olive wiped away her tears and straightened as Morgan came back into the room.

"The front desk just called. Your mom and sister are here."

Olive gave Stella a questioning look. "I can get a ride home with Heather maybe."

"I'm staying. Just tell me where I can wait and not be in the way." Stella intertwined her fingers with Olive's. "Need me to use my pilot voice to talk some sense into your mom?"

Olive gave a watery laugh. "I appreciate the offer. Morgan, do you mind showing Stella where the lobby is?"

As the three women stood, the loud voice of Mary Ellen Murphy echoed from the halls.

Jesus Christ, Olive's mother could walk fast.

Chapter 43

As soon as Olive and Stella walked out into the hallway, they nearly collided with Olive's mom and sister and two silent men, neither of whom was Olive's dad.

"Hi, Father Stiegel. Mr. Adams." She nodded at the priest and then once at the gaunt-faced lawyer. It was probably the dark humor of nursing but the entire entourage together seemed like the beginning of a joke. Two dentists, a lawyer, and a priest walked into a nursing home . . .

"Olive?" Heather asked with a twitch of the head in Stella's direction. Olive's face was still sticky from crying and her whole body ached with stress, so of course she had been too distracted to have basic manners. *Shit.*

"Stella, this is my mom, and my sister, Heather."

Stella donned her most polite smile and shook Heather's hand, since Olive's sister was the only one to offer one. Olive's mom did her usual survey of the room, ignoring Olive and Stella as if they were furniture. She set out five more Christmas cards and made sure they were all evenly spaced. She checked the equipment and settings on the machines at the bedside against a small leather notepad. When she saw what must have been a small amount of dust or grime on the bedside table, she wet a paper towel and then wiped it down with a vigorous scrub.

When she appeared satisfied that all was up to the Mary Ellen Murphy standards, she turned back toward the room and crossed her arms. "Is Jacob's room now a place for socializing? Are emergency family meetings cutting into your date time?"

"Mom—"

"Actually, I *offered* to drive Olive here. I'll just be waiting in the lobby." Stella gave Olive an encouraging smile and then narrowed her eyes just slightly at Olive's mother. A hint of chastisement but no offense. "Take all the time you need, okay?"

"Thank you," Olive said.

"It was nice to meet you," called Heather as Stella walked away.

Stella turned and echoed the sentiment before following Morgan out the door.

A doctor came around the corner. He might have *actually* flinched when he saw Olive's mom and the lawyer.

Olive didn't blame him.

He led the entire entourage into a small conference room near the nurses' station. A few minutes later, Morgan came in and offered Olive a steeling smile as the meeting began.

The family meeting was as depressing as Olive expected. Jake's scans were worse. The nurses had noticed diminishing reflexes and other indications that this was the end.

Her mother sat in uncharacteristic silence during most of the meeting. Her fingers slipping across the beads of a rosary over and over again. Every now and then the priest beside her would place a hand on her shoulder.

It wasn't until the very end that the doctor pulled out a manila folder. "We got the final report from the physician you consulted with, and unfortunately he agrees with our assessments, that—"

Her mother stood, startling everyone in the room. She paced up and down in the small room.

The doctor talked fast as if he also knew there was a tempest brewing. "The team needed to meet with you urgently to make sure that you had the opportunity to make adjustments to your wishes . . ."

"*Our* wishes?" Olive's mother said. "You mean *her* wishes."

Her mother pointed at Olive. "Doesn't preserving a life mean anything to you people here? Why can't anyone understand that we need to give Jacob a chance? Does his life mean anything to you people?"

"Mom . . ." Heather stood, coming to her mom's side.

Olive looked at the lawyer. "What does this mean, if the doctor agreed? Does it change anything?"

Her mother turned to her, and then the yelling began. The meeting devolved from there into ninety minutes of the normal circuitous conversations without any further decision being made until her mother marched out of the room.

Olive lowered her head onto the table. When she looked up, the only person left was Morgan, who had sat beside the doctor the whole time adding in supporting details from her own clinical observations.

"She's never going to accept this, is she?" Olive asked, massaging the tense spots from her forehead.

Morgan shook her head slowly. "You know that sometimes people never do."

Olive groaned. "I know."

A page came from overhead, calling Morgan to room SW413. Jake's room. Olive and Morgan hurried up to the room to help, but it wasn't anything dramatic. Olive's mom wasn't even in there causing a ruckus. Just normal caregiving needs.

She helped Morgan get her brother settled.

When she finished helping, she found Stella outside the door. "Your sister said I should come back up. I'm sorry."

"Why are you sorry?" Olive asked. She hugged Stella. "Thank you so much for staying. I didn't realize this would take this long."

"It's okay." There was a panicky look on Stella's face, one that Olive had never seen there before. Almost like she was going to be sick.

"Stella, are *you* okay?"

"I . . ."

"Stella, what's wrong?"

"I just . . . nothing." Stella tried to keep her mouth from trembling, but every part of her was shaking.

Olive led Stella down to the lobby and through the double doors outside. She seemed to gulp down the cold air. Her shoulders went rigid.

"Stella, please tell me what's going on."

"No, this has been a tough day for you. I'm here for *you*. Want to go get lunch? H-hungry? I'm here for you."

"Stella, today wasn't anything worse than I've been dealing with for almost a year. I'm fine, really. I thought it was going to be worse than that." It would sound fucked up and callous for her to say that it had been good news in a weird way. The idea of Jake's suffering being almost over *would* be a relief. "Can you just tell me what's up? Did my mom say something to you—"

"No, nothing like that."

Stella sat on a wrought-iron bench next to the parking lot. She was quiet for a while, playing with her car keys, twisting them around her index finger over and over again.

"How can you do that?"

"Do what?"

"Everything. All of this. For your brother."

Olive was taken aback. "I . . . I don't have a choice."

Stella stared forward. "I was sitting in the lobby. And someone came in for a tour. They were talking about how they have a whole unit for Parkinson's for when families can't manage the care at home." She swallowed and then her pace of speaking got even faster. "There are brochures. I grabbed one." She opened her fist and the shredded remains of a pamphlet was there. "I just need to know how you can stand watching the person you love fade away. I don't want to. I don't fucking want to, Olive." Her hands trembled as she tore the paper into tinier scraps. "I just want him to be better. I know how selfish that sounds."

All Stella had allowed out before was a single tear, but now they poured out of her eyes. "I'm fine. I'm fine." She bowed her head, angling her face away.

Olive brought gentle hands to Stella's shaking arms. "You're not fine."

After a hesitation, Stella's eyes lifted to meet Olive's gaze. "Isn't *I'm fine* the socially acceptable response when you're having an emotional breakdown in public?" Stella said through tears, echoing their first real conversation in the airport terminal when it had been Olive crying.

Olive wiped a few tears away from Stella's cheeks. "You don't say that if the person with you *wants* to comfort you."

Not if the person you're with would change the world if there was a way to make it stop hurting you.

Stella seemed to read some part of what Olive was thinking in her face, because she cried harder. Olive would never have imagined such broken sounds could come out of Stella. She wished she had something wise to say or something that could help, but there was nothing, so she held her.

"I'm sorry," Stella said. "I was supposed to be here to be your support and now I'm a mess."

"Be a mess. Be a crying goddamn mess about this. That's okay."

"It doesn't *feel* okay," Stella said, taking in a shuddering breath.

"It's not going to feel okay. But it's okay to *feel*."

It was hard to tell after a while if Stella was shaking because she was still crying or because both of them were shivering in the freezing temperatures. "I never cared that I didn't have brothers or sisters. It never bothered me that my other asshole 'father' left us." She used air quotes. "Because my dad was all I needed, but now I'm alone with all this. He's asking me to help him make all these impossible decisions, and I-I-I have no idea if I'm fucking it all up or not. He made me his medical power of attorney a few months ago, and I freaked out. I'm such a coward."

"You're not. You're doing great." Olive held Stella tighter. "Believe me, I know. I see how much you care about everything. And . . . you're *great* at logistics, you told me so yourself. I've heard Stella Soriano knows how to make a hell of an information binder."

Stella gave a shaky laugh.

They pulled apart an inch. The cold making each exhalation visible. Olive dug through her bag to find a crumpled plastic package of tissues buried at the bottom. Stella took one and blew her nose.

"Stella?"

"Yeah?"

"I'm here too, okay."

Stella looked confused.

"I mean, here, just like what you told me earlier. As in if you need to talk about this stuff. Any stuff. I'll help. You can *always* talk to me about it, okay? It's hard to put so much on one person."

"It wouldn't be too hard for you because of Jake?"

Olive shook her head. "I've learned a lot. I just really . . ." *love you.* The words were a gong inside her head, and she swallowed to prevent them from coming out. ". . . want you to know you're not alone in this, okay?"

Shit. She did love her, didn't she?

"I really appreciate it." Stella pulled away and rubbed her hands together to warm them. "D-do you think we could go see my dad right now?"

Olive nodded. "Yeah, of course."

"I—uh—I think I need you to drive." Stella pressed the keys into Olive's hand and headed to the passenger seat of her Prius.

Well, that felt like something.

Chapter 44

Flurries of snow glittered against the night sky as Stella led Olive down a DC sidewalk. Because of Stella's flying schedule, Olive hadn't seen Stella since the emotional tidal wave that was the family meeting day last week. It had ended up being a great night afterward with hours of eating popcorn while watching through Hector's DVR full of historical aviation documentaries and Bravo reality TV shows while Hector provided a hilarious commentary on both.

Olive's embarrassingly wide smile at the feeling of Stella's hand in hers disappeared when Stella stopped in front of a restaurant with a big neon sign. "Surprise." She grinned.

"No, no, no." Olive took a step back.

On their normal nightly phone call a few days earlier, Stella had said someone had told her about a great restaurant in DC and that she wanted to go there tonight. Now it was clear Olive had been played. "No."

"Yes. Yes. Yes." Stella twirled her around and pushed her toward the door.

"I might throw up." Olive covered her face.

"You need to trust me." Stella locked eyes with Olive. They were almost nose to nose. "Do you trust me?"

"Yeah."

"Then to karaoke we go." And Stella grabbed her hand and pulled her through the door. They headed through a maze of tables and a bar area to a hostess desk.

"I booked a room for eight o'clock."

"A room?" Olive cast questioning eyes on the beautiful woman holding her hand.

Stella winked at her.

The hostess in black led them down a hallway to a room that had a large TV screen with a small stage area and a microphone.

"Surprise!" shouted a single voice from the corner.

"Derek?"

He handed her a shot of something sparkly and clear. "Bottoms up."

Stella turned to her. "You don't actually have to sing if you don't want to, but I thought this would be a good compromise. You said you thought you'd die before singing in a room of strangers. I came here a long time ago and thought it was super fun. And Derek said—"

"How?" Olive looked from Derek to Stella, pointing to each of them and then lifting her palms in a questioning motion.

"Stella got my number the night at the bar."

Stella grinned. "Oh, and . . ." She gestured to a table in the corner. "Happy birthday." There was an elegant cake with a few scattered candles and a bottle of champagne in an ice bucket. "It's a champagne cake with champagne."

Olive was truly shocked now. "Happy . . . how did you know?"

"When we rented the car in Georgia and the guy said the thing about his birthday. I didn't know the exact day, so I asked him." She grinned conspiratorially at Derek.

"Traitor," Olive said with mock sass, while grabbing her best friend in a fierce hug.

"I figured checking something off your list and watching your friends make fools of themselves singing would be a perfect compromise," Derek said.

Olive gulped her shot. "Compromise?" she said feebly.

Derek handed her another. "You never want to celebrate your birthday, and I do."

"I think you need to look up the word *compromise*."

Stella's excited expression faltered. "You didn't say she didn't like her birthday . . ." Uneasiness tinged her words.

Olive turned and smiled, stifling the urge to wrap Stella in her arms and kiss her senseless. "I think I'm going to really enjoy this birthday. Usually, I just never want anyone else to be inconvenienced. December birthdays are annoying for everyone."

Derek shook his head at Stella. "She's always been like this."

"Well, this year we just have to spoil her, then." Stella's happy expression returned. "Planning this was fun." She took a shot from the tray. "All right. Should I start with Selena or Dolly?" She pointed to the microphone in front of the screen.

Olive laughed. "Selena."

Derek grabbed a catalog from the table and pushed it into Olive's arms. "We're going to get you drunk enough that we can check this off your list, so pick a song while you can still read."

Olive scrubbed her face, wondering exactly how much alcohol that would take.

✳✳✳

Both Derek and Stella were passable singers, and despite what they said, neither made a fool out of themselves. Olive was in that happy playground of a mind space where she didn't have the spins yet, but the world seemed perfectly splendid. She'd had two pieces of the champagne cake that was indeed her favorite.

Olive grabbed a fry and chewed slowly. After finishing her glass of champagne, she gulped some water. She stood, wobbling a little but not slurring. "Okay."

"Okay?" Derek's eyes went wide.

Olive huffed out a breath. "Okay."

After snapping the binder shut, Olive went over to punch in the track number. She loved this song and was surprised it was in the catalog. She used to belt it out in the car—when she was alone. Since childhood, she only ever sang alone. Her baseline stage jitters were being strongly overruled by the booze and the presence of the beautiful woman. Her parents had pushed her into singing in public when she was little, but her shyness as a child had overwhelmed all their efforts.

The familiar intro of Brandi Carlile's "The Joke" played over the speakers. It wasn't a typical choice, but it was a song she'd loved for years. She knew Stella would like it too.

She held up the mic and began to sing.

Stella's face lit up with shock.

Derek shook his head smugly. He'd caught her singing several times, so he knew.

Olive focused on a spot in the back of the room, not daring to look at either of her friends. But a graceful movement stole her attention, Stella's shiny black hair catching the light as she leaned forward to listen.

The terror she normally felt when someone listened to her sing didn't materialize. Sharing this long-hidden part of herself with this woman felt right. It was easier for the drunk side of her brain to ignore the fact that they were "friends" and that despite all the sex, nothing indicated that would be changing. But with Stella's dreamboat eyes glittering up at her, Olive was happy. And most shockingly, not in any danger of panic-puking.

Being here with her felt right.

As soon as the song finished, Stella leaped out of her seat and applauded. "Oh my god, Olive."

"You're such an asshole." Derek mussed her hair. "Showing us up."

Stella looked in danger of exploding with enthusiasm. "Why were you afraid of karaoke when you could sing like that?"

"Well, I don't like standing up in front of people. My parents used to make me sing in church and for family functions until the time I threw up on the front row of pews." Olive chuckled, and yeah, she might have been slurring now. "And also, when you can sing, you get labeled as that asshole who came to karaoke to show off."

Stella's grin was wicked. "I liked hearing you sing."

"I sort of liked you watching me."

"You're drunk." Stella smirked.

"And you're pretty."

Derek chucked a crumpled napkin at Olive's forehead. "Get a room."

Chapter 45

In addition to being a talented pilot and a credit to the safety standards of the aviation industry, Stella Soriano was also an infuriatingly cautious and law-abiding driver. The letting-Olive-drive thing seemed reserved for moments of extreme emotional distress. They went the speed limit back to Olive's apartment. Stella looked lovely tonight in jeans that did fantastic things to her ass and her sexy leather bomber jacket. A bit of Olive's sloppy birthday drunkenness was wearing off, which was probably for the best.

As if reading her thoughts, Stella's eyes flickered to Olive. "How are you feeling?"

"Good." Olive smiled. "Tonight was amazing."

"It wasn't all me. Derek—"

"Last time Derek planned something for my birthday, it involved a piñata. I had a blast, and I know it was because of you. But I'm glad you invited him too."

"He's great. It makes me miss all of my old friends."

"Where are they?"

"Scattered since we're all pilots. Angie, as you know, lives in Denver." She winked at Olive. "I saw her last week. It's a perk of getting to fly everywhere, I can keep in touch with people. But it must be nice to work with your best friend."

"It is. Derek has been there for me through everything. Forever. All the stuff with Jake. He lost his dad when he was young, so he really understands. I'm not sure I would have survived all that if it weren't for him."

"I'm glad you have him." Stella took her right hand off the steering wheel and twined her fingers with Olive's.

Olive's heart did a time step inside her chest. "You know, you told me that you weren't good at this stuff."

"What stuff?"

"Birthdays and being there for someone." Olive knew she was gushing, but she couldn't will her dumbass mouth to close. "You've been there for me. It's really nice."

"It's been nice having a friend nearby, Olive."

A friend. That word cut through a bit of the champagne haze, but she had the sense that Stella might be trying to convince herself as much as Olive. She was feeling too happy from the best birthday she'd had in recent memory to worry about relationship labels tonight.

Stella blinked rapidly. "I . . . have another small surprise for you. It's not exactly for your birthday. Something to say thank you for what you've done for me."

"Really? What is it?" Olive grinned.

"Patience."

"Not my strong suit."

They stopped at a red light, and Stella pulled Olive into a quick kiss. "We'll be there soon."

The casual affection of the kiss caught Olive off guard. They hadn't touched much at all tonight. Olive wasn't sure if that was because Olive wasn't used to having Stella around Derek or if Stella wasn't used to Derek. But as fun as the night was, it was nice for Olive to be alone with her again.

"I guess I can wait."

Stella squeezed her hand. "Good."

Once they arrived back at the apartment, Stella pulled a gift bag out of her trunk and carried it into the apartment with them. They hung their coats on the rack and toed off their shoes at the door. Gus greeted them with his typical three minutes of enthusiasm before he plopped back on the couch and returned to snoring.

Olive shoved the enormous dog over enough for her and Stella to sit. Stella still held the gift bag in tight fingers, as if she were nervous.

"As I said, it's not really something for your birthday or for Christmas, but I saw it in a shop in Colorado."

"What is it?" Olive peered into the green tissue paper.

Stella gave her a wry smile and held the bag out to her. Olive deftly pulled the tissue paper out to find a vintage airline bag. It was leather and utterly gorgeous. A good balance of kitsch and class. If Olive had a Pinterest board of her aesthetic choices, this bag would have fit perfectly.

"Wow," Olive breathed.

"Open it."

"Okay . . ."

Inside was a teddy bear, a stress ball, and a pack of Swedish Fish. A humor book about worst-case scenarios. A folded-up neck pillow that smelled like lilacs and vanilla. An eye mask. And a cookie that looked like it was from a trendy bakery.

"It's a survival kit for your next flight."

"I can't eat the cookie until I get on another flight?"

"Well . . . the cookie might be for the ride to the airport. Though I didn't really think this through because it will probably be stale by the time I convince you to get on a plane. But—"

"Why is it for the ride to the airport?" Olive raised her eyebrows.

"It's an edible." She stifled a smile and covered her face with her hands.

"Stella Soriano bought me weed?"

"In a manner of speaking. It's illegal to take cannabis on a plane. But there's this bakery I like in Colorado—they actually sell gluten-free . . . um . . . stuff. I thought I would just tell you about it, but then I figured I should bring you back a sample. Maybe it would incentivize you to want to visit yourself."

"How did you get it back here without bringing it on a plane?"

Stella pursed her lips.

Olive gave her a mocking scandalized look. "You broke the law to bring me a cookie?"

Stella's expression became comically earnest. "A cookie that might help you feel better about getting on a plane."

Olive pushed the bag out of her lap and then pulled herself into Stella's. "Thank you." She rested her head in the crook of her neck.

"To be clear, I support you even if you never get on another plane, but after what you said before, I thought I could show you how excited I am at the idea of flying with you somewhere. You deserve to see Italy. You deserve to see everywhere you want to see. And, also I've loved spending time with you. That's not entirely related. I'm not saying you have to fly with me if you're going to fly, but it's true." She let loose a breath as if she'd unexpectedly run out of words.

"Me too."

Olive could tell her now. The feeling had been creeping in for weeks. Like the flicker of a firefly on a summer night. Every text. Every call. Every night spent together. Tiny lights in the darkness, and now the whole world seemed brighter. Olive wanted to tell her she thought she was in love with her and didn't understand why Stella kept her at arm's length. Did Stella know she was doing all the things that a perfect girlfriend would do?

But.

Olive didn't want to destroy the memory of tonight with rejection. She wanted to have a few more days of feeling like she felt now . . . almost giddy? She'd have to say something after the last event on Saturday, but for now, couldn't she enjoy this a little while longer? If Olive brought it up, it would be another example of being too critical and dramatic, just like Lindsay always said. Olive wanted to enjoy the simplicity of the moment, and most of her could. But . . .

That tiny, grating voice in the back of her brain told Olive everything was going to go to hell soon. Everything with her always did.

Murphy's Law.

Stella touched Olive's jaw and tilted her head, and the tenderness broke Olive free from that negative voice stealing her attention. Reverence bloomed on Stella's face. Her lips worked Olive's slowly at first. Tiny brushes. She held Olive's bottom lip with her teeth for a moment, bringing her deeper into the paradise that was kissing Stella. Stella tasted like champagne and smelled like cake, and everything about her was everything Olive wanted.

Stella knit her fingers through Olive's and then stood. Wordlessly Olive followed her to the bedroom. There was no urgency tonight. Olive started a record on the turntable as she entered, the scratch of the needle coming before the quiet melody.

Stella's arms reached around Olive. Stella's palms pressed into her stomach, then lifted Olive's cotton shirt away. Her right hand slid beneath the lace of Olive's bra while the left dipped beneath Olive's waistband. They stood like this for several moments, pausing to savor all of it. Olive melted into Stella's warm touch, and something started to simmer between her thighs.

Turning, Olive stroked the top button of Stella's shirt. She took her time, kissing every new inch of skin revealed as her fingers flicked each button open. Stella undid Olive's pants and pushed them down, dropping to her knees to give a very chaste kiss to a very unchaste part of her.

Clothes came off more quickly now, until all that was left was Stella's sheer purple bra with her brown nipples peaked beneath it as if begging for Olive's attention. Olive slid the straps down Stella's arms, sweeping her fingernails over the perfect curve of Stella's collarbone. Soft. She was so soft.

Without leaving each other's arms they lay on the cool sheets. Olive's legs twisted together with Stella's. Stella's beautiful eyes never leaving hers even as her fingers found those familiar deep places that made Stella unfurl. They moved together, Olive watching for the small reactions she knew so well.

Little moans. Tiny high-pitched whimpers. Stella's hips grinding against her with her beautiful, wet pussy pushing harder and harder against Olive's.

Olive had never had sex like this. So unhurried. So breathtakingly intimate. Eye contact and tender touches. Tonight they explored each other in a way they hadn't yet. Each of them speaking in low murmurs. Asking for what they wanted. Trying and tasting. Sweat shone on their skin, barely visible in the low-lit room.

Stella reached for the nightstand, giving Olive a questioning look.

"Yes" was all Olive could will herself to say. She was so lost in the moment. In the music. In the movement. In the delicious sensation of Stella over every part of her.

They pressed together once more, the hum of the vibrator almost too much for Olive's senses as it linked them together.

With a gasp, Stella raked her nails down Olive's back.

Olive's answering cry had her thighs pressing into Stella's hips. "Stella."

And Stella was right there with her. She lifted her chin high. Olive pushed away Stella's sweat-soaked hair and sucked and licked up the perfect brown column of her neck. Stella's hands took hold of Olive's ass, driving their bodies even more closely together. Her fingers gripped the crease of her thighs, opening Olive the tiniest bit wider.

Olive's forehead rested on Stella's shoulder. "Oh god."

"*Come,*" Stella asked softly.

She did, rocking and writhing through rasping breaths.

After every shudder of pleasure pulsed through her, Olive lay as if broken into pieces. Every muscle limp. Bones looser than they'd been before. Vocal cords barely functional. "I— That was amazing."

She wanted to say it.

That she loved her.

Saying it after sex was an awful cliché.

It wasn't about the sex.

It was about the whole night.

Stella challenged her without making Olive feel like a loser for being afraid of things in the first place. Being with Stella made Olive feel . . . safe.

Stella kissed her once more and offered her a wicked, slightly punch-drunk smile.

Minutes later, Stella was a comfortable weight on top of her. The softness of her body pressed against her like her own personal weighted blanket. Olive opened her mouth to speak several times, before giving up the idea. She closed her eyes and let her mind wander toward sleep.

A thought pricked at her brain, as these thoughts often do in the dark when all is calm and everything should be comfortable and perfect. That looming threat of an expiration date. In four days, it could all be over. Maybe that's all tonight was. The party. The gift. The sex. All a precursor to goodbye.

Chapter 46

The only sound in the room was the rhythmic tidal of Jake's ventilator. Stella was gone for a few days and wouldn't get back until the day of the Pilots' Gala, so it seemed the perfect time to stop in and see him again. The remains of Olive's sandwich sat in the greasy paper on the side table.

She clicked on music from her phone—one of Jake's favorite bands. She'd never let him play it in the car before the accident. She said the singer's voice drove her nuts. It still did. But she missed it for some reason. The smack of his hand as he swatted her away from his fancy car stereo when the song came on.

It was the stupid stuff.

Her eyes followed the walls to the large bulletin board, looking anywhere but at Jake. She hated to admit that to herself. But it was true.

Her family had added a few more photos since she'd last been here. There was one with her parents and her sister's family all together. Probably from Thanksgiving. The room was as cheerful as it could be. Even more Christmas cards were assembled on the side table near a second fake poinsettia.

"Things with Stella continue to be great," Olive said.

Except you obviously want something more.

She took a bite of her sandwich and then chewed for several minutes while considering how to respond to the version of Jake who existed in her head. "I think I'm going to be happy with what we have."

But are you happy or going to be happy?

"I am happy."

Well, then I'm happy for you, Olive.

"I . . . wish you had this. When you were here."

I know you do.

Olive didn't know what else to say.

Have you gotten that therapist yet?

It was one of the last questions he'd asked her in real life too. Therapy had changed his life, so of course he wanted it to help his sister who was afraid of everything. She'd gotten her daily antidepressant from her primary care doc and then forgotten the promise that she'd look for someone to talk to. Looking was overwhelming. Sometimes everything was overwhelming.

At least Jake-in-her-brain had been proud of her when she checked things off the list. She'd come here after every trip to a national park. After everything she'd done that had stretched her idea of what she could do despite all the nature-related catastrophes.

But she still felt empty.

He wasn't here.

Jake was just a fucking memory.

Voices in the hallway carried into the room as footsteps approached. A familiar voice rose above the rest.

"Shit," Olive hissed.

She folded up the rest of her sandwich in the greasy paper while muttering several more curses. She flipped off the music, and braced herself. Every muscle was taut, as if she were the last kid in a dodgeball game waiting for the coordinated attack.

Her mother wrinkled her nose at the smell of the sandwich as she entered the room. "What is that?"

Olive spoke in a small voice. "It was Jake's favorite."

"Oh." Her mother leaned down and kissed her brother's forehead. "Hi, honey." The tenderness was gone as quickly as it came, vanishing completely as her eyes settled on the trash in Olive's hands. "Are you almost done here?"

"Uh . . . yeah." Olive stood and backed away from the chair.

"I didn't think you usually came on Mondays. Don't you usually have appointments?"

Olive's mother's words were clipped. "The office closed early today. We needed to have some plumbing work done."

"Oh. Okay. Everything's okay with the practice?"

"Yes." Her mother sat in the chair Olive had vacated. She scooted it all the way to the bed. She held Jake's hand, kissing his knuckle. She refused to make eye contact with Olive.

Olive crumpled the sandwich wrapper into a tighter ball. "What did the other specialist you called say about Jake's scans? Heather said—"

"Why are you even asking? You've already made up your mind. I know that we think so completely differently about what *preserving a life* means, so why would you even ask me about this?" Her mom's voice was flatter than usual.

"I'm asking because I know it's important to you to get answers." She'd almost made the mistake of saying *closure*.

"That other doctor was a quack." That familiar bite came back into her voice. "That doctor from the family meeting said he was getting worse, but look at him." Her mom gestured to Jake. "He looks much better. Color in his cheeks. I know he's in there." She stroked his face once.

"Okay."

Her mom would find another doctor and another.

Olive gathered her things and took a step toward the door.

"You know, I would think after everything with Jacob you would have learned the lesson of being more wary of online coverage."

"What?"

"Just surprised about all you're doing with that new girlfriend."

"What do you mean?" Olive's gut twisted.

"You were in a magazine, Olive, I'm really not that out of

touch." Her mom wrinkled her nose. "Still, it can be hard for people like you."

"Queer people?" Olive stepped too hard on the trash can pedal and the lid slammed into the wall behind it as she tossed the sandwich wrapper inside it.

"Your father and I have always supported your relationships. Jacob's too." The edge of defensiveness in her voice belied her point. "I'm not being homophobic."

"Right." Technically that was all correct, but it had never felt easy to talk to her mom about dating a woman.

"The people on social media were cruel to Jacob. It didn't matter he saved a child's life. They went into his past and ripped him apart. Watching it happen. Reading what all those evil people said . . ." Her mother stroked Jake's thin arm. Her mother looked thinner too. Her fingers so much slimmer than they used to be.

"I know."

"I'm still rather surprised you seem to be embracing your five minutes of fame as much as you are."

"It's complicat—"

"It always is."

It was strange to have a conversation with someone who blatantly refused to look at you.

Olive shifted her weight, leaning back into the wall. "Why do you do this, Mom? Can't we have a normal conversation? It doesn't have to be like this. It didn't used to be like this."

"I think you know the answer to that." She paused, chewing on her lower lip. "I am trying to forgive you."

"Forgive *me*?"

"Yes."

Olive looked up at the ceiling. "Well, I won't hold my breath. Merry Christmas, Mom."

Her mother didn't deign to respond, and Olive walked out. The hallway was crowded. Nurses and orderlies and other random staff wheeling carts. She had to stop for a moment. Olive braced her fist on the wall, wishing she could punch through it if that would take away everything she was feeling. She gripped a railing that was obviously for the residents and not for family members having a quiet nervous breakdown.

Her own mother thought the worst of her.

It wasn't new, but sitting in the same room with her made the sense of injustice blister worse.

After several deep breaths and waving off multiple staff members, she made it out of the building and into the December cold. The bitter wind felt almost refreshing on her burning cheeks as she trudged back to her car.

Her phone began vibrating. Now that she had service again, a barrage of missed messages were coming though. Service was always spotty at his facility. She wanted to call Stella.

Stella had been right there beside Olive as she fielded calls from her mother's lawyer about payments to Jake's facility and threats about making sure everything was done to keep him alive since that family meeting. Stella cheered her up. Stella made her feel less hopeless in general. Despite what she had said about never being attentive in a relationship, Stella was the best girlfriend Olive had ever had, except for the whole it-was-all-actually-fake thing.

> STELLA
> I hate to ask, but is there any way you can stop by to check on my dad?

Olive couldn't help but be pleased that someone thought she was reliable and a good enough person to be trusted with a loved one.

> OLIVE
> Of course. What's wrong?

STELLA
I think he's napping. But Jocelyn had to leave early today and he's going to be by himself longer than usual. If this is too much to ask, no worries.

OLIVE
It's not too much to ask at all! Done. I'll be there in thirty minutes. Just got out of seeing Jake.

The little circles appeared and disappeared several times. Was Olive making things awkward by bringing him up? Was this what Lindsay had meant about Olive being a bummer most of the time?

STELLA
Are you okay?

Olive typed several things and then deleted them. The conversation with her mother had shaken her. Everything seemed less clear than an hour ago.

OLIVE
Yeah, I'm fine!

STELLA
You sure?

OLIVE
Can I call you later and talk about it?

STELLA
Yes!!!! Of course!!!! I'm about to head into a meeting, but I'll call as soon as I get out.

OLIVE
Thank you 😊

She actually put a smiley face. It was a joke between her and Derek that Olive only knew how to use the facepalm emoji and the grimace one. Now she was apparently a regular smiley-face person. But only with Stella.

Chapter 47

Stella arrived in uniform a few hours before they were scheduled to go to the Allied Airlines Pilots' Gala. Olive had just finished taking Gus for a walk. After Olive hung his leash by the door, Stella dipped her in an almost cinematic kiss.

"Someone's excited," Olive said, kissing Stella one more time after coming vertical again.

"I can't wait." Stella slipped her shoes off at the door, placing them perfectly perpendicular to the wall as she always did. "Oh, and my dad said you stopped by today?"

"He made me promise to come back again because he liked kicking my ass in chess last week." Olive braced herself. "I hope that's not weird. I told him to text me if he needed anything. Mainly, he's just been texting me every day to compare Wordle scores, and he always does better. It's okay that I went?"

"More than okay." Stella grinned. "I think it's great. He really likes you."

"I really like him. He's kind of a hoot."

"He'll like that, I think." Stella smiled and kissed her.

Olive's mind had been clouded all day. Not because she hadn't had a great time playing chess, but because she had. It was weird. She'd found out today that Hector went to the same church as her mom when he still occasionally attended mass. Had he ever met her? Hector never seemed like he let the rigidity of a religion dictate who he was. It was weird to think of someone like Hector Soriano existing in the same space as Mary Ellen Murphy. Maybe Hector had even seen all the candles her mother lit for Jake. All of this left Olive feeling raw,

324 * Andie Burke

because having a loving, kind, supportive parental figure in her life?

It was so nice.

And tonight was the last night of the fake relationship. It was probably weird that she was worried about losing Hector now too.

"You okay, Olive? You went all thoughtful."

Olive fixed her face. "Oh, I'm just nervous that I might accidentally kick that Captain Douchebro guy in the nuts if he calls me sweetheart again. I'm *really* clumsy."

Stella groaned. "Please don't nut-kick anyone tonight."

"Did you just say nut-kick? Is this an aviation-industry term?"

"Very technical. Air marshals are very strict about it."

Olive followed Stella into the bedroom, where Stella removed her earrings and put them in the tiny ceramic plate on the vanity next to Olive's. Olive was staring blankly in the mirror at their reflections when Stella came up behind her. She circled Olive's waist with her arms and pulled her tight.

"I'm glad you're coming with me tonight."

Olive gave herself a tiny shake, trying to focus on the moment. "Me too."

Stella was beaming. That carefree smile always gave the impression of sunlight shining out of her face. Olive adored seeing Stella beaming with excitement. She'd had a meeting with Jack O'Halloran during the previous week. All signs pointed to their plan's grand success. Stella would get her promotion. And Olive had a friend at her side while the fuss over the viral video went on. Her hospital would have the publicity it craved along with a refurbished fish tank. And everything would be great.

Even if it was the end.

She'd tried to bake Stella a cake after getting home from seeing Hector, but after messing up the recipe twice, she gave up. Baking was beyond her today.

"Mind if I shower first?" Stella pointed to the bathroom.

"Of course, that's fine."

Stella grabbed her shoulder bag and went to the bathroom, and Olive plopped down on the bed.

Evidence of Stella had spread everywhere. She had a few hangers in the closet. A pair of shoes she'd forgotten here one night in the corner. A scarf Olive had borrowed from her was hung from a hook. And a clipping from the *People* magazine article was tacked up above Olive's desk.

She crossed the room and touched Stella's face in the photo.

She'd have to tell her tonight. After the party, after everything was over tonight, when Stella was riding high on the success of their plan. Olive would tell her she loved her and needed to know how Stella felt. Olive knew the pain of irrevocably losing someone. The agony over leaving things unsaid. It was a stupidly dramatic way of looking at the world sometimes, but losing Jake *had* changed her. She'd told Derek she loved him many times since, and he'd mostly stopped rolling his eyes about it.

But Stella . . . she needed to know.

Even if it meant the end of things because Olive couldn't go on in this limbo of not truly knowing what they were to each other. They started this with Stella telling her that she didn't date because she was afraid of someone getting hurt. She'd said that she was terrible in relationships. The last few weeks spent together *had* to prove to her that she was capable of being a fantastic girlfriend.

She sat in front of her vanity. Derek was working tonight, so Olive's hair would remain mostly normal, and *normal* meant wild and fluffy, but Stella liked it that way anyway. Olive went to the closet and unzipped the garment bag to check that the dress was still just as perfect as always. She hadn't tried it on for Stella yet, but Derek had said it looked flawless. She hoped to get a repeat reaction from the last time Stella had seen her all dressed up. That glowing look of awe that had seemed to make Sixpence None the Richer crescendo in the background.

Olive's phone began buzzing. She'd left it out in the living room, but she could hear the grating vibration even over the *whoosh* of the shower. She nearly tripped over Gus, who was sprawled over the floor, as she crossed to the coffee table.

Olive's stomach sank when she saw the name. Her father. She never talked to her father on the phone. There were two missed calls that had come before this one. "No. No. No. Not tonight." She swiped her finger to answer and convinced her shaking hands to hold the phone to her ear. "What's wrong?"

"I've been trying to reach you." Her father's voice was flat. Almost defeated? "Your brother passed away an hour ago."

"He . . . no . . ." Tears stung her eyes but she blinked them away.

"Your mother said I should tell you. Said you'd want to know you wouldn't have to be doing any more financial releases or paperwork."

"Mom thinks I cared about the money? Is that why she didn't call?"

"Your mother hasn't been getting out of bed most days lately, Olive."

"What? I thought she was still going to work?"

"She hasn't since Jacob's accident." He cleared his throat. "Heather and I took over a lot of her patients. Your sister's making the arrangements for the funeral at your mother's direction, and the lawyer will be sending you the details."

Olive's mind was reeling. Her type-A mother was spending most of her days in bed since Jake's accident? She was breathless when she spoke again, trying to recall the rest of what her father had said as if the first part hadn't dropped a bomb on her. "What details?"

"About Jacob's will. The release of his money."

Olive swallowed. Grief was a hollow place. An emptiness inside her. He'd been dying as she'd been obsessing over her night with Stella. Shouldn't she have felt it somehow? Like some cosmic rattling of her entire world?

"I don't care about the money, Dad."

Her father's silence was somehow crueler than her mother's spite. "Heather's already set up a meeting with the priest to discuss the service."

"For the funeral?" Olive pressed a hand to her forehead to try to calm her thoughts.

"Yes, Olive, the funeral." Her father grunted. "Your mother's been holding out hope all this time. She knows you haven't."

"I—It's not that I didn't have—"

"The service will be next week. Heather will probably send out an email to everyone in the family about the details."

Everyone in the family. Like Olive was a third cousin or some other distant relative.

A spark of anger crackled like a log on a fire snapping in two. Jake didn't want a religious funeral. "Jake wouldn't have wanted that. He didn't want a Catholic funeral. He wasn't Catholic. Don't you all care what was in his will? He left instructions. He said he wanted—"

"I don't think your mother thought cremating him and sprinkling his ashes on some lake somewhere while reading a poem was a legitimate arrangement." His tone was almost businesslike, but the tremble in his voice was unlike anything Olive had ever heard from him. "It's very important that your mother has this closure. Her faith has been very important to her during this time." Since the accident, her mother had clung so tightly to her religion, Olive barely recognized her mom anymore. There was almost a desperation in her father's tone. Why couldn't he just be honest with her?

"Crater Lake was his favorite place in the whole world. *That* was important to Jake."

"The family deserves a chance to say goodbye with the appropriate setting."

"I'm his family too. I want to honor his wishes. Some big-deal Catholic funeral isn't what he wanted."

"If you're concerned about the expenses, your mother and I will be paying for everything."

"Jesus Christ, Dad. What's wrong with you? Can you just not sound like a robot for a second."

"Don't take that tone with me." Anger. No. Fury. "What's wrong with me? My son—my son is gone." His voice broke. "My wife—your mother—she's fading away. I'm just trying to give her what she needs right now . . ." He paused as if he needed a second to collect himself. Was he crying? "I was hoping that having more time before would help her accept it . . ."

"Time," Olive said, trying and failing to conceal the bitterness in her voice. She didn't say what she wanted to say. *Time for what? Time for Jake to suffer?*

"If you can't be civil, I'd prefer you didn't attend. For your mother's sake."

Olive choked. "What?"

"I have to go. Your sister will be in touch. The lawyer will be too."

"Yeah, well. Bye." Olive ended the call, hanging up before she could tell her bereaved father to go fuck himself.

She picked up the magazines and stacked them on the table. She grabbed a pillow off the couch and screamed into it until pain burned in her throat. She didn't feel better. Her body couldn't decide how to feel. Sad. Yes. She was so, so sad. But she'd been sad for a year. Rage at her parents was the most obvious emotion. Relieved? Not exactly the right word, but she was glad Jake wasn't suffering anymore. Did that relief make her a monster? All of it jumbled inside her. And numbness. It didn't feel real. When would it feel real?

Would she need to see the empty bed at the care facility?

She sat on the ground. Gus ambled over and put his head

in her lap. He seemed subdued tonight. Like some part of him knew.

"I'm s-sorry, big guy." Olive wiped her nose with her shoulder and continued to pet him. "I know you miss him. I do too." A tear slid down Olive's nose and landed on Gus's coat.

"I'm out of the shower, Olive," called Stella's musical voice from the next room.

Olive jumped to standing.

She'd forgotten she wasn't alone in the apartment.

The *party*.

The night she had planned for weeks. The perfect night in a ballroom, wearing her perfect dress happily situated on Stella's arm. And she was going to tell her . . .

She crossed to the kitchen sink and splashed cold water on her face. She fanned her eyes, blinking furiously. Throat constricting.

She didn't want to think about Jake or her family. She couldn't do anything about that. He was gone, and they didn't want her around. She needed tonight, needed to grab hold of some smidgen of happiness, because otherwise she'd completely fall apart.

"Olive?" Stella was in a towel, leaning in her doorway, perfect face filled with anticipation. "You okay?"

"Oh, yeah, I'm fine. Eye was bothering me."

"Did you get something in it?" Stella walked to stand behind her, appraising Olive's eyes with her own. After all of their various shower activities, Olive didn't think she'd ever be able to smell Stella's shampoo without getting aroused.

"Not sure. I'll be fine. I'm going to shower too."

Stella caught her in a quick kiss. "I'm excited about tonight."

"Me too." Olive forced a mirroring smile on her face.

She could get through this.

Chapter 48

Stella and Olive circulated at the event. Having Stella's hand in hers grounded Olive. She smiled at the praise about the news articles and the videos. She answered all the polite inquiries about her without feeling uncomfortable or anxious. She placed walls in her mind around everything about Jake and her father and mother like an encapsulated cancer. It couldn't touch her now. She couldn't think about it.

With those mental walls intact, the biggest issue she was encountering was that Stella's evening dress hugged her hips and ass in a manner that was completely distracting. She'd missed what people were saying a couple of times as Stella walked in front of her. Stella in uniform was dangerous. Stella in a cocktail dress was lethal.

Jack O'Halloran stood with an attractive and much younger woman near the head table. He beckoned them over, greeting both Olive and Stella with a charismatic warmth.

The woman grinned, with the upper half of her face barely moving. "Oh, they're even more beautiful in person, aren't they? No wonder they got invited on the *TODAY* show. I'm Lady O'Halloran."

Olive assumed Lady was her actual first name and not a title, but given the amount of bling around her neck, she didn't feel certain.

"It's lovely to meet you, Mrs. O'Halloran. I've heard so much about you and all your work to encourage the philanthropic goals of the airline." Stella shook Lady's hand.

"I hear you're one of the airline's best volunteers."

Stella flushed.

"She is," Olive said, giving Stella's hand a squeeze. "This holiday party is beautiful."

"We've been putting on this party for thirty years. A tradition in the airline. Glad you're both here. And Jack says he made sure that there was a food you could eat, Stella dear."

Stella's cheeks went redder. "Thank you."

Jack shook his head. "Should never have been a problem. You ladies should have drinks in your hands though. This is a party."

"Yes, go mingle with people other than us older folks." Lady moved to sit at her table, her husband delicately pulling the chair out for her.

Jack waved them away too. "Yes. By all means. Go celebrate your year." He looked at Stella. "Though the new year might be bringing some more good news for you." He tapped the side of his nose.

"Thank you, sir. Thank you."

He sat beside his wife.

Olive and Stella wove through tables to find their seats, and Olive's clutch began buzzing. Derek was calling. He knew where she was, and he wouldn't be calling unless it was an emergency. He'd picked up Gus after they'd left. What if something had happened to him? He couldn't know about Jake? But why else would he be calling?

Olive frowned. "Derek's calling. Do you mind if I . . . ?"

"Of course." Stella nodded. "Do you want me to come outside with you?"

"No, I'll be fine. Stay. This is a big night for you."

"I'll go get you a drink." Stella kissed her cheek. "Come back soon."

God, this all felt so real now. Was it just as real to her?

As soon as Olive hit the lobby, she called Derek back.

Derek didn't bother with a greeting. "You have a Lindsay problem."

"A what?"

"Does Lindsay have a key to your apartment?"

"Uh . . . no, of course not . . . Oh wait, yeah, actually she does. I think I gave her one so she could water my plants when I took that trip to Grand Teton. Half my plants died." She almost crossed herself at the memory of her poor dead ferns, Finnegan and Fergus. "Why do you ask?"

"She put stuff on her Instagram stories about you and Stella. She tagged the TODAY show and People, calling Stella a liar."

"She's angry and wanting to get back at me, Derek. I knew she was going to do something. She knew the last event was tonight. She's known about this for weeks because she saw it on my calendar."

"She found some binder at your place. Said it proved your relationship was fake."

Olive froze.

Oh fuck.

The binder would be suspicious, but not completely damning. It would be hugely embarrassing to Stella, though. It also might mean people would go looking into her account. Looking for anything. It might bring up stuff about Jake too if she was getting bad press. People loved dirt. *Shit.*

She held out a hand to brace herself on the wall, conscious of the way people's eyes glanced her way as they passed. She felt a flush of heat on the back of her neck as if the room temperature had risen twenty degrees. She worked to keep her breathing steady.

"Are you there, Olive?"

"Just dissociating."

"Seems healthy."

"What am I going to do?"

"You have to tell Stella."

"I can't tonight. She's so happy. Everything she wants might finally be happening." Olive didn't want anything fucking with tonight. She had pushed the conversation with her father to the back of her mind. She had pushed everything with Jake even further back. She needed a few more hours before everything crumbled.

"Can you tell her after?"

"That'd probably be better."

But still awful.

"I called Lindsay and told her to take it all down. She hung up on me. Said if you want to talk about it, *you* should call her about it."

Olive tightened her grip on her phone. "I need to get my super to change my locks. Jesus, I can't believe she was snooping in my apartment. Who does that?" A shudder of violation roiled inside her. The apartment where she and Stella had spent such happy times had an intruder.

"Give me your super's number, and I'll call him."

"No, you don't have to do that. I can handle this. I can handle it." Her fingertips dug into her scalp.

"Olive, you can handle everything, but please let me help you with this, so you can have a nice night."

A nice night. Yeah, like that was going to happen. Murphy's Law. "Okay. I'll text you the number."

"I'm sorry all this is happening."

She rubbed her temple. "I was going to tell her I was in love with her tonight. Before . . ."

"You can still do that."

"She's going to freak out about this. Her job's the most important thing to her. What if this puts it in jeopardy? I can't believe I forgot about that stupid key. It hadn't even occurred to me that she would do this . . . I'm such an idiot."

"It's not your fault."

"It is one hundred percent my fault. And everything's going wrong." Tears were threatening. She couldn't fall apart yet. She absolutely could not fall apart here. Tonight was too important.

"What's wrong? This isn't just about Lindsay." A pause. "Olive. What's happening?"

"Jake passed away. My d-dad called. I guess my mom is really not good. I was going to tell you tomorrow, b-but I couldn't tell you today."

A strangled sound came out of Derek. He took a few deep breaths. His voice shook slightly when he found it again. "I-I'm so sorry." His voice steadied into something low and soothing. "You still went to the party?" There was no judgment, just concern and shock.

"My dad said—" Her voice shook. She squeezed the phone harder. "I couldn't do anything for him. Or for them. I didn't want to flake on Stella. I wanted tonight to be good. I needed a distraction."

"Does Stella know?"

Her silence was enough of an answer.

"She would've understood, Olive. She's a good person."

"I know she is. I know. But I don't want her deciding to be with me out of pity." She rubbed her knuckles over her brow ridge. "I—I don't know what I'm going to do."

"Talk to her? Tell her what's going on."

"I don't know." Olive said goodbye and ended the call. Olive's chest was tightening, and not in a floating-happy-in-love way or even a heartbroken-grieving way. It was in a pre–panic attack way. In a she-might-actually-puke-her-brains-out kind of way. When Olive returned to the large banquet hall, Stella was locked in a conversation. There were people everywhere. So many people. There was only one part of all of this Olive might be able to fix. She had to try.

Stella's eyes found hers. With a small, bewitching smile, she beckoned Olive over. The person with her turned. It was an executive. Olive couldn't remember her name, but she remembered her photo from the binder. The binder goddamn Lindsay had stolen.

"I'm s-sorry. I need to make a call." She patted Stella's arm. She didn't want Stella to come looking for her in the lobby. "You stay. I'll be right back. Need to go outside for a sec." Outside was better. She needed air.

Olive couldn't face the walk back through the crowd to get to the front doors. The crowd that had felt friendly before now seemed littered with land mines. She followed the exit signs back through the kitchens to a loading dock alleyway. At the first corner, she pulled her phone out of her clutch and swiped to her blocked numbers list and then held the phone to her ear.

"Hello there, Olive," Lindsay said in a sugared voice.

"Take it down."

"Stella's charade is pathetic, and it might even be fraud. None of it added up. I knew she was using you. I just didn't realize anyone could be that selfish."

"You're saying she's pathetic when you broke into your ex-girlfriend's apartment and stole something?"

"If you must know, since you refused to give me back my stuff, I went there when I knew you wouldn't be there. I didn't expect to find a psycho binder detailing a bogus relationship. Is Stella actually living with you?"

"Why do you care?"

"Was letting her pretend to be in a relationship just a way for you to try to convince her that she really liked you?" Lindsay's tone became pitying. "You thought maybe if she needed something from you, you could convince her to stay?"

Olive leaned against the concrete as the accuracy of this picture sank in. Was she truly just as pathetic as Lindsay was saying?

"Derek probably loves you too much to tell you the truth about this. If Stella is using you to get ahead at her work, she never wanted you. Playing house for a few weeks doesn't make it real." Lindsay's voice slowed down, but the venom kept flowing. "No one at your job is going to give a shit that I put this online, but Stella deserves to get fired for this. If I'm the only person in your life willing to say this, I have to. She's *never* going to want you that way."

"Just stop." Olive held her fist to her forehead as if she *could* stop herself from wondering if what Lindsay said was true.

"I'm just being honest. How long were you going to let this go on? Really, at some point it just seems like you're creating the drama. Like with your brother, why not just let your mom have her way? No, Olive Murphy always needs to make everything harder for herself."

Was that true?

Olive didn't have the emotional energy to respond, so she ended the call. She couldn't stay here anymore. It felt like a weight was pushing against her chest. She needed to talk to Stella, but she was also afraid of that conversation. Part of her just wanted to run.

Her heels clacked against the ground as she moved back to the ballroom door from the loading dock.

A grizzled voice came from around a corner ahead. "Always thought women in Tupelo were the most adventurous. Tell them you're from the big city. They beg for it." Raucous male laughter echoed over the bricks.

Grimacing, Olive scanned the alley for an escape route, but to get to the other side of the building, she'd have to pass them. The air was frigid, but she hardly felt it on her bare shoulders.

Jack O'Halloran and Kevin, the pilot from her flight with Stella, stood leaning on a wall of gray cinder blocks, smoking cigars. They both held whiskey in their other hands, each with the red cheeks that spoke to the number of whiskeys that came before.

"There you are. One of my favorite lesbians," Jack slurred.

"Not that I know too many lesbians. But I can say you're probably my favorite. You know how it is with men—or maybe you don't. Always want what we can't have. Just makes you all the more thirsty for 'em." He slurped more of his whiskey.

Olive stopped dead. "What did you say?" This was too much. She needed to be alone for a second. But the CEO of a company couldn't say gross, fetishizing shit like that. Obviously, it would be pointless to correct him and say she was bisexual and not a lesbian, but the rest of it . . . ugh. Olive's head swam. She hadn't eaten more than a few bites during dinner.

Before Olive could decide how to respond, Jack checked his watch. "I better head back inside, though. Lady will be looking for me." One of his gnarled hands petted her shoulder. He stomped out his cigar on the ground before heading back inside, leaving Olive alone with Kevin.

Olive took a step around Kevin, but he grabbed her elbow. "Come join me. Want a cigar? Just because you like women in your bed doesn't mean you can't celebrate with me. I bet the right man could turn you." *Celebrate* seemed to have an entirely different meaning.

"Get off me." She shot him a look and wrenched her arm away. No, this could not be happening now.

Stella came out the back door, eyeing Kevin's hand, which had been reaching out toward Olive again. "What are you doing?"

"Nothing. I offered her one of my dad's cigars. Being generous."

His dad? Being a nepo baby explained a lot about why his behavior was tolerated.

"I asked what you were doing with your hands on my girlfriend."

"Stop being emotional, Stella. Never could take a joke." Kevin narrowed his eyes. He sipped his whiskey. "You know, I always thought you'd be more like a man."

Olive stood to her fullest height, which meant she barely reached the shoulder of the man in front of her. "I'm sorry. What does that mean?"

"Lesbians. Should be able to appreciate a nice pair of tits with the boys." He narrowed his glassy eyes at Stella.

Olive folded her arms over her chest, anger pushing away the stress over Lindsay and the grief over Jake. "Actually, being a lesbian might mean she's even less interested in being 'one of the boys.'"

Kevin chuckled, giving her the look a circus attendee gives the dancing monkey. "She's so spunky, Stella. Standing up for her girl like a man. No wonder you like her."

Stella took a step forward. "Actually, Kevin, I don't need a man or have to act like a man to stand up for myself. And this behavior is unacceptable." She pointed at him, pressing a perfectly manicured finger into his chest. "And you're being rude, homophobic, and sexist all at once. You should be ashamed of yourself. I don't appreciate your condescending tone or your words."

He nearly cackled in response. "Oh, don't act so fucking self-righteous. Like this is the first time you've seen me act like this. We're all like this. Never bothered you before. You always understood what you have to do on this team." His words slurred. "Does she even know what you've always put up with?"

Olive had no idea where to begin to parse that statement.

Stella's eyes widened at whatever she saw on Olive's face.

Olive was just so tired.

"Now acting so scandalized. Is your sweet little girlfriend so precious"—he affected an exaggerated tone—"that she can't handle a little innocent teasing?" Kevin held out his whiskey to Stella. "So uptight tonight. Have a drink. Have mine."

Then Stella did something that Olive never expected.

She took the drink from him. "Stop being a fucking asshole."

And Stella threw a drink in the face of the CEO's son.

Chapter 49

Olive was having trouble processing everything.

Stella throwing the drink.

Stella standing up for herself and for Olive.

Stella's warm hands on Olive's hips, her laughing as Kevin O'Halloran waddled back into the ballroom with his metaphorical tail between his legs, face dripping. "I'd be worried about him telling his father about this, but given the number of HR complaints about him already, I don't think he'll dare. God, that felt good."

Olive's phone was a lead brick in her hand. The bomb about what Lindsay had said and done tonight waiting there. The delayed grief about Jake beginning to push through the crumbling barriers in her mind. She was shaking. She could barely keep hold of her clutch.

Stella's eyes darkened as she turned back to Olive. "Are you okay? You forgot your coat at the table. Esther saw you go out through the kitchens." She went around behind Olive and pulled the wool coat up over her arms. "I don't want you to get sick again. You're still only a few weeks out from that bad pneumonia. I know that it's just a myth that cold can cause—"

Olive cut her off by lifting the phone with the screenshots Derek sent. The comments were beginning to get nasty about them, judging from his subsequent texts.

Stella's eyes darted around. She swiped through, expression becoming stony. "*Shit*, she put this on Twitter and Instagram. How did she get this?"

"She went to my apartment. I talked to her and tried to get

her to take it down." Olive leaned on the wall. "I'm sorry. I forgot she had a key."

Stella's forehead furrowed. "So she *didn't* break in? She had a key? You just left the binder out when you knew your jealous ex-girlfriend had access to your apartment?" She squeezed the phone in her fist before handing it back to Olive. "Maybe . . . I mean, my bosses don't read random Instagram story threads. No one's going to put any stock in what a random ex says about you. Maybe this won't affect the job. Maybe they won't see it. But oh god . . ." Stella held a clenched fist against the brick wall.

"You're mad at me?"

"I just meant it seems a little thoughtless to forget about Lindsay having the key."

"I've had kind of a lot going on in the past year, Stella."

"Right, I know. I get it." Stella didn't appear entirely convinced. She still wasn't even looking at Olive. She couldn't even make eye contact with her. "None of what she's saying seems credible especially with your history. Honestly, she just comes off a little *crazy*. Don't worry, this shouldn't impact you too much."

Crazy. This was the same word Lindsay had used after watching Olive have a panic attack the first time. The same word she used at the hospital when she talked about Olive and Stella's relationship. Now, the word hit Olive just where it would hurt the most.

"Shouldn't impact me? My name's being plastered around the internet. Exactly what I was worried would happen." Olive paced back and forth outside of the hotel, her ankles screaming from the height of her heels. "You don't understand. I told you. After Jake saved that kid there were posts plastering his name and face all over the internet. Everyone was talking about his story. People wrote horrible things. I'm never going to forget it. I've told you about how this kind of thing makes me anxious."

Stella finally looked at her. "It was awful what happened to Jake, but that's not going to happen with this."

"What if—"

"It won't. In any case, soon I think I'm going to have my promotion, and all the events will be over after tonight." Stella paced back and forth in the small space. Her heels clicked beneath her with each step. Again, not meeting Olive's eye. "None of this matters."

Over after tonight.

"It doesn't *matter*?" Frustration was now added to the slew of emotions roiling in Olive's gut. "The promotion is still all you can think of? Are you even listening to me?"

"You don't understand what it's like to be under this much pressure. My job is stressful, and this is what I've been working toward my entire life."

"Because being a nurse in the ER is just picnics and rainbows? I don't understand what it's like to have a high-stress job? Are you kidding me?"

"I just meant that it's not like nursing was your first choice. I mean, you sort of just went into it after the art history thing didn't work out. It wasn't your lifelong dream. Being a captain at an airline is a *really big deal*."

Olive recoiled as if she'd slapped her. "Yeah . . . okay . . ."

Stella turned back to her, regret lining her face. She clapped a hand over her mouth. But she couldn't take that back. It didn't matter to her. Because Olive didn't matter to her. That was what she was saying.

It was the confirmation of everything Lindsay had said. It would never work. Stella had always known it wouldn't work, because yeah, Stella had big dreams. How could anything in Olive's life or Olive herself compare to the things Stella wanted? They couldn't.

She should have listened. To everyone.

"Oh my god, Olive. I'm so sorry. I was stressed about to-night, and I didn't mean—"

"This was a mistake. God, my mom was right about put-ting my name out there too. I should have known . . . I don't want . . ." All of her worries and anxieties from the past weeks were slamming into her at once.

"I'm sorry. I wasn't being sensitive at all. That was awful." Stella held Olive's upper arms. An expression of sudden under-standing mixed with panic on her face. "Of course this whole situation is triggering for you. Slow down, you don't want what?"

"This." She gestured between them, stepping away from Stella's touch. "I got caught up. And I wasn't thinking. I'm going to get hurt." Olive's mind was moving a mile a minute. Regrets piled on regrets. The articles. The interviews. The fake relation-ship. All of it. It was all an enormous mistake.

Stella had been up front. Stella had told her exactly what she wanted, and Olive had been blinded by dimples and orgasms into pretending that she wasn't hoping for a different outcome. Olive felt like her heart was creased and scored like a movie ticket, ready to be cleanly torn apart at any moment.

This would end in rejection, and she couldn't bear to hear Stella say she didn't want her. Not with everything else going on. Her sister. Lindsay. Her mother. Probably even Derek and Joni. They all knew that Stella was out of Olive's league. That was why they'd all thought this would end in heartbreak from the very beginning.

"I should have listened," Olive mumbled. "To everyone."

Stella seemed to be struggling for words, dread widening her sparkling eyes. "What are you talking about?"

"I'm sick of pretending. You don't even *like* me."

"I do like you, Olive."

"Right. As a *friend*."

The word clanged between them.

Stella went still. Olive had never seen Stella freeze like this.

"I told you, Olive. I-I hurt people. You *had* a toxic ex, but I know I *was* the toxic ex. The one who didn't remember to call. I was the one who left two good people with broken hearts because something inside me is messed up. I couldn't hurt you. But I *did* hurt you tonight." Stella's shoulders slumped. It was as if she was shrinking. "Ugh, I did what I swore to myself I wouldn't do."

"Stella."

Her voice was small now, more tentative than Olive had ever heard it. "After Florida . . . I missed you. We had *just* met, but I missed you."

Olive couldn't figure out what to say that wouldn't reveal how entirely infatuated she'd been after that one day together. No wonder Derek had been trying to stop this.

"I came home and my friend in HR made an offhand comment about how gorgeous you were and how the airline would be on board with anything that would keep the story going. I couldn't stop thinking about you, but I know myself. I couldn't be trusted with someone like you especially with what was going on with your family. I came up with this stupid idea."

"What do you mean?"

"I should have left you alone. But everything was so easy." Stella stared down at the pavement, her black high heel tapping where flattened circles of gum interrupted the grain of the concrete.

The space between their bodies felt tangible, like something Olive could touch if she extended her fingertips a few inches toward the woman she loved. She still couldn't find words.

Stella squeezed her eyes shut. "It's never been like this for me with anyone. The day I found out you were sick and came over, I almost called out of work and dropped everything because I hated leaving you." She shook her head. "That's not how romantic relationships are with me. I always put work first, because if I don't, I'll fail. How could I ask you . . ." Stella's eyes lifted, surveying Olive in a way that made her feel completely bare. "I couldn't ask *you* to be with someone like me, who wouldn't put you first. God, I've been so selfish."

Olive shook her head. "You told me what you wanted. I didn't listen."

"No, I—"

"You're allowed not to want me, Stella. It's okay."

Well, it was okay in the sense that Olive's life already felt shattered. *What does it matter if someone stomps on the glass shards? Fuck,* even Olive's stupid internal monologue metaphors were hackneyed and histrionic.

Olive sighed. "I thought . . . well, you were there for me so many times, I thought maybe . . . But *that's* my fault. You were honest the entire time, and I chose to put my heart on the line. I'm not angry with you. I'm mad at myself for being stupid."

"You aren't stupid." Stella's hand twitched as if she wanted to reach out, but she balled it into a fist and locked it to her side.

Olive understood. Stella didn't even want to touch her because she was so afraid of giving Olive the wrong idea again.

"I'm sorry I've been a distraction from your job and your dad." Olive huffed self-deprecatingly. "I guess I'm just like Lindsay warned you I was at the hotel. Jesus, no wonder you didn't leave me your number then."

Shit, Olive should not have said that. More evidence she was in no mental state to be having a conversation like this. The darkest, most anxious instincts of her brain were on overdrive, forcing words out of her mouth before she could stop them.

"No. You can't think that about yourself. That's not why." Stella took a reluctant step toward Olive. "That night, I thought you were still hung up on Lindsay. You barely said anything after we got back to the hotel room that night after running into her. I thought *she* was your type, all tiny and blond and hipstery and Coachella sexy, and I wasn't those things. She said the thing about overnight phone calls and you had so much going on with your brother." Stella exhaled and crossed her arms over her chest. "Everything about that day was perfect."

How could someone sound so defeated while saying the word *perfect*?

"So perfect you just left?"

"Olive . . . things were too easy between us. Magical romance? This kind of thing—sparks and fantasy—it isn't real. I've never believed it existed. Not for me." She touched the brick wall beside her as if she needed extra support. "We're so different but it just worked. All of it worked."

Why was she saying all of this like what they had together was a bad thing? Like she regretted that it worked.

And then it clicked in Olive's brain. A sharp bolt of understanding pierced the fog. It was that too-familiar voice that always hissed about catastrophe and triggered the worst of Olive's darkest days. That stupid voice now bellowed the truth that Olive had been desperate not to see.

Stella doesn't want you because you're broken.

Olive's hands covered her eyes, messing up the hair she'd been so worried about hours ago. Olive thought of her dad on the phone. He was so devastated over her mother's depression. Olive had days like that. Could Olive inflict herself on a partner?

Lindsay's words continued to echo over and over and over again. *She's never going to want you that way.* Lindsay had been with her for years. She'd seen it too. Broken.

Stella was gorgeous, successful, and perfect. Eventually, Stella would meet someone else. Someone she wasn't embarrassed to post photos of on her Instagram. Someone more successful. More *driven*. To use the same word Stella just did. She needed someone who could actually help her in her career and not tie her more firmly to the ground. Stella was meant to soar. All Olive would ever be was a tether.

Olive had gone into tonight wanting to tell Stella she loved her.

But now, as much as she wanted to, Olive couldn't be that selfish.

She loved Stella too much to ask anything more of her.

Olive willed her voice to be steady and calm. It wasn't Stella's job to take care of her right now. She'd done enough. She straightened and wrapped her coat around her, but it didn't block any of the chill. "I think I need to go home." Olive tried to swallow, but her throat felt thick. "After all, it's time to break up."

"Break up?"

"The fake relationship. Just like what you said. After tonight, the promotion and everything. You should be good. It worked." That hot pressure built beneath Olive's face, but she could hold it back a little longer. "I am so thrilled for you. You really deserve all of it. And I . . . I just want you to be happy." Her hand reached out and patted Stella's. Once. Twice.

No, that was too much. Olive didn't want to let go, but she had to.

"I'm so sorry to leave like this. I just . . . I can't be here right now." Olive paused, wanting the woman in front of her to say *something*, but she didn't. The Stella who always talked in paragraphs and learned breath control so she wouldn't have to pause before her thoughts came out was absolutely silent.

She didn't tell Olive to stay.

She didn't stop her when Olive turned back toward the alley leading to the street in front of the hotel.

All Olive heard was the echoing scrape of her uncomfortable shoes on uneven concrete as her tears froze to her cheeks.

Stella never said anything.

Chapter 50

Derek sat at her kitchen counter, staring at Olive as if she were a ticking time bomb. Her black tights skimmed over the kitchen floor as she put away the flowers Joni had sent and the food she'd dropped off. He pushed a glass of ice water across the granite toward her. She wished it were whiskey, but the new therapist she had seen yesterday thought the drinking might be making the depression worse.

Why did healthy life choices sometimes fucking suck?

She'd sat in the back at the funeral. Her niece beelined to her as soon as the service ended and jumped into her arms, demanding to know when she'd babysit her again. Heather had hugged her once too. They hadn't asked her to help with anything, though. Morgan sat on her right while Derek sat on her left and held her hand the entire time.

Through the priest's homily.

Through the long, drawn-out prayers.

Through the liturgical music.

All things Jake wouldn't have wanted.

None of it seemed like her brother.

Maybe that was why she hadn't cried.

Her dry eyes might have given her mother more ammunition against her, but it hadn't seemed like she'd noticed. Her mother hadn't looked anywhere beyond the casket. Her gaunt face remained flat while Olive's father shook every hand and even accepted the hugs. Her dad let people hug him?

Olive downed half the water in a choking gulp and then walked over to her living room couch with it and collapsed.

Derek sat beside her, his head resting on her shoulder. "I'm sorry, O."

"Today sucked." She set her glass on the coffee table harder than she meant to, and she had to check to make sure she hadn't broken it.

Her phone vibrated in her pocket. She told herself she was hoping it was her sister, who had reluctantly said she'd call later. But every time she had looked down at her phone for the last five days, she only wanted to see one name there.

Stella.

And once again, she was disappointed.

Olive swiped the random junk call away to ignore it, and she let the phone slip out of her fingers and clatter onto the coffee table.

Stella hadn't called her since she left her at the Christmas party. Well, since Olive's heart shattered as she'd walked away from Stella and sobbed all the way home in an incredibly expensive Uber.

"Why didn't she come today?" Derek frowned. "I assumed . . ."

"We're broken up." She tapped the glass with her nails, and a sob escaped her throat. She'd avoided talking about Stella all week. "Well, I mean we didn't ever get together."

"What?" Derek's dark eyes searched hers. "You said the party went well." Uncharacteristically, he hadn't pressed her for details about Stella. He'd seemed as broken as she had been since Jake's death.

Yes, Olive had lied, but Jake's death eclipsed her relationship troubles. She could only manage wallowing in sadness about one thing at a time. The lawyer had called yesterday to try to set up an appointment to go over the will. She hadn't called him back yet.

"It did go well in a sense. I think she'll get the job she wants. That was the point, right?" So much bitterness in her voice these days. "Our relationship ending was always the plan."

"But—"

"I don't want to talk about Stella." Olive shuffled through random journals on her coffee table to find the one she wanted. It had a cactus on the cover. Jake had bought it for her after his first round of national parks travel. The paper she slid out of it bore the scars of creases in two places. It had been folded in Jake's desk when she'd found it. The list was in her brother's handwriting, a slanted mix of cursive and print. She held it out to Derek.

"That's the list?"

"Yup." She grabbed her glass and swallowed another gulp.

"You did most of this stuff that wasn't crossed off." He scanned through, his gaze faltering as he reached the last line. "Oh, Olive."

"Yeah."

She knew why his expression shattered. Hers had too when she'd read it the first time. He'd labeled all the goals with dates. When he made the goal. When he completed the goal. The last couple written at the bottom were ones he had made in the days before his accident, after he'd called her to tell her about the Disney reservation, his insurance policy to make sure she didn't flake on him again.

Run a half-marathon with Olive - - help Olive realize she's worthy of happiness.

"His last goal was for you," Derek said softly.

She leaned her head onto Derek's shoulder. "Do you believe that people know stuff? Like, have some preternatural sense their death is coming?"

"I never did before."

"Me neither." She swirled her drink, making the ice crack and chip on the side of the glass. "He didn't like Lindsay. But I think this was about more than that. I started trying to do everything on the list because I thought it was what he wanted. I thought it would make me feel less guilty about being a disappointment."

Derek shifted his position to face her. He took her hands in his. "No one who'd ever met Jake would think it was possible for you to disappoint him. Ever. He was so fucking proud of you."

She didn't answer. Couldn't answer.

"He loved you. I think all he was saying was that he wanted you to know your worth. He must have known what it was like with you and your mom and Lindsay even before all this shit went down. He was making changes with his life and doing big things, and he wanted you to know that you could too. Don't you think that's why he made the list in the first place?"

Her shoulders slumped. "I miss him." She shielded her face, as if that would hide her tears.

"I know. Me too." He hugged her tightly. "This year has been hell on you."

She sniffed and pulled away. "Maybe I'm ready for a fresh start. Maybe I was thinking about the list all wrong." Maybe it wasn't about national parks or whitewater rafting at all.

She grabbed a pen and turned to a blank page in her notebook.

***

A couple of hours later, Derek was picking up food and she was still scribbling ideas in her notebook. A text came in on her phone, breaking the silence with a loud buzzing that even made Gus jump from where he was snuggled beside her.

> STELLA
> I miss you.

She dropped the pen. Olive couldn't hold it back anymore. When Derek walked through the door she was still crying. Full-on Claire Danes in *Homeland* ugly weeping. He pushed the brown bag onto the counter and kneeled down next to her.

"Shit, Olive." He eyed the phone still clutched in her fist. "Did your family say something else?"

Olive shook her head and hiccuped in an almost comically pitiful way. It was a testament to how much Derek felt bad for her today that he didn't laugh at the ridiculous sound.

She held up the phone to him.

He flopped down beside her again. "Spill everything, Olivia, or I'm not sharing the cheese fries."

"I do really want those cheese fries." She sniffled but then laughed in spite of herself. "Jalapeños and bacon?"

"Yeah." He grabbed a box of tissues from the side table and took it under his arm so he could bring her the bribery greasy potatoes and napkins.

Olive stared at the box of tissues. It was one of the boxes Stella had bought her during her pneumonia. It wasn't even the generic kind. She'd bought her *name-brand* tissues. The memory made her erupt into another round of tears.

Frowning, Derek opened the fries and handed her one. The starch and salt were basically the best comfort food ever created and were exactly what she needed. Fuck, she was lucky to have Derek.

"Since the tissue box just made you lose it more, I feel like you just need to get it all out. What the hell happened?"

She blew her nose once and then every detail from the night of the party came out.

Derek listened without interrupting, and when she finished the story, he stared at her for several seconds.

"Well, shit. You guys goddamn Spider-Manned each other."

"What?"

"The classic film moment of our youth in which Tobey Maguire leaves Kirsten Dunst in—I think—a graveyard after breaking up with her for her own good. Jesus Christ."

"No . . . that's not what happened—"

"You didn't tell her you loved her because you thought you hold her back. She didn't fight for you because she really thinks that she hurts everyone she dates and she had just hurt you after what happened with the photos and Lindsay. She literally said that." He chomped on a fry for dramatic effect. "Spider-Manned."

"*No . . .*" She took her hair out of the neat bun and rubbed the areas of tension on her scalp as she processed his words.

"Stella *clearly* loves you but has never been in love before and was completely freaking out about it and her past and because you were just mind-fucked—and not in a sexy way—by Lindsay you couldn't hear what she was trying to tell you."

Bewildered, Olive replayed the conversation several more times before the weight of what he said sank in.

"You really think she loves me? She didn't want to hurt me so she was afraid of a relationship?"

"Yes, you idiot." He threw out his hands in exasperation. Only Derek would call her an idiot on the day of her brother's funeral and have it be exactly what she needed. "Jesus, did she really say that sappy-ass thing about magic and sparks?" He rolled his eyes.

"Yes . . ."

"She loves you." He patted her knee once and then grabbed his phone. "So, what are you going to do about it?" While she sat speechless, he typed and swiped on the screen and then grimaced. "Also, apparently the term Spider-Manning means something very different on Urban Dictionary, and now I'm going to get some really weird targeted ads. Don't look it up. But, yeah, back to Stella. Plan?"

Snorting, Olive grabbed the notebook from the floor where it had fallen during her mental breakdown. She read over the list she'd written and settled on one particular line. "So, I might have one idea."

Chapter 51

On a scale where ten is completely content with one's life choices, and zero is regretting everything, Olive Murphy was sitting pretty at a negative three. Unfortunately, she was also sitting in the cockpit of a goddamn Cessna.

"How're you feeling?" Esther said from the seat beside her.

"Terrified." She'd taken the Valium as instructed by Joni in conjunction with a conversation with her new therapist. Her panic felt like an indentation on a piece of paper. She couldn't see it exactly, but if she focused on it too long, she could feel where it should be. Esther was performing her final checks, chatting with the people in the small tower at the regional airport. Olive was breathing deliberately slowly. Calling Esther had been terrifying in and of itself, but she knew Stella wouldn't mind.

Esther's cheeks glowed, an easy smile on her face.

"I'm glad you called me. It's been too long since I've been up in the air for the joy of flying. It's a beautiful day. Now I have an excuse to get away from my teenagers for a few hours."

Olive laughed and swallowed, gripping the giant headphones on her ears.

"Anxiety is real and challenging, and I'm not going to pretend I know how to handle it for everyone. But for Margaret we had one particular technique that helped. Would you want to hear it?"

Olive swallowed as she surveyed the mosaic of dials and knobs and screens in front of her. Why were there so many? "Yes, please?"

"We started by acknowledging her fears and how fear can be a blessing and a curse."

"A blessing?"

"Sure, fear at its most basic is a way of protecting ourselves."

"That's true."

"Margaret is a high school history teacher, so she found an Eleanor Roosevelt quote and used it as a mantra. I've heard it so many times, I know it by heart now."

Olive shifted her weight, trying to settle herself more comfortably in the seat. "What is it?"

Esther smiled. "'You gain strength, courage, and confidence by every experience in which you really stop to look fear in the face. You are able to say to yourself, "I have lived through this horror. I can take the next thing that comes along." You must do the thing you think you cannot do.'"

"'You must do the thing you think you cannot do,'" Olive repeated.

"Yes." Esther cleared her throat. "From what Stella told me, you're used to looking fear in the face in your job."

The mention of Stella's name sent a shock of pain through her. "I guess so."

"Getting in the plane was the first step." She patted Olive's shoulder. "You have lived this horror. You can take the next thing that comes along."

Olive nodded.

"Now the next step is getting in the air. Are you ready?"

Olive nodded again. She stared straight out the window, locking in her body. She could do this. She could do this. She *could* do this.

Esther moved through an effortless choreography of the steps for takeoff. Olive stopped trying to guess what it all meant and instead focused on the blue sky, thinking through Esther's words. She thought about all the things she was scared of. Heights. Public speaking and singing. Her fear always seemed like a unilaterally bad thing. A joke her parents would use when she wouldn't do the daring thing on the playground or dive into the deep end like her sister. *"Oh, Olive's just afraid of everything."*

But it had also helped her. Fear had stopped her from proposing to Lindsay or moving in with her, which had been the right decisions. Fear had made her cautious. Which could be good or bad, she supposed.

As the plane sped forward, she thought of times she'd been brave.

Coming out to her parents. Even though Jake had set the tone for that in their family, it had still been hard. Running that stupid half-marathon. Going to nursing school and working her ass off to be good at her job even on the days it scared the shit out of her.

Fighting for Jake even though she'd lost the battle against the lawyers.

I have lived through this horror.

Losing Jake had been the worst thing that had ever happened to her. It had made all the other fears look small afterward. It was why she made herself train for the race. It was why she made it on that stupid plane to Disney World.

You must do the thing you think you cannot do.

And now here she was.

She gripped the seat as the plane lifted into the air.

"Big, deep breaths, Olive," Esther said softly.

She sucked in a breath through her nose and let it out through her mouth. The fear was still there.

But that was okay.

Because it didn't own her.

She risked a glance out the window. She hadn't gotten a chance to look outside at all during the other flight, not that she'd have dared.

"Everything looks so small," she said, somewhat stupidly. Of course it seemed small. She was up in the air. *Thousands of feet* up in the air.

Esther exhaled in agreement. "It certainly is a new perspective. Helps you see the forest for the trees . . . to reverse and bastardize an old aphorism."

"I know what you mean."

"When I first started going up in planes, I loved watching everything become the size of toys. You can still see the big things, but everything else sort of fades. Strange how sometimes you can see stuff from the air that you can't see if you're standing close to it on the ground." She pointed to the baseball field with its tall fence around it. "Just a new way of seeing things."

In a weird way, Olive understood. All the houses seemed to blend together. But a big, shiny lake was obvious from above. The small mountains in the distance. The way the highway off-ramps looked like big clover shapes.

What were the big things in her life?

Her job.

Derek.

Stella.

She shut her eyes tightly, thinking of their last conversation. She'd postmortemed every word several times with Derek since the day of the funeral.

Even the memory of that conversation made Olive flinch. Stella had obviously felt terrible after saying it, but she'd been right too. There *were* big, important things Olive let fear talk her out of. What did she want? What were her dreams? Not Jake's dreams. *Her* dreams.

The dreams she'd scribbled down in the spiral notebook two weeks ago.

To go to Italy. Paris. Cairo. London.

To see all the art she'd read about in college.

But mostly she wanted Stella.

Stella might break her heart, and that was terrifying. But if Stella really did love her, Olive was ready to risk heartbreak for the chance at being with her. Stella had revealed so much in that conversation, but Olive had been too overwhelmed to hear it. It had been a big step for Stella, and Olive had just run off . . .

She'd let Lindsay fill her mind with the idea that Olive was unworthy of someone like Stella. She'd been so in love with Stella, this was easy to believe.

Now she had a plan, and this lesson had been part of it.

This time she'd be up front. She'd tell her she was in love with her. She'd open herself up to whatever hurt might come in the future because the alternative was worse—losing her without even fighting for her. That was the piece that Stella hadn't understood. She was so afraid of hurting the person she loved that she was too afraid to fall in love. Olive needed to tell her that she was worth it. Loving her was *worth* the risk of future heartache. Everything had risks.

"You still with me, Olive?" Esther asked.

Olive jolted. She'd almost forgot where she was. "Oh, um yeah. I'm good."

Right. She was in an airplane.

And she wasn't completely hating it.

"Sure everything's fine?"

"Yeah." She sighed. "Thank you so much for doing this. So, have you—have you seen Stella lately?" Olive's attempt at nonchalance failed miserably.

Esther's mouth quirked to the side. "No. No, I haven't."

"Oh, okay."

"You know she quit the airline, right?"

"She . . . what?" Olive's mouth fell open.

"Not sure I should be telling you this . . ."

"Please. Is she okay?"

"Seems to be. She should have been promoted years ago. She filed an HR complaint about Kevin O'Halloran's behavior at the party and then decided she didn't want to work for the airline anymore. Didn't want to support a company with a culture that didn't value women. Said she was sick of waiting to be valued. I'm looking for a new job too for similar reasons."

"Oh my god."

"I've heard a couple of the younger pilots were pretty inspired by her."

"Does that mean she's got to start over with a new company? What does that mean about her becoming a captain?"

Esther shrugged her shoulders. "Will probably be delayed a bit. Not by much. She's talented and smart, with an excellent record. She'll find a new job. She'll accomplish her goals. She told me that some things are more important than a career. Can't say I ever expected to hear Stella Soriano say that." She smiled knowingly.

The plane shifted in the air, angling slightly. "We're going back now?"

"Yes. Only logged a short flight today. Figured you'd want to start slow."

Olive's leg twitched beneath her; she was desperate to be on the ground again. But not for the reason she expected. "That's great. Thank you. I—uh, there's something I need to do."

Something Olive needed to do right the fuck now. Plan be damned.

Chapter 52

Olive knocked on the door. Stella's car was in the driveway. She must be here. She had to be here.

Olive heard the sound of footsteps from inside. Her heart galloped. Stella pulled the door open, and her eyes went wide. She stood frozen to the spot. Silent. Stella Soriano was speechless.

Olive pushed a plant in a periwinkle blue pot into Stella's arms. "It's a philodendron. Easy to take care of. I named it Seymour Hoffman on the way over, but obviously that's up for negotiation given that it's your plant and not mine. I guess it's also a bit macabre since he's dead. Rest in peace, seriously, he was such an amazing actor. Maybe Collins? Or Wilson? All a play on the whole *Phil* thing . . . you know?" Good fucking god, what was she saying? "I went up in a plane today." Olive pointed to the sky as if to illustrate the point. As if Stella didn't know that planes flew.

Stella still didn't speak. She wrapped her slender arms around the potted plant and stared blankly at Olive.

"I always liked you, Stella. I never fake liked you. I agreed to be your fake girlfriend because of that. Even though my friends thought it was a bad idea, I went along with it because I liked being with you. I liked going to the awards thing. I liked meeting your dad. And talking to you on the phone every night. I know you're nervous about relationships because you say you'll be a bad girlfriend and those other two women got hurt. But there you were this entire time, doing girlfriend things. And doing them so fucking perfectly. I'm not asking for anything beyond exclusivity and the promise that both of us will be willing to try to do things that scare us. I'm not asking for everything to be perfect right away because I'm sure as fuck not perfect. You should know that I have depression and get panic attacks, but I'm seeing a therapist now. And I know you're scared of hurting me, but I'm here to tell you that you are worth that risk. I know who you are. I know you. Believe me, I know there are absolutely no guarantees in life, but I want to be with you anyway. And that's . . . that's what I came to say. With the plant. Not that I was saying that *with* the plant, but you know, accompanied by a plant. Or whatever."

Stella parted her perfect mouth, still mute for several seconds before she spoke in a quiet, tentative voice. "That's the most words I've ever heard you say all at once."

"Maybe you're rubbing off on me."

Stella slid the plant onto the entryway table beside her and stepped out onto the porch. "I'm sorry for what I said at the party. All of it."

"I'm sorry about what *I* said at the party." Olive braced a hand on the railing, focusing on the bare rosebush beside her so she wouldn't have to make eye contact with Stella. Her eyes were too distracting. "I found out right before the party that Jake passed away. Then the whole Lindsay binder thing happened, and I completely spiraled. I didn't hear what you were saying because I was feeling too shitty about myself and everything else. That's no excuse, but it's the truth."

"Oh god, Olive. I'm so sorry about Jake." Stella wrapped her arms around Olive's shoulders.

Olive leaned into the embrace and inhaled the comforting, familiar scent. "It wasn't that I didn't trust you. I didn't want to think about it. I wanted to be happy for a few hours before I had to get into shit with my family again, and I didn't want the entire night to be about that. I wasn't in the best place, but I was too scared of seeming needy to be honest about what was happening."

Stella's mouth tensed as she shook her head. "I should have realized."

With a little shake of the head, Olive held Stella tighter. "No, I should have told you."

"The funeral and—"

"All over now. It was bad. But Derek came." Olive gave a watery nod. "Even though I feel like Jake was gone a year ago, I do feel closure now."

"That's important." She took Olive's hand. "Closure."

"It is." Olive plucked a dried leaf off the bush and then flicked it away. "I really don't regret going to the party, though."

"I'm sorry I was too distracted that night to notice what was going on. And I'm sorry for putting my career above everything else. It's always been important to me, but with what's going on with my dad . . ." Stella combed her fingers through Olive's hair. "I couldn't do *anything*. I can't make the Parkinson's stop. No matter how many lists I make. No matter what I do, he's going to get worse. I think I threw myself at my job because it was something I could control. I focused in on the goal of making captain, but I lost sight of everything that really matters. And then I met you. And I saw what my job was at the party. I saw who I was working for through your eyes."

They were mirrors in a way. Both of them watching their loved ones suffer. Both unable to help in any meaningful way. Both coping—one with work and the other with someone else's list. Both scared shitless of hurting the other one.

Olive gently cradled Stella's face in her hands. "I'm so sorry for what's happening with your dad. I'm sorry if I said anything to make you feel bad about your work or who you are. I didn't mean to."

"No, it felt freeing. Throwing that drink in Kevin's face was one of the happiest moments of my life." Stella's face sobered. "Then you were gone. Which was one of the worst moments of my life."

"I'm sorry."

Stella shook her head. She pulled away and squared herself to Olive like she was a diver in the Olympics taking that deep breath before the plunge. Her eyes shuttered but then opened wide. "Please stop apologizing. I need to say something. At the party . . ." She paused as if the memory caused her pain. "You kept saying that I was honest with you from the start. B-but I wasn't. After that day at Disney, I wanted to claw Lindsay's eyes out when she showed up in the hotel lobby."

Olive suppressed a smile. "You were jealous?"

"Oh my god. You have no idea. I came back home and my dad kept asking me what was wrong with me over and over again." Stella's large, twinkling eyes became gravely serious once more, as if she were about to reveal a secret shame. "I forgot to make *coffee* one morning, Olive. *Coffee.*"

"Holy shit. Because of . . ."

"*You.*" She shook her head. "It was utterly terrifying. I couldn't stop thinking about you. I just wanted to talk to you, and it was confusing. It was never like that with anyone. All I knew is that I wanted to be around you all the time, and that if I tried to be in a relationship I would probably wind up breaking your heart."

"Fuck it all, Derek was right, you were Spider-Manning me too."

"Huh?"

"Never mind. Will explain later, but like, don't google it. Anyway—"

"I thought if we were doing this maybe we could be friends and then I could at least see you." She sighed.

"Stella, I—" Olive nodded, but Stella interrupted before she could say anything else.

"So, I was afraid, and this utterly ridiculous solution occurred to me like I said before, and everything was fine. I thought if we defined the relationship or whatever it would all get screwed up, and I'd lose you." Her laugh was mirthless. "God, I was talking about *your* fear of flying like it was a big deal. Olive, I don't care if you ever get on a plane again."

Once again, Olive was shocked. "You don't?"

Stella folded Olive's hands into her own and looked at her in that blazing way that made Olive feel both perfectly seen and perfectly loved.

"Stella?"

"I'll travel with you by boat or by train. Whatever. I quit my job because it was actually killing me and my self-worth. No dream is worth that. You helped me see that just by being you and watching you fight for your brother and love him so fiercely. You helped me see that my dad doesn't actually care if I make captain, he just wants me happy. I love being a pilot, but I realized other things were more important."

Olive couldn't speak as her eyes grew hazy and warm.

"*You* were always more important." Stella's throat bobbed. "Olive 'Murphy's Law' Murphy, I want to put in a formal request to be your actual girlfriend. Real girlfriend. Saying that aloud alerts me to how absurd that sounds. You know, I couldn't even post the pictures of us on my Instagram because they felt too real. Too personal. I feel like I have no right to ask you to be my girlfriend after how I treated you and led you on when I didn't even know what I wanted, but—"

"Yes."

"Yes, what?"

Olive laughed and covered Stella's hand with her own. "Yes, I'll be your girlfriend."

"Are you sure?" Stella's dark brown eyes glittered with unshed tears.

Olive nodded and kissed Stella's knuckles. "But incidentally, as I said, I was on a plane today. I was gearing up for some big romantic gesture, but this is better. Anyway, I actually didn't hate it. I love that you're a pilot for many reasons, not the least of which being that you look hot as hell in your uniform, and I still have many plans for that necktie of yours."

Stella grinned and clasped Olive's hand to her chest. "Gosh, when we were kissing after the awards banquet, I wanted to rip your clothes off even then. I've missed you so much. Not just the sex, which is amazing by the way, and I would really like to have it all the time with you. Additionally, I'm very interested in all future recreational necktie activities."

Olive snorted.

"But I missed everything about you." Stella traced a delicate line along Olive's cheek.

"It was real before we knew it was real." And Olive brushed her mouth lightly over Stella's. She tasted like chocolate and honey today. "It was always real."

Pulling away an inch, Stella smiled. "If it walks like a duck . . ."

"Exactly. If it texts like a girlfriend and"—Olive spoke between urgent kisses—"and kisses like a girlfriend and fu—"

"I get the idea." Stella's mouth drooped in a sudden frown. "I still think this was all my fault. I messed up your life. I hate I wasn't there for you when you *needed* me. I'm so sorry about Jake." Stella pulled her into a firm embrace. "I should've been there."

"You didn't mess anything up. It was my choice not to tell you about Jake, and it was the wrong one. And just so you know, I didn't have a life before I met you. I mean, I did. But I wasn't living it. I had a plane ticket and a race bib and a checklist. But I was doing it all for someone else. Someone who's gone. It felt like going through the motions. Now I want it all for *me*. I want every experience. And ideally, that would mean spending those moments with you."

"I'd like that." Stella's smile stretched, deepening her dimples.

"When I was on that tiny and scary plane today, I realized I was more afraid of losing you than of dying in a fiery wreckage crater."

Stella pulled away enough so their eyes could meet. "You really do know how to sweet-talk."

"I know how to sweet-talk *you*." Olive kissed her neck. "Label makers." She kissed her shoulder. "Rustic organizational wicker baskets. Color-coordinated binder tabs."

"I hate you." Stella's mouth pushed into an adorable and also very kissable pout, so Olive took full advantage of it.

"Do you?" she said against Stella's lips.

"No."

"That brings me to the last thing I wanted to say . . . Don't freak out." She took a step away and stood to her fullest height.

"Okay . . ." Stella stiffened, looking confused.

"I love you. If there's one thing I learned with Jake it's that I shouldn't wait about telling people how I feel, so I needed to tell you the whole truth right now."

Stella swallowed audibly but didn't speak.

"I love you even though you talk in paragraphs and can't stand messes and you make elaborate binders with multicolor tabs in elegant fonts. I love all of those things about you. I love everything about you because for the first time in my life I'm not afraid. Life can suck. And I know it's going to suck sometimes, but as long as we're together, we'll be fine."

Stella grinned wider than Olive had ever seen her grin before. "I love you, too."

It was Olive's turn to stand frozen, barely believing it.

Eyes sparkling, Stella laughed. "Even though you're surly and a little messy and think airplanes stay up by magic."

"At least we both agree on Swedish Fish." And between the kissing and the laughter, Olive knew everything was going to be okay.

Epilogue

Seventeen Months Later

"How is it possible you look that good after a million-hour flight?" Olive flopped down on the perfectly neat bedspread. "Sleep. Need sleep now." Her voice was a zombielike grunt.

Stella tugged on her arm. "No. Fight it, Olive."

"The sandman cometh. Jet-lag gods are strong." Olive yawned. "Pillows comfy."

Stella whispered sweetly into her ear, pushing aside Olive's wild hair. "We'll get coffee. Or coffee-flavored *gelato*." Stella pronounced each syllable of *gelato* like it was a depraved sex act, making Olive want to stay in bed for an entirely different reason. At least until she yawned again.

"Five minutes." Olive's eyes closed.

"No, if you fall asleep, I'll fall asleep and we only have three days here before our next stop." Stella marched across the room.

Olive managed to convince one of her eyes to open.

The light gilded Stella as she stood at the hotel window. That lovely buttery sunshine of a Florentine morning. God, her girlfriend was beautiful. She flung open the doors onto a small balcony. Olive inhaled, drinking in the smells of the old city coming in on the breeze. She peeled herself out of bed.

She took Stella's hand and stood beside her. After a few minutes of listening to the bustle of the city, Olive kissed the exact spot on Stella's left hand that she hoped would never be bare again after tomorrow.

"Okay." Olive shook out her head in a way rather reminiscent of Gus when he came in from the rain. "I'm going to go take an incredibly quick shower to wake myself up and wash my face. Then we can get moving and get started on your elaborate itinerary."

Stella pouted and eyed the tote bag on the dresser that contained the Stella Soriano comprehensive binder guide to the best-ever, long-awaited European adventure. "I wanted to make sure we made the most of our time."

"By elaborate I meant incredibly thoughtful and wonderful itinerary." Olive kissed her.

"Damn straight."

"Who says damn straight anymore?"

"This beautiful creature in front of you." Stella gestured to herself.

"You are beautiful."

"So are you." Stella pressed her body to Olive's, and Olive brushed a hand down Stella's soft curves.

"Just give me five minutes."

"Five minutes." Stella checked her watch as if she were setting a timer.

Olive rushed through the shower, but it didn't help her wake up. She was as exhausted as she'd been before. She pulled a towel around her.

After opening the door, she blinked twice and then smiled.

Stella was splayed out on the bed. Snoring, drooling, and cuddling a pillow. Olive pulled on a pair of sweats and a T-shirt. She draped a blanket over Stella, lay down, and closed her eyes. They could sightsee later.

Within minutes, the sleep cuddler herself was spooned around her very contented heat source.

Acknowledgments

First and foremost, I want to thank everyone reading this book. I am deeply grateful and honored you chose to spend some of your precious time with Olive and Stella. As a debut author, knowing that people are out there reading this book feels like an absolute miracle to me—a slightly terrifying miracle . . .

To Mariah Nichols, my ray-of-sunshine agent. You changed my life. Thank you for your wisdom and infinite optimism. And thank you, Bob Diforio, for your expertise and for always answering my many, many questions.

To Lisa Bonvissuto, editor extraordinaire and character-development genius—you made this story *take off and soar* (puns certainly intended). Working with you has been a dream come true. I knew from our first phone call that you were the specialest kind of kindred spirit and my stories would be safe in your hands. Thank you for loving my characters (especially Gus) as much as I do. I feel so lucky to be working with St. Martin's. I'm eternally grateful to designer Kerri Resnick and artist Guy Shield, who brought my characters to life on *Fly with Me*'s gorgeous cover. Thank you to Eileen Rothschild, Kejana Ayala, Alyssa Gammello, Ginny Perrin, Austin Adams, Marissa Sangiacomo, and everyone else at SMPG that helped with the publication and promotion of *Fly with Me*. Special thanks to my copy editor, Janine Barlow, particularly for the effort required to correct the capitalization of "Swedish Fish" every single time that candy was mentioned. I owe you a king-sized bag. I am also very grateful to all the incredible romance authors who have offered their support and answered random questions during this journey, especially Ruby Barrett, Chloe Liese, Mazey Eddings, Kate Bromley, and Rachel Lynn Solomon.

Anne Jones—this book would not be what it is without you. Your early developmental edits pushed it in the right direction, and I'm very fortunate to have you in my life. I owe much of my growth as a writer to Anne and my first-ever real writer group, the RPAA. Thank you, Jaclyn Paul, Annabelle McCormack, and Cory Cone.

Sending a manuscript out into the world is frightening, so I was super lucky to have a group of wonderfully dear friends who beta read it. Ciara Trexler Manente, Natalie Levey, Cassie Sanders, Liza McRuer Hainline, Erin Dixon, Chelsey Saatkamp, Maria Effertz, and Liz Beckwith: Your feedback and encouragement gave me the confidence to keep trying when getting published seemed impossible. On that subject, I must say an *enormous* thank-you to all of Bookstagram for being the best community ever. Thank you for rooting for me and cheering with me! Thank you to everyone who participated in my fantastic cover reveal. All of your fabulous recommendations over the years made this story what it is today. And major props go to Julie and our wonderful slackers who made me laugh so much while I was also working on this book. 😃

Olive's character would not be who she is today without all of the brilliant nurses I have worked with during my career. To my favorite rad sedation team—Becca, Kathleen, Gabby, Marla, and everyone at CNI: Y'all are the best. To my fellow former SG Peds ER trauma-bonded Covid dream team—you were my inspiration. I miss you all even though I can't say I miss the bonkers night shifts. Special shout-out to Madison P. for teaching me how to be an ER nurse in the first place. Thank you to Mary Pollard for all of our discussions of nursing culture and, of course, for your excellent taste in hats.

Thank you, Maria, Sara, and Tiffany, for all your check-ins and offers of prosecco. Thank you, Lauren and Haley, for being supersweet. To Ciara, Natalie, and Cassie—you three were my rocks this year. Every message from you was a warm hug offered exactly when I needed it. Thank you to David and Kimberly for offering me words of support during some of the hardest moments of my outside-writing life. Thank you to Diane for all the voice messages that made me smile at times when almost nothing else could. Thank you to Kayla (and Chris) for being amazing friends and answering my earliest aviation-industry questions. Thank you to my therapist . . . even though you make me feel my feelings, which I'd rather not sometimes.

To Ellen, my first-ever reader, who has always been like a sister to me. I was terrified to send that first Word file to anyone, and I will never forget your phone call after you finished it. Thank you for being in my life. I am braver because of you. And to my oldest friend, Karen Jonas (**the incredibly talented, award-winning Gothic Americana singer/songwriter rock star)—you've read more drafts of my manuscripts than anyone else. You've been my cheerleader. You've been my champion. You've let me talk about my characters like they were real people from the very beginning. Because of you, I kept writing. We've come so far from our days busking on street corners with angsty teenage songs, but you are and have always been my creative soulmate.

The biggest thank-you of all goes to my brilliant, big-hearted Amelia and Emerson—you both make every day of my life sweeter and funnier. Thank you for tolerating all the constant typing and living in a house too packed with grown-up books. I am so lucky to be your mom.

ANDIE BURKE writes books with queer kissing and happily ever af-
ters. She was originally an English major who decided to jump into
a pediatric nursing career. Her writing is inspired by over a decade
spent working in hospitals with patients of all ages. After the last
couple of years spent in the pandemic ER, she escaped to an outpa-
tient pediatric sedation unit. Andie lives in a blue house in Maryland
with an alarming number of books and an embarrassing number of
ultrafine-point pens. When she's not writing, she's probably feeding
snacks to the two small human creatures who live with her or trying
not to kill her chaotic houseplants. You can find her adding to her
ever-expanding TBR on Bookstagram or letting her ADHD brain
happily dissociate while listening to Taylor Swift. *Fly with Me* is her
debut novel.